Be Brave
For Me

Elaine Johns

Be Brave
For Me

bookouture

Published by Bookouture in 2022

An imprint of Storyfire Ltd.
Carmelite House
50 Victoria Embankment
London EC4Y 0DZ

www.bookouture.com

"It's the most expeditious and orderly manner in which to move from place to place." in Chapter 30 from Sherman, Margaret, *No time for tears: In the ATS* (London: George G. Harrap & Co. Ltd., 1944) page 13.

ISBN: 978-1-80314-707-9
eBook ISBN: 978-1-80314-706-2

Dedicated to: Loll (for everything). Matt and Sam. My lovely mother who passed on her passion for reading to me. And my lovely da, who bought me my very first 'writing chair'.

16 FEBRUARY 1941

LONDON

Madeline Brady had joined the Auxiliary Territorial Service – ATS – partly to annoy her mother. Maddie's mother was a middle-class snob who didn't think it quite the thing for women to be in the army, to put on a rough khaki uniform. *Uncouth*, was the word she'd used. They should be baking cakes, organising fund-raisers for the war effort or volunteering with the Women's Voluntary Service (WVS) and serving hot tea to soldiers. That was fine. But when Maddie announced that she had passed the ATS driving test at Camberley and could strip down an engine and read a road map, her mother had reached for the smelling salts.

But Maddie Brady didn't need her mother's permission *or* her older brother Richard's to enlist in the army. She was twenty-three years old. A grown woman. Able to make her own decisions.

And she was proud to be in the ATS, proud of the dress-uniform that she wore. It sometimes brought whistles her way, and one chap who took her for a drink in the pub kept on about how attractive women looked in khaki.

The brown lace-up shoes were heavy, though. And the

rough, khaki lisle stockings itched like mad. One of the girls had ditched hers for silk ones – which only the officers were allowed to wear. They'd all been envious until an eagle-eyed sergeant (a large, overbearing woman with a sagging bust) had confined the girl to barracks and had her pay of ten shillings a week cut in half for a month. None of them had complained about wearing regulation lisle-cotton stockings since. But Maddie had swapped her uniform khaki bloomers for some silk knickers. It was as close as she came to rebellion.

She'd also invested ten shillings in the new and stylish forage cap. A private purchase, but most of her ATS friends had bought one. Ten shillings for 'other ranks' and a whole £2 for an officer. It was chocolate-brown with green piping and if you wore it at an angle it gave you a sophisticated 'American' look. It made up for the fact that you weren't allowed to wear your hair long. Regulations. Four inches off the collar. That was the rule. And they all stuck to it.

She was doing what some considered a man's job. And she did it well. At times it could be intriguing, the people she met. Mostly what the other ATS drivers called 'big wigs'. And it was true because, lately, some of the chaps Maddie had to drive around were top brass, as she'd been assigned to the War Office.

On loan, her commanding officer had explained, like Maddie Brady was some kind of property, a piece of equipment, rather than an actual person. But the officer had redeemed herself by adding that Madeline was a *lady*. Knew how to conduct herself in certain company. Could mind her Ps and Qs. See all. Hear all. But repeat nothing that she heard. Discretion! Those had been her orders. To deliver her human cargo safely, without fuss – and absolutely no gossip.

She was to say *nothing* to the other girls in the billet about the high-ranking officers she sometimes carried in the back of her Humber staff car. *Walls have ears*. That was a favourite expression on many lips. And of course, no British patriot would want to let slip even the smallest crumb of intelligence. That would be like handing a gift to Hitler and his cronies. And Maddie Brady considered herself a patriot with a strong love for her country. Britain and its allies needed to win this war. Anything else would be a disaster.

So far, her new posting to the War Office had mostly been routine stuff, apart from a few of the braid-smothered big wigs she'd driven for. There were days it could be a little humdrum. Certainly not the glamour that some of her ATS friends imagined it to be.

Except today promised to be different.

Her journey would be longer than usual, and she'd be driving to a place she'd always longed to see: Cornwall, with its vast moors, the mist clinging to them like a mystical, alien world. And the jagged, jutting cliffs, falling into tempestuous seas at Hell's Mouth cove. She'd heard about the churning seas of Hell's Mouth, wanted to see them for herself. Then there was the natural and harsh beauty of the Lizard Peninsula. Was it as dramatic and awe-inspiring as people claimed? And Deadman's Cove beach, on the North Cliffs. That was supposed to be haunted. She hoped it was.

Maddie drove through the rubble-strewn streets of London towards Whitehall. It was often a challenge, zigzagging your way through a landscape that changed daily; broken water mains and gas mains jutting through the concrete like prehistoric beasts. But, by now, the mental map of back roads and shortcuts through the capital was so ingrained in her that she often found herself driving automatically. Like today.

She'd left early enough but had been held up several times and was five minutes late by the time she arrived at the War Office to pick up her passenger. He was a captain from the Directorate of Prisoners of War DWP (section 5) to be exact – and the War Office liked to be exact.

She was getting used to the confusing number of departments in the place; a human beehive of more than 1,000 offices spread over seven floors. But the building in Whitehall never failed to impress her with its strange trapezium shape and those four magnificent domes. The War Office had been hit several times during the bombing but was still standing. A kind of irony, Maddie decided.

The officer was waiting impatiently for her, his greatcoat slung over his arm and a briefcase clutched importantly in front of him. Her orders were to drive him to Cornwall and be at his disposal during the length of his stay. Captain Ernest Andrews' job in DWP (section 5) was prisoner-of-war camp inspections and camp security.

Maddie had already worked out a route to the hamlet of White Cross, but couldn't imagine what Captain Andrews would have to do in a small Cornish village. Then a sudden, shocking thought struck her: there must be a POW camp there. The grim notion made her shudder. Naively, perhaps, Maddie had never even thought about the idea that Britain, like its enemies, also had prisoner-of-war camps.

The journey was long, and Maddie ended up with a fierce headache, concentrating on the map. There were no signposts anymore. They had all been taken down at the start of the war. No point in making things easier for your enemies.

The wartime roads often meant lengthy detours because of military traffic. You had to be patient and keep your wits about you. But Maddie enjoyed the challenges and that day was one of those days that called for all her ingenuity and skill. Convoys of military hardware and fuel being transported on roads that were already under pressure meant several hold-ups for her staff car, dwarfed by the huge vehicles.

A roadblock, set up at a crossroads in Devon, had made her passenger agitated. At one point he'd even started to blame *her* for the hold-up: 'You can read a damn map, can't you?' he'd demanded. A bit unfairly, Maddie thought, and quite rude. The war was hardly her fault, but he was the one in charge. So, she'd bitten her tongue and got on with it.

After his short outburst, Captain Andrews had become quiet again. And late that night, when they finally arrived at their destination, he'd even smiled at her. Guilt, Maddie figured.

They set her up in a small ante-room off the main guards' barracks. Hardly luxurious, but then there was a war on. And a corporal even brought her some food.

'Just some bread and cheese,' said the soldier. 'And not much at that.'

'That's kind,' she said. 'More than I expected.'

'Bread's that thin you could spit through it. An' you'd need a microscope to find the marge on there.'

'It's the thought that counts,' said Maddie. She gave him a small, tired smile.

The man smiled back and sloped off.

She had no idea what tomorrow might bring: they were due to be there a few days, the officer had informed her. *Tomorrow, I'll instruct you in your duties.* But that would take care of itself.

As for now, Maddie collapsed into the tiny, uncomfortable bunk, feeling none of its hard, wooden slats pressing into her through the thin mattress. It might well have been a massive, luxurious bed with silken sheets and an eiderdown of feathers as soft as an angel's wing, and she Sleeping Beauty, for she immediately fell into a deep sleep. And if she could have hovered above herself, it might have amused her to see the smile on her face.

· · ·

The next morning, the corporal arrived again. Corporal Williams seemed to have taken her under his wing and he brought her a breakfast of stewed tea and bread and dripping. Hardly exotic, thought Maddie. But it was a kind thought and she listened politely as he told her a little about the camp and the neighbouring farms and she watched a smile cross his face. But the smile disappeared when Captain Andrews arrived and barked at the poor man to stop loitering, ordered him out. Maddie turned her attention to the captain as he outlined the day's duties for her.

'You'll find instructions here, Private.'

'Very good, sir,' said Maddie, as she accepted the scrap of paper. Tried to decipher his messy handwriting.

'Not a gruelling task. Only a few items on there. But you'll need to check they've got the measurements correct. Can't trust some of these tradespeople if you're not there to spur them on.'

'Right, sir. Measurements correct. Got it.'

'Place is in Newquay, so I'll instruct them to dig out some petrol for you.'

'Do we know where in Newquay?'

'Address is on there.' He handed her an envelope. 'Give him this and make sure he gives you a receipt.'

'And the other items, sir?'

'Already paid for.'

Nothing on the captain's list struck Maddie as being in the slightest way military: not a single item that might influence the course of the war. Unless you counted the ladies' lingerie she had to pick up from a seamstress. Or the fine leather evening shoes waiting to be collected at the cobbler's shop in a back lane – it had been almost impossible to find – near the train station.

She took the shoes, handed the man the envelope. The cobbler counted out the money inside: a £1 note and a ten-shilling note. £1, seven shillings and 6d – that's what it said on the receipt he gave her in return. The shoemaker pocketed the rest of the money. All that for a pair of shoes!

But being the captain's personal servant did have at least *one* compensation: Maddie got to see the ocean. It seemed only fair, something she'd earned. She walked down to Tolcarne Beach, kicked off her shoes, removed the fearsome lisle stockings and allowed the soft, smooth sand to invade the spaces between her toes.

If you ignored the other beach walkers, promenading in their uniforms, you could imagine yourself on a lonely desert island with just the sound of lapping surf for company. Might even fool yourself into believing there wasn't really a war on.

She walked to the water's edge, dipped her feet into the ice-cold sea. The shock brought her back to reality. There may not be any barbed wire here on Tolcarne, but many of Newquay's other beaches were mined against invasion, and had sinister black gun-emplacements on the cliffs above them. *You might try to forget the war for a few giddy moments, but you couldn't ignore it.* She was on the army's payroll now, and she ought to get back: Captain Andrews might well have drummed up a few more chores to keep her busy. Keep her out of his hair. She understood. For him she was just a lowly private and a *woman* at that. Good for some things, like running his damn errands, but someone to be kept out of the *real* business of war – the serious business. She'd met chaps like him before.

As she brushed the damp sand from her feet and tied her shoes, Maddie took one last look at the ocean and then trudged back up the steep path away from the beach. She got into her car and drove back to the hamlet of White Cross. To Camp 115.

2

17 FEBRUARY 1941

POW CAMP 115, WHITE CROSS, ST COLUMB MAJOR, CORNWALL

Rudi Fischer had been a prisoner of war for almost six months now, although sometimes it was hard to judge the passage of time. One of the first things his British captors had done was to take his watch. He'd tried to hide it in his boot, but an English Tommy had found it. Any other time, Rudi might have called it stealing, but he was a realist. The wedding rings and the watches, the money that had been taken away from them all for 'safekeeping' had never been returned. It had been confiscated, along with the cap badges, regimental insignia and the swastika pins. The booty of war. Rudi had quickly understood that some of the British Tommies saw these things as souvenirs, something they had a right to take from their defeated German enemies.

It had been hard at first. He'd been cold, hungry, frightened. Unsure of his future or how cruel his British captors would be. He'd been part of a bomber crew, after all, a waist gunner in a Heinkel. If you bombed their cities, you couldn't expect to be welcomed with open arms.

But, although he'd been subjected to some initial interrogation, and de-humanised as he was stripped naked for a cold shower and his uniform fumigated, there had been no violence, no real cruelty. His captors had even fixed his broken leg.

There had been hundreds of them at the prisoners' reception centre at Kempton Park – a famous racecourse, he'd heard later, although Rudi had no idea where he was. He was grateful that his father had taught him to speak English. But he knew little about Britain, its geography, or its people, other than the propaganda fed to him at home: about how useless and inferior the British were, not anything like as competent as his own countrymen. Still, he'd been grudgingly impressed by the way his enemies had swiftly processed the milling horde of prisoners.

A prisoner of war. Hard to take in, when all he'd felt was numb. And bone weary. He'd been lucky to survive the crash. Only two of their flight crew had: him and the haughty Berliner, Oberleutnant Karl Hoffmann. Hoffmann was the navigator, an officer and fanatical Nazi sympathiser who, it was rumoured, had been destined for great things in the Nazi Party.

Now that Rudi was in this new, permanent work camp in Cornwall, he'd been allocated clothes and boots that finally fitted. The clothes were a uniform of sorts. An old, worn British RAF battledress, but not royal blue: it was dyed black for prisoners. But it was the miracle of the boots that had put a smile on his face. His own uniform boots had always been far too small for his large feet. He was tall. Big feet came with the package. But when he'd first been issued with his uniform and complained about the boots, they'd all laughed. Germans didn't complain. They were stoic. You were in the *Luftwaffe*. You took what they gave you, and tight boots were better than no boots at all.

These new boots weren't actually *new*, of course. Probably from some dead British soldier. They were scuffed and worn, but at least they didn't let water in. And no more blisters. It was bliss.

And this permanent camp meant they finally knew when their next meals were coming. Two a day, regular as clockwork. Not luxurious meals. One hot, one cold. He was skinny, wouldn't get fat on what they were fed there, but then neither would the guards, for they ate the same thing as their German prisoners.

One of the guards, a Scotsman, was even quite friendly, and had taken a photograph of Rudi outside his hut.

And the camp regime wasn't too harsh. You did what they told you and you got by. It was a boring, monotonous existence, but it was better than facing the flak in the skies, night after night.

He hadn't been keen on fighting a war in the first place. Hadn't joined the Hitler Youth like some of the other young men in his small Alpine village. Rudi had longed to be an engineer, to use his head and his hands like his father, but sometimes you had no choice. And joining the *Luftwaffe* had been better than fighting in the infantry, plus the food was better.

And now? He'd tried to be philosophical. Here, in the middle of the Cornish countryside, he would wait the outcome of the war. And his captors had been reasonable, had even allowed Rudi to set up the camp newspaper, *Die Wochenpost*.

He'd also organised a small, informal group of fellow prisoners who wanted to learn English. Rudi had never imagined himself to be any kind of teacher but found that he enjoyed it and it was a focus, something to hold onto in the boredom of captivity.

There were no guard towers here in Camp 115, no spotlights or coils of barbed wire, no fierce guard dogs – just a perimeter fence and regular patrols. Some of his fellow prisoners even got to go outside the gates, in work parties to help local farmers; or as labourers, working with the locals, fixing potholes in the roads.

But suddenly everything changed, and Rudi Fischer awoke

each day now with a gut-wrenching fear. Not a fear brought on by the British, by his captors. No. The fear had come from his own side.

He knew something important about another prisoner that could get him killed.

Rudi thought back to when his plane had crashed in Kent. How he'd watched Oberleutnant Karl Hoffmann do something strange. The man had changed clothes with the young dorsal gunner, callously stripping the poor dead bugger of his uniform.

At first, Rudi had been confused. But not anymore. That bastard Hoffmann had changed identity, turned himself into an enlisted man, someone who wouldn't be sent to the special interrogation centres reserved for officers and hardliners with Nazi sympathies.

And now, life had changed dramatically for Rudi. It happened the moment he had threatened Hoffmann. Threatened to tell the British who the man *really* was. He had done it because Hoffmann had been bullying younger prisoners. Beating some. If only Rudi had kept his mouth shut, things might have been fine. Instead, he had warned that swine Hoffmann. *Stop the bullying or I go to the British. Tell them everything I know.*

The footsteps behind him were loud and menacing, and a large, meaty hand spun him viciously around. The eyes that stared at Rudi were full of hate, and the broad, brutish face spoke only of vengeance and spite.

'So, I find you here, skulking,' said Hoffmann.

'Skulking? Why should I skulk?' asked Rudi.

'Hiding in the shadows like a frightened rabbit.'

'Now I'm a rabbit? You should write fairy tales, Hoffmann. Something we Germans are good at.'

'A friendly warning, my dear Obergefreiter Fischer.'

'Oh, yes?'

'This camp can be a dangerous place. There are many hazards.'

'I see. Like what?' asked Rudi. But he figured he knew exactly what they were.

'After lights out, many traps can wait in the darkness. And a trip to the showers – a man could easily become careless, could slip. A broken neck. A man should remain vigilant, accidents happen.'

'My thanks, Oberleutnant Hoffmann,' said Rudi.

'For what?' asked Hoffmann.

'Your concern for my welfare. I'll be sure to stay vigilant. Keep my eyes open for hazards.'

With that, Rudi Fischer walked away. He whistled as he left, stuffed his hands in his pockets in a nonchalant, carefree pose. But it was a lie. His hands were shaking, for he had seen the evil in Hoffmann's eyes.

There was no way back now. Escape was the only answer.

Rudi went to the camp chapel, and he prayed. He wasn't a religious man, but he tried to be honourable. Even in war, a man could still have honour and some kind of humanity.

He felt better after he'd prayed, even though he didn't believe in a higher power, in any kind of god.

But, considering the eventual outcome, it would seem that God believed in *him*.

3

Maddie looked over at Captain Andrews. The officer was having an animated discussion with the camp commander, an army major with a piratical patch over one eye and high blood pressure (if the alarmingly red face was anything to go by). Captain Andrews was tall and thin, and the major had to look up at him. Both men seemed to be arguing, although she couldn't hear their conversation. But their exaggerated body language was like watching a silent pantomime. Maddie forced herself not to smile.

It looked as if things weren't going well for Captain Andrews. He kept twisting his handlebar moustache, something she'd noticed him do before when he was agitated. The furrowed brow and the small lines of stress on his face told their own story. At least to Maddie, who seemed to have the knack of reading people; it was a gift that had developed over the years. Not one she was aware of. But her friends in the barracks had told her she was easy to talk to and often got right to the root of their problems.

She liked people. Liked talking to them, hearing about their families. Maybe it was a way to forget about her own family, who knew nothing about the real Maddie: what made her laugh or cry; her hopes for the future. None of them had ever asked.

Instead, they had tried to mould her into this perfect creature: a boarding school education, an exclusive finishing school and elocution lessons that made some of her ATS pals describe her as posh. *Fit to marry the best in the land.* That was the ludicrous phrase that fell repeatedly from her mother's lips. Sometimes Maddie felt as if there'd been a mix-up at birth and the hospital had handed her over to the wrong family, by mistake. She'd always felt out of place.

When she'd first joined the ATS, her mother and brother had discussed her enlistment like she was a troublesome item on their agenda. Something that needed to be fixed. They'd lectured her: she was wasting her life, throwing away her education. She was one of the elite, they claimed. If she *had* to be in the army, why a damn private? Why not an officer?

But Maddie had no interest in being an officer. Or even in becoming an NCO. A non-commissioned officer wasn't the same as an officer – they came up through the ranks – but they could still bark orders. She didn't want to do that. She was happy being one of the many, enjoyed the spirit of camaraderie. The feeling of being part of a sisterhood. In the barracks, there was mutual support. You looked out for each other.

She watched the camp commander walk away, and went across to Captain Andrews, throwing him a smart, regulation salute. Officially, she was only meant to salute her own ATS officers, but for Maddie, it was a matter of courtesy: he was in the army and so was she.

Captain Andrews' salute was returned in an off-hand way, lacking enthusiasm, not crisp like hers. And his eyes didn't connect with her but lingered on her cap badge. Fair enough, you saluted the cap, not the person. *Respect for the cap badge and all it represented.* That was the way of the British Army. Not like the Americans: they liked throwing salutes right, left and centre, even when servicemen weren't wearing their caps.

Her eyes went to the captain's face. Yes, she'd been right. The man seemed distracted. And there were small red veins of stress standing out against the whites of his eyes. Things not going well, maybe.

She waited for him to speak, wondering what was next on his list of errands for her.

'Back so soon, Private?'

'Yes, sir.' She came to attention.

'Mission accomplished, I take it?'

'Yes, sir.'

'And my packages?'

'In the car, sir. I wasn't sure if you wanted me to leave them there, or...'

'Leave them? Good grief, girl. Why would I want you to do that?'

What was she? A mind reader? And girl? *She wasn't a girl. She was a woman.*

'So...'

'Take them to my billet. When you've done that, come and find me. The commander has given me the use of his office. Somewhere down by the water tower, I believe. I'm sure even you can find it.' The captain smirked like he'd made an excellent joke and walked away, leaving Maddie with her mouth open.

That was unfair. She'd only got them lost once on the way there, and it had hardly been her fault as the diversion hadn't been properly signposted. And they'd made it in the end.

Some people just weren't very *nice*, were they? You'd think with the war and the need to pull together that it would make people kind. Most of the officers she ferried around were real gentlemen. Had been gracious, treated her like a fellow human, an equal, despite the difference in rank.

Still – she wouldn't let it get to her, for Maddie Brady recognised sarcasm when she met it. It was a favourite weapon of her mother's, and Maddie always managed to come out on top when those two sparred. But this Captain Andrews had her at a disadvantage. She couldn't bite back at a superior officer, especially one like this chap. She suspected that he wouldn't think twice about getting her into trouble with her own officer. He didn't strike her as a happy man, a man content in his work.

The captain's billet wasn't hard to find: a tiny room in a two-storey house set back from the main gate. She wondered who had been thrown out of the place to make room for the bombastic captain.

After she'd left his parcels on the small bunk bed, Maddie went outside into the garden. It was well kept, the lawn neat and with some sort of small shrubs growing at regular intervals around the perimeter of the grass. Their scent was heady. She had no idea what kind of bushes they were. Gardening, agriculture, it wasn't an area she was familiar with.

A massive, sculpted eagle, its wings spread, wide stood in the middle of the lawn, mounted on a tall stone plinth. She wondered who might have made it and put it there – in the middle of a garden, in a prisoner-of-war camp. But then maybe this place hadn't always been a prison camp.

She might ask Corporal Williams about it. He was a man who seemed to have his finger on the pulse of camp life. And he hadn't just dismissed her, like some of the regular army did to ATS women, as if they were a joke and not part of the *real* army. He'd taken her seriously, given her respect.

Maddie turned her back on the gatehouse and headed towards the tall brick water tower in the distance. The camp was large, with row after row of neat concrete huts. Hard to say how many men would fit into each separate hut, but one of the guards had told her they could house up to a thousand prisoners in the place.

She'd seen some of them earlier that morning before heading off to Newquay. A thin, ragged bunch of men. They'd been gathered in groups around the front of the huts chatting, some of them smoking. Some even laughing. That had surprised her. How could you be captured, be a prisoner – and still be cheerful? Maybe some of them were glad to be out of the fighting. She guessed they'd been about to line up for some sort of roll call. A roll call in the morning and another last thing at night. To make sure none of them tried an escape.

But this was a low-risk camp, as far as escapes went. There had never been any, at least according to Corporal Williams. He'd reckoned this lot were a bunch of Jerries who weren't all that partial to Herr-bleedin'-Hitler and maybe they didn't wish him and his bleedin' Nazis any luck. But most of the prisoners didn't wish him any harm, either. *Fence-sitters*, that's what Corporal Williams had reckoned they were, what he'd told Maddie. They'd been interrogated by intelligence chaps at a holding camp in London, most of them; and some army big wigs had decided these prisoners were *neutral*. Safe enough to be let out to work on some of the surrounding Cornish farms. And still come back to the camp at night.

How strange! That's what Maddie thought, at any rate. Even if you had armed guards taking you to work in the fields, and bringing you back... if there were a lot of you, wouldn't you try to overpower them, try to escape? It was a prisoner of war's duty to escape. To make the enemy use lots of resources and manpower in trying to recapture you.

She passed a flat piece of ground with two sets of makeshift goal posts there and a few men kicking a ball around. A football pitch. The POWs had built a pitch; maybe there was even some kind of league. It was beginning to look more like a holiday camp. No! That was wrong of her. None of these thin, scruffy men looked as if they were on holiday. And the clothes they wore marked them out as prisoners. Those and the white patches on their backs.

Maddie moved on quickly, heard the noisy cheers as one of the prisoners scored a goal. Humanity, with all its faults and quirks, never ceased to amaze her. How the human spirit could rise above trials and find triumph in small things.

Next to the football pitch was a long, low building with a thin, metal chimney on the roof, pumping out steam. A cookhouse. The size surprised her, for it stretched all the way across to the far side of the camp and the perimeter fence. On the other side of the fence there was a railway line. *Strange to see that – right out here in the middle of nowhere.* So far, she hadn't heard or seen any trains.

The camp was neat and well laid out. Not just a collection of mud walkways and huts. Proper concrete pathways connected the long, low buildings and some of the prisoners' barracks even had small patches of cultivated ground out in front of them. No grass here, though, or fancy shrubs. Perhaps they'd been allowed to grow vegetables for themselves. That would make sense.

Growing your own food was important. Not just for these prisoners but for everybody in the country. It saved precious wartime resources. And helped in a time of hard rationing. Dig for victory! That's what the posters said. In the pub, you'd hear a different slogan: *Dig for a bad back.* But despite the odd grumble, people still did it, saw it as their patriotic duty to get out into the allotment and get stuck in. Every available piece of dirt in the country had been turned over and used for growing food.

Maddie smiled as she remembered walking through Kensington Gardens last month, and the bizarre sight of the famous Albert Memorial surrounded by allotments of cabbages, leeks, potatoes, carrots. She felt sure Prince Albert wouldn't have complained if he'd been alive. The prince had been a practical man; he'd have understood. He might even have chuckled that the Tower of London also had the best of veg growing in its moat.

That was all fine, of course – if you liked veg. Maddie wasn't too partial to it. But it was supposed to be good for you, so she'd forced down the limp, overcooked cabbage that they served up in the mess, and the disgusting sprouts.

'Fine day for a walk, miss. Doing some exploring, is it, now?'

The loud voice made Maddie jump, and dragged her out of her head. 'Corporal Williams! Just getting my bearings. It's a big place,' she said.

'That it is. About an 'undred and twenty-odd acres. But we've got a fair few prisoners here. Germans right now, but we used to have Italians till they moved 'em out. They built that fancy chapel over there.' Corporal Williams pointed to a small, whitewashed building some distance away. 'And that grand-looking eagle out front,' he said.

'Ah. I was wondering about that,' said Maddie. 'Impressive.'

'Artistic bunch, the I-ties were. And always singing, they were. And smilin'.' The corporal himself was smiling then.

'You'd wonder they had anything to sing about,' said Maddie.

'Aye, that you would. Lovely choir they had, though. The drop of a hat, the buggers – 'scuse me, miss – would break into song. Bit like the Welsh.' Corporal Williams winked at her: he was Welsh himself.

Maddie gave him a smile in return. The man was friendly, had made her feel welcome.

'I'm looking for the commander's office,' she said. 'Seems like Captain Andrews has commandeered it for the time being.'

'That so?' The corporal grinned. 'And you'd be looking for it in this direction, is it?'

'Down by the water tower, that's what the captain said.'

'You'll be after the Glory Hole then. Least, that's what the lads call it,' said Corporal Williams.

'Glory Hole?'

'That's the only thing you'll find down there. Tiny, pokey place. Storage room, no bigger than a cupboard. Reckon you'd get a desk and chair in there – at a push, mind.'

'Captain Andrews seems to think he's been given the commander's office.'

'Does he now? Well, he'll be tamping then. When he finds out, like.'

'*Tamping?*' Maddie queried.

'What you English call "browned-off". Angry, like. *Very* angry.'

'Ah.' Maddie had seen Captain Andrews upset on the journey down. When he'd been disappointed with their progress. She didn't fancy seeing him when he was angry.

'You can't do it, Rudi. They'll find you.'

'Maybe they won't. There's no choice. I have to try, you know I can't stay here. One way or another, he'll get me,' said Rudi.

'We won't let him. We'll protect you,' said Hans.

Rudi Fischer smiled at his friend. Hans Meyer was a good friend. He'd been a farmhand in a tiny village back home, a bit like Rudi's own. It was why they'd naturally been drawn to each other, helped each other out; kept each other's spirits up when the trials of being imprisoned in a land far away from your country became overwhelming.

But Hans couldn't help him now. Nobody could. Not against that bully Hoffmann. 'Okay,' said Hans. 'Say you even manage to get away from this place. I've been out there, been on one of the farms. It's the back end of nowhere. Where would you go? The whole bloody country is an island.'

'So?' said Rudi. 'Didn't you say you could see the ocean from that farm of yours?'

'What?! All of a sudden you're a sailor?' Hans laughed.

'I know how to row a boat,' said Rudi. 'And I hear that the

Southern Irish don't feel the same way about us *filthy Krauts* as the English.'

But even as he said it, he knew it was a measure of his own desperation. Of course he wasn't a sailor. He'd been on Lake Hintersee near his home, but someone else had been in charge of the boat – and there'd been no waves. Even then, he'd been seasick.

'That's it? That's the plan? You steal a boat. I'm assuming this is a rowing boat.' Hans smiled again and punched his friend in the arm. 'And then – what? You row around Britain, then head across the Irish Sea, where you're greeted like a long-lost friend by some strange Irishman as you pull up on a friendly beach.'

'I never said it was perfect.' Rudi returned his friend's smile. 'Still a work in progress.'

They both knew it was thin. Any kind of escape needed planning, and resources, and friends who could help. But most of all it needed luck. And so far, Rudi Fischer hadn't had a lot of that.

But Rudi had already made up his mind. *Today was the day.* No way around it. He couldn't stay here for another day, and whatever happened, even if the guards discovered him trying to make a run for it, what would they do to him? Send him to another camp – a harsher one? That would be nothing compared to whatever Oberleutnant Karl Hoffmann had in mind for him.

At breakfast that morning, Hoffmann had *accidentally* stumbled into him, had loudly and courteously apologised, smiled, clicked his heels in that polite German way. But quietly, for Rudi's consumption only, he'd whispered in Rudi's ear that that day was to be a *special* day. No prizes for guessing what that meant. Hoffmann had already warned him that an accident could happen. He meant to carry out his threat. Hoffmann was a sociopath who liked to have fun with his prey. To keep them guessing. But even he wouldn't wait for ever.

'It's insane,' warned Hans, when Rudi explained he wouldn't be there for evening roll call.

'Not as insane as staying,' said Rudi.

'Okay, even if you get as far as joining the work detail in the lorry, they always look in the back; do a headcount of those going out.'

'Throw of the dice. Maybe I'll get lucky.'

'Go to the camp commandant. I'll come with you, they can't ignore both of us.'

Rudi slapped his friend on the back: better than words, for there were no words to express the solidarity, the feeling of comradeship they shared. But he knew that Hans would be putting himself in danger too, would end up on that bastard Hoffmann's list – and for what? The British would hardly take them seriously. Would dismiss the whole thing as just rivalry between the troublesome Krauts. And even if somebody did feel their complaint was worth investigating, it would take time. It would be too late.

'I'll be interviewing people for the rest of the day,' said Captain Andrews. He tapped the pile of buff folders on the desk in front of him. It was a large pile.

'I see, sir.'

'I doubt you do, Private Brady. Nevertheless...' He sighed out his frustration.

Maddie tried not to let her feelings register on her face. But really, the captain's ego was large; his people skills small. And she *wasn't* stupid, had a certain amount of intelligence. She could understand all kinds of things, provided they were explained to her. But then, he was an officer. He didn't need to explain himself.

Maybe that sigh of his said something. Could it be that Captain Andrews had been handed the mucky end of a dirty stick and told to get on with it? Sort it out? You never knew. It was the army, but even in war, when everyone should be pulling together, people passed the buck.

'So...' she said. 'What are my orders, sir?'

'Your orders? Ah. Well, I won't be needing a driver for today, or even tomorrow, as I expect I shall be stuck here behind this damn desk all day tomorrow as well...' He eyed the files in front of him malevolently.

She didn't envy him. The office was tiny, and claustrophobic. And the pile of work looked huge. 'Yes, sir,' she replied, her voice neutral. *Not her place to comment.*

'So, Private – why don't you clean the car, or check the radiator, look at the sump... whatever you normally do when you're not driving?'

'Will do, sir,' she said, and threw the man in front of her a regulation salute – he still had his uniform cap on, after all.

'And when you've finished that, take a couple of days off, Private. Drive somewhere. See a bit of the countryside. I envisage driving back to town the day after tomorrow. Until then, you may be on your own devices. Consider it a forty-eight-hour pass.'

'If you're sure you won't need me, sir.' She couldn't believe her luck.

'Absolutely certain. I can think of no contribution you could possibly make to the work I'm about to undertake here. So, off you go – before I change my mind.'

'Do you have written orders for me, sir?'

'Do you *need* written orders? Aren't you supposed to be at my disposal until we return to Whitehall?'

'Those were my orders, sir.'

'Well, then, off you go. And be back here at oh-seven hundred hours the day after tomorrow.'

———

'Look at the *sump*?' asked Corporal Williams. 'That's what he said?'

'Those are my orders,' said Maddie, as she lifted the bonnet of the Humber.

'I wouldn't even know where to find the sump in one of these things.'

'Not sure if the captain would either.' Maddie smiled. 'But we looked under the bonnets of all kinds of cars and lorries at Camberley. A three-tonner holds no mystery for me,' she said, and laughed. 'They taught us how to strip an engine – put a stopwatch on you. We had weeks of studying scale models and memorising all the parts, before they let us loose on the real thing.'

'Doesn't sound so bad,' said Corporal Williams with a grin.

'I loved it,' said Maddie. 'It's good to learn new things.' She thumped the bonnet down with a satisfying *clunk* and inspected the rest of the car. Mud from the narrow Cornish lanes had stuck to it, and the bodywork wasn't as spotless as she liked to see it. The captain was right: it could do with a wash before she went on a sightseeing trip, explored a little. After all, those were her orders, and in the army, you *always* followed orders.

She smiled and watched as Corporal Williams marched smartly away to the sentry box by the gate. He was on barrier duty today, it seemed. A boring but important job that Maddie figured the Welshman would tackle with stoic resignation. He looked back over his shoulder and threw her a friendly wink. She laughed, and thought about her friends back at the billet and how her bunkmate Molly Peters would let out that long, low whistle of hers when there was a hint of romance in the air. Or *lust*.

Molly, a big buxom blonde with a generous heart, was very hot on the idea of lust. She was a confident, happy young woman, glad of the freedom that war had given her and her escape from a stifling family and rigid Catholic upbringing.

Maddie had checked the oil, topped up the water in the radiator and filled the Humber Snipe's hungry belly with a jerry can of petrol. *Just a quick wash and brush-up for the old girl now.* The car was a reliable workhorse if you were good to her: Maddie always thought of the car as a *she*. She'd christened her Harriet. *Harriet the Humber.* Blokes would have sniggered, she knew. But Harriet had become a close ally and, at times, Maddie even found herself talking to the thing. Bizarre, maybe. Still – not as bizarre as being ordered off on a sight-seeing trip. It would be easy to follow an order like that, and the man was her boss, at least for the time being. But would she get in trouble with her own commanding officer back in London? Stuff in life had a way of hanging you, even if you were innocent.

A voice cut through her thoughts: 'You leaving that there all day? You're right in the way of the lorry. All the same, you ATS girlies are; ain't got the sense you was born with.' There was a loud tut. 'Never should 'ave let women join the army,' the man grumbled under his breath. But Maddie heard it.

She looked up at the man, his red, angry face. His sergeant's stripes. She opened her mouth to speak, but he jumped straight back in: a one-sided conversation, then.

'Pull it up over there and leave enough room in front for the prisoners' transport. They'll be leaving soon.'

'I'm washing the car.'

'I don't see no water. Anyroad, you can do that just as easy, parked up over there.' The sergeant pointed to a spot behind her right shoulder, like Maddie's brain was somehow inferior and couldn't work out the directions by herself.

Some of the regular army blokes felt intimidated by women in the ATS, as if somehow the women's army section was tainting the whole service. Had brought it into disrepute. *The man is one of those,* she decided. It wasn't the first time she'd come across that sort of prejudice, and it annoyed her. But she always tried to ignore it. The sexual slurs were harder to ignore – when a bloke sniggered and called you an *officer's blanket.* And it wasn't true: very few of the ATS girls were *easy.*

She watched the sergeant puff himself up with power.

NCOs – the backbone of the army, but some of them misused their position, became bullies.

'I'll get some of them lazy buggers who ain't going out on work detail to bring you buckets and stuff,' he said. 'Do 'em good. Some of 'em think they're on holiday.' The small, fat sergeant guffawed as he marched away.

6

Rudi Fischer felt suddenly positive, cheerful even. A kernel of optimism was growing in the pit of his stomach, and spread itself to his face in a happy grin. Maybe there was a God after all, and He'd finally decided to throw His muscle behind Rudi.

It was the first time he felt that escape might be more than just a vague hope, but a realistic idea. The thought made him whistle as he polished the car. The big old vehicle couldn't really be polished, for like most military vehicles of its kind it was just a dull mat green. But Rudi polished away enthusiastically with his rag as if you might see your reflection in it, and while he was at it, he polished the silver boot latch with equal vigour.

He'd already tried the latch and it had moved smoothly. And the two long hinges at the top of the boot hadn't even groaned as he'd expected, but moved easily to lift the thing like a lid. He'd always thought of his own nation as excellent engineers and manufacturers, for German cars were reliable. Precision, it was a German trait. But maybe the British knew a thing or two as well. Probably used German engineers before the war, though.

He smiled and patted the boot of the car affectionately. It was roomy enough, even though there was a spare tyre in there. Could have been worse. Finally, the sun had decided to shine on him.

He looked at the others busily drying off the car. Four of them had been ordered to wash and polish the thing. Some of them had grumbled under their breath, but not him.

Rudi set about his task with a renewed vigour and cheerfulness, which he suddenly realised might seem suspicious. He cut off his whistle, mid-flow.

The woman in the army uniform turned her head to look at him. He guessed she was the vehicle's driver for she seemed to have a personal interest in the car and had once even patted the bonnet like the thing was a family pet. He'd laughed at that and when their eyes met, there had been laughter in hers as well, and she'd shrugged her shoulders, a kind of admission that she'd been caught out being foolish.

Her eyes were blue. *Sparkling* blue, like he imagined the purest ocean to be, and fizzing with life and laughter. And her hair, a curtain of silky blonde tresses sneaking out from under the uniform cap and framing a strong, but nevertheless pretty face. Not long hair, or the style favoured by Fräuleins in his homeland, but attractive all the same, and the colour of new mown hay. She was unusually tall too. For a woman. At least any of the women Rudi had come across. Her height easily matched his own and gave her a natural elegance that made her stand out in the stark and bleak surroundings. *A jewel in the middle of a rubbish heap* was the description that came to Rudi's mind when his eyes were tugged hypnotically towards her. *Another time, another place*, he thought wistfully, *and things might have been different*.

He might even have been brave enough to overcome his natural shyness and start up a conversation with the woman, tap into the humanity that lay behind that smile. He suspected that she had understanding and empathy, for she'd already apologised to them for having been forced to wash her car. She'd even argued with the sergeant that the men shouldn't be treated like slave labour, should be given the dignity captured prisoners of war deserved.

Rudi had been impressed by the young woman's spirit, but the fat sergeant had only laughed and trotted out some vague insult about allowing women to wear uniforms. Rudi's grasp of English was still only basic, and the sergeant's strange accent hard to decipher, but the downward slope of the woman's shoulders and the sadness in those deep blue eyes hadn't needed a shared language to interpret: that bastard sergeant had made her unhappy.

And for some irrational reason that he couldn't possibly begin to fathom or explain, Rudi Fischer wanted to protect this lovely woman, this stranger he had only just met and never even spoken to. Protect her from any more pain.

———

Maddie knew nothing about the man, other than the fact he was a POW. A German. An enemy. Someone she should hate. But when he'd smiled at her like that, she could find no hate in her for the tall man with the hypnotic, ice-blue eyes. He struck her as someone who would laugh easily, despite whatever sadness the world threw at him, and even now the skin around his eyes crinkled readily into laughter lines. It was a strange contradiction, humour playing across a face with sunken cheeks and sallow skin.

Despite the smile, the man looked ill, emaciated, his impressive height seemed designed for a body with more meat on its bones. *Skeletal* was a word that floated into Maddie's head; she shrugged it off. For she guessed that someone like him, who could find humour in a grim POW camp, would never consider himself a victim.

Gracious!

What? she asked an invisible Molly, as a picture of her bunkmate suddenly thrust itself again into her mind. Molly, the friend who could find romance lurking under every rock. *Well, he is very striking,* Maddie argued with the image in her head. *And those cheekbones – classical, wouldn't you say?* But of course, Molly didn't answer back. And what would she have said if she had? That the man was an enemy?

Maddie had never come face to face with an enemy before, and the reality was a surprise. He didn't look at all like a monster or some strange clone from a race of Hitler's super-humans that the propaganda described. He looked like a normal chap; one she might even talk to if circumstances were different. One thing she knew – some strange chemical reaction had taken place; one she had never encountered before; an indefinable force that drew her towards this stranger, a force she had no control over. But one that she would try her hardest to ignore. She was British, a patriot, proud of her country, and fraternising with the enemy was number one on a long list of things you didn't do.

Even so, after she watched them retreat back to their huts, she wished she'd asked his name.

7

Maddie couldn't remember the last time she'd been this excited. But it wasn't just excitement, it was more than that. If she'd been the superstitious type, she'd have used the word *portentous*.

Yes, that's what it felt like. Momentous, some omen of life-changing importance. But then, she wasn't given to superstition, so maybe the excited shivers working their way from the back of her neck and along her spine were only due to the damp chill of a winter's day in Cornwall. And the cold leather of the car seat tugging at her.

She was off on an adventure; an explorer, eager to grasp each new sensation; intrepid, ready to face the unknown with confidence. But not *entirely* unknown, she supposed, for at least she had a map and was even now heading towards the romance and drama of the Lizard Peninsula, a place she'd read about and dreamed of exploring.

Thanks to the rather pompous Captain Andrews, she was able to follow that dream. He'd ordered her to 'Drive some-where. See a bit of the countryside... Consider it a forty-eight-hour pass'. Well, not quite *forty-eight*: the rest of the day and a full day tomorrow, but more than she'd expected.

Maybe she would even find herself a bed and breakfast lodging for overnight, make it a *real* holiday. Helston was close to the Lizard, there must be places to stay there, for she imagined it to be a fairly large town. And even in wartime, people still had to travel, needed somewhere to spend the night.

Is your journey really necessary? She thought about the words on the railway poster. People were discouraged from making 'frivolous' trips, as resources had to be saved for crucial wartime endeavours. Maddie understood all that. But then, she wasn't taking up a precious seat on a train, was she? *Drive* somewhere, the captain had ordered. Maddie grinned to herself. Maybe her trip *was* frivolous, but orders were orders, right? And she'd already filled up the tank with the jerry can of petrol the captain had instructed Corporal Williams to magically produce.

Corporal Williams had been on barrier duty when she'd driven away from the camp. He, and a squaddie she'd never seen before, had been sheltering from the cold in the small sentry box by the front gate.

Maddie had sat patiently behind the wheel of the staff car, waiting to escape; to start her adventure, butterflies stretching their excited wings in her stomach. But the prisoner transport ahead of her had been held up for ages at the barrier. She'd been lined up behind the canvas-covered lorry for a long time before she'd finally been allowed the freedom of the open road.

There seemed to be some confusion that she didn't understand, and at one stage all of the German POWs had been hastily unloaded from inside the lorry, ordered to wait by the gatehouse, counted twice by Corporal Williams, and made to answer their names in a roll call. While the prisoners were milling around outside, the other British squaddie had gone inside the lorry to conduct a search.

A gaggle of interested prisoners had also gathered around her car. But Maddie hadn't been intimidated by them, for even though there'd been some pushing and shoving, a bit of play-fighting, it had all seemed light-hearted banter, and in good fun. Maddie hadn't got out to discourage or disperse them, as she knew how it went: the squaddie would figure she'd overstepped her authority. She was a visitor, an ATS driver. A woman at that – not a real soldier, then. So, she'd left him to get on with it. But she hadn't failed to notice that one of the men was the tall, thin German with the piercing blue eyes. He'd even smiled at her when he caught Maddie watching him.

The butterfly population in her stomach had doubled.

After the search of the prisoner transport, she'd half expected her own car to be inspected, for there seemed to be some sort of flap on. But Corporal Williams had just waved her on through. He'd added another wink, like they were some sort of co-conspirators.

The drive from the camp at White Cross had been easier and quicker than she'd thought, at least as far as the town of Redruth. Not much traffic on the roads, either. But after that, it became far more of a challenge, and took all her driving skills to keep the staff car safely on the road. *Hardly a road*, she reminded herself, for sometimes the route between Redruth and Helston had narrowed into a country lane. With so many hairpin bends and the abundance of potholes, she'd fought every inch of the way, gripping the steering wheel with an intensity that left ridges in her hands.

Fields of brown slid by her drab, olive-green staff car. Bleak winter colours in the fields, unremarkable, dreary even. And in places, high Cornish hedges, designed as windbreaks, boxed her in on either side. Their claustrophobic presence felt oppressive. The abundance of wild hedgerow flowers that normally clung to them, forcing their way through the buttresses in a riot of colour, were missing. Winter had robbed the hedges of their magic. She'd hoped for something different, more uplifting, to feed her spirit of adventure.

She passed through villages and small hamlets, their grey Cornish granite breaking up the landscape. But even these places seemed to be crouching down in a kind of enforced hibernation. Four Lanes, Pencoys, Burras: collections of houses and chapels, marked on her map, but Maddie saw no evidence of human habitation, as not a single person walked their streets or waved a cheery greeting to her. There was just an eerie silence. She felt suddenly alone, as if she were the last human on some alien, inhospitable planet. *Where* was *everybody?*

And now, as she came onto the moorland again, a thin, wispy mist clutched at some of the low-lying fields with a spectral hand. She shivered. Not excitement, this time, but due to the anxious caveman part of her brain, throwing up ancient fears and superstition.

Her explorer's anticipation slowly dwindled into disappointment. Somehow, she'd expected more. But maybe once she got to the Lizard, headed towards the sea, things would be different.

She shook off the sombre mood, forced herself to smile. *Some people just don't know when they're well off,* she chastised herself. And that seemed to work, because she suddenly saw people. Up ahead, two of them, young girls wearing the brown and green uniform of the Women's Land Army, steering a herd of cows across the road to a field on the other side. Ten cows. Maddie counted them as she slowed to a stop in the road. *You see!* There *were* other people on the planet, she wasn't totally alone.

Once the parade of cows had been safely dispatched, one of the girls came over to the car.

Maddie wound the window down.

'You one of they army women?' The tone was friendly and the young girl's face broke into a grin.

'I am,' agreed Maddie. 'ATS driver.'

'Must be great, driving a fancy car like that. You an officer, like?' asked the girl, wide-eyed. She seemed impressed.

'Nope, just a plain old private.'

'Well, you sounds like an officer. Like a toff, dead posh like.'

'Can't help where you were born,' said Maddie. *Hampstead.* Her parents had moved there because it was where the *right people* lived.

'Ain't that the truth? I were born in a village up the road. All old folk there now, all the decent blokes gone off to fight. Dead dull and boring.'

'Sometimes boring's good,' said Maddie.

'Yeah? Tell that to this lot.' The girl pointed at the cows and laughed. 'Me name's Annie,' she said, and stuck her hand through the window in welcome. 'Very pleased to meet a lady from the ATS.'

'Same here,' said Maddie. 'Pleased to see a friendly face. People seem a bit thin on the ground.'

'They keeps themselves to themselves round here. Don't mean we Cornish don't welcome folk, proper like. Even *incomers.*' The girl laughed again, a high-pitched, friendly sound.

'So, you come from around here?' asked Maddie.

'Wendron. Up the road, after Trenear. You off to Helston? Them's building a new airfield up there. And one out at Predannack as well. Be lots of they gorgeous fly-boys coming through soon, I reckon.' Annie chuckled. 'Wouldn't say no to one of they. If he asked proper, like.'

They said goodbye, and Maddie drove off with the sound of Annie's laughter still hanging in the air. It signalled the return of her own optimism. Maybe this trip would be fun after all, enough to renew her enthusiasm and make the rest of the assignment with the morose Captain Andrews more palatable.

She had no illusions about why he'd given her a forty-eight-hour pass. The man wasn't being kind, he wanted her out of the way. Maybe he didn't feel that comfortable with a woman around while he tried to sort out whatever mess he'd been landed with. But it was the army. They were in the middle of a war. There was always *some* kind of mess.

The village of Wendron, where Annie hailed from, turned out to be a beautiful, picturesque place. Maddie imagined it on a hot summer's day ablaze with the roses that crept around the doors – colour everywhere, tugging the eye away from the stark Cornish granite.

It was a sleepy, picture-postcard place, a Cornish idyll where visitors might come to relish its peace and tranquillity. But she could see how someone like Annie would feel trapped and stifled by it.

After the war, when folk could travel again, they'd go there to remind themselves of another world, another time. They'd walk through the ancient lychgate, explore the churchyard, the defunct tin mines whose engine houses were now mere skeletons on the landscape, a reminder of different times when men worked like slaves prising tin from the earth, so that others could get rich.

She drove on through, didn't stop. Maybe she'd stop in Helston before travelling on, find a café. It was almost lunchtime and Maddie was hungry, hadn't had anything to eat since the breakfast of bread and dripping. That seemed a long time ago now.

The sun had come out, its rays glinting, bouncing off the impressively grand buildings of Coinagehall Street in Helston. Georgian, some of them, and Victorian, the friendly old man had said, when she'd stopped to ask the way to some kind of eatery.

He'd told her where to park the car and given her directions to Coinagehall Street, impressing on her the need to visit the Angel Hotel. 'Historic,' he'd told her, with pride in his voice. ''Course, it ain't what it used to be, what with the blast tape on the winders and the sandbags and the like...' The old Cornishman had shrugged his shoulders, philosophically. 'This bleddy war, eh?' He'd called her *my bird* and given her a full-face grin, and made her feel welcome – even though she was one of *they foreigners* from across the Tamar.

Maddie was getting used to it now – the way the Cornish seemed to classify people by whichever side of the River Tamar they came from. One side Cornwall, the other side England. But there seemed no rancour in the description, no insult intended, no *them* and *us*, just a practical explanation for the differences in folk and a shrug of the shoulders or a scratch of the head when discussions involved 'they English'.

He'd been right about the hotel: it was impressive. And yes, there were sandbags at the front and blast tape on its mullion windows. But the tape criss-crossing the many tiny box-like panes of glass in each window drew attention to the ancient façade rather than detracting from it. The antique building seemed to shout its history from the moment she saw it; Maddie could imagine it as an old coaching inn.

The elderly waitress, who brought her tea, told Maddie that the Angel had once been the elaborate townhouse of the wealthy Godolphin family, who'd owned tin and copper mines. They were proper Tudor gentry, the woman told Maddie proudly.

But Maddie couldn't dismiss the juxtaposition from her mind. Such wealth, side by side with the poverty of the very miners who toiled in dangerous conditions for a pittance to provide riches for the mine owners. Maybe she was just a left-wing socialist as her brother had claimed – he'd used the accusation as a slur, his eyebrows lifting into his hairline in that intimidating way of his. But was it a *bad* thing, being a socialist? If it was, then Maddie didn't mind being bad. Fairness. That's what was needed in the world now. Wasn't that what they were fighting this war for? A bit more fairness and sharing, and people having the same chances of a good, safe life? Equality wasn't a bad thing, surely?

Maddie knew *why* she thought like that, of course. For years she'd watched her mother make judgements about people based on class, treating some with contempt, sucking up to others. Maddie had been discouraged from making friends with anyone *below her*. When she was young, it had confused her – these orders that she was allowed to speak to some people, but not others. Weren't people all just people? Now she was older, she was no longer confused, just saddened that her mother was a bigot and a snob.

'How's the cottage pie? Something wrong? You ain't touched much.' The enquiry from the elderly waitress wasn't a criticism, more of a motherly concern that Maddie should be eating properly.

'Eh?' Maddie dragged her mind away from her mother, back to the woman hovering anxiously by her elbow.

'The pie. Cook calls it *cottage*' – the woman lowered her voice as if she was giving away secret information that shouldn't be shared – 'but if it were *proper* cottage, there'd be some sort of beef in there.'

Maddie caught on quickly, felt she should contribute something to the conversation, especially as the older woman seemed to be going out on a limb. 'So, no beef then. I was never really sure what was in a cottage pie anyway,' Maddie owned up. 'What makes it different from a shepherd's pie? Or maybe they're the same,' she said.

'Oh, no, they ain't the same. Shepherd's pie 'as got lamb in there. Think of shepherds and their sheep, makes it easy to remember,' the waitress added. Her voice had the ring of experience and authority to it, and Maddie believed her.

'I see,' she said. Though to be fair, the whole conversation felt a bit surreal to her.

'*Cottage*, on the other hand – well, that's got beef in there, instead.' The woman chuckled. 'Least it *should* have. You'd need a magnifying glass to find the meat in that one there.' She pointed accusingly towards the pie. 'It's lentil.'

'Ah.'

'Brown lentils. S'posed to be good for you.'

'Really?'

'Minister of Food says so,' said the waitress, a sarcastic edge to her voice. 'But I aren't convinced some fella in London wearing a bowler hat and a fancy pinstripe suit knows what's good for us. Has the bloke even been in a kitchen?' She raised her eyebrows in scorn.

Maddie struggled for a reply. She couldn't say for certain whether or not anyone from the Ministry of Food had ever been in a kitchen, but suspected they had.

She eventually ate all the mock pie – shepherd's or cottage, whichever. It was quite tasty, unlike some of the other strange concoctions she'd eaten in the mess hall that masqueraded as food in these trying times. But folk hardly ever complained; only the odd grumble about powdered egg or the ubiquitous spam, or sausages with only gristle in them and plumped up with water that made them explode in the pan when you tried to fry them. They were given the nickname 'bangers'. Exploding sausages! You had to laugh. *Well, laugh or cry*, thought Maddie. *Two choices. And laughing was always better*.

She laughed quite a bit with her new friend at the Angel Hotel. The elderly waitress was called Lizzie, and for some reason the woman was drawn to Maddie, taking a motherly interest in her. Even persuading the hotel cook to come up with a couple of sandwiches.

'A sort of picnic,' Lizzie said, 'in case you can't find a place to have tea down there in Gunwalloe. It's only a wee place,' the waitress continued. 'You'll not find much there other than the beach and an old churchyard and barbed wire. I hear tell there's even a minefield down there. You'll need to be careful.'

There was a flask of tea with the food, with instructions to return it whenever she was able. 'The sandwiches are only meat paste,' Lizzie complained. 'I'd hoped Cook would be able to spare a bit of cheese, but well – it's the war.' And she assured Maddie that the two bottles of Cornish Spingo would make up for any shortcomings in the picnic.

Maddie was overwhelmed by the kindness and hospitality of the Cornish. And Lizzie Retallack in particular. She tried to pay for the Spingo but the offer was waved away with an airy hand and the explanation that the beer was brewed in the Blue Anchor in Helston, right there in Coinagehall Street, and she was to have it as a souvenir.

Maddie waved goodbye, and made her way back to the car with a smile on her face and a spring in her step. And a home-made wicker basket holding a flask of tea, four meat-paste sand-wiches and two bottles of beer that would *put all but the strongest man on his back.*

You had to laugh. So, she did.

8

It was a black, featureless place, a space where irrational nightmares and fearsome claustrophobia could easily take hold. He had no idea of time, how long he'd been there, but as minutes ticked by, his fear grew. Fear that he would be trapped forever in an airless box with no means of escape.

It wasn't true of course, because the dark space of the car's boot was not a sealed box. It had air. But how much of it, he couldn't be sure. How long before his head became light, his breathing laboured? A long time, perhaps – if he didn't allow the panic of claustrophobia to overcome him.

He already felt sick; the smell of petrol fumes had made him gag at first. He could taste it at the back of his throat, and it had taken all his strength of mind to swallow the cough that had tried to force its way out through his mouth. No traitorous sound could be allowed to give him away.

At first, he'd worried about the different smells. About exhaust gases that could kill. His panicked brain struggled with the idea. Carbon monoxide – or carbon dioxide? Which was it that a faulty exhaust produced? And was it enough to kill him? But then the rational part of him rejected that – there would be no smell. Just a silent killer. And although he knew nothing about the woman driving the car, he imagined her to be someone who took pride in her work. He suspected she was thorough, a professional. She would look after her vehicle, keep it mechanically sound. Unlikely there would be a faulty exhaust on this army car. And the strong petrol smell was nothing to worry about, either. He was sharing the boot of the car with a jerry can.

Rudi Fischer had no idea where he was right then, or where they were heading. The choice had not been his. Fate would now decree where he would end up, what the future would hold in store for him. But whatever it was, it was better than the alternative. If he had stayed at the camp, there could have been only one outcome. He couldn't be sure what form his death at Hoffmann's hands would take, but he could be sure that it was inevitable.

He forced a deep, calming breath through his nostrils, enough to stifle the budding claustrophobia. He steadied his shaking hands and made himself get back to work. His arms and hands ached with the effort of keeping the heavy wrench above his head, clenching his fists around it. His trembling muscles screamed out in exhaustion. But now, finally, he could feel some give in the nut, a definite slackening, and he sensed some sideways movement in the bolt. Like a loose tooth. Yes! He hadn't imagined that. His backbreaking work hadn't been in vain.

He set about the task with a renewed vigour, and optimism now filled the space in his mind where fear had taken hold.

They'd stopped once. He didn't know where, or why, but it had seemed like an eternity. Still, he'd kept on working away at the bolts that held the boot hinges in place and, eventually, he'd felt the motion of the car as it started up again. Noises reverberated around the box that was his home. Engine noise, bumps in the road, and singing.

Singing? Yes, he was right: it was definitely singing. The woman had started up some kind of cheerful song. She seemed happy. The singing went on for a long time. Different songs. She had a good voice, melodic. It made him feel happy too. Despite his situation. His desperation. It made him feel cheerful. And he wished he could see her face. Rudi imagined her face with a smile on it.

――――

This was better. Her face shone with a happy grin, and it wasn't due just to the song that she sang – it was the memories it evoked. Good times. Comradeship. They often sang it, she and her ATS friends.

'The Happy Wanderer'. Her bunkmate Molly loved the song – Molly always enjoyed a good old singsong, getting everybody in the barracks to join in, whether they wanted to or not.

And now, it really did feel like a holiday. And she, like a *free spirit*, a label her brother Richard often used for people who weren't as serious-minded as he thought they should be. *Frivolous*, was another one of Richard's insults. And he would stare at her with that judgemental frown of his, unflinching as he said it.

But her brother was wrong; Maddie was not the frivolous, empty-headed female that his criticism implied. She could be every bit as serious as he was (though maybe not as dull) and was competent at her job. And, sometimes, she wondered if Richard wasn't perhaps a little jealous of her, of her job, which seemed more exciting than his own at the Ministry of Supply – shuffling numbers around a ledger.

Maddie shunted her brother to the back of her mind, eased off on her speed and followed the narrow track on through the hamlet of Gunwalloe, down towards the sea. Church Cove was where she was headed, with its medieval church built right there on the beach.

Lizzie Retallack had struggled with the idea that *anyone* should make a special trip to see the place. 'Gunwalloe's a tiny place,' she'd said. 'An old church, a farm what's falling to bits, and a beach – why would you want to go there?'

But it had all sounded so romantic to Maddie. It conjured up images of Cornish smugglers landing their contraband on an isolated beach at midnight: a doe-eyed young woman with raven-black hair falling in ringlets waiting for her love; an athletic young man jumping easily from the rowing boat into the churning surf, rushing to the woman he loved while his men offloaded the brandy.

She bumped the car to a halt as the track suddenly came to an end. It opened up into a wide flat promontory, a natural parking place. The cast of characters in her head retreated to where they belonged – the pages of a romantic novel.

The scene in front of her was nothing like the images she had imagined.

Maddie put on the brake and slowly got out of the car, shaking the tiredness and cramp from her limbs. Her eyes made a swift appraisal of where her map and her own intrepid exploration had taken her.

She tried to swallow her disappointment, didn't know what exactly she'd been expecting – but not this. She'd parked next to a shabby, rundown barn and supposed there must be a farmhouse somewhere around, though she couldn't see it. And as for the sea! She had a glimpse of it only, but there was no sun glinting on blue ocean as she had pictured it, for the day was grey, with low-hanging clouds threatening rain. And below her, off to the left, stretching into the distance, she could see that the sand dunes, sprouting coarse, tufted grasses, were surrounded by barbed wire – Lizzie had been right about that.

She left the car, following what looked like a natural track downhill towards the small church that must be hiding below. Right then, it was invisible, but she knew it was there. It *must* be there, for she'd read about it. It was old, very old, fifteenth- or sixteenth-century kind of old. She couldn't remember exactly. Saint Winwaloe's, the medieval church at Gunwalloe with its ancient churchyard, perched low on the dunes, stood guard over the sandy beach at Church Cove. The *church of storms*, they called it, because of the powerful storms that often battered this part of the coastline.

She turned a corner and there it was.

Maddie gasped. *This* sight was incredible, dramatic, poetic, beautiful. Nature and man come together as one to produce a miracle, a feast for the eyes. A sight to make your breath catch in your throat.

The tiny church nestled in the sand, exactly as she had imagined, the tower alongside it embedded in rock. Storms would throw up sand from the cove below, and people would have to wrestle with that, clear it from the church. People who cared about the place. The beach itself, that was its own small miracle: fine-grained sand that would be warm to the touch on a summer's day, a calm place to swim and paddle no doubt, sheltered as it was on both sides by ribs of granite headland that enclosed it. But in a storm? Yes, she could picture the fury of an Atlantic storm throwing tempestuous waves up onto the innocent-looking beach. There'd be no swimming then.

The fierce beauty of the place made her emotional. Reminded her of a painting she'd once seen. And she knew this was somewhere she could feel at peace; a place she would always remember. She would keep this precious moment locked away; this first glimpse always in her mind. And it didn't matter that the day was grey, that the sun didn't shine on the water, its reflection on the translucent waves below. Because the sea was crystal clear, blue, green, tiny beads of white foam leaving their echo on the beach as the tide retreated. Miraculous.

She wanted to mark this moment. Run to the beach below. Feel the damp sand between her toes, run out into the ocean.

She glanced at the wooden gate leading to the church; that could wait. There would be time to explore later; to go into the churchyard, read the headstones, imagine the people who had left their mark, their lives echoed only by faint etching on grey memorials. Right then, the sand and the ocean called.

And that's when a voice called. It sounded young, frightened. A cry for help. Followed by a piercing scream.

She turned her head towards the dunes and the barbed wire and the small figure in the distance. The figure had been running, but now it stopped. Frozen in fear. Petrified. In that instant, she saw the flash of flames and a plume of smoke, and heard a strangled shout.

And Maddie knew right then that Lizzie Retallack had been correct and that the barbed wire had been put on the dunes for a reason. There was a minefield there and someone was standing in the middle of it.

She ran towards the wire.

9

17 FEBRUARY 1941

GUNWALLOE

He'd heard the fearful scream just as he was about to set off along the small track back towards some sort of village that he could see in the distance. It was either make his way there, or head towards the sea. And Rudi Fischer knew instinctively that the sea there could not help him. There was no harbour, no boats.

His friend, Hans, had been right. Rudi was no sailor, didn't know the first thing about navigation, and these shores looked treacherous. A man would need to be a seaman in a place like this. So, even though heading towards a village would carry its own danger, it was the only possibility of escape. And he would be careful. Try to steer clear of people.

But then he'd heard the scream. It reverberated around his skull as if it came from his own lips. And there was *terror* in it. And that's when Rudi did something totally illogical, something that might easily change the course of his life. His legs seemed to work independently of his body, taking him not to relative safety, but towards the far-off sand dunes and the source of the scream.

———

Maddie was out of breath, her legs shaking with the effort she'd asked of them, but her reaction had been automatic. Someone was in trouble and that's what you did – went to help. Her body did what she expected, but even so, the speed surprised her for she wasn't a natural athlete.

As she got nearer to the dunes and the barbed wire that surrounded them, she could make out the figure crouched there. A small, scruffy lad. Shaking. Crying.

She reached the wire; saw a hole in it, where the boy had squeezed through. There was no warning sign. Maybe there had been once. Maybe people knew it was a minefield and kept away. But not this little lad. This small, intrepid boy. An explorer, like herself.

The lad's sobs had turned to sniffles now. Tears ran down his dirty face and joined the stream of liquid making its way out of his snotty nose. He wiped it on the sleeve of his jumper, and turned his head towards her, waved an angry hand in the direction of the rutted earth and the sand thrown up by the explosion.

He'd been lucky. The fallout from the explosion of the landmine had missed him by a few feet only.

''E's *dead*, miss,' he shouted. The boy dropped his head onto his chest and his body heaved once more in a massive wail. ''E's 'ad it! 'E never did *nuthin'* to nobody. Why'd 'e 'ave to die?' More snot joined the thin, snail-like trail on the boy's face. He shook his head in disbelief. Carrot-red hair fell over his eyes.

'Don't move!' yelled Maddie. 'Who was with you?' she asked, looking at the heap of earth in desperation.

'Weren't nobody else 'ere, miss. I were on me own.'

'Well, then who—?'

'I were chasing a rabbit. Poor little sod got hisself blowed to bits.' The young lad choked out the words. 'It ain't fair.'

Maddie could feel her whole body shaking with the trauma. Fought to bring it under control. *A rabbit!* So far, the only casualty had been a rabbit. She wanted to cry, to laugh. It was a reaction, she knew. That, and relief. For she'd imagined gruesome bits of body, another child's body, lying out here, peppering the sand dunes. But it wasn't over, she still had to try and get the boy to safety.

'I...' The small lad started to shiver and sank down onto his bottom. 'Wot if I gets blowed up too?'

'What's your name?' asked Maddie. She tried to keep her voice level, to be strong, confident, reassuring. She didn't have any experience with children. But people were people. And this small person had begun to shake uncontrollably, was definitely frightened. *Who wouldn't be?* He'd just seen bits of rabbit evaporate before his eyes.

'Me name's Harry. Harry Foster,' he said, shakily.

'And what age are you, Harry?' It was hard to judge with small boys, especially when they were sitting down. But he seemed very young.

'I'll be seven next birthday,' he said proudly, and puffed his chest out a little.

'Seven,' said Maddie. 'Quite grown up, then. And does your mother live nearby, Harry?'

'Me ma ain't nowhere near here,' Harry said, sadly. 'I miss 'er, *sometimes*. I been 'vacuated. I lives with Mrs Edson in the village, she ain't too bad.'

'So, you're an evacuee, Harry?' she said. 'Must be nice, living by the sea.' *Empty words, but maybe they would help distract him, calm him down.*

Harry drew his bony knees up to his chest and wrapped his skinny arms around them. Thin legs protruded from beneath the worn, short trousers.

She felt suddenly maternal and protective towards this

small, red-headed waif. *Whoever Mrs Edson in the village was,* thought Maddie, *she certainly wasn't over-feeding the lad.*

'We go swimming, sometimes. Me mates and me, like. Jimmy's me best mate.'

'Well, we need to get you back to Jimmy, then. Can you stand up? Just get to your feet, but don't walk. I'll come and get you.' She had no idea how she would do that, but one step at a time.

The young lad didn't answer. Just stared at her wide-eyed, like he was in shock.

'C'mon, Harry. Try to stand up. You're a brave lad, you can do it.' Maddie tried to inject confidence into her voice, a confidence she didn't feel. But there was no point in them both being terrified – that wouldn't get the lad back to safety. 'C'mon, Harry,' she coaxed. 'You can do it.'

'I *can't*, miss,' Harry wailed. 'I can't move me legs.'

'Look, I know you're scared. Anybody would be,' said Maddie.

'I ain't *scared*,' he shouted, defiantly. But the shaking in his body revealed the lie, the bravado.

'Okay, that's good,' she said.

'I'll just sit here for a bit,' said Harry. 'Till me legs feel better.'

'Right, that's okay. You'll be okay, young man,' said Maddie, suddenly making up her mind. 'Don't you worry, we'll get you back home in time for tea. You just stay there, quietly. I'm coming in right now to help you.' Maddie bent down to the hole in the wire, and wrenched both sides apart to make it bigger. She was about to try and squeeze through when she felt a hand on her shoulder. A large hand. A man's hand.

'No! Not you. I go.'

She turned her head towards the voice. Seeing his face, the breath jammed in the hollow of her throat and her head felt light as she tried to work her way through the confusion. 'You!' whispered Maddie. 'But how...?'

He pulled her to her feet and put a finger to her lips to silence any more questions.

'I go,' repeated the man. 'You stay.' He pointed to a spot far away from the wire. 'Stay!' he ordered again, when she didn't seem to be moving to safety.

Stay? What, like a dog? What WAS it with men? How come they were the ones who gave the orders? And what the hell was HE doing here, and how in the name of Hades did he get here?

Maddie wanted to argue with him; after all, she was the one with the uniform on; it was *her* land he was standing on. He was the usurper here, this German.

All the same, when the German prisoner reached out his hand for hers, a pleading look in those blue eyes of his, she nodded her head and took a step back from the wire. She watched his face crease into a smile, his eyes spark with a twinkle for a second and then turn serious again as his hands shooed her away, even farther back, away from danger. That's when she saw the sign, abandoned, rusted, lying on its side in the dunes. The fierce-looking skull and crossbones and the words beneath, faint now, almost illegible, faded by the sun and scoured by sand and harsh winds: DANGER. MINEFIELD. BEWARE.

———

Rudi stepped through the hole in the wire and tried not to think about the odds. They would survive or they wouldn't, him and this small, fearful lad. But at least the woman was out of the danger zone.

He knew that there was no clever, strategic way to do this; nor was he able to put into practice the way they taught you in training: he could not lie on his belly and creep towards the boy, inch by painful inch, probing the ground in front of him. He had no bayonet to do that, no way of painstakingly testing for the tell-tale round metal shape hidden beneath the surface. The size of a dinner plate, but far more malevolent than an innocent piece of crockery, loaded with TNT. Simple but effective killers were landmines. Not too much in there to go wrong: the lethal body packed with explosive, the fuse and the pressure plate.

He tried to remember his basic training. The pressure plate – what kind of weight would set the thing off? The weight of an average man, surely – if they were anti-personnel mines? Even more weight would be needed if they were anti-tank landmines. And he wasn't the weight of an average man, was he? He was a shadow of his former self, his skin loose where the bulk of his body had retreated. He had no idea what he weighed, but it wouldn't be much.

He might be okay. They might both survive. Neither he nor this little chap weighed much. But then he wondered what had made this mine explode. A small animal, maybe. He remembered hearing of shrapnel mines. They only needed a few pounds to set them off. Either way, he'd have to take the chance. There was no other way if the lad was to be saved.

The boy had gone silent now. No more tears. No more shaking. The small body was totally still: shock, he supposed. Scratch that up for both of them; he was a little shocked himself. If his friend Hans had asked what exactly Rudi would choose to do on his first day of freedom, both of them would have been surprised that *this* had been his first choice.

But there had been no choice. Humanity saw no boundaries of race or creed or even country. It wasn't an idea he'd ever put into words before, and not one a German patriot could have voiced in safety. *The master race.* He'd never believed in it. The superiority. The flag waving. Hadn't even been keen on joining in a war in the first place. But still – he was a patriot. You could not deny your own land that easily.

The first raindrop hit him hard on the back of the neck, returning his thoughts to the present. The others followed with a ferocity he hadn't expected, and the sky that had once been merely grey now turned black, a crack of thunder reverberating noisily off the granite headlands to either side of the cove below.

The sudden fury of the storm surprised him and within seconds, he was soaked through. So was the small child cowering and shivering a short distance away. The lad's hair was plastered to his head, like a bright orange cap had been thrown at him, landing randomly, covering one eye.

The comical sight made Rudi laugh. And maybe such strange, boisterous laughter was out of place, but he had no control over it. It might even have been mild hysteria, simply a release valve for his own fear, because the tension that had been building inside him like a curled-up fist finally dissolved. And he moved as fast as he could, not away from the danger, but towards it.

10

Maddie didn't speak, just wrenched the small, wet boy from the man's rigid grip and stumbled back up the track, Harry huddled in her arms. There was no sound of feet behind, and she wondered where the German was. But when she looked around, she saw him still standing there, on the dunes.

He'd picked up the rusted warning sign and was staring at it, transfixed. He didn't move, didn't speak; it was as if he was frozen to the spot.

The lad was silent too, with only the odd shiver running through him, proof he was still awake. Still *alive*.

She looked down at his thin frame, pushed the soggy wet hair back from his face. He didn't resist, just clung on to her, trust mirrored in his huge hazel eyes. Maddie headed back to the car, hardly noticing the weight of her burden. Not much of a burden, for the boy felt light as a feather.

Warm, dry clothes, that's what he needed. And food. And a comfortable bed. A place of safety where he could snuggle beneath the covers and sleep away the trauma. The child had been trapped in a minefield, had seen a rabbit blown to pieces, been terrified for his life. But then children had great powers of recovery. *Didn't they?* That's what she'd heard. But how did that work? Because, right then, the poor little mite was limp, and didn't seem to have a lot of fight in him.

She bundled him into the front seat, out of the rain and howling wind, and walked round to the back of the car, to retrieve the car-rug from the boot.

She gasped in shock.

It had been a day of surprises: good, bad, unexpected; like having a mine explode in front of your eyes. But Maddie, who thought of herself as rational, stoic and in the main unflappable, now threw up her hands in horror. There *was* no boot. Not as she remembered it.

Poor old Harriet! The car was a friend. And her friend had been vandalised in the most dramatic way. The lid of the boot was tilted at a crazy angle, balanced on one hinge only. It gave the car an odd, human-like quality, like a face that had been flattened in a fight, the damaged hinge hanging like a loose tooth.

The *German*. It would have been the German prisoner who did it! Somehow, he'd managed to hide himself in her car, and to punch his way out. And although she'd known nothing of his escape attempt, he couldn't have done it without her. *She* was responsible for helping her country's enemy. *Her* enemy! He'd used her! The *damn* man had used her! Made her into some kind of traitor, if only by default. *Just like Corporal Williams...* she remembered how the man had waved her through and thrown her a wink. He was responsible too. He should have searched the staff car. She wouldn't have minded. She'd expected no less. And now they were both at fault.

Maddie felt the burden of guilt press down heavily on her. She wanted to cry. But you didn't cry over spilt milk. That wouldn't put it back in the bottle, would it? Instead, she thought about young Harry waiting in the car, miserable, soaking wet, thin shoulders shivering with cold. She squeezed her hand carefully into the car boot and pulled out the rug.

Harry hadn't moved. But when she tucked the plaid blanket around him, he nodded, and said, 'Thanks, miss.'

She remembered the Thermos flask of tea Lizzie had given her, and retrieved it from the wicker basket on the back seat. It would warm the lad up a bit.

Harry took it gratefully, cupping his shaking hands around it, slurping the tea noisily. He wiped his mouth with the all-purpose sleeve of his jumper and finally smiled up at Maddie. 'Got any grub in there, miss?' he asked. The smile turned into a cheeky grin.

Maddie handed over one of the meat-paste sandwiches and watched half of it rapidly disappear in one go. *The resilience of youth. The boy must be made of rubber to bounce back like that.*

'Miss...?'

'Yes, Harry?' She smiled. No one had ever warned the lad about speaking with his mouth full. Or if they had, he'd taken no notice.

'I needs to get back, miss. She don't like it when I'm late for tea.'

'Who?'

'Mrs Edson.'

'I see.'

'She's right partic'l'r, miss. Not like me ma. Ma's great, she don't *never* mind how long I stay out. But we don't have such good grub back home,' he admitted, sheepishly. 'That ain't me ma's fault, mind. She's busy, see. Works at the munitions factory. She don't have no time, not for making tea and stuff.'

'Okay, we'll get you home,' said Maddie. 'You can show me where you live. That all right?' She thought about the poor old boot lid, hanging on by a thread, and the narrow track full of ruts – she'd need to drive slowly.

'Maybe you can drop me up the lane, miss? I'll walk to the 'ouse from there, it ain't that far.'

'You don't want me to go in, Harry? Don't you think Mrs

Edson should know what happened? She might be worried. I could explain...'

'Nah, that's alright. I'll tell her I got caught up in the rain.'

'But she should know about this. It was dangerous what you did – you know that, don't you?'

'I won't do it no more, miss. Promise. Cross me heart and hope to die.'

'Harry...'

'What, miss?'

'Mrs Edson – she doesn't hit you, does she?'

'What?! *That* old biddy? There ain't no harm in 'er. She's just a weird old girl. Keeps to 'erself, like. Some of them others thinks she's a witch, but she ain't.'

'So, she's never smacked you?'

'Nah.' Harry laughed at the idea. 'Once she even hugged me. Kissed the top of me 'ead. She'd never belt me, not like me ma.'

'Your mother hits you?'

'Me ma's *okay*,' he said quickly, a challenge in his eyes. 'Only she gets sad sometimes, what wiv the war an' all. Gives me the odd clip round the 'ead. Ain't nuthin' much, and mas are allowed to do stuff like that, ain't they?'

Maddie didn't argue. It wouldn't help. She'd never had kids, and it couldn't be easy looking after them all by yourself with a husband away fighting. Keeping a house, trying to scrape by on the ration, going to work in a munitions factory, bombs falling around you. No, many women didn't have it easy. Would be struggling.

'Okay. Eat up, I'll drive you back. Oh, and Harry...'

'Yeah?' The lad was smiling now, and had requisitioned yet another meat-paste sandwich from the basket.

'I'm glad you're okay. And it's good to be an explorer, to go to new places. But *promise* me you'll never go near those sand dunes again.'

'Said so, didn't I? Crossed me heart an' all.' Harry grinned.

'Right, let's go.' Maddie started up slowly, nosing the car carefully along the bumpy track. Even so, a disturbing grinding noise came from the back of the car. She held onto the steering wheel with a fierce, determined grip and tried to block the unnerving sound from her ears.

'Miss – that bloke were kind, the geezer what saved me. And I didn't say ta. Me ma would knock me block off for that.'

'It's okay, Harry. I'm sure he'll understand.'

'You'll tell him, like?' said Harry, getting agitated.

'Don't worry, I'll tell him,' she said. Though she wouldn't, of course. The man would be far away from there by now, on the run. An enemy escapee. Her fault, and nothing she could do about it. Except report him – at least she could tell the authorities that he'd been in Gunwalloe, last seen on the dunes. But by now he could be anywhere.

'Right, I'll jump out 'ere,' said the lad, pointing towards a decrepit-looking building.

Maddie pulled the car up beside it. It was a pub, or had been. With its flaking paintwork and ancient signboard, the place looked abandoned, like it had sold its last pint years ago.

'You don't live here, do you?' asked Maddie, surprised.

'Nah,' said Harry. 'That's the Ship Inn. Smugglers owned it. Not now, mind. Old boy what owns it now, he's a cranky geezer. Chases me and Jimmy off. Says we're too young to drink.' Harry grinned. 'Wouldn't mind tryin' it, like.'

'The landlord's right,' agreed Maddie, 'alcohol's bad for you.' She thought about the Spingo waiting in the car – she planned to drink it anyway.

The young lad fidgeted in his seat. Bored now. Wanting to get on with more exciting stuff.

'Right, off you go. You take care, young man,' said Maddie. 'And be nice to Mrs Edson, you hear.'

'Sure, miss. And... ta.'

'What for?' said Maddie.

'For the tea and sarnies. Meat paste, they're me favourite.'

Harry Foster grinned and shook her hand with an exuberance and energy that seemed at odds with his skinny body and the frightening events he'd just lived through. He slammed the car door behind him and went running off down the lane, whistling something cheerful as he went.

11

Maddie drove back slowly and carefully along the way she had come, feeling every bump in the rutted track reverberating through her. The Humber's suspension was usually adequate, but right then, it felt as if Harriet was getting her own back for the way she'd been treated.

Maddie's pig-headed determination took her back to the same spot above Church Cove. There was still the old church and the graveyard to investigate later, but first she should tackle the repairs to her car. It would be easier to do that parked on the wide promontory next to the broken-down barn. She'd need to find the police station in Helston soon and make a report about the German who'd escaped. But the damage he'd done to the boot of the Humber made the thing unwieldy to drive. She'd try to fix it first – it shouldn't take long.

The car skidded to a messy halt. She felt its wheels sink into soft earth and stepped out into a quagmire of mud. The brutal rainstorm was over, had churned up the ground, but the wind still howled eerily up there on the clifftop. Its ghostly sound reminded her of a horror film Molly had once dragged her along to see. She'd had nightmares about it.

The icy chill suddenly bit into her and Maddie's whole body began to shake with it. *Funny.* She hadn't even noticed her wet clothes or the freezing air when she'd been sorting Harry out. And Maddie thought about something that had struck her before: the power of mind over matter, and how your brain could fool your body into forgetting pain, forgetting fear, and just getting on with stuff when it was necessary.

Soldiers at the front – that's how it must be with them. Otherwise, how could they do what they had to and carry on after they'd seen such awful things? Finding the courage that was needed? Finding the inner strength to stay sane in an insane world?

Enough! She walked around to the passenger side of the car, opened the door and pulled out the rug that had covered Harry's thin shoulders. And that's when a tall figure appeared behind her, took the blanket from her shaking hands, and wrapped it gently around her.

'You again? Get off me!' she protested.

He didn't answer. Just walked her slowly to the barn, his arms around her trembling shoulders, supporting her shocked body.

Her legs suddenly gave way beneath her, buckling like they didn't belong to her body. *Why would your legs DO that when they've worked perfectly well up to now – were perfectly normal, functional legs that have always served you well?* Her face suddenly felt tight, and a small trickle of tears made its way down it towards her lips, leaving a wet trail that she had no control over. *How can your eyes do that all by themselves, without giving you notice? Like traitors.*

She was a traitor. Had committed treason against her own country. He'd made her do that, even though she might try to excuse her treason. Blame it solely on him.

The man led her to a corner of the barn, lowered her onto an ancient, creaking wooden bench and pulled the plaid blanket tighter around her, as if she was helpless, unable to do such a simple thing for herself. Like some sort of pathetic, useless female.

He didn't speak. Didn't even look back at her as he left the barn. *What? That was it? No apology for ruining her life?*

He had ruined everything for her. Her army career would be in tatters. She might even be court-martialled. For how could she prove she'd known nothing about his bid for freedom, had been an unwilling accomplice? Proving a negative was never easy. But, willing or not, the fact was that a prisoner had escaped in her car. And that's exactly how the army would see it. Pleading innocence wouldn't help, would just make her out as a hapless victim. And weakness wasn't encouraged in the army. It was rooted out in basic training, she knew that.

The unfairness of it all made her angry. She discarded the blanket and went running after him as another frightening thought struck her: what was to stop him stealing the Humber, leaving her there in this remote place?

He hadn't made it far in his bid for freedom. Only to the back of the Humber, where she found him bent over the boot with a wrench in his hand.

Maddie's rage flew from her tight fists, pummelling his back.

The German put the wrench down and slowly turned around to face her, a disarming smile on his face. He took hold of her hands in his. Held onto them tightly.

But Maddie didn't return his smile. She didn't feel like smiling for the frustration and anger bubbled up inside her, looking for an escape. She squirmed in his grasp, pulled her hands away.

'Get away from there. How *dare* you steal my car? This belongs to the British Army,' she shouted.

Rudi laughed. 'I see! So, I am a thief, you think? I *never* steal,' he said, his expression serious now. 'Not from army. Not from you. Especially not from you. I wish no trouble for you, madam. I fix the car for you, is all. I broke it, I must fix.'

'Ha!'

'What is this "ha"? What does it mean?' asked Rudi.

'It means, Mister whatever your name is—'

'Rudi Fischer, Fraulein.' The German bowed his head respectfully and politely clicked his heels. 'And you are?' he asked.

Flustered, Maddie gabbled her name, her finishing-school education coming to her rescue, conquering her anger for a moment. 'It means that I don't believe you. Why would you *not* use my car to get away? Why leave it for me? Why even fix it?'

'I wish you no trouble.'

'Little late for that, don't you think? I'm already *in* trouble, thanks to you. Stable door's wide open, horse has bolted.'

'I don't understand,' he said. 'This horse has what?' He shrugged his shoulders in apology. 'My English,' he said. 'Not perfect.'

'Not important,' she said. 'The horse... just an expression.' Maddie shrugged as well. 'You're an escaped German prisoner. When they discover you've gone, there'll be a manhunt for you. You're not fixing that car to help me, you're doing it for yourself. So – I think you're lying.'

'No, I want to make things fine for you,' said Rudi.

'*Fine?* Ha!' said Maddie again.

'Okay, fifty-fifty, I lie. I do not tell you *all* of the truth.'

'Same thing,' she said.

'Maybe...'

'So?' she said.

'I leave the car for you. And truly, I fix it, so you have no more trouble...'

'And...?'

'I never learn to drive,' he admitted.

She stared straight into those ice-blue eyes of his. Hers was a penetrating stare, searching for the truth.

The German held her gaze, unflinching, unsmiling now.

And that's when Private Maddie Brady threw back her head and laughed.

———

It was growing dark before he finally fixed the damage to the car. Apart from a couple of small scratches inside the boot where the wrench had slipped when he'd been battling his way out, no one would notice. He didn't want the woman blamed for his transgressions.

Rudi was pleased with his efforts. *Peculiar* that he should feel some sort of satisfaction, especially about helping the enemy. Although it wasn't about that. His contentment came from seeing the results of his own ingenuity, his resourcefulness.

He had always shown a flair for working with his hands, discovering how things worked, improving them. His father had been proud of him, had encouraged the young Rudi's curiosity; had allowed him to dismantle things in the workshop, put them back together again. His father had been an engineer, a man of standing in their small Bavarian village. Rudi Fischer had wanted to follow in his father's footsteps but the war had intervened.

Gunter Fischer had been a thoughtful man, respectful of others with different views to his own. A cultured man with liberal, humanitarian ideals, he himself had been respected by others in his village. People had come to him for advice, to share his knowledge, for Rudi's father was not only a man with practical skills but a little of the philosopher dwelt in him as well. That's why he'd engaged with other nations' ideas, had learnt languages other than his own. And he'd taught both Rudi and his younger brother, Werner, to speak a little French as well as English.

That had been fine before the National Socialists came to power. Hitler and his bully boys changed Germany in 1933. After that, the only learning encouraged in schools had been the history of the Nazi Party, of Hitler and the other major figures of the Reich. And no one was expected to speak any language other than the tongue of the Fatherland. Foreign languages were suspect, and knowledge of them could get a person in trouble.

The war had changed everything. Especially for Rudi's father. His liberalism had been considered dangerous, a rebellion against the new regime. Especially suspect were his father's strong views on pacifism. Some 'well-meaning' neighbour had reported him and Gunter Fischer had been put on a register of conscientious objectors. Refusing to fight because your conscience wouldn't allow it was a dangerous thing in this new Germany – the Nazi Party had made it a criminal offence.

It wasn't often that Rudi dwelt on the sadness of the past. The loss of his father was a wound that would always be there. He might put it to the back of his mind, but he could never forget the day they'd taken his father away. Nor the courage it had taken for Gunter to refuse to abandon his ideals, and march off to the camp with his head held high.

The family had never heard from him again. Had no idea if Gunter Fischer was alive or dead.

Rudi grunted to himself, tried to tap into his optimism again. Soon he'd need it. It wasn't often he allowed himself to wallow in self-pity, for there was nothing to be gained by dredging up the sadness of the past.

He heard the barn door open, and turned around at the sound of her voice.

'You're still here then,' said Maddie. 'Thought you'd be long gone.'

'All finished,' he said. He wiped his oily hands on the rag and pointed at the resurrected boot, pleased with his achievement.

He watched her inspect the running repair.

'Mm... hmm.' She nodded her head.

'What will you do?' he asked.

'What will *I* do?' she said, looking astounded. 'I'm not the one with the problem here, am I? They'll all be out looking for you: soldiers, police, civilians. You can't escape.'

Rudi studied the woman: the confident set of her shoulders, head held high, chin thrust out in defiance. She was magnificent, courageous, bold. He wanted to tell her how beautiful she was. How brave he thought her. But the words wouldn't come. Instead, he said: 'Maybe there is no escape. But I can't go back there, I'll die.'

'Such drama,' said Maddie. 'Of *course* you won't die. I'll take you back. We can leave now. I'll say I found you on the road, and that you gave yourself up willingly. It'll be fine, you'll see. You'll not suffer for it. We British have codes – we're not animals.'

Rudi looked at her with sadness in his eyes, with regret. It would be good to share a car journey with her, with this lovely woman. To sit beside her this time, instead of being trapped in a small, terrifying space with little air.

'What? You don't believe me?' said Maddie.

'Codes – yes,' he said. 'Codes are good. We have codes too, we Germans.' He thought about his father. An ethical man, *his* codes, *his* morality. And how he'd suffered for those principles. What the bastards had done to his *Vater*. And he thought about that vicious little dictator Oberleutnant Karl Hoffmann waiting for him back at the POW camp, about Hoffmann's code. 'But not all German codes are the same,' he said sadly, sighing. 'And unhappily for us as a nation, we *do* have animals.'

'Hitler,' she said. 'Yes, I see that.'

'Him and others,' said Rudi. 'But I was thinking of one much nearer. Right here.'

'Here?' she asked, confused.

'In the camp. Oberleutnant Hoffmann. An animal, like the rest of those Nazis. A despicable man.'

'But you're a Nazi,' said Maddie.

'Never!' Rudi spat the word. 'I could never be one of them! It's why I had to run – Hoffmann threatened to kill me.'

'But why?'

'Because I'm not like them. A German, yes. I love my country. But not a Nazi. I refuse to join their vicious little club. And I warned Hoffmann. He was beating up some of the younger men. I told him to stop. He's a bully and a fraud, impersonating someone else. I said I'd expose him. Told him what he could do with his master race and Herr Hitler.'

'You could have told someone he threatened you,' said Maddie.

'And who would listen to a *damn troublesome Kraut*?' He said the words in an exaggerated upper-class English accent. And smiled at her expression.

He watched her face. Saw the look of confusion turn to something else. Pity? Did she pity him? No, not that. Not a sad look. Empathy, but more than that.

And now, the beginnings of a smile, and maybe even friendship.

12

It was dark now. Not pitch-black, for a small sliver of moonlight painted the sky and added a touch of romance to the scene around them. Between that and the far-off sound of surf as it pounded the shoreline of the cove, it was a night of mystical possibilities. At least for Maddie, who remembered the rugged, handsome smuggler she'd conjured up in her mind. He would be pulling his rowing boat into shore on such a night. Off-loading his contraband.

She stared across at Rudi Fischer, slumped on the floor, his back propped up against the wall of the barn. He seemed exhausted. Vulnerable. Not obvious hero material. He wasn't swarthy, not like her make-believe Cornish smuggler. His hair wasn't black, but blond, the kind of blond that was almost white. And his *eyes*. They were neither green nor hazel, but memorable all the same. Mesmerising. An incredible piercing blue. And although he was the enemy, Maddie was beginning to think him a hero as well. He could have run, thought only of himself, his own escape. But instead, he had gone to rescue a small, frightened boy from a minefield.

And that's when her bubble of romance burst. The noise

was incredible and shook the ancient timbers of the barn around them. They both looked skywards at the same time as though it were possible to see through the sagging timbers of the roof: she – pulling herself back to reality; he – opening half-closed eyes in recognition of the familiar sound.

The din went on for a long time and seemed endless. A wave of sound that made speech impossible. Maddie watched his eyes widen, not with fear, but with something else – an old memory, perhaps. He went outside into the chill night, and she followed him.

They both stared up in awe as wave after wave of aircraft passed overhead, heading inland. Black shapes, lit by the moon, silhouetted against the night sky, its shimmering canvas of black satin pierced by occasional stars that glistened like sequins.

It was a breath-taking sight. *Something beautiful and poetic about its symmetry*, thought Maddie. *Majestic*. But at the same time there was a dark malevolence in such power that could take lives so randomly. She shuddered at the thought. She'd been wrong to think the sight beautiful. People who were alive now would be dead by morning.

'Heavy bombers,' she said. 'Headed inland.' She sighed. 'God bless whoever's underneath that lot.'

'Pride of the *Luftwaffe*,' said Rudi.

She looked at him in surprise. He sounded cynical.

'Heinkel He 111s,' said Rudi. 'I recognise the sound.'

Maddie thought she heard sadness in his voice, or maybe even regret for what he no longer had.

'Is that what you flew?' she asked.

Rudi nodded his head. 'I'm sorry,' he said. And then something like guilt crossed his face, reached his eyes.

'What for?'

'For what I did. For what they will do tonight.'

'You dropped bombs?' she asked. 'Is that what you're saying? Were you in a bomber?'

'A gunner, in the waist,' he said. 'But it doesn't matter, does it?'

'What?'

'Whether I drop the bombs, or fire the gun,' Rudi said, with remorse. 'It's all the same. People die. I've killed them. We Germans have killed them. I, Rudi Fischer, have killed.' He said it with passion, his voice getting louder.

'You've killed. We've killed. It's war and I *hate* it,' she said, angrily. 'But we've got to win. Britain *has* to win. You see that, don't you? We can't let that maniac Hitler get away with it – he has to pay.'

Maddie watched him look up once more as the last of the bombers flew overhead. He turned around and headed back to the old barn and as he did so, he seemed to shrink in size, his shoulders drooping as if in defeat. She noticed he had a limp. Maybe the man was tired. He'd had a long, stressful day – they both had. She was tired as well. And hungry. Suddenly, she was very hungry.

She remembered the food in the car and smiled. Harry hadn't scoffed all of it; there must be a couple of sandwiches left. And the tea, although it was asking a lot of the flask that Lizzie had provided for the tea to be anything but lukewarm after all this time. And the local beer, of course. She couldn't remember what Lizzie had called that, but it would be a treat, whatever it was.

That's what made her mind up. The hunger and tiredness that had suddenly crept up on her. *What will you do?* he'd asked her. And until then she hadn't decided. *Drive through the night in the blackout, back to the POW camp? Make her report?* That was one option. Or drive into Helston. Notify the police that there was a German prisoner on the loose. But the struggle with potholes in the road and the narrow country lanes had been hard enough in daylight. No headlights allowed in the blackout. *No point in breaking an axle in the dark.* And even if she left right now, this man wouldn't stay here, waiting to be captured. And she could hardly overpower him and take him with her. She'd report him tomorrow.

Maddie got the basket from the car and the torch from the glove box and made her way back into the barn. The old building might be creaking, but it seemed to be waterproof and would be warmer than spending a night in the vehicle.

He was asleep when she got back. He looked young, the lines around his eyes smoothed out, the thin, sallow face relaxed. She tried to guess his age. *Younger than me*, she thought. Not that she was old: twenty-three was hardly old, was it? Yes, definitely younger, although he acted older, seemed to have a weary sort of experience about him. But then the war did that to people. *Twenty, maybe. Perhaps even younger. Maybe still in his teens.* The idea shocked her. But why should it? She couldn't find a reason. Just that whatever he'd had to do in this war seemed to make him sad.

Maddie unpacked the basket and laid the contents carefully on the barn floor. A sort of picnic. She'd leave a sandwich for him and a bottle of beer. It seemed only right: a small reward after what he'd done for the lad. She poured tea from the flask into its miniature cup and took a sip. She was right; it wasn't hot, just tepid. But still, the trickle of liquid that made its way down her throat was comforting. Like an old friend, rediscovered, remembered.

The unexpected scream startled her, and Maddie knocked the flask over, the precious liquid seeping onto the rough concrete floor.

The German cried out again in his sleep and she ran over to his side.

'*Vater!*' he shouted. He opened his eyes in confusion and looked up at Maddie.

'Water?' she said. 'Is that what you want? I don't understand. I don't speak German.'

He shouted again, a pleading in his eyes this time, and in his voice: '*Mein Vater. Wo ist mein Vater?*' He grabbed her hand urgently.

'Look, I'm sorry,' said Maddie, 'but I don't understand. You had a nightmare...'

'A nightmare?'

'Yes, you were sleeping. You screamed...'

'Oh. I frightened you,' said Rudi.

'What is *meinvater*?' she asked.

'My *Vater*... *mein* Papa,' he explained, when she looked confused. 'Papa...'

'Father – your father?'

'*Ja*. Yes,' he said, and he held his head stiffly, his body taut with trapped emotion.

Maddie rested her hand lightly on his shoulder, felt the small tremor run from him into her fingers. Like electricity looking for an outlet.

And that's when she noticed the first tear. It seeped from the corner of his eye in a slow-motion ballet, as though the man had no control over its beginning or its end. She stopped its progress with a single finger. An intimate gesture, but it didn't feel out of place: it felt right. Other tears followed and she wiped them away.

Like a small, frightened boy, she thought. A boy looking for an answer, searching for a way out of the darkness of his nightmare. She sank down beside him, wrapping her arms around him until his tremors became a part of her, his sadness hers. She listened as his rapid breaths subsided. Their breathing slowly joined together, synchronised, like one body. A magical synthesis – a union of bodies and minds. Hers and his.

And that's when he put his lips on hers. And kissed her. Gently at first, and then with an intensity that spoke of something other than a random impulse. Something deeper. His face was grave and serious as if the weight of his action should not be misunderstood.

Maddie Brady looked into the startling blue eyes of her enemy – and kissed him back.

How can your life change in an instant? Is the pattern of normal life so fleeting, so ephemeral, that it takes only one moment of time to jolt it out of the mundane and into the magical? Into a whole new orbit?

These were questions Maddie asked herself frequently, but not then. Afterwards, and for years to come, yes, but right then, sitting on a blanket in the middle of an ancient barn, eating sandwiches and drinking beer, she could think of nothing but the man beside her.

She'd kissed him.

It wasn't as if she went around kissing every random stranger that she met. But *this* man. The first time she had seen him at the camp there had been an undeniable interaction between them, the déjà vu of meeting someone you'd already seen in a dream. Some magical force had drawn her towards this stranger as if it were outside her control. It was whimsical rather than rational. And Maddie Brady tried to be rational, to stay in contact with reality.

Her romantic encounters in her life so far had been sparse. And that's exactly how she liked it. Her life was her own, and she enjoyed the freedom to do and say what she pleased. Not to relinquish control, hand it over to the whim and unpredictability of some man. She'd never met a man she would trust with that power, one who might treat her as an equal.

She was sure of one thing, however: his face would be imprinted on her memory. It was not a truly handsome face, it was too pale and thin for that. But, all the same, it was aesthetically pleasing to her eye.

Her head reeled when she held his gaze. Or maybe that was the Cornish bitter she'd been drinking. She remembered Lizzie's words: *Enough to put all but the strongest man on his back.* He seemed to be okay with it, though. But then she'd heard that the Germans were big beer drinkers.

She smiled at him again. 'You're a good man, I believe. You could have run away.'

'I *did* run away,' said Rudi, and shrugged his shoulders, confused.

'Not from the camp,' said Maddie. 'When we got here, you didn't vanish. You raced to the sand dunes.'

'The boy,' said Rudi, 'he was in trouble. *Mein Vater*, he taught us—'

'—to care for people,' she said. 'He must be a very kind man.'

'Kind? Yes. He is. *Was!* I don't know...'

'You don't know what?' asked Maddie.

'I don't know if *mein Vater* still lives.' Rudi Fischer swallowed hard. 'They took him away. The Nazis took him away to a camp somewhere.'

'God, no. But why?'

'*Zersetzung der Wehrkraft*,' he whispered, almost to himself. 'That's what they accused him of.' Rudi's body shuddered with the memory. 'It's a criminal offence.'

'I don't understand.'

'They called him a criminal, because he didn't believe in war, in fighting. *Mein Vater* – he was a peaceful man.'

'A pacifist, yes?'

'Just so,' he said. 'And in this new Germany, you cannot criticise the army or the leaders or be an objector to war. It's called *Zersetzung der Wehrkraft*.' She watched him struggle for the English words. 'To try and weaken military force, it means. To undermine it. And that is treason. *Mein Vater* was charged with treason.'

She felt him pull away from her, as if somehow his father's plight was her fault.

'I'm sorry, I shouldn't have asked. I don't want to make you sad,' she said.

'Sad? You don't make me sad, you make me happy. I'm sad for my country. I love my country. You can still love your country and hate what these people do to it – the Nazis.'

'Tell me about your home,' she said.

'*Heimat*,' he said. And there was a strange kind of reverence embedded in the word.

'*Heimat*.' She repeated it slowly. Could see that it was important to him. 'What does it mean?'

'It's something sacred. Especially to a real German. Not Hitler, of course, or any of his bullies,' he said, angrily. 'They don't understand what a *real* German patriot is, or how beautiful an idea *Heimat* is. It means "homeland".'

Suddenly there was a wistfulness in his voice that made Maddie want to cry.

'So, your homeland...?'

'My village. You'd like it, I think. It's beautiful. In a valley, the mountains soaring high above it. A stream running through it beside the road. We only have one road in Ramsau. A tiny place.' He found a smile again, remembering.

'Sounds pretty.'

'Yes. And the church. Saint Sebastian – it's very old. Lots of people travel to Bavaria to see it.'

'I'd like to go there,' said Maddie. 'Do you have snow?'

'Lots and lots of snow,' said Rudi. 'Obersalzberg is nearby, where you can ski. And Hintersee.'

'Hintersee?'

'A lake with icy, crystal waters so deep and clear, and mountains rising up from it to touch the sky. Before the war, people walked all the way around its shore. Artists came. Many artists came to paint it.'

'Must be wonderful,' she said. 'I can imagine you there, on a boat. And swimming.'

Rudi Fischer looked away, embarrassed. 'I've spoken too much,' he said. 'I bore you with my story. It is not good manners,' he added, apologetically. 'But of course, I miss my home, my village. *Heimat!*' he said once again, longing in his voice.

He shook his head, apparently drawing a line under the sadness. 'Now it's your turn. I wish to know of your home, your family.'

Maddie patted his hand. 'Another time. It's late, we should sleep.'

Her cold, passionless family seemed bland and emotionally vacant after Rudi Fischer's; and Hampstead a pale and uninteresting place, not at all like some magical Alpine village bathed in snow-light, nestling at the foot of the mountains.

They cleared the blanket of their picnic and lay down together, huddled close for warmth, for companionship. Finding each other's arms during the long night.

But all they did was sleep.

13

18 FEBRUARY 1941

GUNWALLOE

Maddie wasn't surprised when she woke up next morning and the place beside her on the blanket was empty. Of course, he'd have left early, at first light. Still, she was disappointed that he hadn't said goodbye, especially after that kiss. It had seemed real. As if he felt something special for her. She could still remember the pressure of his mouth on hers, the electricity that went through her when she'd responded. It was more than just a friendly kiss. You didn't kiss a friend like that. And she was confused by it, conflicted – the man was an enemy, after all.

But the way he had shared the details of his home and his family with her. Well, that hadn't felt like an enemy. It had seemed intimate, like he trusted her. Maddie tried to imagine where he might go, this man named Rudi. He would stand out with his poor clothes and the white patch sewn on his back. She'd meant to ask him about that, but it was too late now.

It was strange, but suddenly she felt herself adrift. Wasn't sure what to do next. What she *wanted* to do next. And there was this strange emptiness in her that she had not felt before, like something of value had been suddenly found and now was lost.

She should probably get straight back to Captain Andrews and the camp at White Cross, but she had no heart to go tearing back there before her temporary pass was up. And who knew what she would find. She could be racing back to her own court-martial. But it was exactly what she *should* do. Report on the escape of an enemy prisoner. Tell the guards back at the POW camp where they should look for him. She didn't know why she hadn't done it yesterday. She was a patriot. So, what had stopped her?

A strange melancholy had her in its grip. She couldn't remember walking down to the cove; some internal navigation seemed to be in charge and guided her footsteps unerringly down the rugged path towards the ocean. She didn't question it, offered no resistance to the force that led her to the sea and the ancient church sheltering above its shoreline. For centuries, it had clung on tenaciously to this small strip of land and rock, its fragile hold defiant against the elements. This humble church had survived the constant battering of storms and the sand that tried to invade its tiny realm.

The gate was open, so she walked on through, heading to the churchyard. Something about looking at gravestones, imagining past lives, seemed in keeping with her sombre mood. She'd imagined only ancient souls buried there but was surprised that some from the local parish even now still found their way to this peaceful last resting place: a young girl, eight years old, yet to carve her mark on life, lay buried beneath a simple stone. *Drowned*, the headstone read, *taken back to the ocean that was more her home than the land.*

The unexpected hand on her shoulder made her jump. Not that Maddie was superstitious or frightened that ghostly spectres might inhabit this ancient place, but there had been no warning, no sound behind her as he'd walked lightly across the grass.

'Why aren't you miles away?' she asked, surprised.

Rudi Fischer held out his hands, took hers. 'I missed you,' he said, a roguish look on his face. She thought of her handsome smuggler. But that wasn't right. He was mere fiction.

This man was real.

'You're crazy.' Maddie laughed. 'And I think you're lying again.'

'No,' said Rudi. 'No lies. Well, at least...'

'I knew it.' She pulled her hands away and frowned.

'I *did* miss you. And I wanted to see you again, to keep your face in my mind. I want to remember you and this beautiful ocean.' His gaze turned to the sea. 'And to test my leg – it's not so good.'

'What's wrong with your leg?' asked Maddie.

'It was broken. Your doctors were kind; they fixed it okay, but sometimes—'

'—you have to limp,' she said.

'Yes. A little pain. It needs a rest, maybe just a day to make better,' said Rudi. 'It must be well for a long journey. And maybe I have to run a little.' He shrugged philosophically.

'Okay...'

'You will go back?' he asked, anxiously.

'I have to,' said Maddie. 'But I have one more day of freedom. If I want it. Then I have to drive my boss back.'

'The important man with the fine moustache,' he said. 'He seems angry. I hope he treats you good.'

Maddie shrugged. 'Captain Andrews doesn't have to like me. I don't have to like him. I take orders, he gives them – it's the army.'

'You like the army? Like your job?'

'I love my job,' she said. 'People trust me, and I get to do things women didn't do before the war.'

'So, you must keep your job. That's important,' said Rudi.

Maddie nodded, but looked down. 'But maybe after this, when they find out what I've done...' she said.

'But you've done nothing.'

'I'm afraid the army won't see it like that.'

'The guards were slack, they didn't search your car,' he said. 'The fault is with them, not you.'

'It won't make a difference,' said Maddie.

'Then you must say *nothing*. Let them think I get out over the fence behind the railway line.'

'In other words, lie,' she said.

He shrugged. 'What else is there? You want to go to the sea?' he asked suddenly, changing the subject, throwing her off guard.

'What?'

'The sun begins to shine. We could go to the water.'

'Swim? But I don't have any costume and it must be cold out there,' said Maddie.

'We could put our feet in,' said Rudi.

'Paddle, you mean. Yes, I suppose we could.' *Why not? It's a holiday, isn't it? Bizarre. A paddle in the ice-cold waters of the ocean with an escaped German prisoner of war.* It would a story for the grandchildren.

And what would Molly say? She'd say *Do it!* of course. For if there was one thing that her friend Molly Peters believed in, it was grabbing hold of the moment. Shaking every ounce of pleasure from it. And Molly did that fearlessly, took whatever opportunity came her way, enjoyed every new sensation. And sometimes that had been dangerous, hadn't always ended well, but the strange thing was she had never regretted it. *Regret,* claimed Molly, *is only something you have when you are too frightened to try new things.*

And Maddie, who had argued that love-at-first-sight wasn't real, a myth for novels only, happily followed Rudi Fischer to the ocean, to put her theory to the test.

. . .

She'd sniggered at his attempts to catch a fish. The only way they'd have fish for lunch would be if the fish committed suicide and threw itself up onto the rocks. But you had to admire his persistence. Which she did.

He told her more about his family, his younger brother, Werner, a serious boy. Cannon fodder, a life carelessly thrown away at Dunkirk, Rudi told her. She could see his frustration simmering below the surface. And his mother. He should be there to comfort her! he said. A strong, brave woman. Alone. Left to deal with the idiocy of war. Two sons and a husband gone.

Maddie tried to picture his mother. She could see the fierce pride he had in his family. And the love.

He was a good man, this Rudi. She was sure of it. And her feelings for him were growing into something deeper than friendship. Dangerous feelings, conflicting and traitorous. They were like a runaway train, and she'd need to find the brakes before it was too late.

'Maybe we go back. No fish today.' He laughed.

'Maybe you're a better hunter than a fisherman,' said Maddie.

'Oh?'

'Rabbits.' She shivered, looked across at the dunes, remembering the small furry creature blown to pieces there. 'Then again...'

An unspoken agreement took them back up the shoreline. She watched him stoop to pick up a piece of flint. And she laughed. 'What will you do with it?' she asked.

'A keepsake,' said Rudi.

'A souvenir? You're sentimental.'

'Maybe. Would that be bad?'

'No,' she said.

They walked on past the jagged ribs of granite guarding the beach. Past the tiny church with its ancient bell tower and graveyard. Along the rugged path up to the barn. Hand in hand. It seemed natural.

Friends out for a day by the sea. Or more than friends, perhaps. But was that really what she wanted? To go further with this man than she had ever gone with any man before, to give away something precious of herself. And to one of her country's enemies.

The conflict in her head resolved itself when he led her back into the barn and turned those bright blue eyes on her, and his smile. Both the smile and the eyes seemed innocent to Maddie, not manipulative or contrived.

That afternoon, in a broken-down barn by the ocean, she allowed him into her body. Welcomed him. Gave him the priceless gift of her virginity. Her body, her choice.

It was better than she had ever imagined it could be. Maybe the fact that he seemed shy helped her, for he asked nothing of her, didn't take her love but allowed her to give it freely.

He made love to her slowly, exploring every part of her body, touching places with tender fingers, the surprise of discovery bringing small moans from his lips.

Maddie felt the wetness of her own pleasure even before his body entered hers, but she saw him hesitate. *Didn't he want her?* Why was he holding back? Was he asking her permission before he took this last, irreversible step? Something there could be no return from. Something that changed her from a virgin into a... a what? *A fallen woman.* That's what her mother called them. Loose women who had sex with a man before they were married. But what did her mother know of joy? Of the kind of joy Maddie felt now.

She nodded her head in agreement, and his body joined with hers, gently at first and then with a little pain that told her she had crossed the threshold into womanhood.

He thrust harder and faster inside her, an urgency taking hold of him, until she thought they would both explode with it. And for a fleeting second, she felt fear, not of him, but of what the moment meant, how it might change her. But he seemed to sense her sudden tension, caressed her face with his fingertips, brushed the hair away from her eyes. And then it came, the mountain climbed, the summit reached together, a kind of rapture she had never imagined could exist.

Maddie felt the delicious shudder rush through her. She watched his face, his eyes, his lips, the prominent cheekbones, the tiny mole above his left eyebrow. She imagined that his look of bliss matched her own, apart from one thing. Something she didn't understand.

The tear that trickled slowly from his eye.

14

Maddie hummed all the way into Helston. It was that kind of day, with a cheerful blue sky, peppered with the odd patchwork cloud. A day that winked at her; picked up on her mood of wonder. *Can there really be such unbounded happiness, and in the middle of the misery of war?*

Guilt pricked at the edges of her euphoria, but only for a second. Of *course* you could be allowed happiness. And, like her friend Molly, she would grab it with both hands. She deserved it as much as anyone else. Her newfound bliss wasn't ruined by logic or hampered by anything as mundane as common sense. She had found a special man. One who made her feel complete, and she had celebrated by joining her body with his. They had made love, and there was no going back from that. *And she didn't want to.*

No one could tell her that what she had done was wrong, because she knew deep in her bones that it was right. Even if her mother were to shun her, call her a fallen woman, right then it would not have meant a jot to Maddie Brady. She looked at her hands on the steering wheel. The same hands as yesterday, but somehow different. New. Reinvented. Hands that had roamed over his body. She caught a glimpse of her face in the mirror. The same face, but with an extra dimension. And her mouth, her lips. Well, they seemed the same, but they'd discovered his, so they would never go back to how they were.

She was still humming when she parked the car and made her way up the hill towards the Angel Hotel. She hoped Lizzie Retallack would be there again. It would be good to see her. But although she was bursting to tell someone about the miracle that had taken place in her life, Maddie knew it was impossible. It would be foolish. She could tell no one about Rudi. He was an escaped POW, and folk would feel it their patriotic duty to make sure he was returned to captivity.

This time yesterday *she* had felt the same way. But she would not give him up now. Not to the police or the camp guards, and if that made her a traitor, then it was a price she was prepared to pay. She would square it with her conscience later.

For now, there was only the wonder, the miracle of Rudi.

'Aren't you a sight for sore eyes?' said Lizzie. 'A right *proper job*. Wasson, maid?'

'I beg your pardon?'

'We'll need to teach you proper Cornish, my 'ansum. "Wasson" – I 'spect they English say "*What's on*" – all fancy, like.'

'Ah.' Maddie laughed, finally understanding. 'I brought your flask back,' she said. 'And your basket.'

'You enjoy the Spingo, my bird?'

'Like you said, Lizzie. Knocked me for six.'

Lizzie chuckled. 'You ain't proper Cornish till you've had one of they. You finish your wee holiday, my bird?'

'Leaving first thing tomorrow morning. I wanted to bring your things back before I go. You've been so kind. I won't forget you.'

'Same here. You take care and don't take no chances in the blackout, you hear?'

'Absolutely. And thanks for everything. I'll send you something from London, a keepsake.'

'That'll be nice. One of they fancy fellas would do,' said Lizzie, and chuckled again. 'Hands across the Tamar, eh? You had a pasty yet?'

'What's that?' asked Maddie.

'Can't let you go without a pasty. No meat in them now, mind, just—'

'—lentils,' they both said together, and laughed.

Half an hour later, Maddie was on the road back to Gunwalloe.

Two more bottles of Spingo nestled on the seat beside her, along with two pasties wrapped in a threadbare teacloth. Lizzie had slipped them out of the kitchen when the cook wasn't looking.

Maddie had been worried about her new friend getting in trouble, losing a job she seemed to enjoy. But Lizzie had kept a straight face and tapped her nose with a single finger. A gesture that said she knew a secret, but one she was happy to share with Maddie.

'Smugglers, brigands,' said Lizzie.

'What?'

'Us is *Cornish*,' she said, proudly. 'There's a bit of pirate in all of we Cornish.'

Rudi was outside when Maddie got back. Waiting. Looking serious. Standing propped up against the barn door as if he needed the support.

She thought of it as *their* barn, for no one else had come near it, had shown any interest in the place. It was abandoned to its own devices and to the vagaries of the wild storms that made their way from the rocky shore up to this exposed headland.

'You okay?' he asked, anxiously.

'You were worried?' she said. 'I'm all right.' *It was nice to have a man worry about you.*

'You were a long time. I thought something had happened to you.'

'I'm fine,' she said. 'I'm a big girl. I can look after myself.'

'I know, but you said the pub was just down the track.'

'I changed my mind,' said Maddie. 'Didn't go to the Ship Inn – they might get nosy. Don't suppose they get many strangers down this way, and Harry said the landlord's a nasty sort.'

'Harry. He was a gutsy little chap,' said Rudi. He thought for a second. 'You like children?' he asked.

'Never gave them too much thought,' she said.

'Maybe you have some of your own one day.'

'Maybe.'

'You wouldn't like that?' he asked.

'Kids would be good,' said Maddie. 'If they were like young Harry, full of fire and optimism. And with the right man, of course.'

'Of course! And the right woman. I should like very much to have children. And if I had a boy, I would call him Gunter.'

'After the father you love,' said Maddie.

'Yes,' said Rudi, his voice no more than a sad, hoarse whisper. He quickly changed the subject. 'So, where *did* you go?'

'Into Helston,' she said. 'The large town. It's not far.' She pointed vaguely.

'Clever,' he said. 'What's that?' He pointed to the bundle she held in her arms.

'Lunch. Better than waiting for the fish to give themselves up.' Maddie laughed.

She'd never seen a pasty before. They were like pies but

shaped like an envelope; vegetables wrapped in a pastry crust. She tried to imagine them with meat in them. They would be sublime, but then everything was sublime right then. The world was a wonderful place, surrounded by a rose-coloured aura. But maybe that was just her with rose-tinted glasses on – the world had not changed.

They ate until they were full and shared one of the bottles of Cornish beer between them. And drifted into a lazy afternoon, reaching out for each other, both minds sharing a single thought.

Some might call it shameless, her mother included. But Maddie felt no shame, just a sleepy sort of pleasure as this beautiful man nuzzled her hair, breathed his man-breath into her neck. Lying here in his arms was soporific and maybe even a little decadent. And definitely daring. But not dangerous, certainly not dangerous, for Maddie had never felt so safe before. He made her feel that way. He would never let anything bad happen to her. She was certain of that.

And so they made love again. This second time even better than the first for Maddie, because this time she felt no fear, knew exactly what to expect. A languid slow exploration of each other's bodies as if they could take as much time as they wanted, as if the world had conveniently stopped and the passage of time no longer existed.

They fell asleep afterwards and didn't waken until late in the evening when another wave of aircraft flew overhead. She jumped in terror and then she felt his arms wrapped tightly around her, comforting her. Telling her everything would be fine.

'Are you sorry?' asked Rudi.

'About what?'

'You know...'

'About us? What we did?' she said.

'That and – well, not turning me over to the authorities.'

'No regrets.' Maddie shook her head. He was a kind, compassionate man. Not warlike. Or a Nazi.

'You?'

'About making love to you?' He smiled. 'Never! I've only done that once before,' he admitted, sheepishly. 'I don't know if I'm any good at it. But it didn't feel like *that*. Not half as good as it did with you.'

She felt his hand tremble as he traced a line down from her neck into the cleft between her breasts. Maddie put her hand on top of his, held it there.

'Run away with me,' he said.

'What?'

'Let's run away together. We could find a place... out in the wilds. Somewhere no one could ever find us.'

'Wonderful,' she said. 'Not very practical, though. They'd find us.' She sighed. 'The army is funny about stuff like that. They take deserters very seriously.'

'And you'd never do that,' said Rudi. 'I would never *ask* you to do that – to betray your country. I love you too much for that.'

Had she heard that right? *Did this man just say he loved her?* She'd never had a man declare his love for her before. It seemed such a huge thing to say, if it were true. And when she looked into his face, she saw in that moment that he meant it. And of course that was wonderful. But the rational part of her brain whispered a warning that it was impossible, that it was crazy.

So, she didn't say what she wanted to: that she was crazily, impossibly, earth-shatteringly in love with him too. Even though her whole being ached to tell him those things, she didn't. Instead, Maddie ruffled his shaggy blond hair and changed the subject: 'Tell me about the white triangle on your jacket. What's that for?'

'So that people know you're a war prisoner. German prisoners – we come in different categories. I'm one of the *least* dangerous. Not likely to cause any trouble.' He gave a short, self-deprecating snort and showed her the palms of his hands, a gesture of submission. 'See?' he said. 'Completely harmless. And unlikely to escape.'

'I don't understand,' said Maddie.

'When you're first captured, they give you this whole inter-rogation. Do you like the Nazi Party? Do you believe in their aims? Do you think yourself part of a master race? Would you consider it your duty to try and escape? Ironic, really, as I answered "No" to all of those. And I didn't want to escape. So, they gave me a white triangle – means you're a low-risk pris-oner. Medium-risk, with grey triangles, they go to different camps. And the high-risk, like the *Waffen*-SS and the like... well, they go to some of the *bad* places, and they have to wear black triangles and armbands.'

'Oh, I never knew,' said Maddie.

'No reason you should.'

'So, you didn't want to escape?' she asked, confused.

'Didn't plan on it. I was okay there. Some of the guards were fine, they even let me run the camp newspaper, and I had good friends. I taught a little. Started up a small group to study English.'

'So—?'

'I had no choice. Not when Hoffmann threatened to kill me. I can't go back, he's still there.'

'The bully? But surely there's some complaint procedure.' He frowned at her and she blushed at her own stupidity, her naivety. Complaints from prisoners? Really? Who would care? 'Well, you've got no choice. You've got to speak up, go back and report it. If he's still there, running away won't help. That's the coward's way out,' she said, surprised at the way her voice had risen; at her own passion, her anger.

When he didn't answer, she left him alone, going outside into the night as the last of the German bombers flew overhead with their escort of fighters. She didn't think he was a coward. She didn't know why she'd said that for she didn't mean it, but sometimes her mouth jumped in before her brain had sorted everything out.

She was angry that they would have to leave each other. Had taken it out on him when it wasn't his fault. They'd talked about how things might be, in a perfect world, where they could stay together and just disappear, forget the war. Maybe even meet here again one day, in this lovely place, when the whole damn thing was over. But would they? Both knew that real life had a way of toppling dreams.

Maddie went out to the car and picked up the last bottle of Spingo. But when she got back to the barn, he was fast asleep with his head turned to the wall. She drank the beer by herself.

15

19 FEBRUARY 1941

GUNWALLOE

In the morning, things had changed. Maddie could feel it in the air around her: it was heavy and depressive, and she felt it press down on her; the lightness held yesterday, gone.

The rainbow that had wrapped its arms around her had fled as well. It wasn't her imagination. She had called him a coward, had seen hurt in his eyes at those damaging words. But she couldn't take them back.

It was early, five thirty, but time to start a new day. To face reality. She was an ATS driver and she was due back at Camp 115 in White Cross to pick up her prickly passenger Captain Andrews at 0700 hours. She had been living in a bubble for the past two days, not real life. An amazing dreamlike state, inhabited by an intriguing, charismatic man who had changed her from a girl into a woman. He had said he loved her. And perhaps he did, but now it was time to walk out of her glorious dream and leave it behind on the rugged Cornish shoreline.

All the same, she would like to have said goodbye to Rudi Fischer. But now he was really gone. Vanished without a word. She'd expected more of him, this man who had shared his memories and his love with her. His passion for *Heimat*, a mythical homeland that no longer existed, was in his mind only. She would never forget him, his tenderness, the humanity he showed – rescuing young Harry instead of running away.

No. The man was definitely no coward, and it had been cruel of her to use the word in anger, but it was too late. Even so, Maddie took the torch and walked down to the cove, searched the beach and the small churchyard. She hadn't truly expected to find him there, but hope was a word that still hovered in her mind. Just one last glimpse of him to carry with her. Still, she was glad she'd come down to Church Cove this last time. A chance to say goodbye to this incredible place at the edge of the world. The pounding of the surf on the shore and the surge of the tide as it challenged the land was a symphony of sound that would stay with her. And Maddie made herself a promise that wherever else life took her on the planet, she would return there again one day.

She shuddered in the chill morning air, felt small droplets of saltwater spray her face from the incoming waves, and made her way reluctantly back up the beach. He wasn't anywhere along the path, but in a way, Maddie was relieved. For what would she have said to him after last night? After hurting him with that awful barb.

It seemed silly, school-girlish and sentimental, but she went into the broken-down barn one last time, shone the torch over its walls and went over to the ancient wooden bench, tapped it once. For luck. Said goodbye to their special place. Not a palace but it felt like one.

She turned her back on it, heavy-hearted now, drained. He was gone, but she must carry on. She got in the car and drove the rugged path back up to the hamlet of Gunwalloe, the hooded headlights bouncing off the land.

. . .

The sky had lightened by the time she reached the turn-off from the village and onto the road proper. She turned the car towards Helston. This time she would just skirt around it, no need to go into the town. At the crossroads she had to wait for a convoy to pass, so she pulled up patiently. It was early in the day for traffic, but then as Annie the Land Army girl had told her, they were building a couple of new aerodromes out this way. There'd be a lot of lorries ferrying supplies. Wartime. Bad for most people but good for some. For those who managed to get rich on the back of it.

Maddie turned off her hooded headlights as full daylight filtered through the grey clouds. She checked Harriet's instrument panel, then looked at the leather seat beside her, where the pasties and Spingo had sat, and that's when she saw it.

Something small and white, like glossy paper, gleaming, smiling up at her from the grey leather.

She picked it up and turned it over. It was a small photograph. A tall, thin man, his face emaciated but with a smile that shone with life. A happy face, considering the man was standing outside the hut of a POW camp.

He'd left it there for her. 'Rudi,' she said and smiled with relief. He wanted her to remember him. He'd forgiven her for the damning words she'd carelessly thrown at him. He still loved her after all. And that's when Maddie cried.

She cried most of the way back to Camp 115. She didn't notice the land as it flashed past her, or even the road ahead. All she could remember about the trip back was the sorrow and the pain she felt at leaving him like that. She imagined it was how bereavement felt.

It was strange, driving back in through the camp barrier again. But other than the duty guard checking her military ID card, there was no obvious security flap on, nothing to suggest that a prisoner had broken out. And no one tried to arrest her for aiding and abetting a POW in his escape.

Maddie pulled the car into the parking space where the squaddie directed her and, once she'd locked up, began the long walk down to the temporary 'office' they'd assigned Captain Andrews. She'd half expected to find him waiting for her up by the main gate, stamping around impatiently, looking important, clutching his briefcase – as he'd been when she picked him up from the War Office in Whitehall. He'd said 0700 hours but still, there *was* fifteen minutes to go. Maddie believed in being punctual in her duties, even if her passengers didn't feel the same way.

Corporal Williams crossed over from one of the huts, rushed to catch up with her. 'Back safe then,' he said. 'You missed the fun.'

'Fun?' asked Maddie.

'SNAFU,' he said. 'Situation normal, all fucked up – begging your pardon, miss.'

'Not to worry,' said Maddie. 'I've been in the army long enough to see a few SNAFUs myself.' *And swearing was something you got used to.*

'This one's a beaut,' said Corporal Williams. 'Heads've already started to roll. Our illustrious leader for one.'

'Oh?'

'Major's been reassigned, according to the grapevine. Shit usually runs downhill,' said the corporal, and laughed. 'Looks like it's made its way uphill this time. Can't say I'm surprised – the man's an arse.'

'I don't understand,' said Maddie. Which was true. Well, partly.

'There was a breakout. Two prisoners made it out through the wire, over there.' He nodded towards the railway line. 'One stupid bastard got himself caught in the tracks. Killed stone dead. Train ran over him. Just his legs, mind,' added Williams quickly, when he saw Maddie's face turn white. 'Took 'em clean off at the knees. But his top half was still okay,' he said, as if that made up for it.

'So, you could recognise him?' asked Maddie, urgently. It didn't make sense. And she wanted to throw up.

He couldn't have come back. Couldn't possibly have made it back here in time.

'Yes, I knew him. Arrogant little toad. Always marching around like he was cock of the walk. The other one wasn't bad – for a Kraut, that is. Ran the camp newsletter. That one got clean away.'

She put her hand over her mouth. Felt sick with relief. Some bloke cut in half on the railway line! But it wasn't *him*.

Well, of course it wasn't Rudi. How could it be? Surely, he would still be somewhere on the Lizard Peninsula?

'Right, I'll be off. Stuff to do,' he said. 'You'll find your Captain Andrews down in the Glory Hole.' The corporal grinned. 'Don't suppose he'll come out of this SNAFU with any medals, either.'

'Why?' asked Maddie. 'They can't blame him for...'

'He's from the POW department. Happened on his watch. Lucky you had yourself a 48-hour pass. Did you a service there, eh?'

'How's that?'

'You weren't nowhere near when this kicked off. Right, I'm off for some grub. Pleasure to meet you, miss. Have a good trip back.'

Maddie smiled at the corporal. He seemed like a decent sort. But she doubted she'd have a good trip back, for too many thoughts invaded her head. There'd been a SNAFU all right, like Corporal Williams had said, and – accidental or not – she was right there in the middle of it.

How long before someone with half a brain found out what had *really* happened, and they kicked her out?

She heard footsteps behind her on the concrete path as she headed down towards the water tower. They quickened, and when she walked past the football pitch, their owner caught up with her: suddenly, she was grabbed hold of from behind and pulled around the side of a hut, out of sight.

Maddie tried to scream, but the man in front of her covered her mouth with his hands.

'No hurt,' he said, and took his hands away. 'I no hurt.'

'Who are you? What do you want with me?' Her voice shook. She was frightened, but then this strange man looked frightened as well.

'*Ich bin* Hans Meyer.'

'What?'

'*Mein* name *ist* Hans. *Freund*,' he said. '*Freund!*'

'Friend?' she asked.

'*Ja, ja*.' The man's face relaxed into an expression of relief that she had understood. 'Friend for Rudi. Rudi Fischer *ist mein Freund*.'

'So, you're Rudi's friend. He told me about you,' she said.

'You see him? He escapes okay?'

'He got away,' she told him. 'I don't know where he is now, but for two days they didn't find him.'

'He tells me to cut hole in wire so they don't think *you* do this.'

'My God, he told you to do *that*? And the other man – the one on the railway line?'

'Very bad man,' said Hans Meyer. 'Nazi. Oberleutnant Karl Hoffmann. Rudi try to stop him bullying, but he want to kill *mein Freund*. Rudi must escape. We help him get in your car.'

'You did?'

'*Ja*.' Meyer shrugged his shoulders.

'And this Hoffmann? He wanted to escape too?' she asked.

'*Nein*.'

'No? Then how did he get on the railway line?'

'I go,' said Meyer. 'Roll call. *Danke*,' he said. 'Thanks you.' He shook hands with her before he walked away.

'For what?' said Maddie. 'I didn't *do* anything. And how did Hoffmann get on the line?' she shouted at his retreating back.

Hans Meyer looked back at her and winked. 'Maybe he tripped,' he said.

She could hear him chuckling as he walked away.

16

21 FEBRUARY 1941

HAMMERSMITH, LONDON

'You've changed,' said Molly Peters. 'Ever since you got back from that last job. You ain't been the same.'

'No, I haven't! Still the same normal, bolshie roommate I ever was.' Maddie sat down on her bunk and hid her head in the towel, carried on drying her damp hair. Tried not to start snivelling and give the game away.

'That's just it – you ain't. What you done with that contrary, bloody-minded woman used to bunk here? If I didn't know better, I'd say you've had some sort of love affair and now you're mooning around like a sick cow what can't bear thinking on it.'

Maddie pressed the towel harder into her eyes and hoped the pain would stop the tell-tale flow of tears. But it didn't. And it had been daft to try and hide anything from her friend Moll – the woman was practically psychic.

'I *knew* it!' said Molly. 'Some bastard been playing fast and loose. Sod 'em, Madds. They ain't worth the 'eartache. C'mon, love. Forget the swine.'

Maddie felt her bunk sag, heard the protest of its ancient springs beneath her, as her friend plonked her considerable weight down on it and squeezed in beside her. Then the towel was suddenly tugged from her head and she sat there minus the camouflage, feeling naked and vulnerable. No longer able to hide the truth, or the despair written on her face, in the dark smudges of strain, the ugly red bloodshot eyes.

'Idiot child! Blow your nose,' said Molly, and handed over the hankie she'd fished from the pocket of her old worn candlewick dressing gown.

Maddie did as she was told and handed back the hand-kerchief.

'Well, I don't want it now, do I?' Molly wrinkled her nose in distaste. 'Not after that.'

'He's *not* a swine, Moll. Nor a bastard. He's none of those awful things. He's the sweetest, dearest, most lovely, unselfish man on the planet.'

'Gawd, it's even worse than I thought,' said Molly. 'You got it bad, girl – you're in love.'

She tried to stifle another pathetic sob. But it didn't work, and the shudder travelled right through her body. Proof, if it were needed, that Molly was right. She was undeniably, hope-lessly, irreversibly, impossibly, in love. There was no cure. A problem with no solution. But then her friend, with all her experience, might find one.

'He likely to marry you?' asked Molly.

'I wish!'

'Ah. So, he's been playing away, then?'

'What's that mean?' said Maddie.

'Gawd, woman. You ain't safe to be let out alone. Has he got a wife and half a dozen nippers tucked away back home?'

'No, nothing like that,' Maddie said, miserably. 'He loves me *too*. But it's impossible.'

'What? Just like that, you'll let him go? You ain't the woman I thought you were.'

'You don't understand.'

'No, I don't. You need to hang onto this bloke, if he's that special. They ain't like buses, you know. They don't come along in bunches.'

'I love you, Moll. But I can't talk about this anymore. I just need to be miserable and mope around for a bit. Till I get him out of my system. Believe me, there's no other way. And please don't ask me to explain. It'll get us both sent to jail.'

'Jesus! Gawd! That ain't good.'

'Yeah, I know.' Maddie blew her nose again. No doubt it would look as attractive as her puffy red eyes. She couldn't bear to look in a mirror. Not that it mattered anyway. Who did she have to look good for?

'You need to stop moping,' said Molly. 'We'll go out. Fancy the flicks?'

'What, like this?' asked Maddie, and pointed to her nose. She figured it must resemble a prize-fighter's by now.

'That's it. You just keep on feeling sorry for your poor self. That'll do the trick,' said Molly, unsympathetically. 'We're going down the Gaumont, whether you like it or not. Doctor's orders. Watch a nice flick. A musical or something. Take you right out of yerself. No more arguments.'

'Okay,' Maddie relented. 'But a musical or a comedy. Something cheerful to make us laugh. Anything but a romance. I refuse to sit through another of your soppy romances.'

'Great. Some of the girls've already been to see *Waterloo Bridge*. Supposed to be good. Vivien Leigh and that gorgeous Robert Taylor...'

'Doesn't sound much like a musical,' said Maddie.

'War movie.'

'We got enough war of our own without going out to watch it, Moll.'

'This is different. World War *One*. Our gorgeous Robert will be the hero, I should think.'

'Yeah, okay. But first sign of romance and I'm off, you hear?' warned Maddie.

What Maddie didn't know was that most of their ATS pals who'd already watched the film had come back home to the billet in floods of tears.

Not only was it a war film, but it was also a romance and the saddest film that Maddie had ever been forced to sit through. A two-hankie job, so that she'd had to sacrifice her own best lace handkerchief, the one with the butterflies on, that she kept for special occasions. She'd given it to Moll when she had exhausted her own. But then her best friend had always been a sucker for a weepy movie.

Maddie sat dry-eyed through all of it. She had her own sadness: why would she need to watch it on a screen? As if she didn't have enough real-life drama of her own right then, without seeking out more that was manufactured.

They walked back home arm-in-arm, trying to cheer each other up.

'Next time I'm picking the film,' Maddie said, and dug Molly in the ribs. 'You're useless.'

'Yeah? Well, I didn't know she was going to kill herself 'cause she couldn't have him, did I? They don't tell you these things on the poster. Why couldn't they just have ended up together? Happy ever after.'

'It's called drama,' said Maddie, with a sigh.

Maddie went to bed that night thinking about the film. The image of Waterloo Bridge made its way into her dreams: the two lovers who met there for the first time in the middle of an air raid. And the man who returned there alone many years later, thinking about what might have been. A pain that was too close to hers for comfort.

The handsome actor Robert Taylor magically morphed into her own hero, Rudi Fischer, and she felt his hands on her body once again, enjoyed the same sensations he had evoked in her. And, in the bizarre way of dreams, she ended up being hunted down by a horde of Military Police and an angry gang of squaddies all looking like the ugly, fat sergeant at the camp at White Cross. Just as they fell on her and dragged her off in handcuffs, Maddie woke up sweating.

How long before she was found out? Before the treason against her country was laid out for all to see?

The fear of discovery and the guilt that she had betrayed her uniform – even though the crime was unintended – stayed with Maddie for a while. But like all things, the passage of time made it easier, and gradually she began to feel more like her old self.

As the days moved slowly into weeks, the guilt faded until the strange events in Cornwall turned into nothing more painful than a bittersweet memory. And sometimes, she even allowed herself to stoke the fires of memory by secretly staring at Rudi's photograph, which she kept hidden under her mattress. But the rational part of her brain warned that this was a luxury she couldn't afford to indulge in. *Forget him! The thought of him. The feel of him. The idea that there can be any kind of future for us!* It was ludicrous. He was the enemy.

Being busy helped. Exhaustion, falling into bed after long, arduous days of ferrying officers and equipment through the streets of London. One day, she'd be driving a truck, the next, an ambulance. You went where they pointed you. Drove what they told you to.

Her beloved staff car was no more: it had been crushed to chunks of unrecognisable metal along with others in the garage

compound when the place took a direct hit from a large para-
chute mine. She'd grieved for Harriet even though she knew it
was stupid feeling sad over inanimate things when there were
people being killed. Families being torn apart. Loved ones
dying.

That night, after she dropped her truck off, Maddie trudged
back tiredly to the tall, ugly house in Hammersmith that had
become her home. The building where the ATS women were
billeted was old and often cold, the one bucket of coal a day
they were allowed for the fire in the common room hardly
taking the chill off.

Still, Maddie had grown used to the place and the feeling of
camaraderie among 'the girls' made up for the lack of home
comforts. The water was usually cold, not that warm water
would have made much difference when you could only take
your weekly bath in a miserly five inches of the stuff. But it was
your patriotic duty to stick to the water ration and most of
them did.

And at least they weren't all stuck in a barracks, like she'd
been in basic training. Crammed in together, thirty to a room
with an eagle-eyed sergeant watching your every move. Two
women to a bedroom here, quite luxurious when you thought
about it. Except some bedrooms were bigger than others. She
and Molly had one of the smallest, with only a single long pole
attached to the wall for them both to hang their clothes on. And
the space between their narrow bunk beds was tiny. It meant
they had to get into their bunks at separate times as there was
hardly enough room to pass each other. *Cosy*, Molly had said
when they'd first arrived. But then that was Molly for you: she
usually found something good in everything. Decidedly chirpy
at times was our Moll. And singing a lot. Dragging others into
her singsongs with her.

Maddie managed a smile. It would be good to see her friend tonight after a long, frustrating day. Molly was a proper optimist. And soon they were both due a 48-hour pass, might even pop into the Hammersmith Palais, a cheerful place with its classy musicians in evening dress and impressive revolving bandstand. Or take a trip to the Stage Door Club. That was another favourite of theirs.

She stepped carefully around the rubble of last night's raid. It had been a bad one and the blokes from the Heavy Rescue Squad hadn't managed to get around to clearing up yet. Poor old London – some of its bombed-out streets were unrecognisable. Piles of bricks everywhere, ugly scarred buildings that used to be people's homes. And the smells that pervaded the air for days after a raid were something you expected but, still, they managed to shock. The acrid smoke, the musty smell of damp plasterboard, the nausea of gas from a broken main, and – worst of all – the stench of rotting corpses trapped under the rubble.

Maddie shivered with the thought. Coming home one night she'd spotted a woman's shoe lying among a pile of rubble. She'd gone over to investigate, had dropped her torch in shock and ended up throwing up her lunch onto a pile of bricks. Just beside the shoe was the lower part of a woman's leg, the nylon stocking still in place. Nothing else. There had been no sign of the woman.

She hurried on through the streets. The light was starting to fade, the blackout beginning to kick in. *Don't take no chances in the blackout* – she heard Lizzie Retallack's voice in her head, and Maddie quickened her pace through the darkening streets. She needed to be back home, needed the comfort of her bedroom, familiar things around her.

And her friend Molly's optimism. That's what she needed most. Molly's total belief that things would get better soon and that this crummy war couldn't last forever.

17

APRIL 1941

LONDON

It was hard to believe that over two months had gone by since she'd been to Cornwall. Since the seismic shift in the universe that had turned her from a girl into a woman.

Maddie had weaned herself off staring at his photograph every day now, like a dewy-eyed teenager. She was rationing herself to once a week, taking out the photograph from beneath her mattress. She didn't want to become too reliant on it. On something that could never be.

Where is he now? she wondered. *Still free?* She pictured him roaming the countryside. Sleeping in hedgerows. Stealing food. He would survive, she told herself. He had practical skills. Except for catching fish, of course. She smiled, remembering.

Today had been a lazy, relaxing day. She and Molly were on a 48-hour pass, going up west to see a variety show at the Nuffield Centre in Wardour Street tonight. Billy Cotton was there with his band and comedian Arthur Askey was also on the bill. Molly had been keen to go, for she loved all the silly Askey songs and would be belting them out along with the comic.

Maddie had grown used to the looks from some people when

her friend enthusiastically exercised her vocal cords. *Stuffed shirts*, Moll called them. 'Wouldn't know a good time if it bit them on the arse.' You only get one shot at life, her friend believed, so why waste it being timid, or too embarrassed to enjoy yourself?

Maddie admired that sort of courage and the energy and exuberance that went with it.

'Something I need to tell you,' said Molly as she tried to marshal her bouncy blonde hair under her uniform cap.

'That sounds serious,' said Maddie, suddenly worried. 'You're not...?'

'What? In the club, you mean?' Her friend laughed. 'I ain't that daft. Me ma's had six of us squalling, troublesome, snot-nose kids. That ain't no life.'

'Couldn't be easy for her,' said Maddie.

'Good Catholic woman! Keep them kids coming, says the priest. Mind, he wouldn't say that if it was him had to pop them out and look after them.'

'No, so...?'

'I ain't falling, not if I can help it. What, give some bloke his jollies and then he leaves you with a kid?'

'Put like that,' agreed Maddie, 'it doesn't seem fair.'

'Too right it ain't fair, and until blokes start looking after the kids same as us, I ain't that keen on popping one out,' said Molly with a snort.

'So, what's this news of yours, Moll?'

'Tell you later, when we've had some grub and a laugh at the Nuffield. God bless the geezer.'

'Eh?'

'Lord Nuffield. Weren't for him giving all us squaddies free tickets, we couldn't afford to go up west like the toffs. Not to mention the free STs – the bloke's a gem.'

'Seems like it,' said Maddie.

'Yeah, I reckon every ATS girl in the country sings his

praises when they get their monthlies and don't have to fork out cash for sanitary towels. Man's a decent bloke for a toff.'

Maddie had always thought it odd that they were issued with 'free feminine sanitary products', as the ATS delicately called them. And all at the expense of Lord Nuffield, who had a real soft spot for the services, men and women alike.

'Talking 'bout which,' said Molly. 'I'll take one with me tonight, just in case. Don't pay to be caught out, and my "friend" is waiting in the wings. Should come on any day now.'

Maddie thought about her mother and how she would have reached for the smelling salts if her daughter had talked as openly as Molly did about women's periods while the subject of sex had never, EVER been brought up in the Brady household.

She sometimes wondered how her mother and father had ever managed to produce a family at all. *And the act of love?* How would they have navigated that? Would her mother have found it distasteful, like she did most things? Maybe Phyllis Brady would have worn those long silk evening gloves of hers. Bodies untouched by human hand.

And then something her friend had said struck a distant bell in the back of Maddie's mind.

Monthlies! When did she last have hers?

'Righty-ho! Don't stand there daydreaming, girl. We got a show to see and only an hour to get there. Move your arse,' said Molly.

The show was brilliant. Maddie laughed as much as her friend at Arthur Askey's impression of a bumble bee. He was a natural clown. And the man seemed able to tap into people's need to throw off the sadness of war, to forget it all if only for an hour.

Molly didn't disappoint, joining in Askey's rendition of 'Kiss Me Goodnight Sergeant Major' with a raucous version of her own. A full-blooded contralto that made several heads turn.

By the time Billy Cotton's band came on, Molly was well into her stride, her voice nicely warmed up, ready for a memorable attempt at 'Somebody Stole My Gal'. But by then, there seemed nothing unusual to draw scathing looks from other concert goers, for Molly had worked her miracle of getting others to sing along unabashed.

That included Maddie, who fearlessly joined in for the final song. She didn't have the musical rigour or quality in her voice that Molly did but made up for it with enthusiasm. And soon she was grinning away, like lots of the other servicemen and women in the hall, as it rang to the sounds of a song about a fish. Perhaps the silliest, but happiest, song ever written.

It had been a night to remember, and Maddie's face was flushed with excitement, not to mention the gin that her friend had pressed on her. It was a celebration, Molly had insisted, and they had to mark it with at least one drink.

She wasn't sure exactly what the celebration was, but that didn't seem to matter as they both marched along in the blackout, arm in arm, giggling like schoolgirls and singing 'The Happy Wanderer'. It wasn't until they'd arrived at the YMCA, where they'd booked in for the night, that the evening took a more serious turn. Slipped from happiness into misery.

'This news of yours,' said Maddie. 'Is that what we're celebrating?'

'I've got a new posting, Madds. They're sending me to Camberley.'

In an instant, everything changed. And Maddie wished she'd never asked; that she could turn the clock back, just for a second. Back to the happy little bubble that had enclosed her and her best friend. A friend who was about to abandon her.

'You're being posted somewhere else? And you've known about this for a week already?'

'Been working up to tell you,' said Molly sheepishly. 'It ain't easy. We been friends a long time, Madds. But you know the army – they don't give no mind to friends, you go where you're sent.'

'But a posting like that, out of the blue,' said Maddie, confused. 'They don't suddenly retrain you as a motorcycle messenger. Not when you're doing useful work somewhere else. And you've always wanted to ride a motorbike. *You* did this, didn't you?' she accused. 'You *asked* for the bloody posting!'

'It's the army,' Molly repeated, miserably. 'And it's a promotion, too! Don't get angry, not when I only got a week left. And we can still meet up. Camberley ain't that far. *Please*, Madds,' she pleaded. 'Don't be angry, just be happy for me, eh?'

And of course, her friend was right. It would be selfish to wreck a friendship like theirs over something so stupid. So they made up, because life was just too uncertain and could be short, especially in the middle of a war when bombs were dropping, and staying alive seemed as random as a lottery.

The next day, they went their separate ways: Maddie back to Hammersmith to spend the last day of her pass doing mending and listening to the wireless, while Molly had decided to visit her family over in Hackney.

And it wasn't until three days later, when Molly had already been declared AWOL, that the news finally came out. It was the war, communications got screwed up, people went missing. But Maddie knew her friend would never have gone absent without leave, especially when she was so excited about the new posting and the promotion to lance corporal that had gone with it.

Molly Peters had slept over at her ma's house in Richmond Road, a house that backed onto the railway line. The East End had always been a favourite target for German bombers; the docks, railway lines, they were fair game it seemed. *Bad luck* some of the ATS girls in Hammersmith had whispered. A direct hit. Even an Anderson shelter wouldn't have helped, but then no one had dug one at the house in Hackney.

In one dark, miserable, earth-shattering moment, Maddie Brady lost her best friend. And she knew her pain was small compared to that of Petty Officer Norman Peters, Molly's father. When he returned home from sea, he'd find his house missing and his wife dead, along with all six of his children.

18

19 FEBRUARY 1941

GUNWALLOE

The mental anguish of leaving her was far worse than the physical pain in his leg as Rudi thrashed through the brambles and undergrowth. He'd watched her drive off, had been sheltering behind a rocky outcrop, hadn't wanted to get too close in case she'd picked him out in her headlights and stopped to say goodbye.

He couldn't have managed a proper goodbye. It would have been torment when all he'd wanted was to hold her one last time, sink his head into her hair, nuzzle those soft warm breasts. Just thinking about it was a kind of torture.

So, he'd slipped away. No heartfelt speeches. No lingering over final, misty-eyed farewells. This way was better, would spare them both some pain. He knew that he was right.

And now, he tried to fool his brain into thinking he'd never met her. Tried to block her face from his mind and concentrate on what was important now. One step following another painful step.

Full daylight had arrived. Which was good in one way. At least now he wasn't stumbling around like a blind man in a blackout. But although the light was comforting, it was also dangerous. People would be about, rising from their beds, going to work. He was approaching a village, where strangers were sure to stand out.

He'd already had one scare. He'd just passed the Ship Inn when an old man coming out of the pub with a crate of empty bottles had spotted him. They'd eyed each other suspiciously, until the man had yelled an angry challenge and dropped the empties noisily.

Rudi hadn't stopped to socialise. Instead, he'd abandoned the rough track and taken off through the thick undergrowth. The old man had waved an angry fist and made a half-hearted attempt to follow, but the adrenalin had given Rudi a head start and the man had soon given up the chase.

It had been a painful reminder that capture could come anytime and from anywhere. The old man from the pub might give him up. Might even now be phoning the police or the army – he hadn't looked the benevolent type.

Rudi had no idea where he was. He could work out compass points by the direction of the sunrise and where it set, but that didn't help much when you had no map. And there was no plan, other than the hope to avoid capture for as long as possible. And if the worst happened, what would they do to him? Send him back to White Cross? He didn't think so. He guessed he'd never see that place again, which was fine by him. He'd miss his friend Hans and he'd miss teaching, but at least he'd never have to see Hoffmann again. That had been his *only* aim. Escaping back to Germany had never been in his mind. Not the kind of Germany that existed now. One that would toss aside honourable men like his father in favour of bullies who valued violence over conscience and principles.

Rudi sank tiredly into the undergrowth. Brambles pricked at him, but he was too exhausted to move any farther. He eased off his battledress tunic, removed the piece of flint from its top pocket. He thought back to the walk along the beach with Maddie when he'd stopped to pick it up. She had laughed with that light breezy sound that sent ripples of pleasure through him and accused him of being sentimental, looking for a souvenir.

He hadn't denied it for it was good to have something tangible to remember the day. And an idea had already been forming in the practical side of his brain: a way to use the flint to rid himself of the patch on his jacket.

He shook his head to loosen the hold her face had on his mind. He would never forget her or the incredible days they had spent together, wrapped in the bubble of their fantasy world. But right then, he needed to concentrate.

Rudi turned the tunic over until he could see the large white triangle sewn into the back of it. It stood out starkly against the dyed black cloth of the RAF battledress. It was supposed to. It made him a marked man, and even if civilians had no idea what it meant, it was like wearing a neon sign strapped around his neck. It had to go.

He set to work with the sharp flint, painstakingly sawing across the tiny stitches. When the large patch loosened slightly, it became easier to get the flint in between the stitching. His hands were large and the stitches small, but he persevered, worked tirelessly until his hands were raw and there was blood on them from a myriad of tiny cuts. Then he grinned in triumph for he no longer had a massive white triangle pinned to his back. *Like a target.*

He tossed the piece of fabric into the brambles, and the action made him feel suddenly lighter, as if in an instant he'd also thrown off the label *prisoner*. The ignominy of it. The stigma. His self-esteem returned. He was a man again.

Then tiredness and the trauma ganged up on him, and Rudi sank back into the bushes. And suddenly, there she was – hovering defiantly in front of him, a challenge in those startling eyes of hers. Magnificent, courageous, bold, that's what he'd thought of her – and beautiful, of course. *But had he told her any of that?* He couldn't remember. He fell asleep with a smile on his face.

Rudi woke up cold and shivering, like someone in the grip of fever. What time was it? He searched for his watch; of course, there was no watch. He hadn't owned one since a Tommy had taken it off him. The soldier had grinned, Rudi remembered, like it was a secret joke, and his teeth were bad. Lots of the English seemed to have bad teeth – just something he'd noticed.

Where was he? How long had he been there? He felt groggy and confused and icy cold. He reached over for his discarded jacket lying beside him in the long grass, and pulled it around his shivering body. He needed to get moving. To warm himself up. Hypothermia was no joke and that's where he was headed if he wasn't careful.

He felt his pulse; it seemed weak, and his breathing was slow and laboured. Next would come slurred speech and a lack of coordination. He knew all about hypothermia, as they'd gone through the symptoms in survival training. *Move. Get warm. Get some food in you.* His brain told him these things, sent out small warning messages, but his body was slow to catch up.

Loss of consciousness would be after that. And then what? *Death?* The frightening thought brought him instantly to his feet. He swayed but managed to keep his balance and, like an infant learning to walk, Rudi placed one unsteady foot in front of the other. Baby steps. But if he took enough of them, they were sure to lead him somewhere.

They did. Out of the thicket and onto a road of sorts. He counted his steps at first, always looking down at his feet, mesmerised by their progress, surprised that they managed to find the strength to carry on.

And so he walked on in a kind of trance, finding comfort in the rhythm, the small sound of his own footsteps as they echoed on tarmac, until eventually he became aware of other sounds. Evidence of other humans, of life outside his own. Of noisy machines. Of danger.

'Hey, mate! Look where you're going.' The voice wasn't angry. Just a friendly warning.

'Sorry, mate,' said Rudi. Self-preservation moving his brain and his tongue into English.

'You look done in, pard. They been flogging you to death? Always the same, they sods with their blueprints and their plans, but it's us lot on the ground what has to do the heavy lifting! Let 'em build their own bleedin' runways – see how quick it gets done, eh?' The man grinned.

'Yes,' said Rudi. He had no idea what the man was talking about, but one-word replies seemed safe enough.

'I was you, pard? I'd take a breather. Put your feet up for a spell. Get yourself some grub. Looks like you could use it.' The man pointed towards a line of tents up ahead. Heavy lorries were moving busily about the place, and diggers. 'NAAFI tent's doing breakfast. Ain't like *real* food, but it'll fill a hole. And the ATS girls in there ain't too hard on the eye, neither. Know what I mean?' The workman's grin turned to a leer. And Rudi understood. The language of men was international, body language that needed no translation.

He nodded his thanks and headed off in the direction of the tents. There were rows of them, like a small town all by themselves. Sleeping quarters, maybe, and billets for staff and the workmen. But what were they building here? The man had mentioned a runway, so maybe there was about to be a new airfield rising out of this land in the middle of nowhere.

Rudi stuck his head into a couple of the larger tents. One was empty, but in the last one there were rows of trestle tablets set out with precision: the spaces between looked as if they'd been measured precisely. He'd seen the same thing in the prison camp: meticulous attention to detail that smacked of a military hand behind its order.

Benches were placed either side of these tables, for 'customers' he assumed – military or civilian workers, it was hard to tell. But right now, none of them were occupied, although a woman in an army uniform, like Maddie's, was clearing away the remnants of a meal.

Rudi's eyes were drawn to the head of the makeshift canteen, where a bunch of tables held covered dishes, the smell of food wafting out from them. He remembered what the workman had said, about the quality of the food. Not *real*, but it would fill a hole.

The man was wrong. For the food smelled wonderful, incredible. It was a smell that sent a signal to the juices in his stomach. *Get ready*, it said. *You could be busy soon.* If he was lucky, that was, and the girl in charge of doling out the food gave him some. No questions asked. No ID required.

It was asking a lot of Lady Luck, he knew. But so far, that particular lady had been kind to him, had taken his hand in her own.

Rudi walked up to the girl and smiled. He exuded a confidence that said he had every right to be here, was entitled to eat this breakfast as much as anyone else.

'You're late. Last sitting's just finished,' she said.

'I'm sorry,' said Rudi. 'Got held up.' He pointed to the plates stacked on the end of the table and threw in another apologetic smile. 'Can I—?'

'Go on then.' The young woman relented. 'Still got some milk there, powdered, just as good on porridge, though. When you've finished that, there's a bit of scrambled egg left over, and one rasher of bacon. You're welcome to it,' she said, and handed Rudi his smile back in spades. He wondered absently how you could fit that many teeth into one mouth.

'Many thank-yous,' he said.

'Ain't you sweet? Your accent,' she said. 'You ain't British. One of those Dutch fliers?' she asked. 'And the uniform – I ain't seen that one before.'

Rudi tried to calm his racing pulse, hoped his face didn't show the strange acrobatics that his panic-stricken brain was going through. *Think man, think. The uniform, the accent.*

'Dutch?' He laughed. Like it was a natural question and one he'd been asked many times before. 'No, not Dutch. Polish. I come from Poland.'

'Poland still has an air force?' Her eyes went to his uniform.

'No, Poland was defeated,' he told her, 'but Poles still fly in British planes.' He was sweating now. Hoped she hadn't noticed, this fine young woman who was either about to give him up or give him breakfast.

'A flier from Poland, eh? Thought so,' she said, smugly, and piled a plate high with powdered scrambled eggs and the last slice of bacon.

19

It was strange, how things turned out, especially when you seemed to have no control over them. When you made no contribution to their outcome. *Luck*, he supposed. And Rudi didn't argue with it.

He'd been in the compound for almost a week now, watching the new airfield take shape. He'd got to know the layout and it seemed that if he stayed in the tented part of the construction site where work took place in a noisy chaos, he would be fine. Far away in the distance, where the runways and control tower were being built was a different proposition. Wire fencing. Barricades. Guards checking passes, men with rifles and hard, granite faces. Security was tight over there.

Other than passing the time of day and offering him a cigarette, none of the workers had questioned his reason for being there. A Polish fighter squadron would be based here, or so the rumour went. And wasn't *he* a Polish flier? It was a kind of miracle, but he knew people tend to see what they expect to see, and soon his presence became normal, commonplace.

Eventually he found himself moving freely throughout the

massive site with a confidence born of familiarity, and even managed to bag a bunk for himself in one of the tented billets.

The mess tent served him three meals a day. And soon the cooks and servers got to know his face and smiled when he waited patiently in line. The girl in the army uniform who'd given him breakfast that first day seemed to have taken a shine to him. She put extra-large helpings on his plate, and had dropped some heavy hints about her availability, if he was interested.

He'd tried to remain friendly without giving her the wrong idea. But he had no interest in her, or any woman – not after Maddie. No one could fill that gap. It was hard to look at the girl now, and last night she'd given him a strange, cold stare and pushed the plate angrily towards him like he'd done something wrong. Sometimes, women were hard to understand.

I was right, he thought, smugly. You could melt into a crowd, provided you had the nerve and confidence. It helped that the building site was large. *One thousand acres when it's finished*, one of the ground workers had told him. The football field back at the prison camp had been an acre. Rudi tried to imagine a thousand of them stretched out over the fields here.

Boredom had finally driven him out for a walk. That, and looking for inspiration: what to do next. He'd set off early in the morning and walked into the town of Helston. It had taken three hours, but he'd been in no hurry.

He remembered Maddie telling him about the hotel where the strange-tasting beer had come from. Walking up the hill, knowing he was following in her footsteps, made him feel happy and carefree. And he found that he could think about her now without the crippling pain of loss.

He was feeling fitter, eating regularly. He smiled to himself. Yes, he had every right to feel pleased, proud even. He'd done what he'd set out to do. Here he was, walking through the streets like a free man. What would his friend

Hans say? And if a patrol should challenge him? He had no papers if he was stopped but he would stick with the story. He was an ally. A Polish flier, billeted at the airfield, had forgotten to bring his ID. Two chances. Either it would work, or it wouldn't. And he could always run. His leg was stronger now.

That's when he heard a car door slam, heard footsteps behind him. They quickened, turned into something more sinister that should have rung a warning bell. But there was no bell. No warning of any kind. Just rough hands on his shoulders, pulling him backwards, wrestling him to the pavement and pain in his head as it met concrete.

———

Rudi had been manhandled: roughed up a bit, but nothing fatal – a split lip, one eye swollen shut, a multi-coloured bruise across the side of his face and a headache that took itself seriously. But no bones broken.

He learnt that two British bobbies had been responsible for nabbing him: they'd picked him up and dumped him unceremoniously into the back of their police car.

He was an enemy after all. Maybe even a spy. He couldn't expect sympathy.

But when the intelligence officer had seen the results of the policemen's handiwork, he'd been angry. Had apologised to Rudi. 'We're civilised human beings,' the army officer told him, 'not animals. Those chaps went above their orders.'

'They had *orders*?' asked Rudi.

'Police were warned to keep a lookout. Knew you were down this way somewhere, old chap. Somebody gave you up, I'm afraid. Gave us information that helped in your capture. Or should I say *recapture*.' The man smiled. 'You've done quite well, so far. Impressive.'

'Somebody gave me up?' parroted Rudi, confused. 'But who —? Nobody knew I was here.'

'Hardly matters now who it was, does it?'

'It matters to me,' lisped Rudi. His split lip was painful and when he checked his teeth with his tongue, he found that one was missing. Those policemen may have been old guys, but they'd done a right job on his face. He remembered them taking turns, like it was a game.

'I shouldn't be talking out of school,' said the man. 'Don't suppose it'll make a difference now, though. Not exactly a state secret. A private in the ATS.'

'What?!'

'Lady soldier. Can't give you a name, wouldn't be cricket. But a private in the Auxiliary Territorial Service gave us information that led to your capture. Tick some woman off, did you?' he asked. 'Hell hath no fury like a woman scorned, you know.' The young officer grinned.

She'd given him up? How could that be? It seemed impossible. She loved him. She'd said so. But perhaps when Maddie had got back to the camp at White Cross, she'd had second thoughts about helping her country's enemy. Had she been angry he'd left without saying goodbye? But he'd done that to save her pain. Himself, as well. Still, maybe she'd felt abandoned. *Hell hath no fury*, the officer had said.

The pain in his face was nothing compared to the agony in his mind. In his heart. He felt raw with it. And the more Rudi dwelt on the thought of Maddie's betrayal, the more convinced he became that it was true.

Days went by. Rudi was driven in lorries, travelled on trains with a surly armed guard, was interrogated by several intelligence officers. He answered none of their questions about how he had escaped, or why. It no longer mattered. Nothing mattered to him but the cocoon of misery he had surrounded himself with. He had reached an empty, bleak place in his mind where there was no past, no future, and no point in even trying to survive.

As for love? Rudi Fischer discovered how easily love could turn sour. He took a scouring pad to his memory of Maddie, painfully scouring every trace of her from his life.

A month after he'd been recaptured, they finally transported him on a long, gruelling journey from London to Scotland, to one of the harshest prisoner-of-war camps in Britain. It was one reserved for the most high-risk German prisoners, the ones who were fanatical, hardened Nazis, including the SS and the Afrika Korps. And POWs like him who'd made escape attempts. 'Throwing all you rotten eggs in one basket,' one of the Polish guards had taken delight in telling him when he arrived in his new home.

You have to hand it to the British, thought Rudi. *Clever, using Polish troops to guard the camp*. After what Hitler had done to their country, the Poles in Camp 21 took every chance they could to make life miserable for their German prisoners.

Camp 21, called 'Cultybraggan', was a few miles from Comrie village in Perthshire. The countryside and its scenery reminded Rudi of his own village at home. In another time, under happier circumstances, it might even have been a pleasant place to visit. But nothing about Cultybraggan was pleasant. It was designed for one thing only: as a maximum-security POW camp. It made his last 'home' in White Cross look like a holiday camp.

Instead of the white patch of a low-risk prisoner on his jacket, he now wore a black patch like the other prisoners around him. Unlike Rudi, most of them wore their allegiance to Hitler and the Nazi Party as a badge of honour. Men had died there. Killed by their own countrymen. Guards had been unable to stop it, or maybe they hadn't cared, had turned a blind eye. A prisoner had been hanged in the showers, and all because he failed to show the required enthusiasm for Nazi beliefs.

The irony wasn't lost on Rudi Fischer: the fact that he had broken out of one camp in order to escape a death threat from a fanatic and had ended up somewhere much worse. A place where death threats were commonplace.

20

APRIL 1941

LONDON'S EAST END

Factories, roads, railway lines, people's homes. And 300 civilians. They all vanished in a single night in London: the night Maddie lost her best friend.

The final goodbye to Molly Peters had been sad and brutal, and surreal. One mass funeral with hundreds of coffins laid side by side, in hastily dug trenches. It didn't seem right that her friend had been turned into a name on a clipboard, rather than the funny, generous, life-loving person that she had been. And how could Maddie be sure that Molly and her family were even *in* some of those coffins?

She thought about her own family. Her father in the Home Guard. Her brother Richard, still living at home and juggling figures at the Ministry of Supply. Her mother holding fundraisers. And guilt crept in. It could have been them lying in these trenches. She should get in touch. She would send them a letter. She'd done it before, of course, but maybe this time someone would reply.

Several of the ATS girls had gone to the strange funeral as well. Afterwards, they all headed over to the White Lion pub in Hackney to raise a glass to their lost friend.

'The Irish have the right idea,' said Maddie. 'Celebrating. Maybe it's better than mourning.'

Most of them agreed that the Irish definitely had a handle on things, especially *wakes*.

But Maddie didn't feel a lot like celebrating, and she left them to it after only one drink. She needed to get back home. Needed to do some serious thinking. The sherry had made her queasy.

Most things made her feel sick nowadays, especially in the mornings.

She had finally faced her fears and whispered the words aloud. Words that made her terrified. 'You are pregnant. You are unmarried. You will probably be thrown out of the army. But you cannot get rid of this baby. It is alive in you. It is your flesh. Your blood. More importantly, it is his flesh and blood. His baby too. You must let this baby live.'

Back in her billet, Maddie flung herself down on her bunk and cried. Vicious, angry tears. Tears for her missing friend. Tears for herself. And tears for this poor baby inside her. A child who would have to face the stigma of being a bastard. Born to an unmarried mother.

The tears were cathartic and, in a strange irony, made her feel much more positive. Self-pity was useless, a waste of time. She would have this baby and, when it was born, she would keep it, no matter how much anyone tried to convince her to give it away, or put it up for adoption. She was strong. She could do this. She would be doing it for both of them, for her and Rudi. And if it was a boy, she would call him 'Gunter' after Rudi's father. He would like that.

One thing Maddie knew for sure was that she would *never* go to her family for help.

She'd written her mother a letter, but it was her brother

who'd replied. Maddie's offer to visit on her next leave had been politely, but *firmly*, declined. Mother was busy, he'd said. Unable to take on visitors at this time. A visitor? Is that truly all she was? Her brother had softened the blow, wished her luck, said he hoped her career was going well.

Other than that, nothing was truly sure. She'd gone to see her commanding officer, a woman Maddie had looked up to, the same officer who had picked her for the assignment at the War Office. She'd been given the special duty because she *knew how to conduct herself properly*, her CO had said. Would the officer still feel that way when she sorted Maddie's discharge papers?

It hadn't been an easy meeting, had taken courage. Still, she'd done it. Had stood to attention in front of Chief Commander Helen Worthing's desk, respectfully, but with her head held high, uniform immaculate, regulation shine on her buttons and belt buckle. Spit and polish on her brown leather parade shoes.

Then, in a voice that seemed nothing like her own, she had told her superior officer about her present condition and waited in silence for the angry tirade that would follow the announcement of her pregnancy. But there had been no ranting, no outrage. That might have been better than the look of disappointment on the officer's face, the implication that Maddie had let her down, had squandered the trust the army placed in her.

'You had potential, could have been an officer. Did you not see that?' the CO had asked her mournfully. Then there'd been the issue of the father. Who was he? Was he likely to marry her? Those were questions that Maddie stubbornly refused to answer.

Even so, the officer had remained calm, had ordered Maddie to return to her billet immediately, and to consider herself on temporary suspension from normal duties. Those duties would be taken over by someone else. She was to speak to *no one* about this and was confined to barracks.

The words shook her, although she'd been expecting them. She'd even managed to hold on to the tears that welled up and had banged out a crisp, regulation salute.

And now she existed in a kind of half-world. Neither a civilian nor a member of the ATS. Coming out of her bedroom only for food, spending her time mending, waiting for her discharge. The army would now discard her as if she no longer had a value.

She'd waited for two days already to hear back from her CO with the bad news that she would be dismissed from the service, that she would be required to leave her billet. Find somewhere else to live.

And where will I go then? Where will my baby be born? Our baby, she reminded herself. One of those awful homes for unwed mothers, she supposed, where they treated you like a criminal. A place run by nuns who constantly reminded you of your sin, and the shame you had brought on yourself and your family. Well, she refused to feel shame. And how could something so wonderful possibly be a sin? She didn't believe it. The more she thought about this tiny seed growing inside her, becoming a small person, the more excited Maddie became.

Of course it wouldn't be easy. Nothing worthwhile ever was. It was then she thought of Molly Peters – Molly, who had been about to start a whole new chapter of her life when that life had been randomly and cruelly stolen from her. It wasn't fair. How she wished her friend could be there to talk to, to share this miracle with. Her friend had been fearless, and now Maddie would need to follow her example.

The next day she was called to Chief Commander Worthing's office. Helen Worthing had been harried by so many problems lately that she hadn't left the office in days, just grabbed a few hours' sleep on a camp bed in the corner. Those around her, her adjutant for one, as well as a sergeant known for her shrewdness and common sense, had grown increasingly worried about the CO. About the dark smudges that had arrived under her eyes and the way she'd begun snapping at anyone who walked through the door.

Chief Commander Worthing seemed disturbed. And now, as she waited for Private Madeline Brady to arrive, she did something that her office staff found strange: she dismissed all three clerks and her sergeant from the outer office. Told them they wouldn't be needed until after lunch.

She wanted no one to be aware of her meeting with Maddie. And no record to be kept. She'd been in the army long enough to know that if you went out on a limb, there was always someone eager to saw it off.

Maddie was surprised to find the commanding officer on her own. It unnerved her. But then maybe the CO was being thoughtful, was about to give her a bawling out and was sparing her the embarrassment of others eavesdropping. That didn't sound much like the army, though. The ATS had no room for sentiment, or weakness, or giddy women going feeble at the first sign of trouble. You were expected to be as tough as the men – even though you didn't earn as much as them.

'Sit down, Private,' said Helen Worthing.

The order threw Maddie. She hadn't expected to sit. They usually made you stand to attention for a dressing-down. She didn't move.

'Sit. Sit!' ordered the CO and pointed to the only other chair in the small space.

'Yes, ma'am.' Maddie stared vacantly at the crown and pip on the officer's shoulder, insignia that marked her out as a chief commander. She remembered to sit.

'Have you any idea how many ATS units I have under my command?'

'No, ma'am,' said Maddie. How was she supposed to know that?' she wondered. She'd never even thought about it.

Maddie was confused now – about where this interview was going, what she was expected to say.

'No, of course not,' said the officer, wearily. 'Why would you?' A heavy sigh left her lips and she took off her uniform cap, placed it carefully on the desk in front of her. Pulled a hand through her thick, wavy brown hair.

The move made Maddie even more confused, and she stared at the cap, fascinated, as a snake's prey might before being struck. Why on earth had the CO done that? It seemed like a deliberate action. A way to bring the interview down to a more intimate level, less formal. As if the officer were somehow setting aside the stiff military rules and protocol. Still, maybe she was reading too much into something simple – she sometimes did that.

'Twelve ATS units. That's 22,000 personnel,' said Helen Worthing. 'Scattered all over the place. One of the largest in the country. Enough to keep me busy, wouldn't you agree, Private Brady?'

'Yes, ma'am,' said Maddie, carefully picking her words. 'I *would* agree. A very large responsibility,' she added. Not sure where it was leading, what she was supposed to say. Or even if it was one of those rhetorical questions that people didn't expect an answer to.

'Yes, indeed,' said the older woman. 'Enough problems to last a while, don't you think? So why then, Maddie, would you hand me one more? I thought you were different from the others; serious, thoughtful. A girl who could keep her mind on the job. Someone I could rely on. You have gravely disappointed me.'

Maddie dropped her head to her chest, stared intently at one of the buttons on her uniform. A button she'd just polished with Brasso. She could find no words to reply. Anything she said now would sound like an excuse, and she had a feeling that this woman across the desk didn't want that. Wouldn't accept it. And she'd called her Maddie. *Why would her superior do that?*

'Someone with leadership qualities, with potential. That's what I thought. And it grieves me to find you in your... present condition.'

'Yes, ma'am,' said Maddie. And this time she raised her head, looked the officer in the face, saw that the older woman meant it. That she really did seem sad.

'Maddie, do you like being in the ATS? Is the army important to you?'

'I *love* the service,' said Maddie. 'It's my life.'

'And you mean to go through with all this, I presume?' Helen Worthing waved her hand vaguely towards Maddie's stomach. There was no evidence yet of the baby cocooned inside.

'Yes, ma'am. It isn't this baby's fault. And I won't kill it,' said Maddie.

'*Admirable*,' said Helen Worthing. 'Admirable, but a little inconvenient for you, eh?' And for the first time, Chief Commander Worthing smiled. 'But then I would expect no less of you, Private Brady. You strike me as a woman of principle. And that's why I intend to help you.'

'What? I mean, I beg your pardon, ma'am?'

'If you found yourself out of the army, where would you go to have this baby? Would you go home?'

'No. I wouldn't go home. I'm not sure right now what I'd do, how I'd manage it, where I'd have my baby. But no, I would do this on my own.'

'Right. Here's what I need you to do, Private. You are to return to your billet immediately. You will clear out your belongings and you will head to the address inside this envelope. You'll also find a railway warrant in there.'

'I don't understand, ma'am.'

'No, I don't suppose you do. You should, of course, be

picking up your discharge papers, but let's leave all talk of that for the future. Consider yourself on long-term sick leave, Private. And please, do not discuss this with anyone else in your billet. Just catch the train as soon as you can and go to this place, where they will look after you and help you give birth.'

'But...'

'No buts. You said you had nowhere else to go. So, if you're agreeable, you may have your baby at this place in Cornwall. *Is* it agreeable, Private Brady?'

'I don't know,' said Maddie. Her brain was racing around in circles, trying to understand.

'You could always go home.'

'*No.* I can never go home, not now.' She paused. 'This place in Cornwall – is it run by nuns?'

'No. No nuns. I've spoken to them on the phone, and I believe they understand your situation. They seem like good people. You'll go, then?'

What was the alternative? Maddie came to a decision. One she hoped she wouldn't regret.

'I will,' she said. 'And thank you, ma'am.'

'Let's wait and see about that – if you're still thanking me later, Madeline.' Helen Worthing smiled again and stood up from her desk; put her uniform cap back on. A signal.

'Ma'am?'

'Yes, Private Brady?'

'Am I still to wear my uniform – on the train and at this place in Cornwall?'

'Why not?' said the CO. 'You're still in the army, aren't you? Okay. Dismissed, Private.'

'Thank you, ma'am.' Maddie produced a perfect salute, turned on her heel and marched smartly from the room.

Still in the army. How had *that* happened? She was amazed, baffled. Maddie walked through the outer office. Still no one in there, which was odd, for the place was normally a hive of activity: at times orderly, at times chaotic. But she'd never known it as quiet as this. Or as empty. Strange. Confusing!

Maddie wasn't the only one confused. Once the door closed, Helen Worthing sat back down at her desk and wondered about what she had just done. And *why*. That was the big question. It was one she'd asked herself several times already. And the answer was glaringly obvious: it was something very personal – and she was supposed to be above all that. Supposed to treat all those under her command exactly the same. Pregnancy was an automatic discharge, so why was she covering up for the girl? And at the risk of her own career.

But she'd always had a soft spot for Madeline Brady: the girl was a professional, had done a competent job and never complained, unlike some of the others. And when she looked at Private Brady, she saw the spitting image of her own daughter, or what her daughter would have looked like, had she not died when she was fourteen.

It was a kind of healing realisation, to finally own up to it. But had she actually helped Maddie, or made things more complicated for her? That was the question. But whatever the outcome, life had to go on and Chief Commander Worthing had a stack of papers in front of her that needed immediate attention. Lots more problems that would keep her up at night. Including that limb that she had just taken herself out onto. She wondered who might find out about it. *And try to cut it off.*

21

7 MAY 1941

HAMMERSMITH, LONDON

It hadn't taken Maddie long to remove all traces of herself from the bedroom that she and Molly had shared. They'd laughed in this room, cried, sung the most ridiculous songs and talked about love and romance.

The thought of returning to Cornwall again sent a small shiver of expectation through her. Surely it was fate? There must be mother-and-baby homes in London, and yet Commander Worthing had sorted out this one in Cornwall for her.

Everyone was at work when she left the house in Hammersmith. No one to say goodbye to. And with a small sigh of regret, she left her key on the hall table, feeling a little sorry for herself. Deflated, as this part of her life came to an end with hardly a whimper. She had been happy there with the rest of the ATS crew and her friend Moll. She'd miss the camaraderie, the banter of the common room, as they huddled around the fire, listening to the wireless.

Maddie struggled through the front door shouldering a kitbag, canvas gas mask holder slung across her chest and carrying her small suitcase. *All her worldly goods.* But then life was more than the sum of your possessions. And her life was about to change in the most radical way. It was exciting, but also a little frightening; the part that caused her a trace of sadness was that Rudi would be unable to share this with her. The marvel of their child.

The train was crowded and uncomfortable, scores of servicemen and women going on leave, coming back from leave, travelling to new postings. Civilians too, many of them standing in corridors, waiting anxiously for seats in packed compartments. Excitement, boredom, sadness: Maddie read all those emotions on the faces of her fellow travellers. *What could they see on hers? The miracle of her child?* Was it already written in her eyes?

She often thought about her baby, had even begun talking to it. Was that quite normal? Did every pregnant woman do that? Maddie had no idea. How naive she was. Sex. Her own body. Pregnancy. Those things had never been discussed in her family.

It seemed ludicrous that there she was, about to bring another life into the world, and with only a vague idea of the process of giving birth. She'd looked for a book in the library, but there'd been nothing there to help, only a medical book that had been more terrifying than reassuring. She'd put it back on the shelf.

The train slowed to a walking pace, and they were shunted into a siding. Wartime traffic on the railway, it was always slow. Passenger trains had to give way to freight trains carrying goods and ammunition. It was the way things were, it didn't help to complain.

Her journey from Paddington was to take six hours, arriving in Truro at four o'clock. Then a short trip on a branch line to a place called St Agnes. That's where this home was – Rosemundy House – and they would send a cart to the station for her.

She'd read the letter from her CO several times now. Chief Commander Helen Worthing had even included her home telephone number. She was beyond kind. She had also included some details about where Maddie was going, and Maddie tried now to get some sense of this Rosemundy House, the home where she would introduce her baby to the world.

A home for unmarried mothers. Not run by nuns, though. Commander Worthing had assured her of that. The full force of her new reality hit her. The place where she was about to spend the next few months of her life was a home for *bad* girls, for sinful girls, those who had fallen short of society's unwritten rules. *Not a holiday camp, then. It would have some kind of regime It was sure to.* So what? She was used to the army, could take orders, wasn't any kind of weakling who ran at the first sign of trouble. And really – just how bad could it be?

The train finally arrived in Truro station at eleven thirty. Almost eight hours late. It was all a bit wearisome, but what could you do, other than make the best of it?

Maddie sat on one of the hard, wooden benches with her luggage around her. That's when it started to rain. And a tall, elderly man came out of the booking hall.

The man jangled a massive bunch of keys as he whistled a cheery sort of tune. Maddie couldn't put a name to the song, but it was a popular one that she remembered Molly singing in her more exuberant moods.

He came across to the seat and smiled at her. 'Having a rest, miss?' the man asked.

'Something like that,' said Maddie. 'I missed my train.'

'Oh?'

'I'm going to St Agnes. I was supposed to catch a train from here this afternoon, but the one from Paddington was late.'

'Dearie me,' he said in commiseration. 'Train schedules nowadays, they're sometimes just guesses, though I shouldn't say it. We tries our best, miss, but it's the war, you know.' He grinned at her again, his eyes taking in her ATS uniform.

Maddie thought he looked like a sort of ragged, ancient teddy bear. A face that was worn but still perfectly serviceable. He could easily be someone's favourite grandad. Not hers, of course. Her grandfather had been a very stern gentleman, who never grinned. 'Do you think I could stay here until my train comes?'

''Fraid not, miss. Last train on the branch line's long gone. Won't be one along now till tomorrow morning. First one leaves seven thirty.'

'Then maybe I could just wait here till then. I won't cause any trouble.' Her eyes pleaded with the old man.

'I'm sure you're a fine young lady, miss. But you can't stay here overnight. GWR's fussy about things like that. I got to close up straight after the last train.'

'I understand,' said Maddie. 'I wouldn't want to get you in trouble with the railway, Mister—?'

'Bentley. Edward, but you can call me Ted. That's what friends call me.'

'Happy to meet you, Ted,' she said. And she meant it because he seemed like a very pleasant chap. *And 'Ted'!* That was priceless, considering her thoughts about his resemblance to a teddy bear.

'Right, I'll see you out.' He jangled his keys. 'You'll have somewhere to stay, miss?' he asked, a concerned look on his face.

'I'll walk around for a bit,' she said. Maddie struggled to her feet and picked up the suitcase once more, made her way towards the exit.

'What?! In the blackout and carrying your luggage? It's

pouring cats and dogs. Can't have a fine young woman like yerself doing that. You'll catch yer death. Besides, it ain't safe.' Ted looked at her for a moment. 'Tell you what, my sister lives over the road there in one of they railway cottages. Brother-in-law's a shunter with the railway, cottage comes cheap for they pair. You could stop overnight. They wouldn't mind.'

'You're a kind man, Ted. But we can't wake your sister up in the middle of the night,' said Maddie.

'*Gesson!* She'd be right pleased to meet you, same as me.'

Maddie smiled back at the ancient Cornishman. She'd been confused when she'd first come to Cornwall, by the language that was almost English, but not quite. Their own brand. But Maddie was used to it now. In fact, she preferred *gesson* to *get on*. And *wasson* to *what's on*. Somehow it seemed more friendly, less harsh than its English equivalent.

'But you don't know anything about me,' she said. 'I'm a perfect stranger.'

'Ain't none of us *perfect*, miss,' he chuckled. 'So – what's yer name, then?'

'Private Madeline Brady,' she said. 'And my friends call me Maddie.'

'Maddie it is, then,' said Ted Bentley. 'See – you ain't a stranger no more.'

Ted's sister, a Cornish woman with the romantic-sounding name of Morwenna, was every bit as kind as he was. She was a few years younger than her brother but with the same cheery outlook, despite last night's surprise invasion into her tiny cottage.

Morwenna was a down-to-earth, practical woman, with a careworn face that could still produce a smile and long, steel-grey hair. A woman with a sense of humour too. She treated Maddie like a long-lost friend. The same couldn't be said of her husband, a disagreeable sort of man whose frown showed exactly what he thought of his night's sleep being interrupted. But Morwenna had just winked at Maddie and put a pillow down on the sofa for her. Better than spending the night sleeping on a railway platform with the rain pouring down, she'd said.

And now, the next morning, Morwenna Davy had produced a cup of tea and a ginger biscuit. A proper Cornish one, she'd said proudly. A *fairing*, baked right there in Truro.

'Brilliant, thanks,' said Maddie, as she gratefully accepted the tea. She hadn't had a thing to eat or drink since yesterday morning. 'But I can't take one of your biscuits. What about the ration?'

'Eat, eat! Looks like you could use it. And you'll need to keep your strength up – for the babe.'

'What... but how...?'

'Don't worry, you aren't showing,' said Morwenna. 'Just a feeling I 'ad. No need to cry. Tis a wonderful thing.'

The tears had been automatic. The long journey and the feelings of being alone. It had made Maddie feel sorry for herself. 'Sorry,' she said. 'I'm an idiot, and you're right. It *is* a wonderful thing.'

'There you go. Proper job! You wipe your eyes, maid. And enjoy yer biscuit.'

'What about your husband, won't he need breakfast?' asked Maddie.

'He? He's been gone hours. And don't you pay he no mind. The man can be teasy at times, but 'tis the hard life and the war.'

'You didn't tell him I was pregnant...?' asked Maddie.

'Women's work.' Morwenna laughed. 'Hard enough without men getting in the way. So, you on yer way to Rose-mundy House?'

'How did you know?' asked Maddie.

'Put two and two together. Yer off to St Agnes this morning. 'Tis a small place, not much else up there for a lady like yerself.'

'Maybe not such a lady, Morwenna. Not to get like this.' She patted her stomach.

'Aye, there's some that'll say as much. Even they up there at Rosemundy. But not me. You was only one part of the transaction, ain't that right? Blokes got the easy bit – they can walk away.'

'Not HIM!' said Maddie, and she was surprised at the strength in her voice. At the passion.

'Oh? Yer man didn't walk away, then?'

'He doesn't know. Don't suppose he'll ever know. And he's a wonderful man. A kind, sensitive man. Not a rotter, like you might think.'

'So, he can't help – but your family...'

'Ha!'

'What – you ain't got one? Father? Mother?'

'Not all mothers are like you, Morwenna.'

'Right. Well. You find yerself in need of a friend – if this thing gets tough – you can always come an' visit. Give they lot in St Agnes the slip for the day.'

'I'll keep that in mind. Thanks for your kindness.' She stood up to take her leave – it was nearly time for her train. 'Please give my best to your brother.'

'No need. You'll find he over the road at the station already. First one there in the morning, last one out at night. Railway's his life.'

Pockets of kindness. You could find them everywhere. She'd found several of them in Cornwall: the waitress Lizzie Retallack at the Angel Hotel in Helston, and now, here in Truro in a tiny railway cottage and a woman she instantly liked. A friendly Cornishwoman who had instinctively known about Maddie and her problem; had offered help but hadn't judged her. It was enough to make her feel optimistic for the world.

22

''Tis a friendly place, St Agnes,' the man sitting next to her on the train had told her. He'd gone on to tell her about how people pulled together, helped neighbours out with the harvest and stuff. Brought vegetables to those who needed them and the odd chicken to supplement the ration for those struggling to feed their kids.

There were farmers, fishermen, folk who worked in the grand city of Truro, but most of the young men had gone now, off fighting the war in some strange foreign place that many had never heard of.

There used to be copper, tin and even arsenic mines too, Maddie had learned. Lots of them spread around, at one time. Loads of folk worked the mines, but there was no tin being mined now and most of the mine stacks had already been pulled down. Dynamited. 'Quite a drama for they what watched it,' the chap had told Maddie. It didn't do to give the Jerries landmarks that could help when they tried to bomb the nearby airfields at Trevellas and Portreath.

The man beside her had been like a history and geography book rolled into one. He'd been proud of the place, of his heritage, and wanted to talk. So, she'd just relaxed back into her seat and listened, throwing in the odd nod now and then to show her interest, her appreciation. He hadn't asked why she was going to St Agnes, so Maddie hadn't offered a reason or anything personal. But she figured that her uniform was enough. There must be lots of servicemen and women in the area. The thought made her a little homesick for her ATS billet, her friends there and the laughter, and life-force that had burned so vividly in one particular friend.

They got out at the station together, as well as a young woman clutching a squalling toddler. The woman threatened all kinds of retribution if the small boy didn't quit his screeching and pulled him by the arm in what Maddie thought a callous way. It didn't seem very motherly. But then maybe kids did that to you. Made you frustrated. But how could you ever forget that you loved them? That they were part of you. She'd find out soon enough, she supposed.

What kind of a mother would she be?

'This *is* St Agnes, I suppose,' she asked the man who'd regaled her with the local history.

'That's right, my 'ansum,' he assured her. 'Why? Wasson?'

'But I don't see any town.'

'Village is that way.' The man pointed over his shoulder. 'Few miles up the road. Don't take long to walk it.'

'A few *miles*,' she said. 'But why would they call the station St Agnes if it's nowhere near the place?' she asked him.

The man shrugged, as if such things were beyond his under-standing and made no difference anyway. 'GWR ain't likely to consult us folk about where to put their stations. This ain't bad. You should see some of they halts. They ain't nowhere *near* the places they're named after.' He shrugged again. A philosophical gesture that said he was happy enough with how things were. The status quo was okay by him.

Maddie looked down at her suitcase in despair. No taxis.

And the cart that was supposed to have transported her to the village had been promised last night, not that day.

'Whereabouts you headed?' the man asked.

'St Agnes,' she said, confused.

'Lots of places in St Aggie: Churchtown, Rosemundy, Peterville, Trevaunance...'

'*Rosemundy*,' said Maddie, gratefully grasping hold of something she recognised.

The man gave her an odd look and his attitude towards her underwent a subtle change. 'Out the road, turn right, keep going for a couple miles till you hits the crossroads and take a right. Couple hundred yards on, you'll find a hill. That's Rosemundy. House's near the bottom of it,' he said, tersely. And he disappeared quickly without saying goodbye.

The young woman had finally rounded up the toddler to her satisfaction. She walked over to Maddie and pushed her face in closer, a threatening look on it. The woman's anger was obvious but inexplicable to Maddie, who had never met her before.

'You're all the same, you lot.' The woman spat the words out.

'Who?' asked Maddie. 'What?! I don't understand.'

'Oh, you understand right enough. Come down here like *that*. Flaunting yer bleddy self. Tempting the local lads with yer sinful ways. Got yerself up the duff and no bloke willing to take you on? Well, you can't have *ours*. Yer a bleddy disgrace. Shame on you.'

After this venomous tirade, the woman marched off out of the station, pulling the youngster by the arm. Almost dragging the poor lad off his feet in her anger, her haste to get away from the unholy sinner behind her.

And that's when Maddie knew for sure. That not everybody would be as understanding or kind as Morwenna. Some folks would be judgemental, might treat her like a leper, not fit for normal society. Her mother had a saying for girls like her who had fallen from grace – 'They make their bed, they lie in it.'

Maddie Brady stifled a sob, drew her invisible armour around her, picked up her luggage and headed bravely down the road to St Agnes.

It took Maddie an hour to get there, stopping every so often to change the hand holding her suitcase and moving her ATS kitbag to the opposite shoulder. The gas mask holder clunked noisily against her chest as she walked, beating out a regular rhythm: a strange sort of natural percussion. If Molly had been here with her, no doubt they'd both have laughed and sung 'The Happy Wanderer' to its background beat. The thought cheered her up.

Maddie followed the directions the chap from the train had given her. One of the right turns led into a long street with shops on either side. They were beginning to open, queues already forming outside the butcher's. Women with wicker baskets on their arms and hope in their eyes, ration books in their pockets. A greengrocer. A chemist. A pub. A school. And a chapel. The elements of civilisation.

It might be just a small village, but it seemed like a busy, bustling sort of spot, ancient and new mixed in together. *It's a friendly place, St Agnes*, the man had told her. And so far, it looked promising. Some folk had nodded to her as she passed. A couple had even smiled.

She looked across at the pub on the opposite side of the street. WE'VE GOT BEER, the chalkboard outside proudly boasted. Beer was often in short supply. She knew that already. Hop fields got bombed. No way around that. There would be some sort of quota system, she imagined. But the landlord there seemed to have things under control, had a few barrels tucked away for regulars, no doubt. The sign didn't say what kind of beer, but she supposed that didn't matter, for some folk would always complain that it was watered down no matter how good the stuff was. The chalkboard announced that it was 1s. 2d. per pint of beer, while cider was 9d.

The pub was called the Railway Inn. Maddie smiled. Miles away from the railway. Had some optimistic builder imagined the train station would be built in the middle of the village, instead of being marooned on a patch of land so far away?

She stopped to get her bearings. And there it was, a few yards ahead on her side of the road: a street sign on the wall, almost covered with ivy, the letters faded with age.

Rosemundy.

Maddie tried to recall the directions. Rosemundy was a hill, the man had said. And at the bottom of it was the place that would be her home.

She blew out some air, checked her tie was straight, adjusted her gas mask and walked boldly down the hill, head held high. Her parade shoes clicked sonorously on the cobblestones and the sound of Molly's voice invaded her thoughts: *You are strong, you are fearless; you are unbeatable. You can do this.*

The house was large and imposing, and *grey*. Everything about it seemed grey, including the high stone walls that enclosed the house and gardens and outbuildings, as if to hide it all from prying eyes. *Or keep its inmates in seclusion from the outside.* A kind of quarantine from normal society, so that Rosemundy House might not taint it.

The trees rescued it. Woods behind it and on either side gave the place a softer, more humane touch, took the edge off its brittleness. And the massive lawn in front, stretching across to some of the smaller outbuildings, was evidence of the home's real purpose. Rows of prams already sat out on the grass, their tiny occupants washed and fed and either sleeping or wailing in protest. Maddie noted with alarm that no one took any notice of these protests. Not the uniformed nurse sitting in a chair writing up notes, nor any of the women busily crossing the lawn and disappearing into the outbuildings.

She walked along the path and up to the impressive front porch flanked on either side by grand-looking columns. Maddie rang the bell. And waited. Maybe she should have gone around the back, like a tradesman, or a servant. That's what the place felt like: as if it was meant to intimidate. But she refused to be intimidated.

The door suddenly swung open, and a woman stood there. 'Yes?' she asked. Her tone was clipped.

Not a friendly voice, thought Maddie. Not angry exactly, but certainly not welcoming.

'I'm expected,' said Maddie, and moved closer to the woman blocking the front door with her over-generous frame. What she lacked in height, she made up for in width, and Maddie wanted to laugh at her stiff, sentry-like pose as guardian of the door. But she didn't. She was respectful. 'My name is Madeline Brady and I believe you've had a letter about me from Chief Commander Worthing.'

The woman took a pair of metal-rimmed glasses from the pocket of her nurse's uniform and peered through them at Maddie. Her inspection was both intense and critical. 'You were expected, yes. But that was *yesterday*. Where have you been?' she asked, fiercely.

'The train was held up. If I might come in,' said Maddie. 'I've walked all the way from the station.'

'If you'd have been here on time you wouldn't have had to walk, would you? I can't think why Matron even agreed to send the donkey cart in the first place. What are you, royalty?' the woman asked, with a sneer.

She finally opened the door and ushered Maddie inside. 'Quickly now. Don't dawdle. First office on the right, off you go.

And knock on the door,' she added. 'Wait until you're summoned. And don't go through your whole life story in there, Matron's a busy woman. She'll show you around. Well, what you waiting for? Shoo!'

Shoo? Maddie didn't know whether to scream at the woman, or cry. But she did neither of those things. Instead, she drew herself up to her full height, a good few inches above this domineering bully who had tried to browbeat her into submission, and remembered why she was there. She was doing this for her and Rudi, and their baby. And no tyrant could take that away from her.

23

She followed the matron up the sweeping, majestic staircase. It must once have been impressive, the gilding on it glistening in the light from many fancy candelabras hanging from the high ceiling.

Maddie only imagined the candelabras. There were none, and the gilding had worn off in most places. But it would have been a magical place. Where balls were held, and landowners came from miles around in their carriages. The home of gentry or mine owners perhaps, in years gone by.

But Maddie didn't ask, and the matron didn't offer an insight into its history. Whatever it had once been, Rosemundy House was no longer a grand mansion. It needed some repair, the plaster crumbling in places. It was cold, and a damp smell pervaded the air.

'This staircase,' said the matron, 'is *never* to be used again in your time here, only today as part of your induction. For the rest of your time with us you will use the back stairs that lead from the servants' quarters. Is that understood?'

'Perfectly,' said Maddie. She'd been right. Had picked up on the pecking order immediately. Didn't need it spelled out for her. She, and the other *naughty* girls like her, would be at the bottom of the ladder. The staff, on the other hand, appeared to be just one rung below God Almighty Himself.

The matron studied Maddie's face for any sign of insolence in the reply. She nodded. Seemed satisfied that all was in order. She'd introduced herself as Miss Robertson, and Maddie hadn't missed the slight emphasis on *Miss*, as if the matron wore it as a badge of honour. 'However,' she'd said, '*you* are to call me Matron at all times.'

People were sometimes strange, thought Maddie. *You couldn't always work them out. Their motives.* But whatever she did, no matter how hard Maddie tried to be perfect, she knew this woman would never like her. Held some sort of grudge against her from the beginning. Maybe it was a power thing. Or prejudice. Miss Robertson knew nothing about her, but maybe it was enough that Maddie was an unmarried mother, a sinner in the matron's eyes.

Miss Robertson was a small husk of a human being who looked as if all the humanity had been drained out of her, leaving only bitterness and dryness in its place. Her movements were precise and fussy. It was hard to guess her age, but old certainly, Maddie decided. For she had the sort of voice you sometimes heard in the elderly: high-pitched and with a slight quiver. Despite this, she carried an air of authority that dared anyone to challenge her.

Her dress was black, plain and unadorned. It flowed to her ankles and climbed back up to her chin, its tight collar constricting, as if the woman would need to make a special effort to breathe. No neck was showing, just her small head that pushed itself alarmingly up out of the constricting collar.

Maddie was convinced of one thing, that Miss Robertson, for all her small stature, might be every bit as much a tyrant as the buxom nurse who had opened the front door to her. She hadn't smiled once.

'You may wonder why I wear no nursing uniform,' the matron had said.

It hadn't crossed Maddie's mind.

'I am in charge of this entire home as well as its staff: two nurses, a midwife, a laundry matron and a cook. But my role is not medical.'

'No?' said Maddie, who felt something was expected of her. A reply of some sort.

'No, my role is far more important than that, young lady. I am trained in moral welfare. That is my task. To bring sinners like you back to the path of light. And to train all who have brought shame on themselves and their families in the proper spiritual and moral values that are expected of you. It is my job to *instruct*.'

The woman spoke like a zealot. Maddie had met such people before. They poisoned the air with their religious fervour, which rarely had the true ring of sincerity about it. If they truly believed in God, wouldn't they be kind?

That's it, then. No hope of sympathy would reside within the walls of this old and crumbling mansion. Not that she'd truly expected any, but it would have been good to find support and understanding at a time when she needed it, a friend when she was alone. An empathetic ear at least.

She'd been right about the matron's proximity to God. The first place Miss Robertson led her on her induction tour was the chapel. It was a small room with a few chairs and a makeshift altar, but at least someone had put fresh flowers in there, their perfume heady and sweet in the tiny space.

It was the most important room in the building according to Matron. The mothers and mothers-to-be were expected to turn up to the chapel every morning at ten. Bible study also took place in this small room, taken by a minister from the village church, a man responsible for the souls of the girls.

Next, there was an inspection of the dormitories: two long,

bare rooms with flagstone floors, fifteen bunks in each. Thirty pregnant women all in one place? She hadn't expected so many. Like a barracks. Something she knew and understood. It reminded Maddie of basic training and a feeling of nostalgia flooded her. *I can cope with this*, she thought. *It isn't so bad.*

That feeling quickly faded when the matron marched her into the maternity ward. Even worse was the 'birthing room'. Not a welcoming space designed to put an anxious woman in labour at her ease, it had more in common with Victorian customs than the twentieth century; it was a frightening place. A small, narrow bed, complete with leather foot stirrups, stood in one corner – a harrowing-looking sight that made Maddie shudder. The other bed dominating the centre of the room looked wider and more comfortable, but had a strange-looking metal affair attached to its sides, with padded knee rests.

A medieval torture chamber would have been more inviting.

Both rooms were freezing cold. Hygienically sound, no doubt. And medically sterile. White walls. Cold white tiles. Chrome. Glass. She tried to block the images from her mind before they overwhelmed her. No point in worrying about things you could do nothing about, things you couldn't change.

She was pregnant. She would end up in this awful room one day.

That was a hard fact, irreversible. And she would face it head-on. With acceptance and as much courage as she could muster.

The next stage of her tour was the final one and far more cheerful and uplifting. She could feel her optimism drifting back, bit by bit. She followed Matron into the nursery wing. It wasn't so cold and sterile in there. Two small electric bars hung from the high roof, sending heat into the cots below. There were lots of cots, but only one was occupied. Maddie assumed that most of the babies were out in the prams she'd seen on the lawn.

She wandered over and looked in the cot. A tiny figure was trussed up tightly in there, moving its head from side to side and issuing a small whimper now and then. *Why did they need to be wrapped up like that, like they were being suffocated? Surely it couldn't be comfortable for the poor little soul?* Not that she had any experience with babies, but some maternal instinct made Maddie want to pick up the poor little mite and pull off all the swaddling clothes, and just cuddle it.

A nurse was busy in one corner of the room, putting things away in a cupboard. Her movements were practised and confident, as if the nursery was a place she was used to. She raised her head to look at them and Maddie saw that the nurse was young, with an earnest face, but there was kindness there too. The girl nodded towards Miss Robertson, an acknowledgement that the authority in the room had shifted with the matron's entrance. Then she looked at Maddie – and smiled. It was the first time anyone had done so since she'd arrived. It was a beaming smile. A welcoming smile.

An angel, thought Maddie. At least there was one angel in this place.

24

It soon became obvious that the underlying philosophy of the home was that the women who ended up there deserved their fate. Deserved to be punished. It was not a place of joy. But Maddie did her best to spread cheerfulness among her fellow inmates. She'd taken to thinking of herself and those around her as prisoners, because none of them had any real freedom of choice. There were strict rules that had to be adhered to, and if they weren't, there were *consequences*.

One young mum-to-be had gone into the village without permission and had been brought back in disgrace and confined to a separate room away from all the others for a week. No company, no food. Maddie had smuggled in bits of her own food to the poor girl but had been found out and had to suffer a lecture from Matron about responsibility and Christian duty.

She'd thought it *was* her Christian duty to be kind and concerned for those around you. But Miss Robertson's ideas were different from Maddie's. Matron favoured the Old Testament values of fear, punishment, retribution. Those were top of her list, which didn't leave much room for kindness. And the woman's anger could indeed be biblical. She was also very big on 'atoning for your sins' and took every chance she could to remind her *girls* that they were sinners who needed to repent.

Maddie didn't feel like a sinner. And she wasn't a girl. She was a woman. At twenty-three, she was one of the oldest there. Some of them were just sad, confused children who had discovered their sexuality and been taken advantage of. One fourteen-year-old had been raped by her uncle. Where was the retribution for him?

Her determination not to be cowed into submission by Matron, and the fierce midwife who had opened the door to her, made Maddie's life more complicated than some of the others in Rosemundy. Some were okay with the place, were given an easier ride. Those who were prepared to turn up to chapel every morning and tug their forelock. And attend all the patronising lectures. But that wasn't for Maddie. She didn't want to be a hypocrite and sometimes she made it worse for herself. She was not being awkward, or arrogant, as they'd accused, only trying to keep her self-respect. But Sister Bennett, the midwife, had taken an instant dislike to her. She had no idea why. Jealousy, perhaps. For Maddie had stood on the doorstep in her ATS uniform, towering above the small, rotund nurse, confident and unrepentant.

That was the first thing that had been stripped away from her. Her uniform. It had been like losing a friend. It was taken away and, in its place, she'd been given the uniform of the house: a dark brown, shapeless smock with long sleeves and a white pinafore over the top, like a servant's uniform. It looked as if it came from another century. This was to be worn for work and at meals and for walking out in the village, should permission be given.

The new uniform got her into trouble. Unfairly. But then Maddie hadn't been expecting fairness. Showing too much leg! 'A harlot,' Sister Bennett had called her. Most of the other mums and mothers-in-waiting were shorter than her and their uniforms came to a respectful place in the middle of the calf. More in keeping with the modesty that was expected. Maddie's smock came only as far as her knee. She'd let out as much of the hem as possible, but it still wasn't satisfactory.

Nothing she did would ever be satisfactory for the hard-nosed midwife. Even so, Maddie set about her work every morning in a cheerful, uncomplaining frame of mind, willing to take on the back-breaking work in the laundry.

The laundry was far away from the main house, in a small outbuilding, its antiquated equipment – including the heavy mangle and ancient copper heated by a fire underneath – dealing with the immense amount of dirty washing. It also held a huge concrete laundry sink, twice the length of a Belfast and even deeper, with a massive draining board. Someone shorter than Maddie would have trouble reaching to the bottom of that beast of a sink.

She lit the fire under the boiler at night, soaked the sheets soiled with childbirth and the nappies in the copper, rinsed them over and over again, battling with the heavy linen. Put them through the mangle, hung them out on the rows of lines in the garden if the weather was fine, or wrestled with the pulleys in the laundry's porch, filling the wooden racks with wet washing and pulling them high up to the ceiling. A job that made the muscles in her arms ache for days.

Some thought that working in the laundry was drudgery, a thankless task. But Maddie was happy there. By herself. Away from everyone. And it was satisfying seeing all those fresh, clean clothes flapping in the breeze. She didn't even mind the mounds of ironing with the old flat iron. And when she came to the end of it, she felt proud of the tall piles of clean, freshly ironed sheets surrounding her. She'd even found herself humming a tune. One of Molly's favourites.

When Sister Bennett overheard it, she'd immediately reported Maddie to the matron. And her duties in the laundry room had been curtailed. She'd been switched to floor cleaning. The flagstones were brutes to scrub and after hours of it, Maddie had red, swollen knees and hands. This time, she hadn't just hummed, but sung: it made her feel better.

That was the first time Nurse Ryder had come to her. Ethel, her name was. And she was the angel Maddie had seen in the nursery on her first day. The girl was young, around eighteen, Maddie guessed, although she carried herself with an assurance and dignity that spoke of an older, more experienced woman. Someone who had seen and heard extraordinary things. But someone who did not judge. She reminded Maddie of a younger version of Morwenna.

'You mustn't do that, you know. They won't like it. Although *I* do,' she added quickly, and smiled that serene smile of hers.

'What?'

'The singing. It sounds far too happy.' The young woman chuckled. 'You're supposed to be sad and show remorse. They expect it.' She nodded in the direction of Matron's office. 'It'll make your life a whole lot easier.'

'I like to sing,' said Maddie.

'I know,' said Nurse Ethel. 'I've listened to you.'

'You have?'

'Yes. And I like to sing too. But the only singing they like around here is hymns.'

'For God's sake!'

'I guess so. Don't you believe in God, then?'

'I haven't worked it all out yet,' admitted Maddie. 'I think there must be someone out there bigger than us. But whether or not He's directing things, well – I don't know.'

'Sister Bennett says I'm to keep an eye on you. She says you're a heathen – and you need to be watched.'

'Does she now? And is that because I sing, or because I don't sing hymns?'

'Bit of both, I reckon. But you need to be careful, miss. You don't want to get on the bad side of Sister Bennett.'

'Oh, and why's that?'

'Don't know about you,' said Ethel, 'but I wouldn't fancy having *her* help birth *my* baby. Know what I mean? I've seen it before. She doesn't like somebody, she makes sure they have a hard time. She thinks they should suffer – for their sins, like.'

'Sweet Jesus! What is this – the Middle Ages?'

'You're a nice lady. Confident, clever, with a mind of your own. They don't like that. They likes you to be humble.'

'Not *that* clever, Ethel – am I?' said Maddie. 'Otherwise I wouldn't have got like this now, would I?' She wrapped her hands around her stomach. Protecting the baby inside her. The baby she'd felt move in there for the first time that day.

'Unless the man was special, maybe.' The nurse smiled. 'And you loved him. *Did* you love him, miss?'

Maddie tried to swallow but the lump in her throat made it hard. And her breath came out in a small gasp. *Shouldn't breathing be automatic?* Except it didn't feel like that, not now. A fine film of tears misted her eyes and then slowly made their way down her flushed cheeks.

The nurse took hold of Maddie's trembling hands. 'You *do* love him then! He must be a wonderful man. But why are you crying?'

'Because,' said Maddie, 'you're the first person here who's asked me that.'

25

NOVEMBER 1941

ST AGNES, CORNWALL

They found Rudi's photograph under her mattress.

That was the lowest point of her stay, the day they took him away from her. There was the promise that she would have it back when she left, along with her uniform.

She didn't believe it. Because the nurse who'd found it had searched the bedding on the orders of Matron, and seemed gleeful to have discovered something that might get Maddie in trouble.

Trouble was something that dogged her heels. There were the lectures on 'moral decay in the younger generation' that Matron was proud of, and that Maddie had refused to attend. And the numerous refusals to give her baby up for adoption had brought scorn from some of the staff. How did she expect to look after a child and keep a roof over her head? There were times she wondered that as well, but it was hardly their place to condemn her for wanting to try.

Already six months into her stay, with her baby due anytime now, Maddie was a whole lot larger than when she first arrived. And she was used to the home's regime. Understood the staff, their jealousies and those who were callous and vindictive. That was most of them, apart from Nurse Ethel and the laundry matron, a genial woman from the village, but even she would think twice about standing up for the girls if it meant going against Matron's wishes.

The worst of all was Sister Bennett, the midwife. She struck Maddie as being not only a waspish woman with a sharp tongue, but sadistic. There were stories from some of the girls who had already given birth about how the woman treated those in labour. 'Paying penance for your sins' was a favourite expression of hers. And it appeared she was not going to make the process of birth any easier if she could help it. Suffering, it seemed, was good for the soul.

Maddie hoped that when her time came to go into labour, the doctor would be there as well. Or Ethel, that sweet, quiet-spoken angel of a nurse who sometimes helped the resident midwife out.

Maddie had sat night after night in the cold, damp sitting room, all of them trying to squeeze in close to the small fire burning in the hearth. They had to take turns collecting firewood for it from the wood at the bottom of the large garden, but it was strictly rationed to make it last. Matron didn't need wood for her fire. There was always a hearty coal fire ablaze in the hearth in her office and quarters.

The coal was kept under the stairs, and one night an expectant mother had slipped in there and stolen a few lumps of coal, hidden them in her coat and arrived in triumph in the sitting room.

The girl had been thrown out of the home the next day. Nowhere to go. No money in her purse and disowned by her parents. Maddie had run up the hill after the youngster and given her a ten-shilling note, some of her army wages from happier times. But they'd gone after the girl, taken the money off her, and Maddie's wallet had been confiscated. Taken into Matron's office for 'safe keeping'.

She still had nightmares about the girl. *Was she out there lying in a ditch somewhere?* And for her part in the fiasco, Maddie had been punished with solitary confinement for three days with little food, apart from the remnants of breakfast that Nurse Ethel had managed to sneak into her.

Ethel Ryder was a strange young woman. There was a serenity about her and a maturity that belied her youth, but over the months Maddie had come to realise there was also sadness in her pale, thin face. Despite the threat of discovery, Ethel had stayed a while with her, and they talked about Maddie's baby, and Ethel's family living a few miles away in Trevellas. The girl looked after her mother: a sick woman who seemed kindly, at least kinder than Maddie's.

And for the first time ever, Maddie told someone the name of her baby's father: Rudi Fischer from Ramsau, a small Alpine village in Bavaria. A place that sounded as beautiful as he was. And Ethel hadn't been shocked that he was a German. Or that he was a prisoner of war. Maddie knew that her secret was safe with this girl.

Ethel had hurried away, reminding her that this was a punishment and she should show remorse, but there was a smile on the nurse's face. They were both alike. Understood each other. Rebels. Ethel Ryder's rebellion was a quiet one, Maddie's not so much – but she was learning.

As for her punishment: if it was meant to upset her, it didn't. It had the opposite effect. Solitary confinement was good, it gave you time alone to think. Time away from the petty squabbling that often punctuated the evenings of knitting and sewing and mending in the girls' sitting room.

Everyone was expected to knit clothes for their babies and sew a layette. Maddie found that part restful and even pleasant. She took pride in fashioning her baby's wardrobe and was surprised at how such simple things could give you so much satisfaction. She had never had time before. And she sang songs to her unborn child. Told him or her about their father. She hoped the baby would be a boy, but it didn't matter either way. As long as the babe was well and healthy and happy... She would do her best to make sure of that.

The visiting doctor came. He pronounced Maddie fit and well.

A relief. Not that she felt ill, but she could have done without the back pain, the varicose veins and the heavy weight pressing down on her bladder. Still, it was all in a good cause. A precious small person was waiting at the end of it – that was worth any amount of extra lavatory trips.

Dr Harries, a tall, imposing figure, put the stethoscope away in his bag. Instructed her to get up from the couch in the birthing room.

'Strong as an ox,' he said, gruffly. 'No complications, unlike some of the younger girls, and your baby's heartbeat is strong. You have a lusty child there.'

Maddie blew out some air and struggled to get herself up from the narrow bed. She fought to find her core muscles that seemed to have taken a holiday. No one offered to give her a hand, neither the doctor nor Sister Bennett. The midwife had a smirk on her face. Maybe the image of one of her bad girls struggling like a beached whale brought her satisfaction.

'Any day now, Miss Brady,' the doctor confidently predicted.

'Really?' asked Maddie.

'Should I be otherwise engaged when you go into labour, you can safely rely on your own midwife, here. She's done this many times before. I have total faith in the abilities of Sister Bennett, a professional to her fingertips.'

At this point the midwife smiled at Doctor Harries, a sickly sweet, angel-of-mercy sort of smile. With a touch of humility thrown in. *Pure fiction*, thought Maddie. But the doctor was impressed.

'So, would I be well enough to walk up the hill with the others tonight?' asked Maddie.

'Up the hill?' he asked.

'Some of the girls have permission to go to the cinema, Doctor,' explained Sister Bennett.

'That's very kind. You're not spoiling them, are you?' the doctor asked.

'Oh, well... Our young ladies are very special to us, as you know. We mustn't blame them for their condition. *To err is human, to forgive divine.*' The midwife simpered under the approving gaze of Doctor Harries.

'Very humane, I'm sure,' he said. 'And I suppose, if you feel well enough, young lady' – he turned his attention to Maddie – 'then I don't see why you can't join them at the Regal. Bit of a hike up there, but you're fit enough.'

'Thank you, Doctor,' said Maddie. 'I appreciate your trouble and concern.'

'Yes... well...'

'That will be *all*, Miss Brady, thank you,' said Sister Bennett, sharply. 'Run along. I think we've kept the doctor long enough, I'm sure he's busy.'

A tight expression around the midwife's mouth and the stern look in her eyes was one Maddie had seen before. *A warning signal that all is not well.* Maddie doubted she'd be seeing the cinema tonight. Sometimes they were allowed to walk there, hand in hand in pairs, a crocodile. Like children walking to school. The girls were allowed to wear their own clothes for the visit, not the dreary uniform dresses of the home. Except they were expected to wear a green armband, something to mark them out from ordinary people.

She thought about Rudi and the tell-tale white patch on the back of his uniform. Something else they had in common. Both of them now, seen as different from others. Kept separate from them. In the small cinema, the inmates from Rosemundy were all seated together, at one side of the aisle; like a contagion that couldn't be allowed to spread to the rest of the community. Especially the impressionable young lads.

Maddie had only been there once before. Had sworn she would not put herself through the ignominy again, as a few of the villagers had hissed and booed at them. It had been a relief when the lights went out. Not that all the villagers were like that. Many people were kind. They took pity on the girls and even gave them sweets at times when they walked up the hill to the shops.

Permission had to be given by Matron to go outside the home. Then for a few hours in the afternoon, after your morning work was done, you could take a walk, maybe even go down to the beach. But you had to be back by five or Matron would unleash her full range of imaginative punishments on the culprits.

Maddie went straight back to work after the doctor examined her. He had decreed her fit and here, that meant fit for work. The only women who got out of work were the ones who had gone into labour. Some of the girls wished for those gruelling hours of childbirth, just to get out of laundry duty. Some even wished that something might go wrong, so they'd be sent to Redruth hospital. *A much more pleasant experience*, it was said. Not that Maddie believed that.

She had searched her heart, taken out her fear and examined it at close quarters. She wasn't looking forward to labour, not after some of the grisly stories they bandied about in the common room, but at least it would have to end sometime.

She was on her knees, stripping the wax from the hallway floor, when she heard loud footsteps. Heavy shoes and the sharp pungent smell of sweat. She knew who was hovering behind her. The breathing was laboured, like someone bulky and overweight.

Someone who was upset.

'How *dare* you speak to the doctor like that?' said Sister Bennett.

'What?'

'Forward. And with *such* familiarity. But then, we could hardly expect anything else from a person who gets herself in your disgusting state.'

'Forward?' said Maddie. 'I just thanked him for his trouble and care.'

'Exactly. And that's not your place. You are very lucky, young woman, to have someone of his stature look after you. If you were left to your own devices, you wouldn't be able to afford that. The good people who fund this place have soft hearts. If it wasn't for the Moral and Social Welfare Association, Miss High and Mighty, you'd be out on the street having your brat. And as for the cinema tonight, you can forget all that.'

With that, the midwife stamped off in anger.

Maddie collapsed into a flood of tears and dropped the scrubbing brush. It was the second time she had cried since she'd been here and she vowed that they would never make her do it again. She pictured Rudi and their baby and her wonderful friend Moll, and she wiped her eyes with the stupid pinny. Picked up the scrubbing brush again. *Well, if she lost her job in the army, at least she could always get work cleaning.* She'd become an expert.

The thought made her laugh and she started to sing at the top of her voice.

26

Her uniform was lying on the bed. The on-duty nurse had brought it, told her to change into it quickly. The jacket wouldn't pull together, and Maddie had had to pin the blouse where her bountiful bust had threatened to rip it asunder. The skirt had always been a generous fit, but even it was struggling to look decent.

Then Maddie was ordered out into the garden to wait – she didn't know why. 'Visitors,' was all the nurse would say. Her wallet had been returned as well.

Visitors? But she'd not had any visitors in all the time she'd been here. She wondered who it might be.

Morwenna, perhaps, coming from Truro? That kind woman whose generosity of spirit was so far removed from her own mother's. How wonderful it would have been to have had Morwenna as her mother. How different life might have been. More smiles, at least. More laughter. Less money, of course. But then money didn't matter that much, not when you weighed it up against important things like love.

But her visitor wasn't Morwenna. Maddie could hardly

believe the figure that made her way towards her across the path.

'You look well,' said Helen Worthing. 'I'm sorry I couldn't make it down before. I wanted to check on you, but you know the army. Paperwork up to my armpits,' said the CO and she smiled.

Maddie struggled up from the bench. Managed a salute, but it was silly of course, for everything was far from normal, and she knew her uniform looked bizarre.

'Ma'am – what a wonderful surprise.'

'I hoped it might be,' Helen said. 'Although I did tell the matron to warn you, in case you'd be upset.'

'No. It's super, cheered up my day.'

'I'm pleased. You're really okay then? This place…?'

'It's fine,' said Maddie. *No point burdening her CO with the truth. Not when Commander Worthing had been so kind and arranged it all.*

'That's good,' Helen said, relieved. 'You hear stuff about places like this, but I did some research and I was happy that this was the one for you.'

'Thank you.'

'I've brought you a little something. A few apples and a slice of cake.'

'Ma'am! That's very kind, ma'am.' Maddie grinned.

'You can take them with you to the cinema tonight.'

'How did you know…?'

'Matron. She tells me her *girls* often have little treats like that. She's an old-fashioned woman, but she seems decent.'

Maddie didn't answer. What was there to say?

'And you and the baby – you're both fine? Any time now, Matron tells me.'

'Yes.' Please God it would all be over soon, and she could get away from this place.

'It looks lovely,' said Helen. 'The garden, I mean. I guess they bring the babies out here.'

'When it's a fine day,' said Maddie, and she smiled warmly at the woman who had helped her, had thrown her a lifeline. The smile slipped when she saw Miss Robertson heading their way.

'Well, you ladies seem to be having a nice visit.' The matron nodded.

'Miss Robertson, lovely to see you again. Your garden is beautiful here,' said Helen.

'Yes, our young ladies take great pride in keeping it that way.'

'The mothers-to-be? They work in the gardens?' asked Helen, surprised.

'Fresh air is good for them. And a little light work never hurt anyone, did it now?' The matron turned to Maddie. 'So, you're off to the cinema tonight, I hear?'

'Really? But I thought Sister Bennett said it was off-limits,' said Maddie.

'Nonsense! You leave Sister to me. Go and have a good time, Madeline. Abbott and Costello are just the right sort of medicine, you enjoy it.'

The matron left them sitting together on the bench. Two women, both in uniform, both with different expressions on their faces. Helen was smiling. But Maddie's face was wreathed in confusion. Confusion that turned into understanding. *Of course.* The visit to the Regal was back on and the aura of sweetness and light that had exuded from Miss Robertson was purely for her commanding officer's consumption. Not that it changed anything. But a bag of apples and a slice of cake plus Abbott and Costello later...

All in all, not a bad day.

'Well, I should be going. Don't want to miss the last train. Services seem a bit patchy.'

'It's the war.' They both said it together, and the two women laughed.

It was the first time Maddie had laughed in ages.

'You get yourself well and settled with the baby. Then we need to talk, of course,' Helen said, suddenly serious.

'Of course,' said Maddie. 'I totally understand. And I'll come to see you when I get back to London, if that's all right, ma'am.'

'That would be best. But phone first before you come. Things may be difficult. You have my home number there still?'

'Yes. I still have the letter. And, ma'am, thank you again for all you've done.'

'Fine. Fine. Must rush.'

And then she was gone. Maddie was left alone in the garden, wondering what had just happened. Not really understanding why her commanding officer had rushed off like that. Or why she had taken the trouble to travel all the way down to Cornwall. And why she was crying.

The doctor might have pronounced her fit, but fitness was a relative thing, she guessed. She certainly couldn't have marched for the hours she had in her ATS basic training, or run the miles expected of her in those first six weeks.

Marching up the hill at Rosemundy was enough to almost finish Maddie off. But the others had surprised her – comradeship that she hadn't expected – when two of the girls walked on either side, held onto her arms and almost frog-marched her up to the cinema. For a minute it was like being back in the old billet.

She shared her apples with the other three and they all settled down to watch the screen. Bud Abbott and Lou Costello, two American comedians, were acting in a silly sort of movie called *In the Navy*. It was an unlikely plot, a mixture of comedy, romance and musical. She thought about Molly. *Molly would have loved it.*

She laughed at the daft antics and so did the others around her, including people on the other side of the aisle: the villagers who wanted a night out to take them away from the hardship and worries of the war. And this time, no one had made the four women from the home feel any different or complained about having to share the same air as them. People were just people when you came down to it.

Maddie laughed so much she almost cried. And suddenly, she heard a strange popping sound, like she'd sat on something that had collapsed. And a tiny trickle of wet ran down her leg.

She leaned into the girl next to her, a worldly girl for her seventeen years. Young Alice had come to Rosemundy with dyed blonde hair, but it had almost grown out now, dark brown roots forcing their way through. Sister Bennett had called her a harlot, too. That was something both she and Maddie had in common: the way they seemed to annoy the resident midwife.

'I'm embarrassed,' whispered Maddie. 'I've laughed so much that I think I've peed myself.' She felt a hot flush of shame push itself up her neck and into her cheeks.

'Shush! Wait... What did you say?' the girl asked.

'I've wet myself,' she whispered again.

'Is it a lot?'

'Not much, I don't think. Just a trickle. And there was a funny popping noise like a rubber band going ping.'

'Gawd, girl! Sounds like your waters broke.'

'No. Can't be,' said Maddie, worried now. 'Not yet. And I feel fine. Just damp. No pain, nothing.'

'So? Just sit there then. We ain't going back, not till the end of the flick.'

'But what if I'm in labour?' said Maddie, panicking now, feeling sick.

'You ain't – not yet. You said you ain't got no pain.'

'Yes, but I'm all *wet*.'

'Worse things in life, Madds. Enjoy the flick.'

Worse things in life. And it turned out that was right: there were much worse things.

27

Although the journey back was downhill, it was harder than the outward one. If it hadn't been for them practically dragging her, Maddie might not have made it. Not on her own.

Her saviour was Alice, who chivvied her along. This was Alice Wainwright's second baby, and she had a straightforward way of explaining the future Maddie had let herself in for. No drama. No grisly details. And a lot of common sense – far more than Maddie had credited the girl with.

'Just remember, you'll need to be seen soon. And the pains might come any time.'

'But my waters,' whispered Maddie. 'You said they'd just broken.'

'Don't take no mind to that. Sometimes they goes with a whish just before. Sometimes the babe comes out on the wave of them, like it's swimming. And sometimes they breaks in the cinema in the middle of an Abbott and Costello flick.' Alice chuckled.

'But I don't know what that *means*.'

'It means that now this little babe of yourn has lost the sack around 'im, it could be dangerous for the kid. Could be infection, least that's what my ma says, and she should know. She's had six of us. And lost two.'

'So...?'

'So, get Nurse to give you an internal. And cross yer fingers and think of England.'

'Oh... right?'

'Don't help to scream,' said Alice, helpfully. 'That only upsets the babbie and holds stuff up. And that crabby old midwife loves to hear you scream. So don't give her no satisfaction.'

'I'll try to remember that.'

'You ain't nowhere *near* yet,' grumbled Sister Bennett, following the rough internal exam. The woman had large hands and being gentle hadn't been her priority. 'Stop making such a fuss and get yerself on to the dormitory. I'm off to my bed too, and I'll check on you in the morning.'

The pains came throughout the night. In waves, as she'd expected, but not nearly as bad as Maddie had feared. Then they went away again. Gave her a bit of a rest. And the next morning, she was ordered to work as usual. Washing dishes, light duty.

They did have a heart here, after all.

She was sent out to scrub the front step. 'Work and exercise,' Sister Bennett told her. 'The best medicine for girls like you.' The woman grinned at her. 'No doubt we'll be seeing each other later, Miss Brady.'

'But what about Doctor Harries,' asked Maddie, 'shouldn't we call him?'

'And what makes you so special?' said the midwife. 'You got nothing I haven't seen before.'

'But my waters,' said Maddie, 'they've gone already.

Shouldn't we be careful? I don't want my baby to get an infection, to get sick.'

'So, you're the expert now? Maybe I'll just take myself off for a wee holiday. Seems you won't be needing me.'

But she needed *something*. She wasn't sure what. Anything to take her mind off the agony that held her in its grip. Hour after hour. Getting fiercer as the time went on, until at the end of the day, Matron came and ordered her into the birthing room with its austere white tiles and its grim medical instruments.

The old woman sat with her for a while; she even smiled once. It was a little bizarre: Matron rattling on about social responsibility and patting Maddie on the stomach to remind her that what she had in there was a life she would need to take care of, bring up under the eye of The Almighty.

Time and again Matron stressed just how *difficult* that would be. People would be against her. She would be a pariah, an outcast. Annexed from normal society. 'Will you be able to do it?' the woman asked. The inference was that she couldn't. That Maddie would be unable to look after a young baby, all by herself; that the best thing for this child of hers would be to give it up.

The voice in Maddie's ear was persistent. And maybe the old woman was right, for she'd seen a lot of babies born there. It would be easy. So easy just to close her eyes and block this baby from her mind. Except *easy* was never good. And she wanted this baby now with a passion that had turned to fury. Fury against the woman sitting on the end of her bed, droning on in her self-righteous voice.

Maddie raised herself painfully from the bed and threw a pillow at her.

Matron stormed from the room, vowing all sorts of Old Testament retribution.

But Maddie didn't care. What more could they do to her? Her

whole body was already in the grip of a massive vice that threatened to swallow her up in its waves of indescribable pain. She imagined Rudi's face in her mind. Held onto the image. Spoke to it. Told him she was doing this for him, for them, for their baby. They'd packed a lifetime into two short days. They'd talked and laughed and loved. She remembered the things he cared about: his homeland; his father, Gunter; his brother Werner who had died. His mother, still waiting for her son. And *her*. He loved her too. *A special love*, he'd said. She prayed that he was safe, and made herself a promise – that he would get to meet his child.

Another wave of pain crashed over her, and she thought of Alice in the dormitory. Alice who had told her that screaming was no good. That it didn't help.

But in the long night there was a lot of screaming. People drifted in and out of her feverish vision. The midwife. Matron, standing there with her arms crossed, a frown sketched deep into her face. But no doctor. And no angelic nurse. Nurse Ethel Ryder had gone to look after her mother, wouldn't be back for days. Maddie had hoped to have her here, mopping her brow, holding her hand in comfort. Maybe then she would not have screamed so much.

And finally, born on the end of one of those many terrifying screams, came a final tsunami of pain and a tug and the sound of ripping skin and a strange sloshing noise, and a baby shot out of her.

But no cry. No small infant noise.

Sister Bennett slapped the small person on its tiny bottom. She did it several times, and still there was no cry. Maddie weakly raised her head, reached out her arms, aching for her child. Imploring, begging them to bring her baby to her side. But they ignored her. Instead, the midwife rushed urgently from the room. But not before Maddie had seen the glance between them. A look of concern.

· · ·

There was a lot of activity. Maddie could hear feet moving noisily and doors being slammed and soon a nurse came in to see her and delivered the placenta. The woman also put some stitches in where Maddie had torn giving birth. Pain on top of other pain. Layers of it. But she didn't scream, didn't complain. For the worst pain of all was in her mind, and that would go when they brought her baby back.

'I need to feed my baby,' she said.

The woman didn't reply or look at her. It was the nurse who'd taken such delight in taking Rudi's photograph.

'And I want my photograph back,' she said. 'I'm leaving here, I'll be taking it with me.'

The woman left the room in a hurry. She seemed flustered.

Young Alice popped her head around the door nervously. Came over to sit on the bed and took Maddie's hand in hers. 'I'm sorry about your babbie. We're all sorry. How d'you feel?'

'What?' said Maddie. 'What about my baby?'

'Better run,' said the young girl. 'They find me here, I'm dead meat.' With that, she was gone, as silently and swiftly as she'd come.

Maddie heard herself scream. Except the voice wasn't hers, but some stranger's.

Sister Bennett came into the birthing room with a wheel-chair and pulled Maddie roughly from the bed. 'Stop all that fuss. You're being moved next door to the lying-in room. Some-body's just gone into labour,' she said, tersely.

It was surreal. The trip in the wheelchair with the ceiling above her head spinning around like she'd had too much to drink.

'Right, you need to get yerself in bed now, young woman. I haven't time to fuss. In you get.' The midwife tried to coax her out of the chair, but Maddie wouldn't move.

'What's wrong with you?' she shouted. 'Why haven't you brought my baby? I need to feed my baby.'

'You won't have to do that. But we'll get you something to dry your milk up.'

'Where's my baby? I want to feed my baby now.'

'*What baby?*' said Sister Bennett. 'Did you hear a baby cry? There *is* no baby. God's retribution for sinners,' she said, cruelly.

Maddie lashed out and smacked the woman hard across her smug, self-righteous face. A small trickle of blood ran down where Maddie's nails had caught.

The midwife reeled in shock, wiped the blood away with the back of her hand. 'You'll be sorry you did that,' she said, angrily. 'I was going to help you, but not now. And you can sign these papers.' She pulled a document from the pocket of her uniform, thrust it in front of Maddie along with a pen. 'Right there. Sign it.'

Maddie could hardly see the thing for the tears choking her. Her baby. There *was* no baby. She'd lost her and Rudi's baby. Maybe it was her fault. Something she'd done. She'd been selfish and gone to the cinema and her waters had broken and her lovely little baby had got an infection, like Alice said.

'What is it? What's it for?' She pointed at the paper.

'It means you can leave here. That's what you want, isn't it, you ungrateful girl? It releases you. Sign it and you can forget all about us.'

Maddie didn't even read the document – she just signed, because this awful woman was right. She didn't want to stay there a minute longer than she had to.

28

Had they forgotten her? Maddie had been left in the lying-in room for hours now. Just her and the black cloud of despair that hovered around her.

One of the girls had smuggled a little food into her: brittle toast with a scrape of jam. Hard, unappetising food that stuck in your throat. When what she really fancied was soft food. Some porridge or gently scrambled egg. Food that didn't choke you – or make you feel sick.

Maddie thanked the girl who had taken a risk coming to see her. The staff wouldn't like it. If she had been a pariah before, what was she now? She'd slapped the midwife across the face and thrown a pillow at Matron, not the sort of pliable patient they expected to fall in with their archaic rules and punishments. But Maddie was unrepentant.

She wanted to howl, like a demented, wounded animal. Her baby was gone. A boy or a girl? They wouldn't tell her. And when she'd pleaded to hold her child, she'd been ignored, treated like a leper. As if she were the one to blame. *God's retribution*, Sister Bennett had called it. But even now in the depths of her pain, Maddie could not believe that. If there was a

God that she could believe in, then He would be a kinder, gentler sort of deity, one who used His powers for good. Not to kill small, innocent babies, or punish their mothers.

So, Maddie Brady didn't howl. Or scream. Or seek revenge on those who had treated her unfairly. But the emotional scars would stay with her, like the hole in her heart where her baby should be. Yet she had to carry on, despite the mental pain.

The physical pain was still with her. Her body was encased in it, and she felt weak. But that would go. It had to. Because she needed to get dressed, pack her suitcase, and leave this place behind. She was free. She'd signed the release papers that Sister Bennett had thrust so callously in front of her and they couldn't keep her there against her will.

The door opened again, and a nurse came in.

'I'm to wheel you out to the ambulance,' she said.

'An ambulance?'

'Yes. You're off to Redruth. They'll sort you out at the hospital. We've got two more births on our hands right now, you're best off there.' The woman dropped her head, couldn't look Maddie in the eye.

'But my things, and my uniform...'

'All packed. In the ambulance already.'

'And my photograph?'

'Everything's packed,' the nurse mumbled. 'Best you forget everything and move on.'

She was pushed out to the waiting ambulance, helped in by the driver – an old man who looked as if he should be sitting in a fireside chair with his feet up. Yet there he was, still working. Taking the place of younger men, so they could go off to war.

The man gave her a cheerful grin. 'Soon have ye back on yer feet, my 'ansum,' he said kindly, and winked. 'They lot at Redruth know what they're about.'

'Bless you,' said Maddie. She could have kissed him. Right on the top of his grizzled head. Or on his wrinkled cheek.

Another small pocket of kindness in what had been a barren desert lately. She didn't know whether to laugh or cry.

You see, said the small voice inside her head, *there* is *a God*. And for a moment she forgot her terrible grief. For the first time in days, Maddie smiled.

———

Maddie got her strength back after two weeks. But they kept her in for three at Redruth hospital – *convalescing* was the word the ward sister used.

Maddie had to prove that she could walk around unaided. And that she could sit down, comfortably. The comfort part might take a bit longer, and the chairs would need to be padded, but at least now she could sit without her eyes watering. And the tugging pain in her breasts had finally gone. No more steeping them in Epsom Salts as her milk dried up. That had been a psychological hurdle to overcome, knowing there was no milk now. Another sadness to be conquered. The symbol of a missing baby.

The three weeks in hospital put some distance between her and her stillborn child, although there would never be enough distance to forget. And she didn't want to. Each year she would remember the birthday: 10 November in the year 1941 was the date of a birth and a death. And she would add a year, *every* year.

No one from Rosemundy had been in touch with her. If there had been a funeral already, no one had invited her. 'Forget it and move on,' the nurse had said. A cold, callous thing to say.

Maddie might move on, but she would never forget. That much was sure. Another thing she was sure of now, she would *never* go back to Rosemundy House again. At first, she'd thought she might. She'd wanted to go there and ransack Matron's office, force her to hand over the precious photograph of Rudi. It hadn't been returned in her suitcase as the nurse had promised. And to pick up her baby's death certificate. And birth certificate. Would there even be one? She didn't know. And what difference could it make, anyway? It wouldn't bring her baby back, nothing could do that.

'Well, you've had yourself a nice little holiday, Maddie.' The ward sister smiled. It was a tired smile. Most of the nurses were busy there. Rushed off their feet. But they usually took time to smile at you.

'Three weeks of lying around and not a single floor to scrub. It really was a holiday,' said Maddie.

'They make you girls scrub floors? Not when you're in labour, surely?' The woman was astounded.

'Good for the soul, Sister,' said Maddie.

'You hear things, of course, but I never imagined they were true. That's appalling.'

'I think so too. You could tell someone,' said Maddie. 'They'd listen to you.'

'I will...' The woman nodded once, briskly. Then: 'You'll be leaving us tomorrow, going home.'

'Thanks for getting me on my feet again,' said Maddie.

'It's what we do,' the sister said and smiled.

Going home? She wasn't sure where that might be.

She had the name of a lodging house not far from her old billet in West London. Nothing fancy and a reasonable price. She had some money saved. It should be enough until she got sorted with a job. That was one good thing about this war: lots of jobs. War work in factories. If you were young enough, it was your duty to sign up for some kind of work, unless you were in the forces.

She phoned Commander Worthing. She'd promised to. It was a sad call, for both of them. She knew that Helen Worthing was used to being in control, used to thinking on her feet, assessing changing situations. The army had done that for her.

She heard it in her CO's voice – the shock. The sadness. That the baby Maddie had refused to give away – had fought so hard to keep – was no longer there.

'You're to come and see me in my office when you get back. I'm still your commanding officer.'

She'd agreed, of course. It was an order. And technically, Maddie supposed, she hadn't been mustered out, must still be in the ATS, if only for a day or so until she saw the commander.

She sorted out her new lodgings with the landlady in Hammersmith Grove. 'The attic,' the woman said defensively, waiting for Maddie to complain. 'The only room I have left. But there's a war on, lots of people need lodgings. People bombed out.' But Maddie didn't complain. Whatever it looked like, it was a roof over her head. A safe space where she could regroup and contemplate the future.

Even though that was a future without her best friend Molly. And a future without her baby.

29

1 DECEMBER 1941

LONDON

It had been a special day for Maddie. The rekindling of her optimism. The reason was simple, not profound: one kind gesture on the part of the ward sister and the staff at Redruth hospital that morning, as she picked up her suitcase and waved them goodbye. A card wishing her good luck, and the gift of a small black cat with a shamrock pinned to his neck. The cat was stuffed. The shamrock was real.

She'd tried not to cry. She tended to cry at any show of kindness now. A strange phenomenon. Maddie had thought that the harshness and unkindness she had lived through lately would have made her cry. But maybe she'd always been like that. For, as Molly had pointed out, Madeline Brady was a contrary, single-minded woman who often did things arse-about-face.

The train trip back to London wasn't bad. And she'd bagged a seat for most of it. Then there was the surprise when she'd arrived at her new lodgings. Her landlady wasn't nearly as fierce as the voice on the phone suggested and had even made up a supper plate for her newest lodger: a tiny sliver of cheese, a slice of bread and marge, and some kind of cold meat, along with homemade pickle. The meat was a bit on the rubbery side.

Hardly a surprise that it turned out to be whale. 'The butcher was keen to offload it,' Mrs Green the landlady had revealed, taking Maddie into her confidence.

The room was clean and small. Some of the wooden floorboards sagged, but she soon got used to those. She'd been given one half of the attic space, with a fellow lodger on the other side of the wooden partition. Maddie spent her first night listening to the sound of rain running down the roof and splashing into the gutters; its echo amplified, bouncing off her bedroom walls. A pleasant sound, comforting, the feeling of being cocooned inside, safe from the storm.

She thought she would like it there. She fell asleep to the thrumming of the wind on the roof tiles, and the pattering rain. Tomorrow, she would start her new life.

But in her dreams Rudi came – and brought their child. Maddie couldn't see its face. And that was when she cried.

———

Maddie wore her uniform, even though the fit was still a little cramped. Not that it mattered, for soon she would have no use for it.

This time the outer office was staffed by two busy, efficient-looking women. She saluted the pair of them. They were both officers. The salute came automatically, and Maddie felt at home once more, her place in the universe confirmed, a place where she had been happy, had fitted in comfortably.

One of the women nodded towards the door. 'You're to go straight in,' she said.

The inner sanctum. The holy of holies, thought Maddie. But it held no fear for her – she'd been there before.

Maddie marched in and fired off another crisp salute to the woman sitting behind the desk. A surprising woman. A busy commanding officer who had come all the way down to Cornwall to visit her. Had brought apples and cake; an oasis of hope in the middle of despair.

'Sit down, Private,' said Helen Worthing.

'Yes, ma'am,' said Maddie. The chair was hard. A few weeks ago, she wouldn't have been able to sit down on it so easily, but things had improved, and she didn't even wince.

'I have new orders for you.' Chief Commander Worthing tapped the papers in front of her.

Maddie said nothing. Just hoped her separation from the ATS wouldn't be bound up in too much red tape. Perhaps this would be it. Here in this office. One single blow. No traipsing around from place to place, handing in her uniform, swapping it for civvies, a final pay call. Although she didn't suppose the army owed her any back pay, considering the circumstances.

'Aren't you at all interested in what might be in store for you, Maddie?'

There it was again! The woman had called her Maddie. Odd. And she'd taken off her uniform cap once more. It must mean something, for the gesture seemed pointed, deliberate.

'What's in store? I don't follow, ma'am,' said Maddie.

'The future. Where do you see yourself in the future? What would you like it to be?'

'My future? Out of the service, I presume. And I'll need to find a job in war work somewhere. A factory maybe...'

'And is that what you'd like?' Helen Worthing smiled. 'Speak freely, Private.'

Madeline Brady took a deep breath and plunged in. 'What I'd like, ma'am? What I'd *really* like is not to have to look for work. To stay in the service. It's a place where I feel at home, somewhere that I'd hoped to be able to serve my country in her time of need.' She stopped short. Realised just how pompous that sounded. How exaggerated and lame. But she couldn't take it back.

'Commendable,' said Helen Worthing, 'if a little over the

top.' She managed a smile. 'The service needs good people, Private. And that's why I'm sending you back to basic training.' She put up a hand to silence any reply. 'I know you've already been through all that, but in the circumstances, I feel it's warranted. And not the full six weeks. Let's call it a refresher. You'll go to the training depot for three weeks and then I've sorted out a posting for you. It's not what you're used to, and no doubt you'll see it as some sort of step down. But considering what might be happening to you, I'd say it was a step *up*.'

'You mean I'm to stay in the army?'

'That you are, Private Brady.' The CO put her cap back on again.

'I don't know what to say.'

'Say nothing, then. Much easier. And your record will show that you've been on a prolonged sick leave. Let's keep it at that, Private. Oh, and one more thing...'

'Yes, ma'am?'

'Go to Stores and see the quartermaster sergeant. Draw yourself out a new uniform. That one leaves a lot to be desired.' Helen Worthing stood up and handed across the papers from her desk. 'Your new orders. *Dismissed*, Private.'

Maddie took the orders, saluted, did a regulation about-face, and left the room smartly, but with a grin on her face that showed almost every tooth in her head.

———

Another railway warrant and another train that stopped everywhere. But Maddie didn't mind the hold-ups. This time she hadn't managed to get a seat in a compartment, but had been content just sitting on her suitcase, crammed into an already packed corridor. She didn't mind. Because against all odds, she was still in the army and had even drawn back-pay. A miracle. But she supposed the miracle had a name: Chief

Commander Worthing. Why her commanding officer had thought fit to do that was still a puzzle to Maddie. But sometimes it was better not to question a miracle or go looking gift horses in their accommodating mouths.

But what did seem ironic, and maybe a little strange, was the location of the training camp she was headed for. The West Country again. But this time Devon. A place called Honiton. There must be camps nearer London, surely? Still, that was the army for you, and orders were orders, even if they didn't always seem logical.

It was only three weeks. She could manage that. Only half the time spent at her basic training centre. And she already knew the ropes, so it shouldn't be that difficult. It could even be good for her, a refresher, like the CO had said. And the square bashing and PE that was sure to be on the cards might get her figure back, and improve her fitness. Not that Maddie was interested in looking good for its own sake. A special man had once told her she was beautiful. She didn't need to hear it again from another man's lips. For there would be no one else. She didn't want anyone else. Not after Rudi.

30

3 DECEMBER 1941

HONITON, DEVON

'So, what did *you* do wrong?'

'Wrong?' asked Maddie. 'I don't follow.' She looked at the young woman beside her, who was also on her knees scrubbing the barrack room floor. Déjà vu for Maddie. It didn't seem that long ago since she'd been on her knees scrubbing another flagstone floor.

'You and me. Like bleedin' parlour maids.'

'It's the army. They like to keep us busy with these little jobs. The devil finds work for idle hands and all that.' Maddie laughed. And why had she said that, that stuff about the devil? She was beginning to sound like bloody Matron.

'But scrubbing it with a nail brush? That smacks of punishment.'

'It's called discipline,' said Maddie.

'Yeah? You see anybody else here doing the donkey work?'

'Somebody's got to do it,' said Maddie, cheerfully. She was quite happy with her lot. After all, she could easily have been picking up her discharge papers.

'Well, ain't you a chirpy little thing?' the girl said, and laughed. She wiped a soapy hand on her overalls and stuck it out towards Maddie to shake. 'Me name's Gertrude, Gertrude Wilson,' she said, 'but Gertie to me pals.'

'Delighted to meet you, Gertrude – *Gertie*,' said Maddie. 'I'm Madeline Brady. Friends call me Maddie.'

'And ain't you posh? Chirpy *and* posh. Still, I got a feeling we'll get on right fine, Maddie Brady.'

'Thanks, Gertie.'

'I been here three weeks already, how come I ain't seen you before?'

'Just got here. I'm on a refresher course, three weeks' basic instead of six.'

'They sent you back? Thought so. You been a naughty girl. What you done then, Maddie?'

'Nothing,' said Maddie, quickly. 'I've been sick. Been on extended sick leave. I guess my officer thought I could use a refresher.'

'I ain't been nowhere yet – just here. But don't reckon the sergeant likes me, that's why I got me a floor cleaning job with a nail brush.'

'Just discipline,' said Maddie. 'It's the army. They like to keep their floors clean and...'

'Somebody's got to do it,' they said together, and laughed.

They laughed a lot, she and Gertie. Not only in the barracks, but when they went out with other recruits on a weekend pass. Gertie was a tiny bundle of energy. There were some who got the wrong impression of her, dismissed her because of her diminutive size. Others thought her a bit odd. But not Maddie. Her new friend may have been small in stature, but her confidence and personality were huge. And so was her heart. The underdog need never fear if Gertie Wilson was in their corner.

Gertie was a Londoner, proud to be an East Ender born in Bethnal Green. Molly had been an East Ender too, except she had done her best to shake the dust of Hackney from her, glad to be away from her family's poverty, but still tugged back there by loyalty.

In some ways both women were alike. Confident, outspoken, practical. Except for appearance, of course. Molly had been an attractive, big, bouncy blonde. Sexy, though strangely unaware of the charismatic effect she had on men. Gertie, on the other hand, could never have been called attractive, but there was something about her confidence and that remarkable red hair of hers that made her memorable. She was *striking*. Yes, that was the word. And a large port wine stain on her neck that might have made other women feel embarrassed was never an issue with Gertie.

Maddie thought her courageous but her new friend had dismissed the idea. 'What, me? Brave?' She'd laughed at that. 'I am what I am,' she'd told Maddie. 'Why try to hide it with a stupid scarf? If people don't like it, if they want to be ignorant and stare, then that's their problem. Why would I make it mine?' she'd asked.

But Gertrude *was* brave. And young. She'd be eighteen soon, she'd said proudly. But, young as she was, life had already dealt her some blows. Her mother had died giving birth to her, and her father was a merchant seaman who'd drowned on one of the convoys in the North Atlantic. But she didn't wear the grief like a badge; instead, it seemed to have given her a maturity far beyond her years and the confidence to speak her mind.

Despite the five years' difference in their ages, Maddie found herself drawn to the youngster. They called themselves Tweedledum and Tweedledee, though it was obvious that they were by no means the identical twins Lewis Carroll envisaged. Maddie was tall and slim with blonde hair and Gertie was small, verging on the rotund, with glorious red wavy hair.

Neither envied the other, and perhaps that was the glue that cemented their friendship, although Gertie had immediately scored her new friend Maddie '100 on the cor-blimey scale'. A compliment, it seemed. And blokes would be falling over themselves to get to her. But she didn't want chaps to do that. One man had already made sure that no one else could ever fill his shoes.

'Skivvies, that's all we are – bleedin' skivvies,' grumbled Gertie.

'You're in the army now, girl. Minute you picked up your military ID card and army paybook, you were doomed.' Maddie grinned. 'The army had you in its clutches.' Not that she minded being in its clutches and she didn't feel at all doomed. Maddie loved the ATS, the comradeship and even the discipline had its place, made you feel part of something big and important.

'Maybe I ain't that excited about scrubbin' floors and making some snobby officer's bleedin' bed,' said Gertie, a sour look on her face.

'You want to get paid, don't you, Gert?'

'Sure, but not to be a bleedin' skivvy. This ain't what I signed up for.'

They had only been at their new posting for a couple of days, but it was obvious that Gertie was right. Neither of them had been picked for further specialised training. There were all kinds of jobs that ATS women were trained for: telephonists, teleprinter operators, drivers, mechanics, motorcycle messengers and working on Ack Ack batteries. And what had they got? They'd been posted to Inglis Barracks at Mill Hill, working as mess orderlies (glorified chambermaids) and waitresses in the officers' mess. Cleaning the bedrooms and the lounges, sorting out the laundry, serving meals. Polishing the regimental silver.

Maddie didn't mind the work, was pleased to still be in the army. And she remembered what her commanding officer had said: a *step down*. She might think it a step down. But she didn't.

She was proud of her ATS uniform, thrilled to still be wearing it.

But Gertie had been hoping for something else. Something more exciting. Driving an ambulance, maybe, or a motorcycle. Or a mechanic. Learning about engines. Learning to do the things that men took for granted. She was a practical young woman, could have done all kinds of work, and she had an adventurous spirit.

'It's because we wear skirts,' said Gertie, coming back to her theme of the day.

'What is?'

'Women's work! Housemaid, parlourmaid, kitchen-bleedin-maid, bleedin' bottle washer, cook...'

'I can't cook,' said Maddie, and laughed.

'And you can stop that right off. This ain't nothin' to laugh at,' said Gertie.

'C'mon, Gert. They seem like nice, decent blokes. That captain even offered to walk us back to our new billet.'

'Course 'e did!' Gertie jutted out her lower lip even further, like a kid in a huff. 'Well, I for one ain't no officer's-bleedin-blanket. They can forget all that.'

'Think he got the idea, don't you?' Maddie smiled and poked her friend in the ribs. 'And some of them did their best to make us welcome.'

'Bleedin' snobs, that's what they are. Them and their regimental service-dress for dinner and their regimental silver what's got to be cleaned *every* week. Right particular, ain't they?'

'Tradition. Something to be said for tradition and I don't mind serving them,' said Maddie, 'or cleaning their silver. Somebody's—'

'—got to do it,' finished Gertie. Then she laughed too. 'There're worse things, I guess, like cleaning out toilets. Like some of them in basic training had to.'

'Sure,' said Maddie. 'Marching with mops and buckets to the latrines. Keeping in step at one hundred and twenty beats a minute...'

'With a damn mop slung over your bleedin' shoulder like a rifle. Bleedin' marching!' said Gertie.

'Well, you know what the army says about marching, Gert: "It's the most expeditious and orderly manner in which to move from place to place."' Maddie's impression of their pompous drill sergeant was spot on, and both women laughed.

'You idiot!' said Gertie.

'See?' said Maddie. 'Life's not that bad. We got a half-decent billet to go back to and a weekend pass coming up soon.'

It was true. All of that was true if you saw the glass as half full, if you were an optimist. If you forgot the sadness of the war and how some good friends had been lost to it. There were many pluses for both of them.

They'd been billeted in Mill Hill with three other ATS girls in a rambling old Victorian house in Sunnyfield, where open fields reached out to the north. Fields smothered with bluebells in the summer. It sounded idyllic. Except now it wasn't summer, and the ancient house was cold.

Still, the billet was convenient for their new posting. It only took fifteen minutes to walk to work in the mess at Inglis Barracks. And, right then, the whole mess looked very jolly, all decked out in paper chains and a Christmas tree in one corner of the fancy dining room.

Christmas Day tomorrow – and they were both to report for duty to the mess officer, who would give them their orders. It sounded like a long day ahead, but then, as Maddie had pointed out, at least someone else would be doing the washing-up. So what if they missed their own Christmas celebration? There was always the New Year to look forward to.

The barracks was home to the Middlesex Regiment, a group of soldiers nicknamed the 'Die Hards'. Gertie had sniggered, claiming the nickname had obvious sexual undertones, but it turned out that this venerable old regiment had paid dearly for the name. In the blood of soldiers from many wars when they wore their famous red coats with pride. The coats were long gone now, but the pride remained. *Pride* – it was something Maddie could understand. A sense of belonging was good. And to have something to believe in.

31

MARCH 1942

SUNNYFIELD, MILL HILL, LONDON

Maddie had settled into a routine. And routine was always good to hold on to. To stop her mind lingering over the bad stuff. But mostly things were good. Decent food, which might have been strange, had they not been serving in a posh mess where the cooks sometimes gave them illicit titbits to take home to their billet in Sunnyfield.

The first weeks had been hard. Gertie especially found it tough, had looked forward to bringing in the New Year. Maybe even the odd glass of porter back at the billet with the rest of the ATS girls. Instead, they had run themselves ragged, making sure the officers had enjoyed *their* New Year's Eve celebration.

Gertie pointed to the unfairness of life but Maddie had been relieved, for celebrations made her maudlin nowadays. A few drinks and she would dwell on past sadness. Things she had lost. People she had lost. Her baby. Molly. Rudi.

Some of the officers were kind. Others didn't even recognise the existence of the two young waitresses who served them in the mess, who tidied up after them in their quarters, made their beds like chambermaids, scrubbed their floors.

Gertie's quick evaluation had been ruthless: the higher up

the ranks they crawled, '... the more up theirselves these blokes become.' When a visiting brigadier had taken a cup of tea from her hand, and not even looked at her, nor said thank you, Gertie had complained: 'What are we – invisible? Bleedin' snobs!'

But Maddie saw most of these young men with different eyes. She watched sadly as some of them left for action. Men who might not return. The war wasn't going well. And did it really matter what rank you were? Dead was dead.

Gertie had settled down after a few months. Maddie had even heard her friend humming as she went about her work, and yesterday she'd noticed a massive grin on Gertie's face. The reason was obvious: Bill Adams.

Gertie had met the man a month ago at the local dancehall. She'd dragged Maddie along to the Palais de Dance, because if there was one thing Gertie was keen on, it was flinging herself around the dance floor in a Lindy Hop.

It never ceased to amaze Maddie just how energetic and fearless her friend became the minute her feet touched a sprung dance floor. Gertie never held back. And the Lindy Hop was surely invented with her in mind – its freedom and exuberance.

And apparently, Lance Corporal Adams felt the same way.

The man was slight and small in height, only an inch or so above Gertie: if some higher deity had designed the pair of them with a match in mind, he had made a decent go of it. They had hit it off from the beginning and as dance partners went, they were impressive.

Maddie watched in awe as Gertie's feet left the ground in the acrobatic air-steps. But Bill Adams was always right there to catch her. It was a breath-taking sight and other dancers would be forced to make way, for fear of being knocked over like skittles.

'My kind of gal,' Bill had said. 'Full of gusto.'

And Maddie couldn't fault the man's observation. Gertie certainly had life force. Especially now that she'd found this one special man, someone who seemed to fit her like a well-worn glove.

But it left Maddie with one small problem. For some reason, Gertie kept insisting that she go along with them both to the Palais. Maddie didn't dance with any of the chaps who asked. And sometimes she ended up wandering off to the balcony or ordering tea in the restaurant high above the ballroom. A safe place to watch without ending up with somebody in your lap, for the dance floor was usually packed with hundreds of couples, all making their way around it in a circular motion. One-way traffic. Except rogue elements among the dancers didn't always follow the flow.

And so they passed their Friday nights. The start of a weekend pass was spent sitting at a table in a fancy ballroom, drinking tea or weak beer. A strange trio: Gertie and Bill, two lovebirds, who should be alone, and Maddie, feeling out of place, playing gooseberry, watching others – couples who laughed and joked and gazed into each other's eyes.

Her friend was being kind. Didn't want Maddie to be on her own back at the billet. That's what she guessed.

———

A bomb fell close to their house in Sunnyfield. It was a reminder to Maddie that living or dying in this war was a random thing and that she should live every day like it was the final one she'd been allotted.

Bill Adams turned up soon afterwards, worried about them. He'd brought flowers for Gertie and the two of them went off to the nearby fields for a walk. Maddie watched them leave hand-in-hand, saw Bill slip an arm around her friend's waist. An intimate gesture of protection. Of love. They were such a natural match, an equal match, and they were both content with that.

Give and take, it was a simple idea, men and women giving

each other equal respect. Maddie believed in it and her friend seemed to have hit the jackpot with a man who did too. Not all men did.

Maddie was happy for them both. Her friend Gertie was a rough diamond, an honest woman who spoke her mind, despite the trouble it got her into at times. But it was a gift to have her as a friend, with her loyalty and downright common sense. No frills, no pretension. You got the real thing with Gertrude. And now, she'd fallen in love. And Maddie was glad, even though the thought was bittersweet. For she'd once been in love herself.

Hours later, Gertie came back from her walk, alone. Looking serious. 'He's asked me to marry him, Madds.' She looked as if she might cry.

'That's *wonderful*,' said Maddie. 'Well – isn't it?'

'I guess so. It's just that...'

'What?'

'I'm scared.'

'You! Scared? Of what?' Maddie asked.

'When you're really happy – you sometimes get it taken away from you.'

'But that's daft. If you love him and he loves you and you want to marry him – why wouldn't you?'

'I couldn't bear to lose him, Madds. His lot's set to go off any time now.'

'But that would happen whether you marry him or not,' said Maddie.

'I know, but. Well – what if he cops it?' She started to cry.

Maddie pulled her friend in close to her. Held her tightly while Gertie cried out her fear.

'I won't lie to you,' said Maddie. 'Life doesn't come with guarantees. He might be killed. *Any* of us could get killed at any minute. But isn't it better that you have time with him?'

'You think I should do it then? You *really* think I should?' asked Gertie.

'Not up to me, is it? But if somebody loved me the way that daft beggar loves you – I'd grab him. And I'd enjoy the time together. No matter how long or short that turned out to be.'

A month later, Gertie became Mrs Gertrude Adams and she disappeared to Blackpool for a week's honeymoon. A whole week with the man of her dreams, she told Maddie. All that and the Tower Ballroom as well. They'd be able to marvel at the Wurlitzer organ as it magically appeared from below the floor. Maddie tried to picture the ballroom and Lance Corporal Bill Adams flinging his bride in the air. The adoring looks on their faces.

A postcard arrived from Blackpool showing the illuminations. A reminder of how things used to be before blackouts and rationing. Maddie pinned the card up on her bedroom wall and went downstairs to join the others in the lounge.

She missed Gertie, of course, but the atmosphere in the room was friendly. And two of the younger girls, Sissy and Dot, who usually found something to squabble over, even seemed to have called a truce. Everyone was in a cheerful mood as they listened to a dance-band on the wireless. They gathered around the blazing fire, toasting bread on the end of a long fork. And drinking tea.

So very British, thought Maddie, and smiled. Her thoughts rewound to another place, another time. The tea was lukewarm but she'd drunk it gratefully from the flask Lizzie Retallack had given her. In a barn. In Gunwalloe. And then Rudi had wakened from his nightmare.

Her mood changed now: high spirits plunging to gloom as she thought of him. Of missing him. Of wanting him. Of touching him, here and now, not only in her dreams.

Rudi, where ARE you? she screamed. But it was only in her head.

———

Bluebells arrived in the countryside close to Sunnyfield, trumpeting the beginning of spring. Acres of them spread out in a carpet of cobalt-blue. In not so very long now, farmers would be thinking about building their haystacks. Some of the ATS girls, who'd been in the billet for a while, described the delights of sneaking across the fields and climbing the giant hayricks in summer. With some willing chap perhaps. Maddie hadn't asked.

Now that the Americans had joined the war, there was no shortage of men in exotic uniforms with time on their hands and plenty of money in their pockets. The American GIs were paid far more than a homegrown British Tommy and weren't shy about spending it. *Overpaid, oversexed and over here.* It was a familiar refrain. But, so far, the arrival of what people were calling 'the Yanks' had been a friendly invasion.

The weather was fine, and when they were off duty, Maddie cajoled her friend into going for long walks with her. Anything to stop Gertie mooning around and take her mind off Bill. After their honeymoon, Lance Corporal Adams had been swallowed up once more by the giant machinery of the British Army, confined to a special training camp somewhere in the wilds of Scotland. He wasn't allowed to say where. And all leave had been cancelled.

Maddie worked hard at keeping up her friend's flagging spirits. She understood the misery of finding love and having it wrenched from your grasp. And there were times when she caught that faraway look in Gertie's eyes, a wistful expression like the world had offered her its riches and then betrayed her.

32

AUGUST 1942

SUNNYFIELD, MILL HILL, LONDON

It was a Sunday morning and when Maddie went into the kitchen, she found a gaggle of excited ATS girls gathered around Betty Wooten.

Betty was a kind of unofficial den mother. Some of the younger girls went to her with their problems for she was much older than the others. Exactly how old was hard to tell, and Betty never revealed a number. Someplace in the forties, Maddie guessed. Her hands weren't too lined, but her face had deep ridges in it.

Her skin too had an odd yellow tint. At first, Maddie assumed the woman was jaundiced, but strands of her hair were also a peculiar orange colour. 'Got this in the munitions factory,' Betty had explained when she'd seen Maddie staring. 'Sulphur. And all those toxic chemicals we had to mix. They called us canaries. Coloured yellow and we sang as we worked. Sweet, eh?'

Maddie was appalled. No wonder the woman had joined the army – a whole lot safer.

'Okay, listen up,' said Betty. 'You lot'll be amazed.'

'We're in the army, ain't we? Ain't nothing they do could

amaze me,' said one girl. She huffed cynically. Sissy was the youngest one there, but not always the smartest.

'Nothing to do with the army,' said Betty. 'They've re-opened the outdoor baths up the road. We can go swimming.'

'Terrific!' said Maddie. She loved to swim.

'Yep. From now on, girlies, we can strut our stuff by the pool. And they got water slides and fountains in there.'

'Ain't *we* died and gone to heaven, then!' said Sissy. The young girl gave another of her cynical snorts and walked away. She wasn't an outdoorsy type. And the only exercise she took was of another sort, usually with some bloke who brought her cigarettes.

But for Maddie and the rest of the Sunnyfield billet, it truly was a miracle. Hours of laughter and innocent fun. Building friendships and fond memories they would reminisce over in years to come. Throwing each other in the pool.

Time away from duty was different from then on. Gertie smiled again, the pain of separation from her new husband fading. And Maddie was especially thrilled for she was a keen swimmer, spending hours in the pool till she looked like a giant pickle.

Weekends were the best, especially when the sun was out. But Maddie still swam in the rain and when the water was icy cold. Some of the others laughed. Sissy called it *kooky*, swimming miles and miles to nowhere. But it took her mind off other things. Like obsessing over Rudi and her baby. Took the edge off the sadness. And, sometimes, she even imagined him here beside her, laughing, joking, smiling, swimming.

One day, they would do those things together. Her intuition told her so.

———

As far as Maddie could see, life was like a balance sheet: good things on one side and sometimes bad on the other. It didn't pay to get too excited about the good stuff, like spending time with friends and basking in the summer sunshine by a pool, because you always seemed to pay for having fun. The gods in their heaven threw in a liberal sprinkling of sadness as well.

While she was plodding up and down a pool, people were being killed. Servicemen and women and civilians, they were taking their final breath. Of course she could do nothing to change that, so Maddie Brady came to an agreement with her conscience – she would relish these good times without guilt. And as soon as this hateful war was over, she would try to make recompense. There would be people who came out of it broken and sad. She would make it her business to help them if she could.

Many people had been kind to her, had helped her in times of need: Gertie, Molly, Lizzie Retallack in Helston, Morwenna in a tiny railway cottage in Truro, Ethel Ryder in St Agnes, and her old commanding officer, Helen Worthing. She would pay their kindness forward in any way she could. For that's what one did with kindness: passed it on.

Life lately had been almost too perfect to be true. Their posting was enjoyable – hard work at times, but often satisfying when there was appreciation from the officers and even smiles from some of them. Not to mention those fancy leftovers that Cook sometimes passed on. And the picnics in the surrounding countryside or a swim in the pool – they were small rays of sunshine that Maddie would hoard away and always treasure.

Count your blessings. And she did. The sorrow of the past would never be forgotten. People had been right when they said it got less: it faded, but it didn't go away. The loss of her baby had been consigned to a safe place, tucked away in the back of her mind. And although its rawness had retreated, the dull ache would always be there. What would it be like, to have a child?

The small life she'd lost – had it been a boy or a girl? Did it have Rudi's beautiful eyes? And then there was the guilt. She'd run away. Hadn't even gone back to Rosemundy House to find out about the funeral.

Now Gertie had some news that brought it all back. Maddie was conflicted, her feelings all over the place. On the one hand she was truly thrilled for Gertie. Gertie who was younger than she, and already married. And now, Gertie was *pregnant* – about to become a mother. And, although that was wonderful, it reminded her of what she had missed in her own life. No baby. No Rudi. And no one knew. She could tell none of her pals, for what could they do, except look at her with pity in their eyes?

Women at the billet pampered Gertie, and knitted baby clothes, and Maddie watched her friend grow bigger. Pregnant women were supposed to bloom, and Gertie did, like a bud opening into an exotic flower. Her cheeks filled out and she smiled a *lot*.

Maddie's thoughts returned to Rudi. Would he survive? She'd tried to tell herself that he was safe, that when the war was over, the strength of their feelings for each other would lead him back to her side.

But what if she was wrong?

33

18 AUGUST 1942

POW CAMP 21, CULTYBRAGGAN, SCOTLAND

Rudi Fischer didn't think of himself as a coward, but maybe he was. Otherwise, why would he still be sitting there in the mess hall, weighing up the options? Surely there was only one option? *Speak up. Try and prevent a massacre. Even if that meant telling the camp guards what he knew: that the fanatical SS prisoners were planning a mutiny.*

It was the right thing to do, wasn't it? Moral, ethical, principled. The things his father had taught him to believe in. The action of a brave man, certainly. Because if the guards didn't believe him or couldn't protect him from the wrath of the *Waffen-SS* prisoners, then Rudi knew what his fate would be: he would end up dead. Maybe they'd make it look like a suicide. They sometimes did that. And this time there was no way out. No one escaped from this camp. That was why the British had built it in such an inaccessible place and with such water-tight security.

He shouldn't even *be* there. Not in Compound B, the place where they dumped German SS prisoners, the hardened fanatics. He wasn't one of them. He was an airman, a member of the *Luftwaffe*, not one of Hitler's *Waffen-SS* thugs. But the fact that he'd already escaped from a camp in Cornwall had sealed his fate.

All four main compounds in this high-security camp looked exactly the same, even though they were separated by soaring barbed-wire fences and guard towers. Barracks, mess hall, showers, latrines – all the usual things that were necessary to keep so many men securely penned in one place. Interaction between the different compounds wasn't allowed. Some had tried. It hadn't been anything sinister. Just one German soldier spotting a friend on the other side of the wire. Waving. Shouting across.

Rudi had heard them. Seen them both walk towards the barbed wire. One man with a smile on his face. It seemed like a harmless and innocent meeting of old friends. But one of the guards hadn't thought so, and Rudi had watched in horror as a perimeter guard fired his rifle at one of the men. The young man fell to the ground, the smile of welcome wiped from his face.

Rudi had watched the man writhe in the dirt. Had seen the Polish guard casually sling the rifle back on his shoulder and bare his teeth in a smile. He'd shot only one man. A warning to the other prisoners. An example of what to expect if they tried to fraternise with POWs from another compound.

That had been months ago now. But it had been an important lesson for Rudi Fischer. That's when he knew for sure that Camp 21 was a dangerous, lawless place, a sort of Wild West of POW camps. The danger came from many places: British guards, Polish guards and even your fellow countrymen – fanatical Nazis who expected you to feel the same as they did.

He took out his last cigarette, lit it and inhaled the acrid smoke. *God knows what was in the thing.* Not real tobacco. But pulling the smoke down into his lungs had a calming effect.

He made his decision. There had only ever been one real choice. And he'd known that all along. Only one option existed if he was to stay true to himself. Keep his self-respect and that of the father he loved. Time to make out that last will and testament. *Burial or cremation, which should he choose?* He smiled to himself. Always good to drag out the odd bit of gallows humour – it helped you to keep perspective.

It was a rebellion with little hope of success. Rudi had known that from the moment he'd first been dragged into the plan, been told to play his part in the takeover of the compound. 'You are *in* or *out*,' he'd been told. 'Make up your mind.' And so that there could be no misunderstanding about what exactly *out* meant, two POWs had held him down, put a homemade shiv to his neck. The drops of blood it drew were real. The knife was real, fashioned from a razor blade stuck into the end of a toothbrush. There were other weapons, too, all equally as lethal: shards of glass with crude wooden handles attached, toothbrushes from Red Cross parcels had been hoarded, their innocent handles honed to sharp points. Up-close weapons, meant to threaten the guards.

A 'takeover', they'd explained. A 'bloodless coup d'état'. But Rudi wasn't stupid: nothing about this enterprise would end up bloodless, for these were hardliners, prepared to put their lives on the line for their Führer.

It was all about the Führer. Otherwise why would that particular date have been chosen? Tomorrow – 19 August. The anniversary of the date that Hitler, their 'glorious leader', had first been given the absolute power to rule a broken Germany. The right to call himself *Führer*.

Tomorrow. The day when things would change in the camp. For better or worse. And Rudi had been selected as part of the spearhead. Right up there at the sharp end. They'd chosen him because his English was good and because sometimes he'd been asked to work as a translator in the warden's office, the man who ran Compound B. But Rudi Fischer was under no illusions.

He'd been chosen for another reason as well: if it went wrong, he was expendable.

There were fellow prisoners who doubted Rudi's allegiance to the cause of the Third Reich, saw his translation work for the British as a betrayal. So, this was a test of his loyalty. His task was to walk into the office, overpower the officer in charge, disable the phone and wait for reinforcements. All with the use of a flimsy, homemade knife. A crazy far-fetched plan that even an experienced and gifted commando would have had trouble pulling off. Rudi put his own chances at zero. Not that he had ever considered seeing the thing through.

He left the mess hall in a fatalistic frame of mind. The choice had been made. It had been a difficult one, because he was still a German after all, didn't want to be a traitor to his homeland. But neither did he want to align himself with these SS thugs whose idea of *Heimat* was so different from his own. But he would keep his honour. Give up no names. Just a warning to the British that tomorrow, the prisoners would take action.

Rudi strolled past the rows of Nissen huts, tried to look casual, like the last thing on his mind was betrayal. He stuffed his hands deep into his pockets and stopped to watch a game of *Schlagball*. He remembered laughing with his friend Hans Meyer and joking that the British were a bunch of sissies with their cricket, for their bats were flat and wide – much easier to smack a ball with one of those than with a bat in *Schlagball*, a similar game but more complex and regimented.

Something we Germans are good at, he thought and smiled. *Precision.*

They were probably watching him right now. These men who wanted a Germany where Aryan blood ran pure. A master race with no room for the sick, or the weak; where difference was weeded out and 'learning' a thing to be shunned. A nation of automatons who flung their arms high in a Nazi salute and followed like sheep.

And what would be left, Rudi wondered, if these robots who burned books and despised free thought, succeeded? A land ruled by fear, with no place left for tolerance or kindness or sentimentality.

The more he thought about it, the more frightened Rudi Fischer became for his homeland. The place he loved. If Hitler had his way, it would be a terrifying, brutal place, lacking any kind of morality.

He took a final look around. No one, it seemed, had any particular interest in him. So, maybe they believed him to be loyal, weren't keeping a close watch on him. Either way, it didn't matter. This time tomorrow he would probably be dead. Just another dead Kraut that the British wouldn't waste too many tears over.

Rudi walked slowly towards the administration building. It was a strong-looking concrete structure, and some part of his reasoning brain tried to analyse the chances of their insane coup succeeding tomorrow. How could a ragged bunch of prisoners possibly take this building and hold it? Fanatics, admittedly, but armed only with flimsy knives. Knives against guns.

He was only a few metres away now. Despite the coldness of the day, sweat ran down the back of Rudi's neck, seeking a channel beneath the collar of his uniform. What would he say to the British to persuade them that he didn't agree with these *Waffen*-SS fanatics? And how would he have any credibility if he wasn't prepared to hand over names?

But in the next few moments, these questions became theoretical, academic: simply wasted brain power on Rudi's part.

He heard the footsteps behind him, but by then it was too late. A heavy boot caught him behind the knee, and he folded over like grass in the wind, hands still in his pockets, unable to save himself. His face hit the hard earth, its smell dusty in his nostrils, its sour taste invading his mouth, making him gag.

He cursed himself that he hadn't been prepared, had allowed himself to be taken. He tried to speak, but no sound came from his dirt-encrusted lips. Hands grabbed him roughly by the hair and forced his head back so fiercely that he feared his neck would snap. He felt something being pulled over his head: a heavy cloth hood. It blocked out the daylight and made him feel claustrophobic. They pulled him to his feet and dragged him along the ground. One on either side of him.

No one spoke. But they didn't need to. Rudi Fischer knew the score, what would happen next. He'd been careless, had somehow signalled his treachery. Everything else was just details that wouldn't make a difference to his future.

He didn't need a crystal ball to predict what was in store for him. A kangaroo court. A beating in the showers. And the final ignominy – being stripped naked and left to hang from one of the pipes. It took a while to die that way. Or so he'd heard. Because he wouldn't be the first one that it had happened to.

The black cloth hood moulded itself to Rudi's face as he tried to suck in air. He clamped his eyes shut tightly, as if to ward off any fearful images that might make their way from his imagination to his eyes. But one image made it through. A surprising one. And not in the least terrifying.

A picture of Maddie Brady impinged itself upon him, her eyes smiling, her lips inviting. How on earth had he conjured her up? He hadn't thought of her for so long now. The woman he had loved for a time. The woman who betrayed him.

34

He woke up gradually, his eyes half lidded, unable to focus. They felt like they'd been washed in sand. He moved his head slowly from side to side, a pain shooting through his neck. His throat was raw, and his mouth was parched, like an arid desert. His tongue felt swollen, a tight fit in its allotted space. He could hear himself moan but could do nothing to prevent the sound leaving his cracked lips. *My God, he was still alive. How could he be alive? Maybe the rope had snapped.*

Rudi prodded his sluggish brain into action. It made the pain in his head worse and he winced. He bit his tongue, tasted blood in his mouth. The very last thing he recalled was being hauled off with a hood over his head and his fear of a hanging.

But the hood was gone. And there had been no hanging. Not that he could remember. And, surely, your brain would keep check on something like that? But then maybe it had been so horrific that he had blocked it from his mind.

He raised his arms to touch his neck. His arms were fine, both in good working order. And his neck – it seemed okay, no rope burns or groove where one might have bitten in, no broken skin. But moving it sent a sickening jolt of pain through his body.

He let his head sink back. Noticed that it rested against something soft. A high-backed chair, maybe. He was certainly sitting down in a chair, for his legs were pressed against it. But his stupid, addled brain refused to cooperate. Gave him no more information, other than the pain and the fact that his eyes didn't seem to be working normally.

He heard a door close nearby. And Rudi's brain finally sprang into action from the ancient caveman instinct that was attuned to danger. His eyes opened fully, and his body jolted upright with the adrenalin surge that pulsed through his system.

More pain. But more information too, although it only added to his confusion. His brain fished for some memory. No, he had never been in this place before. This was not the barracks: no lines of bunks, no wooden floor. No pencil drawings on the walls. Not the mess hall either. And definitely not the shower block.

It looked more like someone's front room. Drapes hung at a window, and the high-backed chair that he sat on had a twin in another corner of the room. There was a heavy wooden desk at one end with a seat behind it. And a low table in front of him. A painting hung on the wall. *Bringing in the harvest*, he thought, incongruously. It showed a young couple sitting on a hay wagon, their faces wearing happy smiles. A picnic of some sort sat beside them. And a hayrick was in the background. A friendly, country scene.

The door opened and a man in uniform stepped inside. Rudi lumbered to his feet. His head reeled with the sudden movement and a shower of coloured lights passed in front of his eyes. He held onto the chair-back to steady himself. There was only so far adrenalin could take you, it seemed.

'Sit!' The man in front of him ordered. 'Before you fall down, old chap.'

'What? Who…?'

'Yes, I know, old man. Confusing, eh?'

'Where am I?' asked Rudi. 'And who are you?'

———

'So many questions. I have some as well – *obviously*,' the officer said politely, and smiled. 'But I don't see why we can't do a little horse-trading, as they say. One for you and one for me. Right, I'll go first. My name is Major Arnold Dunstan – Military Intelligence.'

The major was a specialist from the War Office. He belonged to a small but elite group of men called MI19 set up by the Directorate of Military Intelligence for one reason only: to obtain information from enemy prisoners of war.

Arnold Dunstan was proud of his role, a cross between an intelligence boffin and an actor. In peacetime he had pursued his interest in amateur dramatics and found that his skills came in useful during the war.

'Your turn, I believe,' he said now. 'Why were you going to the administration building in Compound B?'

Rudi swallowed hard. 'Some water…' he said. 'My throat…' His voice cracked.

'Yes, of course.' Major Dunstan went to the desk, poured water from a jug and handed it across. 'Sorry for the drama, the hood and the rough stuff,' he said. 'But speed was of the essence. I'm sure you'll understand.'

'I don't understand *anything*,' said Rudi. '*You* did this? The British? I thought it was…' He stopped before he said anything more.

'Confusing, yes. As I said, we had to get to you quickly before any of your *friends* saw.'

'My friends? They're not my friends,' said Rudi, and he gave a mirthless laugh.

'Yes, we know, old chap. But we couldn't let you carry on. You'd have mucked the whole thing up,' replied the major.

'Mucked up? What's that?'

'Compromised an operation. Something we've put a lot of time and effort into.'

'I thought you were them,' said Rudi. 'I thought I'd be dead by now.'

'Ah, yes. A trip to the showers. A fatal slip on the wet floor. A broken neck.'

'Or a hanging,' said Rudi.

'It's been done before. That's why I'm here, *Herr* Fischer. I want to save you from all that.'

'That's kind,' said Rudi, sarcastically. 'But why?' He hadn't missed the major's emphasis on 'Herr', as if Rudi was no longer Obergefreiter Fischer of the *Luftwaffe*, but had been stripped of all military standing.

'For us, as much as for your sake.'

'For me?' He shook his head in disbelief. 'Yes, you people are real humanitarians. Especially perimeter guards who use us for target practice.'

'That was unfortunate,' said the major. 'We don't encourage that sort of thing. But it's wartime. Bad things happen. Men get overzealous. The guard has been removed.'

Rudi said nothing. But his brain was working overtime, trying to catch up. He thought about the perimeter guard. He hadn't seen the soldier for a long time, so maybe it was true that the man really had been removed, and this intelligence officer was telling the truth.

'Look, I know this may sound a little unlikely to you, but we don't want to find you – or anyone else, for that matter – hanging in the shower. Surely that much is obvious?'

'Nothing about this is obvious, not to me,' said Rudi.

Arnold Dunstan meticulously brushed an invisible speck

from his uniform. Rudi suspected he was only pretending to be distracted, to buy himself thinking time.

'Number one, I know about your little coup.' The major held a finger up, then added a second. 'And number two, I believe you were coming today to warn us.'

'What are you – psychic?'

'More or less. We have ways of keeping tabs on you chaps in there behind the wire. Intelligence methods.'

'What ways?' asked Rudi. 'What kind of intelligence? No one is talking, as far as I know.'

''Fraid I can't tell you that, *Herr* Fischer. You're an enemy prisoner. But if you don't go ahead with your part in this little coup d'état tomorrow, you will have ruined a whole intelligence operation. And that would not only be bad for me and my operatives, but would not play out well for your own future health.'

'So?'

'So, what I need from you, old chap, is to just go back as if nothing had happened here and when tomorrow comes, you are to play along and do exactly as they ask.'

'But why?' asked Rudi, even more confused.

'Because I need to find the men behind this little venture. I know that it's happening. I know when. I know where. But I need the ringleaders... need to root them out.'

'Ringleaders?' said Rudi.

'Names, Herr Fischer, I want names. But if you were prepared to give them to me...'

'I can't do that. I won't do that. I can't give you names. No matter how much I disagree with them. I'm not a *traitor*.'

'No?' The major raised an eyebrow, fixed Rudi with a stare. 'Maybe. Maybe not. You know what I think?'

Rudi said nothing.

'You're not like the rest of them. The warden tells me you tried to get transferred from Compound B. And I think you don't want any more bloodshed. That's why you're prepared to warn your enemy but not prepared to give up any names. Not a traitor, you say. And if what you say is true, that makes you a conflicted man. Maybe even an honourable man. Am I right, Obergefreiter Fischer? Are you an honourable man?'

'I try to be,' said Rudi. 'I never asked to fight a war, but you can still be a human being.'

'Quite so,' said Major Dunstan. 'And that's why we need to get you back right now, before anyone knows you've tried to warn us. Things must go ahead tomorrow as planned. Otherwise, you could have a whole lot more blood on your conscience.'

Two men appeared and replaced the hood. They took him back to a spot behind the shower block. Left him there as if nothing had happened.

———

Once Rudi had left the office, Major Dunstan removed a cigarette from the silver case that had been his father's. A souvenir, passed on by his father's regiment. His father had been a professional soldier, and a man of honour.

The major read the inscription once again and thought about the man who had had it inscribed 'Country first. Family Second. Self last. God can take care of Himself'. He wasn't sure if his father believed in any kind of god. Probably just hedging his bets with that inscription.

In some ways, Rudi Fischer reminded him of the father who had died on the Flanders Fields in World War One, fighting alongside his men. Being honourable. He hoped he wasn't wrong about Obergefreiter Fischer and that he too would do the right thing. That he would go along tomorrow as if nothing had happened. That he wouldn't warn the others.

This attempted coup must be allowed to take place. Otherwise, the months of painstaking intelligence gathering, the preparation of the expensive listening equipment and the hours of transcribing prisoners' conversations would all have been in vain. But the Germans had been careful, hadn't used each other's names. And he needed those names, needed to bag the ringleaders. Take them away from this place to somewhere they couldn't infect others with their fanaticism. Throw away the key.

Major Arnold Dunstan had to do all that without the Krauts knowing how he did it. His pressure microphones, the miles of wiring and the hours of listeners in the basement keeping a watch; it only worked if the surveillance went undiscovered. He believed secret surveillance and eavesdropping would play an important role in intelligence-gathering in the future. He hoped this exercise of his would finally persuade the powers that be of that. He knew he could gain useful information from the POWs, but only if the Germans felt secure enough to speak freely – both now and in the future.

The prisoners must suspect nothing. And if that meant this chap Fischer was injured in tomorrow's violence, then so be it. Although it would be a pity, for the German seemed like a decent sort – for an enemy, that was. Yes, it would be a bonus if Obergefreiter Fischer came out of this alive for he might prove useful in the future. But for that to happen, the gods would need to be on Rudi Fischer's side. Ready to hand out miracles.

But so far in Major Dunstan's experience of war, miracles were thin on the ground.

35

AUGUST 1942

SUNNYFIELD, MILL HILL, LONDON

The screaming began as soon as the telegram arrived. Gertie didn't open it, even though it was addressed to her. That depressing task was left to Maddie, who picked it up from the floor, where her friend had flung it.

People rarely got telegrams. Normal people at least. They all knew that, and a couple of the girls from the ATS billet hovered in the background, keeping a respectful distance. Sometimes telegrams announced happy things like marriages and the arrival of a baby. But mostly they were the overture to grief. Like this one.

Maddie read it in silence. Then she took her treasured friend Gertie by the hand, gently led her into the lounge, settled her by the fireside and used up most of her own tea ration on the strongest brew either of them had drunk in a long time. Maddie was recklessly lavish with the sugar ration as well, heaping spoonfuls of the precious stuff into Gertie's cup. And then Betty Wooten arrived, clucking in a motherly way and emptying the last few precious drops of her brandy supply into Gertie's cup.

Maddie eyed the older woman and nodded her thanks,

watched Betty leave. Everyone had gone now, leaving the two of them alone to their grief. People were kind, mostly. But they didn't always know what to say. Not that she did, either.

She moved her mouth into a smile. It was meant to be reassuring, but instead it felt alien and false on her lips, not a proper smile.

When would she find one of those again?

She rested a hand lightly on Gertie's shoulder, a gesture of support, of love. But it was rejected, shrugged off angrily, like an unwanted intrusion. At least the screaming and the tears had subsided now. Gertie had lapsed into an eerie, unnatural silence, head stiff, eyes staring straight ahead but glazed, seeing nothing. Her friend's face was white with shock, Maddie noted, surprised at her own sense of calm. Her eyes were drawn to the port wine stain on Gertie's neck, which seemed even more pronounced than usual.

The silence was a blanket of fog between them. Maddie had no idea where to start. How to break her way through it. She took the telegram from her pocket. Even as she'd read it to herself, digested its meaning, it had been hard to believe: *KIA. Killed in action.* The language had been formal, and stilted, just one of thousands of such telegrams sent since the war had begun.

Maybe some clerk at the War Office had a template in his desk drawer. Just had to fill in the name, date and place.

Gertie's eyes flicked down towards the telegram. 'Well, read it out then,' she ordered, her voice brittle and hostile.

A fragile tear built up at the corner of Maddie's eye, wound its way down the contour of her cheek. Soon, other tears followed: silent proof of her pain. They trickled their way to her chin in thin, messy trails. But she said nothing. How could she read these words out? They were cruel, poisonous.

'Read the bloody thing, Madds!' Gertie ordered again. 'You're my pal, ain't you?'

''Course! But maybe you should wait till you're—'

'What? You ain't got the stomach for it? Seems to me you were quick enough to offer advice before.' A fleck of spittle flew from Gertie's mouth, along with the angry words.

'What? I don't follow,' said Maddie.

'Oh, you follow all right. Wasn't it *you* said I should marry Bill, even when I was scared he might cop it?'

'Gert, don't do this. It's nobody's fault.'

'I wanted to wait. I *should* have waited,' wailed Gertie.

'It wouldn't have made any difference, would it? He'd still be...'

'Go on, say it! You can't, can you, Maddie? My Bill would still be *dead*. There you are – I said it for you. Give me that thing.' She grabbed the crumpled telegram and finally read it.

Then Gertie let out a howl of anguish again, angrily side-swiped the crockery from the table beside her and rushed from the room in tears.

Maddie's mind refused to accept any more sadness. There'd been enough. So, it slipped into automatic pilot, and she found herself picking up the pieces of broken crockery, mopping up the debris, tidying. She swept the floor. Then she moved on to the kitchen and cleared away the breakfast dishes. It wasn't her turn for the washing-up, but she did it anyway. Anything rather than think or pick her way through the emotional maze that was lying in wait, ready to trap her.

The kettle whistled. Maddie didn't recall filling it again, putting it on the stove, but she must have done. She freshened up the tea in the pot, put the cosy on and set the tray, took it through to the lounge.

No one else was there. The house was quiet now, as if it too was holding its breath. Like Maddie.

She should go to the bedroom, try to comfort Gertie. But something told her that it was too soon. Or maybe she just wasn't ready, wasn't brave enough to face more guilt, more recriminations from her friend. Instead, Maddie slumped down gratefully into a chair. A tiredness had overtaken her – maybe the tea would help. *Good for what ails you.* That's what the WVS ladies always said, standing behind their huge tea urns, after a raid, when people were scared, and friends had died. Maybe it was true. Maybe tea was a magical elixir that could heal all wounds.

Maddie poured the tea. It was thick and black. No milk. No sugar. Its bitterness seemed fitting.

She thought about poor Bill Adams. Dying out there in a foreign land, far away from all he knew and loved. She'd liked him. He'd been a decent man: not handsome, or particularly clever, but kind and thoughtful to those around him, and he'd treated Gertie with respect and love. He would have made a good father.

According to the telegram, Lance Corporal William Adams had given his life for his country on 27 July 1942. Maddie was shocked: surely that couldn't be right? August was almost over. Did it really take that long to get the news to relatives? She read the telegram again. They'd probably got the date wrong. And did it even matter? The poor man was gone. He had died *valiantly as befitted a soldier of the proud Eighth Army.*

Valiantly. Maddie wondered if they always wrote that to loved ones. And where exactly was El Alamein? Somewhere in Egypt, she guessed. The Eighth Army was fighting in the desert as far as she knew, but some things passed you by when there was so much going on in this war.

She tried to imagine it. A place with burning sand beneath your feet. Flies everywhere, and getting thirsty in the stifling desert heat and having to fight in that. She wondered what might have gone through Bill's mind. She hoped there had been no time for fear or pain, just an instant and the poor man hurled from life into death. If there was a choice, that's what Maddie would have picked. But war was unpredictable. And who said you got a choice?

———

Maddie finally took matters into her own hands. As soon as she came off duty, she organised a doctor to pay a home visit to the house in Sunnyfield. Gertie had refused to leave her bedroom for four whole days now, had locked the door. At first there'd been sobbing, but then silence, which was even worse. And the trays of food Maddie had left for her were still languishing in the hallway, ignored, uneaten. It couldn't go on – she'd make herself and the baby ill.

Someone found a spare key, and the doctor, a fussy old gentleman with an ancient suit, a colourful bow tie and a battered trilby hat, had smiled at Maddie and winked. 'We'll get her well again,' he'd promised.

He'd been a man true to his word. He'd only been in there for a few moments when he rushed out to the telephone in the hallway and called for an ambulance. It worked like clockwork. A military ambulance arrived ten minutes later, driven by an ATS girl. Someone Maddie knew, which made her feel confident and happier. She relaxed. The doctor was right: it would be okay. Everything would be fine. They would take Gertie to Redhill County Hospital and sort her out. There was even a maternity unit in there.

But when Maddie saw the small, pale face that peered out from beneath the hospital blanket and looked down at the shrunken figure on the stretcher, she was frightened for her friend. Gertie's face was not only sallow, but terrified; the firm, round cheeks that had filled out with the rosy bloom of pregnancy had collapsed inwards, leaving a harrowed look.

Maddie gasped. Could four days of starvation really do that

to you? She reached for her friend's hand, took it in her own. Squeezed it.

'I'm frightened, Madds,' said Gertie, her voice no more than a hoarse, childlike whisper.

'No need. I'm coming with you,' said Maddie and smiled. 'Tweedledum and Tweedledee, remember? You can't have one without the other.'

'They won't allow that,' said the doctor. 'You know how these places are.'

'Oh, no?' said Maddie. 'This is the best friend I've got on the whole planet. I'd like to see them try and stop me.'

And with that, Maddie Brady climbed into the back of the ambulance.

36

There was nothing they could do. That's what the doctors had said. On the fifth of September, a day that was as black outside as the depression inside the tiny room where Maddie now sat at her friend's bedside, Gertrude Adams had lost her baby. Its tiny heart stopped beating.

The elderly doctor who examined her had been kind. Had explained that sometimes these sad things happened and there was no one to blame. She mustn't feel guilty. She just seemed frozen when they'd told her, her face immobile as if in shock, but it was her eyes that upset Maddie the most. They had a lost, empty look in them. And Maddie understood. For her friend had joined the sad ranks of sorrowful women whose babies had died in the womb.

Stillbirth. That's what the doctor called it. A small, inno-cent-sounding word which made it seem even more brutal because Gertie had lived for months with this new life inside her. She'd knitted baby clothes, her face wreathed in smiles. Had spoken to her child. Told it stories. Told this baby about its father, a brave man off fighting for his country.

Maddie tried to picture it. The baby, still there, in Gertie's womb. Still. Unmoving. No longer alive. Her own labour had been bad enough, but at least she'd always imagined that there would be a child to cuddle and love at the end of it. *But to go through the pain of childbirth, all the time knowing that your baby wouldn't be alive? To deliver a dead child?* Maddie could only imagine how terrible that would be.

She'd held Gertie's hand as they wheeled her precious friend off to the theatre, already in an induced labour. It had been hard to prise that hand from her own, but Maddie understood. And the pleading look in Gertie's eyes – she understood that as well, for they were like twins, the pair of them: Tweedledum and Tweedledee. But this was something that Gertie had to do on her own. No one could take that physical or mental pain off her.

Maddie had tried to be strong, as she'd waited in the draughty corridor painted a bilious green and the overpowering hospital smell of disinfectant making her queasy. The smell revived the memory of her own pregnancy and images of Rosemundy House spooled vividly across her mind. The frightening birthing room.

Once again, Maddie Brady relived her own failure. She'd failed at the most basic thing a woman could do. Failed to bring her child safely into the world. To protect it. The guilt that somehow it had been her fault was embedded too deeply in her to be erased. She hadn't told Gertie that she *too* had lost a child. And now didn't seem the right time to talk about it, to muscle in on her friend's grief. And Gertie knew nothing about Rudi or anything that had happened in Maddie's life before the two women met. Maybe one day they would share the grief of their missing children, but for now, her own sorrow needed to be smothered, had to take second place. For she had lost a baby, it was true, but Gertie had lost a baby *and* a husband.

She sat rigidly in the hard chair, the sounds of hospital life filtering through her sadness. Somewhere in the distance a baby cried. The shrill first cry of a newborn. The sound of new life sent a jolt through her raw nerve endings; the thought that while Gertie's baby had been dying another was being born.

Maddie wanted to cry, but no tears would come. It wasn't until a friendly nurse came along with tea for her that the dam finally broke its fragile banks. Kindness could do that every time.

She mumbled her thanks to the nurse and warmed her hands on the tin mug. No fancy china teacups here. But the tea tasted like nectar. And Maddie marvelled at the resilience of folk who managed to carry on through the trials of war and still maintain their humanity. The woman was professional without being overbearing. Kind without being sentimental. Nurses were a special breed, staying at their posts throughout the bombing and the exhaustion of long shifts. *Heroes, all of them.*

———

Maddie woke up in bed with a sickening jolt, instantly thrown into the sorrow of the day. She'd organised the funeral herself, for Gertie had neither the strength nor energy for the task, nor the space in her head to deal with any more grief. Maddie had taken the burden off her friend's shoulders.

Gertie was home from hospital now, back at the billet, but she was still weak. And there seemed to be a numbness inside her that appeared to swallow up the confident and vibrant, life-loving person that had gone before. The woman who had fearlessly danced the Lindy Hop.

Two funerals in one. A strange affair that hadn't been easy to arrange: a funeral for a tiny baby girl called Alice, and a symbolic funeral for her father who was buried somewhere in a distant desert. A father that little Alice Adams, even had she lived, would never have met. But maybe they would both be together now. In that magical place that people spoke of.

Heaven. Maddie liked to think that it was real, especially now, when her friend Gertie needed the comfort of such a place. Were father and daughter together in that beautiful place in the sky, surrounded by rainbows, laughing, each finding joy in the other?

Maddie truly hoped so. But she didn't think so.

They stood arm in arm throughout the melancholy little ceremony. Only a few people had been at the graveside: some ATS friends and two of the younger officers from Inglis Barracks. They were representing the Middlesex, which Maddie thought was kind and decent of them but Gertie didn't even notice they were there. And afterwards, the chaps had come back to the house in Sunnyfield, had brought a bottle of sherry with them. But they didn't stay long. It wasn't a celebration. Or even a wake.

The day was a sad affair. Just a vessel for grief. But it was necessary, thought Maddie. The whole while Gertie clung to her, afraid to let go, as if Maddie was the one constant in a world that had been flipped on its head.

Later, they both sat in armchairs by the fire watching the patterns in the flames. Only three of them were left in the room now; people had slipped away, self-conscious – it was easier to leave than try to find words of comfort. There were none. Only platitudes. Betty Wooten stayed, practical as always. Doling out the sherry. Being a mother hen.

Maddie had tried to smile at her friend. The sort of comforting smile that says *I'm here. Ready to help. To hold you up in your grief.* But Gertie had just stared back with those huge saucer eyes of hers. Eyes now sunk into a thin, pale face. It had been a look of fear, not like the courageous woman that used to live behind that face.

'Maddie? You won't ever leave me, will you?'

'What?'

'You're the only family I've got left now. No husband, no baby. No Ma, no Pa.'

'Gertie, I'm right here. You know that.'

'I know, but promise me. Say you'll always be here. I need to hear it.'

'Of course I'm here,' said Maddie.

'*Now*, yes. But promise me. Tell me you won't die. You see, everybody dies on me.' The last words were said in a flat, emotionless monotone. Like their truth was obvious, could not be disputed.

Betty suddenly materialised right behind them. As if she'd been hovering, preparing for a moment like this. 'Now that's just daft, isn't it?' she said, her voice crisp with authority. 'I'm here. You're here. Maddie's here. Nobody's going anywhere.'

'I know, but...' Gertie trapped an escaping tear, knuckled it away fiercely.

'Listen, kiddo,' said Betty, 'people die in wars, it's true. But that ain't *nobody* here in this room. You got that?'

'Got it.' Gertie sniffed.

'Right, get yerself off to bed,' said Betty. 'I'll bring in some of that nice Bournville cocoa you like. Steadies the nerves.'

Betty was right about one thing. People did die in wars. Hundreds of thousands of people. But she was wrong about something else. Only two of the three ATS women in the lounge in that rambling old house in Sunnyfield would see the end of the war.

37

28 SEPTEMBER 1942

LONDON

It was five o'clock in the morning of a very special day. Maddie's twenty-fifth birthday. It didn't feel much like a celebration though, and no one else in the billet even knew about it. Only Gertie, who had other things on her mind, who was still swamped by sorrow. Besides, Gertie wasn't even there. She'd gone off to the seaside in East Sussex to convalesce.

Maddie was thrilled that her best friend hadn't been discharged from the army, although Gertie herself didn't seem interested one way or the other. They'd sent her off on compassionate leave for a month. Someone pushing a pen in an office somewhere had decided that a month was the amount of time it took to recover from the trauma of losing a husband and a baby.

One of their ATS friends who'd been posted to Hastings had offered to share her room with Gertie for a short holiday. The boarding house wasn't far from the seafront; not that it mattered, as no one could walk on the beach anymore and the seafront was surrounded by barbed wire. The whole South Coast was a mass of barbed wire and Ack-Ack batteries. Ginger Barclay, an ATS pal from basic training, was a Predictor operator on one of the huge gun batteries.

Working on an anti-aircraft battery – Maddie knew it was the kind of job Gertie had once hoped for. Important, challenging, exciting. Working beside the men. It was the men who loaded and fired the guns, for women weren't allowed to use live ammunition. But still, ATS women played a crucial part in the gun batteries. And operating a Sperry Predictor was a complex job that needed steady, cool nerves in the middle of an enemy air raid.

Their friend Ginger was one of a specialist team of six women working together on the Predictor, an impressive, futuristic piece of kit, smothered in dials and levers. It was heavy to manoeuvre, square and box-like, and could rotate on its large base to follow the trajectory of enemy planes as they moved across the sky. And with it, the ATS women could calculate the length of fuse needed so that the anti-aircraft shell would explode at the correct time, in the right place.

Ginger's job was vital, took skill and training and high levels of concentration. But some things they couldn't teach you. Like how to ignore your fear when planes were screeching overhead and bombs were dropping around you. It wasn't unusual for operators to burn out with nervous exhaustion.

Maddie was pleased about the sabbatical. A chance for Gertie to recuperate and gain her strength back. But it wouldn't be a miracle cure. There was no such thing. It couldn't turn back time, or bring Bill back, or a tiny baby called Alice who had never uttered her first cry. But the change of scene couldn't hurt. And there was something to be said for bracing sea air, even if you couldn't walk on the beach.

Maddie missed her friend, missed their chats, and Gertie's straight-talking, no-nonsense outlook on the world. That had faded since Bill died, and the world had become a bitter place, but you could still see some of the old Gertie in there, in small flashes of defiance. When she came home, though, would she still be content to be a skivvy, happy to return to her mundane duty as a mess orderly at Inglis Barracks? Or would she be tempted to chase down a more exciting posting after watching Ginger on her Ack-Ack battery?

She remembered Gertie's frantic words: *Say you'll always be here!* Her friend had no one else now, had extracted a promise that would make them both family. Tie them together. *You won't ever leave me, will you?* Plaintive, pleading words born out of grief and tragedy. But they were a plea that could just as easily have come from Maddie's lips. She had no one either. No one in her family had sent a birthday card. She hadn't expected one from her mother, and her father wouldn't go out on a limb to do so, as he liked an easy life. But her brother, he could have tried. A letter at least, to mark the day.

Enough! Feeling sorry for herself wouldn't do. There were beds to be made in the barracks. Silverware to polish. Tables to be set out in preparation for tonight's regimental dinner. A celebration to mark an anniversary for the Middlesex. It should be easy enough to forget her own anniversary in the middle of all that. A special birthday.

Twenty-five years old. A quarter of a century. It seemed impressive when you said it like that. A kind of landmark in your life. And she was thankful for every one of those years, even if some of them hadn't been ecstatically happy. She'd had her moments of joy. And in a world marked by sadness and turmoil, that was something not many could say. Something positive to hold onto. Her glass may not be filled to the brim, but at least it was half-full.

In the beginning, the war had generated a feeling of optimism and comradeship: people had helped each other build Anderson shelters, waited patiently in queues to collect an elderly neighbour's ration at the butcher's, happily spent nights down public shelters permeated with the smell of stale sweat and overused toilets to the sound of cheerful singsongs. But the third year of a war that looked like having no quick end had made folk weary and resigned. Dented their optimism. Many had started to complain about the lack of food, petrol rationing, clothes coupons being cut back. You tried to do your bit, it was the patriotic thing to do, but really – how long did they expect people to get by on one bath a week, and in only five miserly inches of water? And toilet rolls? One a week for a large family? You had to be frugal.

It had been a busy day for Maddie, but a happy one, a much better birthday than she had expected. People had smiled at her in the street, as if they had known it was a special day for her. And when she got back to the billet that night, it got even better. So good that Madeline Brady ended up with tears coursing down her cheeks. Happy tears. The best kind.

The girls had used up their rations to make a cake. And by some miracle, Betty had managed to find a birthday candle. A single candle blazed proudly in the middle of a sandwich cake that was slightly lopsided and looked in danger of collapsing. But it was perfect. The most wonderful cake she had ever seen. There were presents as well. A tiny bottle of perfume. Only a cheapie, Betty had apologised. *Evening in Paris* from Woolies.

Maddie held the small, thin flask of perfume gently, as if it was made from precious metal. It was deep blue glass shaped like a tube, with a stopper in one end and a fancy tassel attached to it, meant to fit snuggly in your bag. She'd seen them in Woolworths but had never bought one for herself. It looked truly exotic, French perfume.

'Betty, you shouldn't have,' she said.

'Have it back then, shall I?' Betty laughed.

'This is wonderful,' said Maddie. She took off the stopper and used the dropper dispenser to put a little behind each ear. 'Here, have some.' She offered the perfume around.

'Nope, it's all yours,' said Betty. 'We figure you need it.'

'What? You think I smell?'

'No, you daft beggar! But you need to start going out and about a bit. Find yerself a bloke. That there's called *dating* perfume.'

A bloke? she thought. *And dating?* Not something she would do.

'Here, we got you these as well. You got yerself some good legs there, just need to show them off a bit.'

Maddie stared at the silk stockings in disbelief. 'But where did you—?'

'Get them from? That bloke of Sissy's. He's a spiv. We all clubbed together, like. But he gave us a bit off.'

'My God, you lot, you're incredible. You're the *best*.' She cried again.

'No more blubbering. Just cut the damn cake,' said Betty.

She cut the cake, and someone carried in tea, and they sat around the fire and listened to the BBC Home Service and laughed at the Tommy Handley comedy, *It's That Man Again*. It was a kind of safety valve for people. It poked fun at some of the small-minded government regulations and wartime sanctions that they had to put up with.

It was the best birthday that Maddie could ever remember having.

'Can't believe you lot did this,' she said. 'And how on earth did you know? I didn't tell anybody.'

'Yeah, we know. But Betty's been reading the tea leaves.' Sissy sniggered. 'She's got the gift.'

'You believe that?' asked Betty.

'No,' said Maddie. 'And I don't think you're psychic, so how...?'

'Gertie! She gave us the nod. Sent a postcard. Sent you one too.'

. . .

Maddie cried again that night. In the privacy of her room. Reading her birthday postcard. They were tears of happiness, and relief. For in the midst of all her misery, Gertie had still found room to remember a friend. Her best pal, the card had said. *Now and forever*. It was twee. It was over the top, but all the same it sounded wonderful. And Gertie wouldn't leave her. She would be home in a few days, she promised. Reporting for duty. She'd missed Maddie, she said. And it would even be good to see the girls in the billet again, despite the petty squabbles.

But the strangest thing of all, at least to Maddie, was that she was ready to start work.

> *Looking forward to scrubbing the barracks floors. Side by side with my best pal. It's a messy old job, but somebody's got to do it!*

38

If there had been a corner to be turned, Gertie had turned it. Slowly, she became less melancholy and threw herself into her ATS duties, as if she really enjoyed being a 'skivvy'.

One day, just before Christmas and the first anniversary of their arrival at Inglis Barracks, Maddie asked her friend why. *Why* she seemed so content now with her duty as a mess orderly.

'You know, when you went off to see Ginger, I didn't think you'd be back,' said Maddie.

'Really? Why ever not?'

'All the excitement of her job, I guess. Sort of exotic, up a notch from what we do.'

'We're well off, Madds. The guys here treat us like queens; appreciate the things we do. Proper gents, they are. Not like some of the blokes Ginger's got to work with. Always sniping away: "Women shouldn't be in the army, specially not on guns and on stuff like the Predictor, what needs brains instead of tits."'

Maddie looked shocked.

'Swear to God, Madds. It's what them idiots say. Girls on

her battery take some stick. Sergeant told her she'd be better off lying on her back. Don't know how Ginger stands it, that and the bleedin' stress.'

'You believe we've made it through to our first anniversary?' asked Maddie.

'Maybe we'll get to celebrate Christmas this time.'

'Shouldn't think so,' said Maddie. 'Maybe New Year, eh?'

They both smiled. Because really, did it matter what day of the year you celebrated on? They'd have a weekend pass coming up, for sure, after the officers that were still left in the barracks had enjoyed their own Christmas dinner. No turkey. But a friend of the cook had killed a few chickens and somebody else had caught some salmon. And maybe, if they were lucky, there'd be a bit left over to make its way back to their billet at Sunnyfield. Life had lots of riches, you just had to look for them.

———

New Year's Eve was a wonderful surprise. There was the miracle of the steak and kidney pie, courtesy of Cook, and a bottle of her homemade elderberry wine, along with half a bottle of port.

It was a night to remember, with gummed paper chains decorating the lounge at the billet, and they all wore bizarre-looking paper hats in the shape of upside-down flowerpots that somebody had made out of hoarded newspapers. And just when Maddie thought that couldn't be topped, Betty arrived from the kitchen with a massive grin on her face, and with the flair of a magician, had produced a huge bottle of pickled onions. They went wonderfully well with the steak and kidney pie. And the elderberry wine, although a primitive concoction, was full-blooded, just one notch below dynamite.

'It'll blow yer head off,' said Gertie, after only one sip. And she took more than one sip – they all did.

The wine went first and then they started on the port. Maddie had never been a lover of port, but she took a hefty swig from her tin mug without even tasting it. By then, her taste buds had been overwhelmed by the grip of the elderberry wine and her tongue had gone numb.

There were jokes and laughter and somebody sang. And nobody argued. And at twelve o'clock, they all held hands and squawked out a noisy rendition of 'Auld Lang Syne'. Furniture was moved and in a raucous conga that started in the lounge, they all made their way downstairs and onto the street. Somebody tripped over the outside step in the blackout. Maddie couldn't be sure who it was, but the culprit picked herself up and sniggered. Drunken giggles came from both Sissy and Dot.

A figure on a bike loomed out of the darkness in front of them. An air raid warden. 'Keep the noise down and put that bleedin' light out,' the man said, pointing at the miserable light filtering onto the street from the hallway.

'It's New Year,' said Maddie. 'And it's only a *little* party.'

'Think Hitler's having a party?' the warden asked.

'Well, *we* didn't invite him,' said Gertie, her words slurred. She hiccupped. Said pardon. And coyly put a hand in front of her mouth.

'Women in the army?' said the man. 'Bleedin' joke!'

'Like we ain't heard *that* before,' Betty shouted back.

'Shall we, ladies?' asked Maddie. And she led the ragged conga back into the house, only a slight wobble in her step. The bloke was angry, but fair enough: it was New Year and there he was, out working while others were celebrating. Making his rounds on an ancient bicycle in the dark, with only a small hooded lamp to light his way. A perilous business. An air raid warden had died last year in the blackout. Had taken a wrong turn and ridden his bike straight into the Regent's Canal. Drowned before they could haul him out.

With luck, the warden wouldn't report them for not keeping

a proper blackout. But it had been worth it at any rate. It had been one of the best nights they'd shared together and one that Maddie and her friends would recall for years to come. Silly hats made from newspaper and pickled onions the size of golf balls. And goodness only knew where the steak and kidney had come from for the pie – some miracles you didn't question, just got on with and enjoyed.

———

It was a fitting and optimistic welcome to the year 1943 and maybe it meant that the war would take an optimistic turn for the country as well, thought Maddie. Everyone needed some good news.

But, good news or bad, the British Bulldog would take a bite out of Hitler wherever it could. The country would grit its collective teeth and carry on regardless. And so would the feisty women of the ATS, on their gun batteries and driving their ambulances, on their motorcycles and in their offices, sorting out schedules and troop movements and cooking in kitchens. And those waiting tables and cleaning floors in the officers' mess.

Women had stepped up to be counted. Women from all social backgrounds and races were showing they were equal to men, could do all kinds of jobs. They were working in the navy, in the army and the air force, facing arduous shifts in hospitals, going out fire-watching; and some were even having their hair dyed orange by toxic chemicals in munitions factories, like Betty Wooten.

They were freeing men to go off to war. Men who did what their country asked of them in its time of need. Ordinary men like Bill Adams, whose final sacrifice made them extraordinary, turned them into heroes.

One day, there would be a grim accounting of young men's lives and the thousands of civilians killed in countries around the world. Would it all be worth it? Maddie Brady fervently hoped so, but only time would tell.

———

When the calendar worked its way around to May 1943, they went back to the outdoor pool again. Even managed some picnics. And there were visits to the cinema. Lots of people went to the flicks not just to lift their spirits but to keep warm. The cold, draughty old house in Sunnyfield was beginning to feel its age. Still, Maddie was glad of it, ancient or not. A roof over her head and a room to herself was a luxury nowadays. Not things to be taken for granted. Especially when you saw the bombed-out buildings, the fronts of houses ripped off, exposing their innards. Floors miraculously still hanging there, suspended. And tables and chairs in place; ornaments and pictures bizarrely sitting on shelves. The minutia of people's lives left there for all to see.

But there was one thing that Maddie and her best pal never did again in the remaining years of war, and that was go to the Palais. Or go dancing anywhere. It was just too painful for Gertie. Like a trip to Blackpool would have been. Too many memories of her husband, Bill.

Gertie sometimes spoke of Bill, but not often. And she *never* talked about her baby. So, Maddie didn't either. And as for her own? As time went by, it grew harder to introduce the subject. To tell her friend that she too shared that same hollow space in her heart.

And Maddie made a vow, that for every year that passed, on that sorrowful anniversary in November, she would add another year to the age of her baby. A child that never was.

39

New housemates had come and gone in their billet in Mill Hill, but Maddie was pleased that both she and Gertie and even Betty had been left to their own devices. There had been the odd inspection by a superior officer but, luckily, they'd always been prepared and the house and their quarters had passed muster.

Then one day, out of the blue, Chief Commander Helen Worthing, her old commanding officer, arrived. The woman looked even more exhausted than the last time Maddie had seen her, and Maddie knew she'd been right not to let them pressure her into becoming an officer.

Gertie had made tea for the visitor and then hung around uncomfortably until it was obvious that this was to be a private and perhaps confidential meeting.

'You look well,' said Helen Worthing.

'You too,' lied Maddie.

'This posting obviously agrees with you.'

'I've been content here,' said Maddie.

'Just *content*?' asked the commander. 'You don't feel it's a step down, then?' The woman smiled.

'I'm happy in my work, ma'am. And I'll do anything the army and my country asks of me.'

'Right. Does that mean that if I asked you to drive an ambulance again instead of scrubbing floors at Inglis Barracks you'd do it?'

'I'm sorry, I—'

'Would you like to have your old job back, Private Brady?'

Yes! No. Maddie paused. 'I... I don't know. I like living here. Sunnyfield's not far from the barracks. And my best pal and I work well together at the officers' mess.'

'But if you could still stay here in this billet, would you be interested in a driving job then?'

'I need time to think, ma'am. I'm used to being with my friend...'

'Ah, Private Adams, I believe. But surely your friend would understand, and you could still be together in your off-duty time? We need good mechanics and drivers.'

'Yes, but Gertie needs me too. She's had a bad time and I'm her friend. I've promised I won't leave her.'

'Not the sort of promise we can make in wartime, though, is it, Private? But I understand. Your friend Gertrude Adams has been through a lot. Lost her husband. Lost a baby. I can see where you two have a lot in common.'

Maddie said nothing. She wasn't being rude. Or insubordinate. She was confused. And unhappy. Commander Worthing had reminded her of her baby and asked her to make a decision that would split up her and Gertie.

'Tell you what, Private Brady, I'll give you some time to think about this.'

'Do I have to accept the new post?'

'I thought you enjoyed driving. And you were good at it. Steady, dependable, careful. And an excellent mechanic. Don't you want to do that again?'

'I'm not sure.'

'Seven days, Private. You've got seven days to decide. Phone me at headquarters with your decision.'

They exchanged salutes at the front door and Helen Worthing left the house and got into her car. A staff car like the one Maddie used to drive. An ATS driver was at the wheel.

Maddie stared after them wistfully. Stayed there on the front step until the car was far out of sight.

Gertie was waiting for her in the kitchen, her face taut with anger. 'So, you leaving then? Taking this fancy new job?'

'You were listening? Did you eavesdrop, Gert?'

''Course I bleedin' listened! Stood behind the kitchen door! What d'you expect me to do when brass like her turns up, looking all official? I was worried for my mate. Worried you were in trouble. Turns out I needn't have bothered. Seems you got it all sewn up, Madds. How long you known about this? This fancy new job?'

'If you listened carefully, then you already know. It's the first I heard of it. The woman used to be my commanding officer, but I haven't seen her for over a year. And I can't believe you're getting shirty. I didn't accept, did I? I told her about the promise I made you.'

'Sure! Like I'm some pathetic charity case. Well, I don't need no soddin' charity.'

'Gert, don't do this.' Maddie pulled out a chair at the kitchen table and sat down next to her friend. 'Don't get angry, let's talk about it.'

'Oh? You want to talk, Madds? *Now* you want to talk? So, let's talk about what we've got in common. What did she mean by that?'

'I don't get you,' said Maddie.

'Sure you do. That officer seemed to know an awful lot about you – about *me*. She knew about Bill getting killed. About my baby...' Gertie sniffed and pulled a sleeve roughly across her eyes to trap the tears. 'What ain't you told me,

Maddie? Did *you* lose a husband as well? Is that what she means?'

'No!' said Maddie, adamantly. 'I never had a husband.' And now she was angry too. Why did Gertie have to do this? Dig up the sadness of the past. Some things were better off buried.

'So, not a husband then. What else could it be?' asked Gertie. 'A husband and a baby, both taken from me. Have you lost something too?'

Maddie's head sunk to her chest and her shoulders heaved as she struggled to suck in air. Plump tears fell in heavy drops onto the kitchen table in front of her and burst in random patterns.

'Jesus, Mary and Joseph! You lost a *baby*. That's it, ain't it?'

Maddie couldn't speak. Even if she'd wanted to, it seemed that the power of speech had been taken from her. Suddenly, her head felt much too heavy for her body to hold. She rested her arms on the table, dropped her head on top of them.

The poignant silence lay thick and heavy on the room, enveloping the two friends.

Gertie was the first to break it: 'Well?'

Maddie had nothing. No words would come. The passage between her brain and her mouth seemed blocked. Any meaningful words had dried up.

'And when was this? Before we met, *obviously*,' sneered Gertie, answering her own question. 'That's it!' she said, remembering. 'You got sent back to basic for a refresher; you told me so. Said you was on *sick leave*. Gawd, how thick am I? Right under my nose.'

Maddie still couldn't speak. Nothing would make a difference to the way Gertie felt.

'But you know what kills me, Madds? The thing I can't get my head around? The thing I may *never* be able to forgive you for? Is that all the time I was suffering, you could have told me I wasn't alone. That the same thing had happened to you. You could have helped me. Told me it wasn't my fault.'

'Of course it wasn't your fault!' shouted Maddie.

'She speaks,' said Gertie.

'Look, let's not do this, not now,' said Maddie. 'You're angry. We'll talk about it later, when we can be rational.'

'Rational! You think you've been rational? And yes, I'm bleedin' angry. What you expect? You betrayed me. I thought you were a friend, that we had no secrets. That we looked out for each other. But you know what?'

'What?'

'Sod off and take the bloody job. Go off with your fancy commander and your fancy new posting and I don't care if I never see your face around here again, Maddie Brady. And that's the truth. Chew on it till it chokes you.'

And with that, Gertie ran from the kitchen and slammed the door noisily behind her. The sound rang in Maddie's ears like a death knell.

40

SEPTEMBER 1943

SUNNYFIELD, MILL HILL, LONDON

It had been five of the longest, unhappiest days of Maddie's life. Five days of total misery. Leaving for work alone. Coming home and passing her friend in the hallway. And Gertie giving her the cold shoulder. She'd smiled, tried to strike up a conversation, but Gertie had just given her a stare that had made its way from the Arctic. But Maddie didn't give up. And neither did Betty Wooten.

Betty waited until they were both in the kitchen making food, awkwardly passing each other in silence. The clatter of dishes the only sound to break up the painful and spiky atmosphere.

'Incredible!' said Betty.

They both stared at her, but neither of them spoke.

'You pair! What age are you? Ten years old? I've a mind to knock both your heads together.'

'It's her fault,' said Gertie with a pout. 'I never asked for any of this.'

'No? Seems to me you're both to blame. And you, Gertrude Adams – you're acting like a spoilt kid. *Sending her to Coventry*.

Your best friend. I never heard anything so pathetic. Ain't one war enough for you?'

Nobody answered her.

'Right, here's what's happening. The pair of you, you'll sit down and tell the other one why you're unhappy. And I'll be here to referee. I want to see fair play from both of you. And then you'll drink your tea and shake hands, and both apologise to the other for whatever crime you figure's been committed. And then we'll all hug and make up and act like grown-ups for a change. And if you do all that, I'll take you both out to the flicks. My treat.'

It wasn't easy, but neither was it as hard as Maddie imagined it might be. Still, a lot of that was down to the common sense and practical moderation of Betty, who steered them towards a resolution, where no one was truly to blame for the idiocy that had taken place over the last few days.

Peace talks, Betty called them. They lasted over an hour. A raw and emotional discussion punctuated by tears, but – thanks to Betty – there was no anger allowed, and no blame.

It cleared the air, allowed the two women to start over. A new beginning. A fresh reappraisal of their friendship. They both agreed on one thing: neither of them would dwell on the pain of lost children. A bunch of flowers and tears shed, once a year. They would do it together. For both of their babies. But they would never forget – it wasn't something you could ever forget.

Now that both Gertie and Betty shared the secret of Maddie's child, she was relieved. No one had passed judgement or asked about the father of her child – and Maddie was glad of that.

The love she felt for Rudi Fischer, and the love he had given her in return, had been a miraculous thing, a tiny precious bud of hope in the middle of a war. Two enemies who should have hated each other, but who had loved instead. She wanted to hug the marvel, the wonder of it all, to herself.

'*You*,' said Gertie, looking at Betty in admiration. 'You should be in the War Cabinet.'

'And waste all those filing skills?' Betty laughed. She hated filing. It was a boring job, but better than the munitions factory.

'So? We going to the flicks or what?' asked Maddie.

'Said so, didn't I?' Betty grinned. 'I get to pick the movie, though. Seeing as I'm paying.'

'Seems fair,' said Maddie. 'Long as it's not some silly, mushy romance.'

'And what's wrong with romance?' asked Betty.

'Let's just have a laugh, eh?' said Maddie. 'Think we've earned it, don't you?'

'And maybe a glass of porter on the way home?' suggested Gertie.

'Sure,' said Betty, 'but I ain't paying for that too.'

'This is very grand,' said Gertie. 'First time I've been here.'

'Shush!' An angry voice came from behind them in the front stalls.

'I'm trying to watch the bleedin' film,' said another.

'Sorry, I'm sure,' giggled Gertie.

But she's right, thought Maddie. The Ritz was *very* grand. Luxurious and a little ostentatious, maybe. What she imagined American cinemas might look like. And exactly what they all needed right then. A bit of pampering to liven up the dull wartime restrictions and shake off the misery they'd gone through over the last few days. All friends again, and revelling in those beautiful surroundings, which could easily have been Hollywood rather than the Ritz in Harringay.

Even the outside was impressive, a huge neon sign with the name of the cinema on it. Very modern. And chic. She wondered about the blackout. Maybe they switched the sign off when the customers had gone inside. Or when the blackout kicked in.

Betty had bought them all tickets for the front stalls. The cheap seats. *But then she is paying for all three of us, so fair enough*, thought Maddie. The front stalls were cheap because you were so close to the screen that you had to crane your neck up to see the film. Back stalls were more expensive and the place where couples usually went. More room and manoeuvrability if you wanted to try anything adventurous. The front upstairs circle was the most expensive of all – people usually went there if they were trying to impress.

Betty had picked the film *and* the cinema. This week's 'fun feast', the advertising had said. It sounded fine – they could all do with a feast of fun round about now.

They Got Me Covered had a strange, complicated plot, but Dorothy Lamour and Bob Hope picked their way through it as best they could. Maddie gave up trying to follow it in the end, and just waited for the jokes. There were a couple of hilarious bits that made the film worthwhile and the Nazi spies in it were booed when they came on the screen, but they came to a sticky end and the audience cheered.

It was a fine evening out and ended on a cheerful note when Maddie bought bottles of brown ale to take home with them.

Back at the billet it was cold: no roaring fire to gather around in the lounge, for their coal supply was rationed now to one bucket a week, but all the same it didn't matter. The three of them sat there with their greatcoats on and happily drank brown ale.

'Not much of a "fun feast", was it?' asked Betty. She sounded disappointed.

'Oh, I don't know,' said Maddie. 'It had its moments. I thought it was a grand night. Thanks, Betts.'

'Yeah, thanks, pal. For everything,' said Gertie. 'You're the best.'

'Well, we're mates, ain't we? The three musketeers, right?'

'You said it,' agreed Maddie. 'All pals together. All for one, and one for all.'

'Right,' said Betty. 'It's time for bed for us senior citizens. Check the blackout and kick the cat out, you pair.' She laughed. There *was* no cat.

When she left, Gertie became suddenly serious. 'Don't want to open up no old wounds, Madds, but I need to say something. That okay?'

'Sure,' said Maddie. 'Go ahead. Promise I won't blow a gasket.'

'I'm not sure how you really feel about this thing with the commander. But I think you should take that job she offered. It'd be good for you. And you'd still be billeted here. Only if it's what you want to do, mind. It's up to you, Madds. But I really don't mind...'

She didn't blow a gasket, but the tears Maddie Brady had been holding back for days now suddenly broke through their barricades.

'Sorry,' she said. 'That was ridiculous of me.'

'You sad?' asked Gertie.

'Sad? No! They're happy tears,' said Maddie. 'You're a wonderful friend, Gertrude Adams. And I'll never forget you as long as I live.'

'I should bleedin' well think not. Now, does that mean you'll be taking the job?'

'And you wouldn't mind if I left you on your own at the barracks, if I gave up being a mess orderly?'

'Don't worry... Truth be told,' said Gertie, 'you ain't the most *natural* skivvy I ever come across.' She gave Maddie a friendly punch in the arm. 'It ain't like they'll have a problem replacing you.'

'Swine!' said Maddie, and grinned. 'Okay, bedtime. Let's find that damn cat.'

41

JUNE 1944

LONDON

Time rolled by at a brisk pace: birthdays, Christmas, New Year. And the year 1944 brought many changes with it. Rationing was still as painful as it always had been, but people were philosophical now about the sacrifices that came with fighting a war.

Life was hectic for Maddie, and her duties meant that sometimes she didn't see her friends in the billet for days. Her new rota turned the clock on its head as she was often on night call, working while the others slept.

Although Maddie loved driving, navigating an ambulance through the blackout to get to people in distress could often be frightening, especially if the sirens wailed out their warning of a raid. And now, there was a new threat to civilians: the horrendous V-1s of the Germans. Doodlebugs, or buzz bombs as some were calling them, were bringing back the horror of the Blitz. Bombs with wings, that's what they were, powered by jet engines. And the most terrifying thing about them was that you could never tell where they would explode. The only warning you had was when the engine ran out of fuel and then the fearful buzzing noise would stop, and the things would tumble from the sky. *When the noise stops, run.* That was the advice.

Or, if you were driving an ambulance, you just gritted your teeth, clenched the steering wheel, and hoped that the lucky black cat sitting on the seat beside you would work its magic. The little toy cat, the parting gift from the wonderful nurses at Redruth hospital, had so far done its job. She'd had one near-miss, driving through a raid, but she was still there.

Sometimes, Maddie would have company in her ambulance. A medical orderly called Tom Winston. A fine young man with huge sad eyes and a heavy heart. A young man who had never been to war, who believed that mankind could resolve its conflicts through peaceful negotiation. He was a Quaker and a conscientious objector. And although Maddie liked the young man, and understood his brave ideals, she thought him naive. For once war became a reality, really you had no choice but to go and fight beside the rest. It was unfair to make others do your fighting for you. *Well – wasn't it?*

Tom reminded her of Rudi Fischer. Not that they looked anything alike, apart from their blond hair – but she remembered Rudi's father Gunter had the same high-minded ideals. Principles he'd had to pay for dearly.

She wasn't sorry when Tom was transferred to other duties. His perpetual sadness had rubbed off on her, and sometimes overcame her natural optimism.

And there was a lot to be optimistic about. It had been a good year for the British and the Allies. A year when they had started to believe that the war might soon be a distant memory. A nightmare finally ended.

In June there had been a huge invasion: masses of men and equipment had been landed on the beaches of Normandy along the French coast. They were calling it D-Day; she didn't know why. But the Germans were slowly being defeated and any day now, the British and their Allies could be in Paris.

What a day that would be! How the French would celebrate the liberation of Paris, their beautiful capital city, occupied for the last four years! She tried to imagine the celebration. Flags out. Parades in the streets. People singing and dancing and hugging and kissing each other. And wine. There was sure to be wine, for wasn't France famous for its wine? Of course you would celebrate. The way people in London would celebrate when Hitler finally got what he deserved and his army, his navy, his air force were defeated.

Rudi had been in the air force. She wondered how he would have looked in the uniform. She wished she still had his photograph, though she could still see his face in her head when she closed her eyes and concentrated hard. That thin, pale face of his and the startling blue eyes. A face that could crease in amusement and eyes that could still smile, even after all he'd been through.

She thought of him in her quiet times, remembered that final day, how he'd slipped away without a last goodbye. At first, she'd felt abandoned and deprived. But now she understood how brave he'd been, to save them both a harrowing farewell. She imagined him back home in his beloved Alps, at that lake he'd told her about.

She prayed he'd made it that far.

Maddie yawned and forced herself to shrug away the tiredness. She got off the bus and walked the last half-mile home in the early morning fog. Gratefully, she turned her key in the lock and climbed the stairs, flung herself wearily into a kitchen chair.

'Some tea in the pot for you,' said Gertie, cheerfully. 'Heard those clodhoppers of yours on the stairs.'

'Sounds good,' said Maddie.

'And we're making kites,' said Gertie.

'What?'

'*Kites*. We been collecting newspaper and string. And Betts has nicked some glue from the office. Trying them out on the common on Saturday morning, early. You coming?'

'That's a bit strange,' said Maddie.

'Strange? Different, maybe,' agreed Gertie. 'And fun. But since when has fun been bad?'

'Why not?' said Maddie. 'And these kites, do I need to make mine?'

'Already done,' said Betty.

'You're a star, Betts,' said Maddie.

'We aims to please, ma'am.' Betty Wooten tugged her forelock.

And they all laughed. The trusty trio of musketeers. Good friends. Good company. The pride of the ATS.

And what memories they made to cherish. Maddie was happy she'd gone to fly her daft newspaper kite that dive-bombed into a tree. And when the others laughed at her attempts, she laughed with them. They had gone back home and drunk Bournville cocoa. Small things made large treasures.

And when Paris was finally liberated, on 25 August 1944, Maddie and Gertie had sat in the cold house in Sunnyfield and used up a half-bucket of coal on the fire and toasted the people of France with powerful elderberry wine.

'Rocket fuel,' said Maddie. 'Up to Cook's normal standard.'

'Lift yer head right off,' agreed Gertie. 'Pity Betts ain't here to enjoy it.'

'We'll save her some,' said Maddie. 'Only fair.'

But they hadn't. Somehow the whole bottle disappeared. At the time it didn't seem important, but greedily guzzling the elderberry wine before Betty Wooten could have her share was something that would sit guiltily on Maddie's shoulders for a long time to come.

26 NOVEMBER 1944

SUNNYFIELD, MILL HILL, LONDON

Maddie Brady had some dates scorched into her memory. And apart from the day she'd met Rudi, they had mostly been anniversaries that heralded sadness. Now, she had another to add to this growing litany of sorrow.

It was a Sunday when they heard the news. She would always remember that. And Sunday would have a darkness attached to it from then on, that even in cheerful times Maddie would find hard to dismiss.

At first, she'd been confused. The arrival of a serious-looking Chief Commander Worthing at their house in Mill Hill had been an unusual start to the day. Maddie had assumed she'd done something wrong, was on the carpet for it. But nothing came to mind. And when Helen Worthing had insisted that she needed to speak to both her *and* Gertie, it had only deepened the confusion.

They'd had to wait for Gertie to get dressed. Maddie had tried to find a calm space in herself, but her heart had pounded as if it might force its way out through her skin.

She made the officer some tea. The woman looked as if she needed it. And then Gertie arrived, sleep still in her eyes and her unruly red hair like a wig perched on top of her head. The sight made Maddie relax and she even managed a smile. Her friend Gert wasn't at her best early in the morning and it usually took two mugs of tea to shake her brain into action.

Chief Commander Worthing pushed her chair back from the table, and her face took on a sombre, funereal look. That's when Maddie knew for sure. Only bad news followed an expression like that.

'Private Elizabeth Wooten...'

'Elizabeth? Who's Elizabeth?' asked Gertie, confused.

'Betty – our housemate? She's not here right now,' said Maddie. 'She went into town shopping yesterday. Hasn't come back yet. She had a seventy-two-hour pass. Can we give her a message?'

'A message...' said Helen Worthing. She took another sip of the tea. Her hand shook.

'Unless you'd like to wait for her, ma'am,' said Maddie.

'Betty – Private Wooten. A good friend?'

'Yes, ma'am. The very best. The three musketeers, that's what we call ourselves,' said Maddie, blushing. Feeling slightly embarrassed at the juvenile idea. 'She's a great friend to everybody at the billet. Bit like a mother to us. Smashing lady and wears the uniform with pride,' she added. She didn't know if Betts had got herself in trouble but call a spade a spade – Betty Wooten was a loyal friend and a good soldier. Worth standing up for.

'Have you got any more sugar?' asked the officer.

Maddie pointed lamely to a cupboard and watched fascinated as Chief Commander Worthing walked across to the tap and refilled the kettle, put it on the stove and took the sugar canister from the cupboard above the sink. She made them all tea and filled three ATS-issue tin mugs to the brim, using up most of their sugar ration for the week.

When all three of them were seated around the table,

drinking the tea, Helen Worthing took a deep, shuddering breath and composed herself. 'There's no other way to do this,' she said, 'but I'm afraid I have bad news.'

'No!' Maddie was no psychic, but you didn't have to be to guess what that news might be.

'You won't have heard anything about this yet. The powers that be want to keep a lid on it for a while. Not good for morale,' said the officer. 'But it happened yesterday, right in the middle of a busy shopping district.'

'What? What happened yesterday?' asked Maddie, her voice rising to a high-pitched crescendo. And she distractedly grabbed hold of Helen Worthing's sleeve. Tugged on it.

'Jerries knew *exactly* what they were doing. They launched one of these awful new terror weapons we've been hearing about, the V-2 rockets. Timed to fall over London right when people were shopping on a Saturday. When it would have maximum impact. Your friend was killed in the blast...'

'Gawd Almighty,' said Gertie.

'One hundred and sixty-eight people killed outright. Thirty-three children. Some were babies still in their prams. Over a hundred injured.' The officer's voice was barely a whisper now – now that she'd delivered the horrific news.

'Where?' asked Maddie. Her voice shook. And she suddenly noticed the hand that gripped the commander's sleeve. Looked at it in surprise and let it fall to the kitchen table, where it trembled with shock. Helen Worthing put a comforting hand over Maddie's.

'I'm so sorry. No other way to tell you both. I know it's an awful shock, especially when she was such a good friend. We lost six more ATS girls in the atrocity as well. A heinous act, a deliberate act of terror designed to murder as many innocent civilians as possible.' The officer choked on the words and took another sip of her tea.

'Where?' asked Maddie again.

'New Cross. The large Woolworths store there took a direct hit, but the blast radius was massive. Shops, nearby houses, cars exploding, people working in offices had their desks blown out from under them. Pure carnage. Poor devils didn't stand a chance.'

'But maybe it wasn't Betts,' said Gertie. 'We can't be sure, can we? People make mistakes. It's wartime, things get scrambled up.'

'I'm so very, very sorry, Private Adams,' said the officer. 'I'm afraid there's no mistake.' Helen Worthing reached into the pocket of her greatcoat and took out the identity disks, one green and the other one red.

Both still intact, Maddie noted with a strange sense of detachment, as if her body didn't belong to her. *No damage to the ID disks, no blood.* No evidence of the carnage the officer had spoken of, but then maybe they'd been cleaned up.

Maddie shuddered as her imagination grappled with a scene of blast damage. Bodies scattered everywhere, blood, survivors stumbling through the rubble of buildings and broken glass; smoke and dust finding its way into their eyes and nostrils. A struggle for breath. And hysterical screams as the trauma hit them.

She shook her head in denial. 'Not Betts. Not our Betts. You've got that wrong. It couldn't be her, she's a survivor.'

'That's right,' said Gertie. 'She promised us! Nobody in this house would die. You remember, Madds?' Gertie's shoulders heaved with grief.

Maddie went over to her friend and put her arms protectively around her. 'I remember.' She looked across at the officer. 'No chance it's a mistake?'

'No, I'm sorry. They got a positive ID from her military identity card. That and the disks...'

'So, her face…?' asked Maddie.

'Not a mark on her. Looked like she was sleeping,' said Helen Worthing. 'Not like some of them…' The commander's face lightened by a shade as she remembered. She'd been one of the officers called to the scene because of the ATS victims, and it was a picture of horror that she would find hard to wipe from her mind.

'Gawd Almighty,' Gertie swore again.

The officer nodded in what might have been agreement. She turned to Maddie. 'She'd put you down in her Army Book 64 as next of kin, Maddie. So, you'd better have these.'

Maddie stared blankly at the identity disks. 'Me? Next of kin?'

'She didn't tell you? I guess she had no one else.'

'Yes, but…' And that's when Maddie truly understood. Betty Wooten had treated them like family, she and Gertie. So, maybe it was true then, and they were all she had. And she remembered Betty bullying her to write to her own family. Family's precious, she had said.

'Can I do anything for either of you?' asked Helen Worthing. 'Would you like me to contact the welfare officer? Or the padre, perhaps?'

'No!' They both answered at once.

'I think God has done enough damage for one day,' said Gertie, bitterly.

'I can sort out some compassionate leave…'

'Thank you,' said Maddie. 'You've been very kind. We've got each other, that's enough.'

When the officer had gone, Maddie made more tea. And they cried together until it seemed impossible there could be any more tears left in the world. And then they started to recall all the things they'd done together with Betty.

'Elizabeth? She was *never* an Elizabeth, was she?' said Gertie.

'No. She was our Betts. Always will be,' agreed Maddie. 'And at least she got to fly her kite. But I can't forgive myself for not saving her the wine.'

'She'd understand,' said Gertie. 'She's probably up there laughing at us now.'

'Maybe,' said Maddie. But she had her doubts. Betty Wooten was gone, not hovering above them playing a harp. But she certainly wouldn't be forgotten.

She and Gertie still had their memories of her; the laughs they'd had together. That's how Betts would live on. Maddie turned the ID disks over in her hand. Read the name on there: Elizabeth Wooten. Gertie was perfectly right. Betts had never been an Elizabeth. A Lizzy, maybe. But they would always think of her as Betts.

'You think it's right – what Sissy said about those things?' asked Gertie.

Sissy had claimed that the two identity disks they were expected to always wear around their necks were coloured red and green for a good reason. The green one, she'd said, was waterproof, so that if you died in a drowning, they'd still be able to read it and identify you. At least then your family would have something to remember you by. And the red tag? She claimed it was fireproof.

'I shouldn't think Sissy was right about many things,' said Maddie. 'She had some odd ideas. A good kid, but still a bit of growing up to do.' Maddie smiled, remembering. Sissy had started lots of squabbles when she'd lived at the house in Sunny-field, but they'd all got used to her. Had missed her when she left.

And it was rubbish, of course. Just a myth born in Sissy's wild imagination. But even so, the idea took root in Maddie's head. And that, along with horrendous visions of a V-2 rocket landing, gave her vivid nightmares for weeks to come. And *Woolworths*! She might never be able to go into any of them again. It was – had been – Betty Wooten's favourite shop.

43

Although the war had moved into its sixth year, you could see the optimism on people's faces now. The news from the different battle fronts was encouraging and it seemed to Maddie that it would take a heavy-duty miracle for the Germans to turn around defeat. And they *needed* to be defeated, there was no doubt of that in Maddie's mind. Hitler was a vicious bully. Some were calling him a power-mad maniac. Because of him, millions of people had died, including her friends Molly and Betts. It was his bomb that had fallen on Molly and her family. And his V-2 rocket that had put an end to Betty's life.

Even so, Maddie's thoughts were sometimes conflicted. Could you really blame the German people for Hitler's sins, people like Rudi's mother, who had lost her youngest son Werner at Dunkirk and had no idea if her husband was alive or dead? And Rudi, of course. She wished him no harm. Things were often complicated.

She and Gertie would sometimes sit by the fire in the evening, listening to the wireless, and if there was any cocoa left, they would raise their tin mugs in a toast to 'lost pals'.

Then Maddie came up with a plan. It was a daring plan.

And a little rebellious. And if it went wrong, she could end up in hot water. She was not a natural rebel, but in the circumstances, it was the least she could do for her very special friend, Gertie Adams.

Gertie had no mother, no father, no brothers or sisters. No husband, no lover. And one important date was coming up for her when a family was needed to help celebrate it. So, Maddie had decided that on 1 March she would do something novel for Gertie to mark her twenty-first birthday.

Fortune favours the bold it's said. And maybe luck favours them as well. Maddie had never thought herself bold, but now it seemed that she must be. Because events just fell into place, and her plans for Gertie's birthday treat worked out even better than she could ever have imagined.

Most of it was down to one wonderful American major in the United States Army Air Force. An interesting and rather attractive man, she had driven him in her staff car a few times now. She was on rota to drive him to a meeting during the afternoon and then to take him to a theatre in Central London.

She'd logged in as usual, picked up the car and then the major. But when Maddie had tried to pin down some sort of schedule from the man, he'd been intrigued and extracted the whole story from her.

'So, you'll just drive this friend of yours around in the black-out. Is that your plan, Private Brady?'

Maddie felt herself blush under his quizzical stare. 'Just a skeleton plan, right now,' she said. 'Only an idea, not too much flesh on the bones. But not the blackout, no. I thought perhaps while you were at your meeting, sir, I could give her a trip out in the staff car. And then collect you later, sir – deliver you to the Playhouse...'

'Not much of a treat for a twenty-first birthday,' said the major. He raised an eyebrow in amusement.

'More than she's expecting,' said Maddie.

'No, it won't do at all,' he said. 'So, here's what we'll do. You'll take me to my meeting. Go and collect this pal of yours, drive her around for a bit. And then the pair of you will accompany me to this play tonight.'

'But I can't do that,' said Maddie, appalled. 'I'm on duty.'

'I see, young lady. So, you were prepared to steal one of the British Army's staff cars, but you're not prepared to go out to the theatre when you're asked?'

'I don't think it would be right, sir. Nor proper. Going to the theatre when I should be on duty. It's not professional.'

'And if I were to call it an order, instead of an invitation?'

'I don't know...' said Maddie.

'Well, I do. Plus, you'd be doing me a favour. This play tonight will likely be the most boring thing I've ever had to sit through. But it's being put on by the American Forces Theater Unit, so it's obligatory to attend. Flying the flag, so to speak. The company of two fine young ladies might ease the pain somewhat.'

Maddie could think of nothing to say.

'And if you're worried about reputations, Private. I promise to be on my best behaviour. You have the word of a Southern gentleman.'

'That's not what I'm worried about, sir.'

'Nothing more to say, then. Log me in on that timesheet of yours, Private Brady, and log me out when we finish. And I won't tell if you don't.'

44

1 MARCH 1945

LONDON

Major Anderson had been wrong. The play had not been boring. It had been thrilling and a little thought-provoking and sad. *Our Town* was a story about Grover's Corners, a small town in America, but really it could have been in England or France or anywhere.

Maddie cried when the heroine, Emily, died. Smiled when Emily came back as a kind of ghost to visit her family and told them to enjoy their lives before it was too late. Even the small things were important: listening to the magic of ticking clocks, wearing newly ironed clothes, looking at sunflowers, watching loved ones while they slept. That's what Emily had told the ones she'd left behind, although none of them could hear her. But she was totally right. Maddie agreed with her: the small things in life were *definitely* the most important. And that's when Maddie had cried again. But she wasn't alone for when she looked at Gertie, she was crying too. And Gertie grabbed for her hand. Held onto it.

But there weren't only tears that night. There was joy too. Pure joy in Gertie's eyes when she rode in the staff car, and wonder when she realised she was going out to the theatre.

. . .

'You stole the car?' asked Gertie, amazed.

'Not technically stolen. Yeah, okay – maybe,' said Maddie.

They'd come home to a cold house and there was no cocoa left, but that didn't matter a jot. The night had been incredible, like something from a dream. And besides, who needs cocoa when a fine, upstanding Southern gentleman has given you glasses of bubbly?

'Cinderella, that's what I feel like. Ain't it great?' said Gertie.

'No more than you deserve. And I feel like Cinderella too.'

'And wasn't that guy just the sweetest man you ever met?' said Gertie.

'A decent bloke,' agreed Maddie. 'I was only going to borrow the car.' She laughed. 'It was his idea to take us both out to the theatre.'

'Think he fancies you.'

'Nonsense,' said Maddie.

But Gertie had already moved on. Her voice took on a dreamy quality. 'And all those gorgeous American actors. How d'you think they got those?'

'They're here already. All service guys who act in their spare time. Overpaid, over-sexed and over here.' Maddie grinned. It had all been worth it. And it felt good being a rebel. Okay, maybe only a small-time rebel, because she might just get away with it. She'd delivered the car back to the vehicle-pool and the log said that she'd taken the officer to the theatre after his meeting and on to his billet. *Could be perfectly fine.*

'I'm a wee bit tiddly,' said Gertie. 'Just two glasses of that stuff, but I ain't used to champagne.'

'Off to bed then, Cinderella,' Maddie ordered. She didn't think it had been real champagne. But even so, it was an unexpected bonus, like the one she'd had in the post today.

Her brother Richard had sent a card. Laid out in careful bullet points. So precise it made her smile. So very *Richard*.

1. He'd had a promotion. 2. He'd rented a flat of his own. And 3. He invited her to visit. An open invitation, and he would cook for them. He'd called her *sister*, a surprising declaration that had made her want to cry.

The whole day had been a feast of emotion. A time to treasure after the interludes of sadness both she and Gertie had lived through.

————

After that night's celebration, the war seemed easier to take. And to Maddie it felt as if the whole sad business was gradually coming to an end, although she had no idea when that might be. Maybe Mister Churchill did. She trusted him, for he had steered the country through its darkest days. She suspected there were times when even he had given up hope, but you could never tell because he was always so fired up and positive in his speeches, knew exactly what to say even when things had been so black that you couldn't see a way out.

Now there was real hope on the horizon. Everybody said so. *And the future?* During the last five years, Maddie hadn't dared to think about it. But now she did.

The dream she'd harboured as a child resurfaced once again. She'd buried it deep, for her father had scoffed, and her mother had dismissed her as a fool. 'Chickens in Hampstead?' they'd said. 'Ridiculous!'

So, she'd cast the dream aside. But things were different now. She was no longer that six-year-old, didn't need their permission to keep chickens or get herself a dog. A smallholding, with lots of animals. What a great idea. And maybe she'd use it as a kind of therapy, not only for herself, but others too. People traumatised by the painful memories of war.

That's it! That's exactly what she'd do, just as soon as she was demobbed. Start looking for somewhere. Maybe Gertie would be interested too. They could find a place of their own. In the country, somewhere peaceful, far away from any city and the ugly scars left behind by the bombing. She didn't need a reminder of the ugliness of the last six years. The only thing she wanted to remember was the kindness of people she'd met and their courage and resilience. She had a little money in the bank. Money from her grandmother. Both she and Richard had been gifted a small inheritance.

She would do it.

'You sitting here talking to yerself again?' Gertie laughed.

'What?'

'You'll *do* it? What's that mean? What you planning now, Madds? Some new caper? Next step up from stealing staff cars would be bank robbery.' Gertie pulled her chenille dressing gown tighter around her and grinned.

'Just thinking about things,' said Maddie.

'Oh? What things?'

'Afterwards. When this lot's over and done with.'

'Think they'll throw us out of the service?' asked Gertie, panic in her voice.

'We'll all get our marching orders. Don't see why the ATS would keep on going, do you?' said Maddie.

'And if it did, would you stay on, Madds?'

'Shouldn't think so. Fresh fields to conquer. New things to try. I've got lots of exciting ideas,' said Maddie. 'Might buy a small place somewhere, nothing fancy. By the sea maybe, or in the countryside. Some cheap place that needs fixing up. But I'd need a friend to help me. Somebody who doesn't mind roughing it for a bit.' Maddie raised a questioning eyebrow.

'Me? You mean me?' asked Gertie.

'Do you see anybody else here, you silly goose?'

And so, it was settled. Rough plans were sketched out for

the future, whenever that might be. It didn't matter when or where. She could wait. Just the thought that they would both be together in an adventure was enough to go on with for Maddie. For both of them.

———

Cheerful whistling could be heard coming from Gertie's bedroom periodically over the following weeks. And Maddie found herself joining in, although the art of pitching a whistle tunefully was one she had yet to master. But enthusiasm went a long way.

There were lots of reasons to be optimistic: British and Allied victories that made them proud of the chaps at the front, putting themselves in danger every day. But Hitler's terror machines, those damn V-2 rockets, were still finding their way into the heart of London. Still, the farther the British troops progressed, the more launch sites were being overrun. It was only a matter of time before the Germans couldn't use them anymore.

And Maddie had come to an arrangement with her conscience – she wouldn't blame the German people for either the Blitz or those awful terror weapons. And the reason for that was a kind of trade-off: her own country's air force had done something just as horrific when the city of Dresden had been firebombed, its ancient streets enveloped in fire storms. Three continual days of bombing. Over 20,000 people killed. Its cathedral reduced to rubble. She felt pity for the ordinary Germans who'd been trapped in the hell of Dresden. But no more than she'd felt for poor old London and the East End that had been pounded relentlessly during the Blitz.

Maybe now that madman Hitler would give up. And sanity could return. And they could put the lights back on. And take the blackout curtains down. And smile like they really meant it.

45

1 MAY 1945

LONDON

They'd just finished eating a gloopy macaroni thing for tea. Maddie had almost heaved, but she'd eaten it anyway, for it had been kind of the cook at Inglis Barracks to think of them. She often sent strange leftovers back home with Gertie. Giving food. A sign of love. *Not to be dismissed out of hand just because the macaroni has stuck together, and the cheese is unrecognisable as any kind of real dairy product.* So, Maddie ate it gratefully and told her friend to thank the cook. A stalwart woman who never gave up trying to work miracles with meagre wartime rations.

Maddie made tea in their tin mugs and both women settled in to listen to the news on the wireless.

'This is today's news, and this is Alvar Lidell reading it,' the announcer said. '*And cracking good news it is too.*'

'What?!' said Gertie. 'That's odd.'

'It is,' agreed Maddie. 'He's never said *that* before.'

Maddie stared intently at the wireless set, her mug clutched so tightly that it left small indents in her fingers. She turned to Gertie, who seemed to be holding her breath in anticipation. Mr Alvar Lidell had one of those proper British speaking voices, a bit like the king and queen, and he had always been so calm and measured in his delivery of the news. Even when a bomb had landed outside the studio, he had carried on, sitting there behind his microphone in evening dress. Very British. Very proper.

Whatever kind of news he'd had to report throughout the war, good and bad, he had never been carried away by emotion. He was someone you could rely on to be cool in the face of terrible news. A man with credibility. Someone you could believe in. That was why you invited him into your front room.

Yet here he was being... being what? Emotional, Maddie supposed. There was no other word for it. He'd become excited and his voice cracked in several places as his words speeded up until he sounded quite breathless.

As Maddie listened to the news bulletin, her mug of tea hovered forgotten in mid-air. And when she next looked at Gertie, her friend's eyes were wide with shock.

'Bastard!' said Maddie. 'A cowardly, bullying bastard.' Her voice shook.

'God and all his angels be praised!' said Gertie.

'I think you'll find God had nothing to do with this. Now the devil...' said Maddie. She stared at a space in the distance, but her thoughts were somewhere else. 'Bastard,' she said again. 'Cowering in a damn basement bunker, not man enough to face the Russians. Killing himself. *And* Eva Braun. *And* his poor bloody dog,' she said. 'The *dog*. Why would you do that?'

'Reckon he wanted to see if the cyanide would work. Tried it out on the Alsatian first,' said Gertie. And a huge tear ran down her cheek – Gertie loved dogs.

'Cyanide *and* a bullet. The coward wasn't taking any chances, was he?' said Maddie. 'You know what this means, Gert?'

'It's over?'

'It's over! Maybe not today, but soon. Very soon.'

Gertie started to shake, and she dashed from the room. When Maddie caught up with her, she was in the bathroom, throwing up. A mixture of gloopy macaroni and black tea. She was shivering and kept on muttering one name over and over again. *Bill.* Her lovely husband.

Maddie got her to bed and put an extra blanket on top: her own blanket. *Shock.* It could do that sort of thing to you.

Then she went back and freshened up the stewed tea with another shot of boiling water and sat down in the lounge. Hitler had committed suicide. The coward had killed himself yesterday in a dank cellar beneath the Reich Chancellery, leaving his troops to carry on fighting and dying in a useless battle to save Berlin. So much for his master race and a Reich that was meant to last a thousand years.

The wireless was still on. Playing cheerful jazz music from some big band or other. And Maddie wanted to be cheerful too. To sing along with it. But all she could think about was the waste of the last six years and all those poor souls who had given their lives. Men, women and children on *all* sides of the war. So, instead of singing and cheering with happiness, Maddie Brady sat in the freezing-cold room alone. And cried.

46

8 MAY 1945

LONDON

Maddie waited in the room next to the garage. She wasn't alone. Lots of other drivers and mechanics were hanging around waiting for their assignments as well. Some were sitting, like her; others were caged lions, pacing back and forth. The lance corporal who normally handed out the rotas was nowhere to be seen. The woman had disappeared an hour ago after bellowing orders that all drivers were to 'stand by' and await further instructions.

Every so often one of the younger women would grumble about the hold-up, but Maddie was content to sit and wait and enjoy the respite. Especially after yesterday, when there'd been palpable excitement in the air, as well as curious theories about Hitler's death. And work was frenzied. Maddie had christened it 'Manic Monday', and she'd fallen into bed late last night, exhausted. She'd spent the day ferrying officers between the War Office and different government ministries non-stop. Her vehicle log had taken up three whole sheets, and nowhere on there had it mentioned lunch. *Or* tea. So, not only had she gone to bed late, but hungry and cranky as well. And this morning, she'd woken up with a headache.

Two WVS volunteers arrived and set up trestle tables at the far end of the room. Another pushed a trolley with a tea urn on it and a stack of plates.

'Know what's up?' asked a young woman, who'd sidled up to Maddie.

'Not a clue,' said Maddie. 'I guess we'll find out.'

'You're not curious?'

'It's the army,' said Maddie. 'They'll tell us when they're ready.'

'The trusting type, eh?' said the woman. She gave Maddie a sarcastic smile.

'I beg your pardon?'

'Know what I think? None of 'em's got a clue what the hell's going on.' The voice held a challenge in it.

Maddie closed her eyes, ignoring the woman. She wasn't often rude, but she had a fierce headache and the young woman wasn't making it any better. Maddie had met her type before. Barrack-room lawyers, they were called and most people ignored them for they were always ready to complain about something, trying to stir up trouble where none existed. Making bullets for other people to fire.

'Charmed, I'm sure.' The woman walked off in a huff.

The WVS ladies returned with another trolley, the smell of food wafting from it. And a small procession of officers arrived; one of them, a captain Maddie had never seen before, lifted a ladle and banged it noisily on the table.

'Ladies, ladies! May I have your attention, please?'

A hush fell over the room and everyone who'd been sitting sprang to attention, firing off a ragged volley of salutes.

'At ease, ladies.' The captain smiled. 'You've all done an incredible job and I'm proud of you. It's not been easy – long hours, battling through blackouts... and yesterday... well, I expect there are many of you exhausted today.'

A few heads nodded in reply. There were some ironic smiles as well. And Maddie heard a theatrical cough.

'Right,' said the officer. 'These ladies behind me will be serving you all breakfast. You've earned it. After that, there will be new orders posted with the dailies in the office. Most of you won't be going out today. Instead, you may return to your billets and at fifteen hundred hours, you would be well advised to turn on your wireless sets. You will be on the rota for a forty-eight-hour pass.' She smiled. 'Some of you will need it, I feel sure. And when you return to duty, there will be further instructions from your section head. Carry on, Corporal.' She turned to the small woman beside her, nodded and handed the corporal the serving ladle, like handing off a baton.

Once the captain left, the noise in the room grew to a din. Drivers and mechanics asking questions, everyone speaking at once. To be given breakfast? This wasn't normal. And a forty-eight-hour pass?

The corporal wielded the ladle with military precision and a hush fell over the room. 'You heard the officer,' she said. 'Form an orderly line for breakfast and when you've finished, you may come to the office to read your new orders. Only three at a time, please – the clerks already have their hands full in there. Carry on, ladies.'

Breakfast was wonderful. Maddie had seconds, to make up for yesterday's shortfall of food, and when she finally made it to the office, only the lance corporal was there.

'You're on a forty-eight. Report back at oh-eight hundred hours on Thursday. Dismissed, Private.'

Maddie made it home around lunchtime and fell wearily into a chair in the lounge. She'd walked back to the billet, from one side of London to the other. The buses were sometimes hit-and-miss, but today had been one of their *miss* days. She thought back to the strange morning and the way the forty-eight-hour passes had been handed out like confetti. Odd.

And there had still been an odd tension in the air. There'd been speculation that the war was over, but no one could be sure.

She should do something to celebrate her unexpected leave but the house was silent and cold. No one to share this free time with. And that's when the idea came to her.

She would use some of the week's coal ration and build a fire. She imagined the others would be pleased, coming home to a warm house.

The ashes had been cleaned out, but no one had set the fire in the grate yet. Still, there was something therapeutic about twisting newspaper into concertina firelighters and crisscrossing the shavings of kindling around it like a wigwam. She placed small nuggets of coal carefully around the whole construction. There was an art to coaxing a fire into life, but it was one Maddie had mastered during these frugal years of rationing. And there was a special magic when you stared into the flames bursting into life with their incandescent colours: orange, yellow, red and sometimes a strange blue haze. It was a kind of alchemy.

She sat back on her heels in front of the fire, watching with satisfaction as the flames grew and made their way up the chimney to the sky above. That's when the unexpected clatter of heavy shoes and a cheerful whistling announced her friend Gertie's arrival.

'Get you,' said Gertie. 'Throwing coal around like we lived in Buck House.'

'It was freezing,' said Maddie. 'Besides, it's a celebration – I've been given leave.'

'You too? The mess officer just sent me home and gave me this. Told me to enjoy myself.' Gertie produced a bottle from her rucksack. It was half-full and she held it up to the light so that the liquid inside shone like amber.

'Brandy?' said Maddie, confused. 'Sergeant Johnson gave

you a half-bottle of brandy? Why would the grumpy old guy do that?'

'Said we should both enjoy ourselves, Madds. Don't know what he meant but he winked as well.'

'Maybe he fancies you, Gert.' Maddie grinned.

'Shouldn't think so. He spends most of his time complainin' I ain't up to snuff.'

'All bark and no bite, though,' said Maddie. 'He hasn't got the teeth for it.'

They both giggled at that. Sergeant Johnson was always having trouble keeping his loose-fitting false teeth in place.

'Right, let's have the last of the cheese,' said Gertie. 'I'm starved. And maybe a nip of that brandy.'

'But it's the middle of the day!' said Maddie. 'It'll send me to sleep.'

'No, it won't and that's an order, Private.' Her friend sniggered. 'Get your feet up, enjoy the fire and I'll make you lunch. Got to look after you pensioners.'

'Cheeky monkey! I still got some useful mileage in me,' said Maddie. All the same, it was good to be fussed over.

'And put the wireless on,' ordered Gertie as she headed for the kitchen to do battle with the hard bread.

Maddie hummed to herself as she thought about an afternoon away from work, sitting by a blazing fire, listening to music on the wireless and drinking brandy.

Life didn't get much better than this.

Life *did* get better. A whole, humongous, incredible lot better. They both drank their brandy and battled their way through heels of stale bread that, as Gertie pointed out, would have been a challenge to Sergeant Johnson and his dodgy teeth. And just before three o'clock in the afternoon, a BBC Home Service announcer warned that listeners should stand by for a very special programme. Then there was a loud trumpet fanfare. And that was the moment that life truly got better.

Mr Churchill addressed the nation in his usual charismatic way.

The war was over.

The Germans had signed an unconditional surrender the day before and Churchill called for national celebrations. But he warned that it wasn't the end. Victory! But only in Europe. He was calling it VE Day.

Maddie grabbed her friend, hugged her and rushed out excitedly onto the street with Gertie in her wake. They passed an old woman draped in a Union Jack flag, sitting on her front step, a massive grin on her face. There were people everywhere, shouting, laughing, waving flags.

She joined a conga line making its way along Sunnyfield and, in an ambitious move, not unlike the impressive choreography of the Lindy Hop, she pulled Gertie into its line.

She could feel the uninhibited joy, the excitement pulsing through people as they clung to the person in front. The strange line of dancers wobbled its precarious way along the middle of the road, tall people, small people, old people, young people; people whose pinched, grey, worried wartime faces of yesterday had miraculously transformed into beaming, happy faces. Two lorries stopped to make way for them all, honking their horns in celebration. It was as if a wonderful madness had gripped everyone. People laughing, kissing strangers.

Maddie broke away from the line, dragging Gertie with her. They linked arms, marched along the pavement together, grinning the same idiotic grin that was on faces all around them. *Freedom. Liberation.* They were words that went round and round in Maddie's head. Suddenly, miraculously, they were cut free – untethered from the fear that had held them down. The fear of dying. The fear of losing friends. The fear of never feeling normal again.

'Let's go up town,' said Maddie.

'What, now?'

'Sure. It's what we should do, celebrate properly. The Strand. Trafalgar Square. The Mall. Whatever... Let's just go mad. And Gert?'

'What?'

'Let's get the brandy. That's what he meant it for. The sergeant must have known.'

They went back home for the brandy – and their army greatcoats. It looked like being a long night, but one to remember.

The excitement was at fever pitch. Strangers hugging each other like long-lost friends, dancing 'The Lambeth Walk', all packed together like sardines wriggling in their cans.

On the Strand, they were hoisted up onto the back of an open army lorry. Maddie clung on precariously and when a bump in the road threatened to dislodge her, a uniformed soldier hauled her back. He held her tightly round the waist and planted an exuberant kiss on her lips. It was the first of many kisses from total strangers but it was all in good sport, part of the atmosphere of euphoria and boisterous happiness that enveloped London and its people that night.

When the road became blocked by hundreds of revellers, they abandoned the lorry and joined the mass of bodies pressing on towards The Mall.

'Let's go and see the king,' yelled Maddie over the racket. 'And Churchill. I want to see Churchill!'

It took ages to get through the roaring crowds lining The Mall but Maddie was insistent: she wanted to get as close to the gates of Buckingham Palace as she could. She intended to see Churchill and the king and queen, and maybe even Princess Elizabeth would be there. The princess was one of them, just like her and Gertie. In the ATS. A driver and mechanic. It had been brave of her to push to join up, to be normal – and for the king to let her.

Someone handed her a bottle of brown ale and she shared it with Gertie. She didn't want to get blotto and miss out on the excitement. They'd already had some of the brandy and Gertie carried the rest of the bottle in her backpack.

Maddie thought back to the captain's words that morning. About the forty-eight-hour pass and how some of them would need it. She'd imagined that was because of their exhaustion from long hours on duty, but it hadn't meant that at all. *The officer had known about this.* Had suspected there were some who would have sore heads tomorrow, would need the time off.

They bludgeoned their way through the dense crowd, Maddie in front, refusing to be knocked off course. And by some miracle and a lot of good-natured banter when toes had been stood on and folks elbowed out of her way, Maddie made her objective. Close enough to the palace to see the figures already out on the balcony. Churchill was there, right next to the king and queen. The rightful place for him, she felt.

Someone behind them knocked her uniform cap off and she struggled to retrieve it, but the old man gave her a good-natured, toothless grin and replaced it with a party hat. She smiled at him. There was no room for anger that night – there'd been enough of that. Churchill's words were awe-inspiring, their power resonating, amplified through many speakers placed around the vast space. Words that seemed to find their way straight to the hearts of people, for the cheering was so loud from the thousands packed in front of the palace and all the way down The Mall that the prime minister had to stop until the noise died down.

Maddie's throat was raw from screaming and cheering along with the rest. But when she turned to Gertie, she saw that her friend was silent and tears were streaming down her grief-stricken face. *Bill... Of course it would be Bill.* Victory was great, but for Gertie it must be bittersweet. Bill had helped to pay for it, but he couldn't be there to enjoy it. Or take his wife dancing. There would be a sad stock-taking now, not only for her friend Gertie but for millions around the world.

But that was for tomorrow. That night was for celebration. Maddie thought about the other people, in countries far away from here. The Allies would be celebrating too, wouldn't they? Would the lights all be blazing in Paris now, as they were here in London? That was an amazing thing. A crazy, wonderful thing when you were used to a blackout: to see the lights blazing away on The Mall, and Buckingham Palace lit up like it was Christmas.

She took Gertie's hand, squeezed it in a gesture of under-standing. And Gertie smiled at her. Nodded her head. Mouthed the words, 'It's okay.' And maybe it would be okay. But losing your husband, losing your family, your friends – it wasn't something that would soon be forgotten, and neither should it be.

Gertie had found a soulmate, only to have him ripped from her grasp. And although they had only known each other for an eye blink in time, Maddie felt the same way about Rudi. She hadn't forgotten him. And didn't think she ever could. They had shared something powerful. It had felt natural to love him, and she knew he felt the same way for he'd told her so.

Where was he now? Was he free or a prisoner? And if he was, *he* would hardly be celebrating, not like her and Gertie, or these Londoners, and people throughout the country. Folk would be celebrating in France, in Belgium, in Holland, in New York, all over the place. But the one country that wouldn't be having parties that night would be Germany. Rudi's family wouldn't be celebrating, would they?

'Let's go, shall we?' said Gertie, suddenly.

'Go? Go where?'

'Don't know. Feels weird being trapped here. Need to breathe,' said Gertie, her breath coming out in short bursts. Her eyes had a wild look of panic in them.

Maddie reached for her friend, held her up by the elbow, for Gertie's legs had buckled under her. And now Maddie was worried, tried to stay calm. Collapsing in the middle of such a massive, excited crowd would be dangerous: a person could easily get trampled and others might not even notice.

She turned to the man next to her, tugged urgently at his uniform, pulling him towards her. The American airman laughed and kissed Maddie smack on the mouth. His breath smelled of something strange, something she hadn't come across before. She didn't kiss him back. Instead, Maddie shouted in the young man's ear.

'Can you help us? I need to get my friend out of here – she's ill.'

'Ma'am,' he said, politely, and gave a mock salute. 'We're allies, ain't we?' He winked.

And in a night full of weird and wonderful happenings, it didn't seem out of place, this young man grappling with her friend Gertie, pushing her through the sea of humanity. Most people were good-humoured and gave way. Some, Maddie noted, were downright squiffy. Pubs had been handing out free beer most of the day. Hopefully, chemists would be handing out free aspirins tomorrow.

It took the three of them almost an hour to make it down The Mall. The man – his name turned out to be Al – left them there and carried on to Trafalgar Square, but Maddie steered her friend towards the park. Maybe the crowds were thinner there and they could sit and catch a breath and watch the ducks. Were the pelicans and ducks back in St James's Park? Had they even left? Maddie didn't know. The last time she'd been there, there had been no war. Now it had a massive air raid shelter in it.

'Well,' said Maddie, after they'd collapsed onto the grass. 'Quite a night. Feeling better?'

'Yeah.'

'You gave me a scare.'

'Sorry. Not sure what happened there. Panicked, I guess.'

'All those people,' said Maddie. 'Claustrophobic.'

'Yeah.' Gertie blew out some air. 'Some of 'em weren't bad-looking neither,' she said. 'Specially that last one.'

'Our knight in armour, you mean.' Maddie laughed.

'You get his name and address?' asked Gertie.

'His name was Al. And no – I didn't get his address.'

'Missed your chance there, girl. And those baby blues? Gorgeous. Like a film star.'

'Thought you were too busy fainting to notice,' said Maddie.

'I was poorly, not dead. Blond hair too. Not like a bloke. Reckon he dyes it?'

'God, Gert! How would I know? I only just met the bloke.'

Gertie reached down and took the brandy from her rucksack. 'Might as well finish it.'

It was a cold night. A good-enough excuse for finishing off the brandy. And it wasn't as if they'd be able to get back home before morning now. So they drank, sitting on the ground in the park, huddled up in their army greatcoats. Watching people passing by. Gazing in awe at fireworks going off in the distance.

'You still want to do that thing like you said, Madds – you and me in a house somewhere?'

'Absolutely!'

'By the sea?'

'Hope so.' Maddie smiled. And the sigh of contentment that came from the friend beside her – well, it couldn't all be about the brandy.

'That bloke...'

'What bloke?' asked Maddie.

'Our rescuer,' said Gertie. She had trouble with the word. Tiredness and alcohol taking their toll.

'Al. He said his name was Al.'

'Yeah, Al. *Blondie*,' said Gertie. 'Looked kind of German, don't you think? Jesus, Madds! You don't think he was a German, do you?'

'No. How could a German be walking along The Mall? He was a full-blooded American GI. Chewed gum the whole time.'

'Yeah, but how can you be sure?'

'He was no German. I've *met* a German,' said Maddie. 'I *know* a German,' she said wistfully.

'You do? How? Who—?'

'Can't tell you that, Gert.'

'But I'm your best mate,' said Gertie.

'You are. *Friends forever*,' agreed Maddie. 'But I can't tell you. Not now, not yet. It's not safe.'

'What?! That don't make sense.'

'It will – one day. I'll tell you one day. That's a promise.' Maddie stared off into the distance and tried to remember his face. A feeling of panic gripped her. *Rudi*. How could it be that she'd forgotten his face?

47

29 SEPTEMBER 1957

CHURCH COVE, GUNWALLOE, CORNWALL

Maddie counted the waves as they crashed dramatically onto the rocks. Every tenth wave sent up an enormous blast of white foam thrashing into the granite backbone of the beach.

She always counted the wave-sets there and they were rarely the same. Some days you'd wait five minutes for a huge titanic wave to batter the rocks, throwing its spume over the slick grey boulders. But there was always a pattern to it. A rhythm. One you could rely on.

The scenery on the Lizard Peninsula was breath-taking, and sometimes it moved her to tears. You could easily imagine it as the very edge of the world, with its jagged rocks and deep, treacherous gullies waiting for the careless or the reckless to step too close to the cliff edge.

The drama of the Cornish seascape there in Gunwalloe might seem violent to some, primal even. But for Maddie it was soothing, brought her peace. It was also healing. Cleansing the sadness of loss, leaving just a bittersweet memory of the very first time she had been there.

It seemed so long ago, when she'd first watched these same

waves in Church Cove. The date – 17 February 1941 – would be etched in her mind forever.

Nowadays, she often came down to the cove to think. Or when her flagging spirit needed prodding back into action.

And today? Why would the world need to cosset her today? She wasn't feeble. Had lived through far worse than this. They all had. She'd survived a war, for God's sake. *And turning forty wasn't such a big deal.*

Things were good. No more rationing. No more fear. And a new decade: the fifties. It all sounded so modern, contemporary.

Count your blessings, woman! Maddie thought to herself. *You're alive. You've got a washing machine, a fridge, a vacuum cleaner, and one of those fancy new hairdryers. No more taking hours drying your hair in front of the fire. And the farmhouse has a new roof. No more buckets catching drips. Turning forty shouldn't be such a disaster. Well, should it?*

It was the anti-climax, that's all. After her birthday party yesterday, and all the fuss. And now, dropping her brother into Helston to get his train.

He was leaving Cornwall, heading back to London and the bright lights. Though she doubted Richard ever saw the bright lights. In bed by eight with his cocoa and his bank reports. Still, it suited him. Not *everybody* could afford to be a free spirit, he'd said. Funny how he always said stuff like that around her.

Maddie picked up a pebble from the beach. The stone was round and smooth. Years of patient sculpting by the waves of the Atlantic had turned it into a work of art. Perfection. She was tempted to keep it. Take it home and add it to her hoard of treasures.

Instead, Maddie threw the pebble as far as she could out into the ocean. Then she turned her back on the foaming sea, walked past the ancient church and trudged back uphill to the car. She always parked there, in the same spot on the promontory. Like a kind of ritual. Beside the old barn, ancient now, but still stubbornly clinging on; she went over and touched it. Another ritual.

Memories washed over her. Memories of the two of them together. Joined for the first time. She hoped life had been kind to him; it wasn't always. She shook her head, trying to dislodge the melancholy that had attached itself to her. It wasn't welcome. And it wasn't like her. She wasn't normally sad.

It wasn't just the birthday, of course. It was the thought of saying goodbye to Gertie as well. Side by side for most of the war years. Working together in the ATS. Laughing together in their billet. Crying together when they'd lost pals. It was Gertie who'd organised the surprise birthday party and now, she too, would be going home to London.

Maddie drove the ten miles back to the village of Pendurran in a kind of bubble. Didn't notice the lush fields, the grazing sheep, or the countryside as it flashed past. She was on automatic pilot – not the best way to operate a lethal weapon that could reach up to fifty miles an hour with a following wind. And do untold damage to any sheep that crossed her path.

She pulled up next to the village shop. Milk, bread; that would hold her till she could do a larger shop in town. And she'd check on the post. Save old Mr Bingham trudging up to her farm.

'Miss Brady. Alright, my 'ansum? Got your post here,' said Rose Trevelyan, and handed across two buff envelopes.

'Thanks,' said Maddie. *More bills.*

The woman dropped her voice and leaned in closer. 'And – there were some young fella asking for you just now,' she said.

'Really? Did he leave his name?'

'Didn't say,' said Rose. 'And I didn't ask. Not my place. But he weren't local. *Foreigner*, I should say.' Rose Trevelyan sniffed; a significant sniff, disdainful. That, and the raised eyebrow, left no doubt as to how the postmistress of Pendurran felt about foreigners.

Maddie tried not to smile. Rose considered most folk east of the Tamar *foreign*, to be eyed with suspicion; she made some exceptions. Maddie herself had finally been accepted as a 'villager' by the old woman, but it had taken ten years – and several boxes of eggs from Maddie's chickens – to grease the process.

'So...?'

'He asked directions to your place.'

'Did he go up there?' asked Maddie.

'I don't give out no private information like that,' said Rose, and she tapped the side of her nose in a knowing gesture.

'So, he left?'

'Looked like he was heading to the Old Forge. Might still be there,' said Rose.

'Thanks,' said Maddie. She pocketed the bills and left, forgetting to buy her milk and bread. She was distracted and intrigued. Maybe she'd go to the Forge Café, find out what the man wanted. Besides, a cup of tea would warm her up, and Gertie wouldn't mind if she didn't get back straight off. Her friend had been happily sitting in the farmhouse parlour reading her new book. Feet up. Not often Gertrude Adams got to do that nowadays.

The Old Forge had lately been given a new slate roof, for the ancient one had started to sag dangerously but, other than that, the old village smithy was pretty much as it had been for decades now, at least on the outside. Villagers were proud of its history, the fact that the forge had been standing since 1805 and that they'd only stopped having a blacksmith working there in 1939: the year war broke out.

Lots of things had changed that year.

The old building was sturdy. Looked like it could go on for years to come. Battling the Cornish weather and the winds that seemed to blow in from the Arctic at times. The locals were used to the harsh winter weather and the mist that often clung to the low-lying village of Pendurran. The building had been turned into a café, a popular destination for holidaymakers looking for their authentic Cornish cream tea. And now, in September, a time when most of the tourists had gone home, it was returned to the locals – a cosy haven where friends could meet for a catch-up and a decent lunch of homemade steak and kidney pie.

The only thing that marked it out as a smithy now was the heavy anvil that stood outside the door. Black and shiny, repainted lovingly every year, like the thick cob walls that were sparkling white in contrast. Colourful winter pansies hung in baskets either side of the door. *Happy little flowers*, Maddie always thought.

The old-fashioned bell over the door tinkled as she went in.

Rachel came over straight away, a friendly, polite young woman, looking neat and competent in her smart black uniform and white frilly apron and matching mobcap.

Maddie followed the young waitress to a table and smiled at her. Rachel's face opened in a wide beam – the girl had excellent teeth.

'I love what you've done to your hair, Miss Madeline.'

'You do?' When she left the army, she'd allowed her hair to grow; it was easier to manage, scrapped into a ponytail. She had no time for fussing with her hair. But Gertie had badgered her into a new style, shoulder-length. She hadn't been convinced. Maybe a bit too young, she'd thought. *Hark at that. Thinking like a grumpy middle-aged woman already and she'd only been forty for a day.*

'Dead glamorous. 'Zakly like Grace Kelly,' said Rachel. 'And Marilyn Monroe sometimes wears it that way. All sleek and smooth, glossy like. And turned under in a pageboy. Mind, you're lucky.'

'Oh?'

'Having blonde hair.'

That's what the hairdresser had told her as well. So maybe

it was true. But then she was taking your money, so that's the sort of thing she would say. Blonde hair and blue eyes, and tall and willowy. *Score 100 on the cor-blimey scale.* That had been Gertie's verdict when they'd first met in 1941. *Blokes'll be falling over theirselves to get to you*, Gertie had assured her when they'd become friends.

But somehow it hadn't worked out that way. After Rudi, she hadn't been interested in taking on another man. She would always be thinking of him.

'Bring you some tea over, shall I, miss?' asked Rachel.

'That'd be lovely. And one of those toasted teacakes of yours,' said Maddie.

'Right you are, miss. Quick as a wink,' Rachel said and did a funny little bob, like a curtsy.

Maddie looked around for the stranger. He wasn't hard to spot, for there were only two other people in the café. One was old Mr Bingham – 'Alf' to his mates. He was proud of his job working for the Royal Mail. He always emphasised the word 'royal' when describing his illustrious employers, and he wore the uniform cap at a jaunty devil-may-care angle. Maddie wondered if the ancient postman ever took it off.

The other customer looked uncomfortable in the quaint surroundings of horse brasses and memorabilia of the old smithy. Looked vaguely out of place in his suit and tie. The fedora hat placed on the table in front of him reminded Maddie of something she'd seen in a gangster film.

The young man looked up, caught her watching him – and the hand that held his teacup shook. His jaw slackened, and a strange look came over his face.

Maddie couldn't pin it down. Surprise? Recognition? A revelation of some kind.

He stared at her. Like he knew her. And he tried a smile, but it didn't work. It slipped into a nervous grimace. Still he didn't look away.

She didn't know him, had never seen him before. And yet he insisted on staring at her, his gaze intimate, disturbing. It made her feel on edge. And the warm flush of embarrassment stung her cheeks.

Maddie didn't wait for the tea. She searched her purse for change, left the money for her bill and got ready to leave. But the young man walked to her table and put a hand out towards her. He didn't touch her.

'Miss Brady?'

'What do you want?'

'Won't you stay?' he asked. 'I've come a long way to meet you.'

Up close like this, she could see that he was very young. Sixteen? Seventeen at the most. Still a gangling, skinny teenager with spots fighting their hormonal battle on his face. A young man dressed up in old man's clothes.

He pointed to a seat at her table, a question in his eyes, the hat held nervously in front of him, like a shield.

Maddie sat down again, and he took the seat opposite.

He will be quite handsome, she thought. *When he matures. Once the spots give up their hold.* 'Who are you?' she asked.

'I offer my apologies,' the lad said, a little stiffly. 'I would have written to request a meeting, but I wasn't sure I had the right place. I came from Munich to find you.'

So, Rose Trevelyan was right: he had come from abroad. But he was no foreigner. She could detect no accent, although there was something about his stilted use of language that made her wonder. Like someone who has become used to the strange syntax of a foreign tongue struggling to remember his own.

Germany, he said. He'd come all the way from Munich to see her. But why her? Maybe he'd heard about the centre? People came to her from all over the country. But *this* country, never from abroad before. Nor was the centre very large. But word got out, she supposed, when you were trying to do something like she was. Something unusual, like a retreat.

It had all started in a small way the year after war ended. Just the land and the ancient, decrepit farmhouse. Maddie had been idealistic, trying to change the world, or at least a tiny part of it. And Gertie? Going along for the ride, because she couldn't think of anything else to do in the vacuum the end of the war had left. The pair of them, living in a cold, leaky caravan until they could get the old place brought back to life. A bit of self-sufficiency. The chickens, the goats, a couple of lazy pigs. Just your typical smallholding.

But then, not really typical, was it? Maddie had encouraged any women she'd found who'd been disturbed by the war and its consequences to come and find an oasis of peace. Not only soldiers got shell-shocked. Or knew the trauma left by war. Those women, who'd stayed behind, fighting their own private battles on the home front, had had their fair share of anguish too.

Maddie wasn't a doctor, or psychologist, or one of those fancy therapists that were springing up all over the place now, but she'd given them a sympathetic ear, someone to listen to their pain. Some had found contentment looking after the chickens and the goats. Many women had made their way to her door. She'd prided herself that several had left the centre feeling stronger, more able to cope with the trauma left behind by those years of war. Some had needed only weeks, a breathing space, to pull their lives together. Others stayed for longer, sometimes leaving, then returning. There was no rule. The centre was a life-raft.

And not only for the women, but for Maddie, too.

'So, you've heard about the centre?' she asked. It was rather flattering. Or was that wrong of her? Too arrogant maybe. 'The centre – is that why you've come?' asked Maddie.

'Centre?' he echoed, confused. 'I don't understand anything about a centre,' he said.

'Well then, why? What do you want?' Something about the way he was staring at her was making her feel uncomfortable again.

'I came for *you*. This is the *only* reason I came. To find you. A son should know his mother. A mother should know her son.' The lad smiled. A sad, wistful smile.

'What?! But that's crazy!' said Maddie. '*You're* crazy. You're not my son. I don't *have* any children. I've never had any children.' Her voice was strident, not like her. The denial adamant.

But anyone who truly knew Maddie Brady might have wondered at the fleeting expression on her face. It could easily have been guilt.

'And I suppose you'll tell me you don't know this man.' The lad reached into his pocket and took out a dog-eared photograph, held it up in front of her. Close to her face.

The body was thin, the face in the picture emaciated, but still able to produce a smile. He was standing outside a hut, maybe his own barracks, she couldn't remember, not after all this time. But those startling eyes that had sparked when he laughed... his was a face she saw often in her dreams.

'*Rudi*,' she whispered.

And that's when Madeline Brady passed out.

48

'His name was Rudi?' asked Gertie. 'The guy in the Old Forge?' she added, when Maddie looked as if the words were in a foreign language.

Maddie was disoriented. She stared at her friend, searching the worried face beside her for a clue, watched Gertie's hands tighten on the car's steering wheel.

'Look, I know you don't want me to run you to the hospital, but at least let me get Doctor Handy. You fainted,' said Gertie.

'I'm fine.'

'You don't look fine. What day is it?'

'Day? I don't know,' said Maddie.

'What year is it?' asked Gertie.

'It's...'

'It's 1957. We're in Cornwall. Your name's Maddie Brady, mine's Gertie Adams. We're best mates, have been for years, although I'm the younger and better-looking one,' said Gertie.

'Oh? And who says so?'

'My Arthur, that's who. But it's well-known that blokes go for us redheads. Now, what the heck's going on here, Madds?

You look like you've seen a ghost. And you fainted, that ain't normal.'

'Nothing's going on. Just drive me home, will you? And I don't know why everybody's making such a fuss. Or why they dragged you out.'

'They dragged me out – made me walk away from a lovely warm fire and a bloody good book – because, Maddie Brady, there was no way you could drive yourself back home. Not looking white like that and with a gert big lump on your head and muttering the name "Rudi" over and over again.'

'Rudi?'

'Yes. That's what they said in the Forge. Was that the name of the young bloke who upset you in there?' asked Gertie.

Maddie's head throbbed and she fought hard to stop the bile in her stomach from reaching her throat. Maybe she was hungry. Should have had some breakfast that morning before dropping her brother off for his train. That would be it. That would be why she fainted, like they'd said.

But that wasn't it, of course. Her reluctant brain finally brought the strange events into focus. And she remembered the young man. Saw his eager face as he told her that he was her son. That she was his mother. Bizarre.

Because of course she didn't have a son. She would like to have had children – and a son would have been good.

'*Rudi?*' said Maddie. 'No – I don't think his name was Rudi. The young man... he didn't tell me his name.'

'He tried to help you when you fainted, then it seems he disappeared.'

'He's gone?' asked Maddie.

'So Rachel said,' said Gertie. Then: 'Right, we need to get you home. You should be in bed.'

'No bed,' said Maddie. 'I'll just rest a bit and you can make me one of your famous cheese sandwiches with lots of onion and that runner-bean chutney of yours. Your cheese sandwiches are as good as any medicine Doctor Handy doles out.'

'Fair enough. But you'll need to take it easy for a while. I'm staying on a bit longer, and I don't want no arguments from you, miss. You've been doing far too much, lately. Nice as it is to do stuff for other folk, Madds, comes a time when you got to be kind to yerself too. *Got that?*'

'Got it,' Maddie said, and smiled.

Maddie watched her friend start the car, letting out the sticky clutch. She'd need to get that fixed soon, like so many other jobs piling up; things that needed money to sort out. Money she didn't have right then. She noted the rigid set of her friend's shoulders, the determined look on Gertie's face that meant there would be no arguments. And there wouldn't, not from Maddie. Truth be told, she was glad and maybe even a bit relieved that someone else would be in charge for a while. It *was* good to do things for other people and the centre gave her a feeling of satisfaction, a sense of purpose – her life hadn't been wasted – but it could be exhausting and frustrating as well.

And in her quiet moments, when she allowed her own feelings to surface, Maddie Brady had to own up to regrets. Her family were almost strangers: her mother hadn't bothered to make the trip to Cornwall for Maddie's fortieth birthday, and her brother was a reserved man who found it hard to show emotion.

Gertie was like a sister to her, always had been. A younger sister, but then Gertie had always been older than her years. Life had forced her to be. But now Gertie had her own life. And, although the few remaining women in the centre were a family of sorts, it wasn't the same. She had no special man to share her life with, and no children. It seemed such a simple thing to ask, to long for. A real family to have Christmas with. To go to the beach with. To make birthday cakes for.

She put her hand on top of Gertie's, squeezed it gently. A

gesture meant to reassure her friend. Gertie was precious, a diamond in the rough; worth more than a hundred *real* families. And she'd always been there in times of trouble.

'You know I love you, don't you?' said Maddie.

'You goin' all mushy on me? 'Cause if you are, you can forget the cheese sandwich.'

'No mush,' promised Maddie.

'And you'll rest? Put your feet up for a bit?'

'Yes.'

'Yeah!' Gertie threw her a cynical look. 'And those damn pigs of yours might grow wings and fly up to visit the Queen in Buck House.'

49

Arriving at Pendurran Farm never failed to give Maddie a warm feeling of pride, of truly coming home. Although she'd lived in many places, none of them had evoked the feeling that this hotchpotch of buildings did.

But the centre was more than just an odd collection of buildings: a barn that would soon need a new roof, a vegetable garden, a pig pen, a ramshackle shed for the two crazy goats and a fancy chicken coup. It was her life. Her happiness. Her security. Her reason to get out of bed each new day, even though some of those days might seem difficult to others.

She sighed as Gertie pulled the car into the yard.

'You okay?' asked her friend.

'Fine. Glad to be home. Been a strange day,' said Maddie. She thought again about the young man. What an odd thing for him to say. That he was her son. Of course, he'd got that wrong, had mistaken her for someone else. But it brought the sadness back to her, from that awful day. The cruel way they'd told her of her loss. First, the midwife, then the nurse. There'd been no kindness, only blame. *Move on with your life*, they'd said. Callous and insensitive.

A voice broke through her melancholy thoughts.

'Rusty's still getting free rides, then.' Gertie grinned and they both watched the cheeky hen launch herself at one of the pigs and perch on its back.

'Identity crisis,' said Maddie, and laughed.

'Yeah? She's come to the right place then,' said Gertie.

'Rusty's one crazy, mixed-up kiddie,' Maddie said. 'She lays eggs with the other hens, but she hops over the wire and steals the pigs' food. Doesn't know whether she's a pig or a hen. Can't imagine why the pigs put up with her.'

Maddie eyed the scene in front of her with satisfaction, like a proud parent.

Pendurran Farmhouse had once been a sad, neglected place. At least when she and Gertie had first arrived there, back in 1946. She'd had a second-hand caravan towed there and had immediately started planning, making drawings, excitement oozing from every pore. Excitement for a future free from bombs and sadness and fear. A future inscribed with hope. Hope that they could both find peace here. And maybe even do some good.

The refuge idea had been Maddie's. Gertie had lent her practical skills, apparently happy to be led, willing to go along with something that would take her mind off her sadness. Both women had stuck together, guiding each other through the residue of war. Making a new life. Offering a home to women scarred by war. Women with nowhere else to go. But Gertie had never truly been a country girl. Still, she'd given the project three years of her life. Had worked hard to help it succeed. Maddie knew why she'd done that; why she'd stayed so long – she'd done it for *her*. *The mark of a true friend*.

Maddie climbed slowly and laboriously out of the car.

A small dog immediately jumped at her. Barking and yelping a high-pitched welcome. It was the sort of greeting she'd come to expect from Wilma. Enthusiastic. Robust. Excited.

Punching way above her weight. For Wilma was a tiny dog, a Pembroke Welsh Corgi, and a useful ally on the busy smallholding. She was a natural herder, fast and agile, and had been known to round up many an escapee chicken making a bid for freedom.

'Good girl, Wilma!' said Maddie.

The dog stopped barking, satisfied her welcome had been understood, and cocked her head on one side in that smug, knowing way of hers.

Both women made their way up to the house, ignoring the shaggy-haired goats in the yard, eating the washing they'd ripped from the line.

———

Maddie felt a little better. A bit of fussing from a friend in her no-nonsense, tough-love way. A tiny powerhouse of a friend like Gertie Adams, who took the idea of loyalty seriously. Then there was the huge mug of tea, strong enough to float a spoon in, huge doorsteps of homemade bread lagged in creamy butter freshly churned at a neighbour's farm, chunky runner-bean chutney, and *real* cheese that crumbled into powerful little flavour bombs when it hit her tongue.

Surprising what a difference a friend giving you lunch can make. And sitting in a chair by an open fire, logs crackling away.

The strange noise in her ears – like a rushing waterfall – had retreated and Maddie could breathe normally again; the weird, spongy feeling in her legs had gone back to wherever it came from. Still, she didn't move, just carried on drinking her tea with her feet up. 'Raise them above your heart,' Gertie had ordered. 'It's good for you.'

Her friend came and sat down in the chair opposite. Gertie warmed her hands by the fire. It was September, a cold day, and the farmhouse wasn't perfectly insulated against the cold; despite the cob walls, draughts found their way in.

'Right,' said Gertie. 'Forget about the rampant goats and the leaky roof in the barn.' Her face became serious. 'You need to start thinking about yerself. That episode this morning in the café, it was the universe giving you a warning. You fainting like that. You got to start looking after number one for a bit and stop worrying about this place. Take yerself off for a wee holiday. Let them all get on with it for a change...'

'I can't do that,' said Maddie, appalled. 'People rely on me.'

'People? You've only got four of them, right now. Four grown-up people who could just as easily look out for themselves. *Strays*. You never could resist them.'

'I know, but...'

'No bleedin' buts. You collapsed this morning. You need to think about that, give yerself a rest.'

'I fainted this morning because...' She paused.

'Yeah – because?'

'Not because I was tired or sick. *Or* overdoing things. I love it here. It's my reason for being, for living, for carrying on each day through all the petty problems like paying bills, and goats that eat my laundry. It's what I do. It's what I love. Don't ask me to give that up.'

'Yeah, but you fainted. And don't tell me it's because you were hungry. I ain't that daft. You been hungry before and you ain't fainted.'

'I passed out because I'd had a shock, Gert. That's all. Nothing sinister, like health stuff. I'm perfectly okay, or at least I will be once I've had this little rest and the shock's worn off.'

'What shock? Look, I'm your best mate. Well, aren't I?'

'Of course.'

'I tell *you* everything. And I mean *everything*, girl. Including my love life. I reckon my Arthur would have a fit and lose even more of his hair if he had an inkling of the sort of stuff I told you about him and me. So...'

'It's complicated.'

'Tell me something that ain't.' Gertie laughed.

'It all happened a long time ago, during the war, before I even met you. And I've never told anybody about it.'

'So? Maybe it's time, then,' said Gertie.

'Yes,' said Maddie and sighed. 'You're right. Maybe it *is* time.'

'Wait. I'm *right*?'

'Sure. Haven't I always said you're a very wise woman, Gertrude Adams? So, *yes*, you're right. "*The time has come, the Walrus said, to talk of many things...*"'

'And one of those things? That would be this Rudi, would it?'

'Yes,' said Maddie. '*Rudi.*' She whispered the name. A sad, plaintive sound.

The fire was warm on her face as she stared into its depths, and Maddie Brady was surprised at just how easy it was to slide back into the past. 'It's *all* about Rudi,' she said.

50

29 SEPTEMBER 1957

PENDURRAN, CORNWALL

The sound of Gertie throwing logs on the fire pulled Maddie from her reverie. It catapulted her brutally from the past and her memories of Rudi, the time they'd spent together, to the present. The day after her fortieth birthday, sitting here in the farmhouse parlour in her beloved Cornwall.

She was cold, didn't know how long she'd been sitting there, narrating a story that belonged to the past. Was it real or a fantasy her mind had conjured up? A love story that the passage of time had turned into an exotic fiction? Maybe she had simply made him up, this handsome German, and he was nothing more than a wish. A dream. A dashing hero whose face she could no longer visualise. Only in dreams. He often came to her in dreams, and then his face was perfectly clear.

She had told Gertie everything. Held nothing back. Including the curious visit from the young man and his bizarre and impossible claim that she was his mother.

'So, this is *it*? The secret you couldn't *bear* to share. Not even with your best friend?' Gertie's voice held a sharp, cutting edge. And she flung the logs angrily, sending cascades of tiny sparks flying up the chimney.

'That's not fair, Gert. I made you a promise. That I'd tell you about a German I knew. And I'm keeping that promise.'

'Oh, sure! VE night. That's when you made that promise. And it only took twelve bleedin' years.'

'C'mon, Gert. Better late than never.'

'And don't try that. Don't make this into a joke. It ain't no bleedin' joke, Madds. Just admit it...'

'What?'

'You didn't trust me with your secret. This Rudi was the love of your life. The father of your child. You don't think I'd have understood that? We're like sisters, Madds.'

'I know. And that's why I couldn't tell you, not then. Didn't want to get you in trouble. He was an enemy. I'd been fraternising with the enemy...'

'Sure, I get that. But the war was over. You could have told me, right there in the park that night.'

'No, it was too soon. I'd no idea where Rudi was, where he'd gone when I left Gunwalloe. It could have been treason, the things I did. No way I'd drag you into that.'

'But it was a hell of a burden to carry by yerself. To take through the war with you. Wondering where he was. If he was alive or dead.' Gertie's voice tapered off into a whisper. 'I know how that feels,' she said.

And of course, she did. They had both lost men they'd loved. Pals they'd loved. Babies they hadn't had a chance to love.

Gertie was right: they were sisters, in more ways than one.

The fire grew cheery again, its heat comforting, leaving a pink flush on Maddie's cheeks. Or maybe that was the memory of Rudi.

'I'll get some tea,' said Gertie. 'We both need it.'

Tea. *Good for what ails you.* Maddie thought back to the WVS heroes with their huge tea urns. Those women were right, a cup of tea never hurt. The British answer to problems great and small. She managed a smile.

A heavy weight felt as if it had suddenly slipped from her shoulders and maybe now, finally, she could draw a line under those years of war. They hadn't all been bad; some had been good. Friendships endured if you were lucky. Hers and Gertie's. And although they'd both been sad about friends they'd lost, memories of Betty and the brilliant times they had all shared by the pool in Sunnyfield and the picnics eating cold rice pudding could still make them laugh.

'Get that down you. It'll warm you up,' said Gertie, and she handed over one of the tin mugs salvaged from their ATS kit. A souvenir. A happy reminder of their old billet.

'Ta.'

'Brought you some seedy cake as well.'

'Hummm, that's good,' said Maddie. 'I love seedy cake. You made it?' she asked.

'Don't sound so surprised, I can be domestic,' said Gertie. 'Now, we need to talk.'

'Thought we'd done that already,' said Maddie.

'This lad...'

'What lad?' asked Maddie, her mouth full of seedy cake.

'You know exactly which lad. The one who's turned up with Rudi's photograph.'

Maddie didn't speak. She was still conveniently battling with a rogue seed that had stuck between her teeth.

'How d'you suppose he got that? And why would he say he's your son, Madds? Kind of odd, don't you think?'

'Of course, it's bloody odd,' said Maddie, angrily. 'I don't have a son; you *know* that, Gert. A son would have been great. Kids would have been great, but...'

'And yet he's sure you're his mother. Odd. And the photograph. Don't it make you wonder how he got it? I mean, you said they took it away from you at that awful place.'

'They did.'

'So, how come it turns up in the pocket of a tall, skinny lad from Munich with acne on his face?'

'How would I know?'

'Well, now, that's a real puzzle,' said Gertie. She had that determined look on her face. One that Maddie recognised as her friend's dog-with-a-bone look. No way Gertie was about to give up that bone if she could help it. It made her who she was. A determined, bloody-minded woman, and a champion of the under-dog. A friend with true grit.

'Yes.'

'And we need to find the answer. So, finish your tea,' ordered Gertie Adams. 'We'll go and look for this lad. Ask him his name. And then, you and I are going to this place in St Agnes.'

'*Rosemundy?*' gasped Maddie. 'No. I can't go back to Rosemundy. Never. Not ever!'

'Oh? You sure?'

'Besides, it won't even be there. Times have changed. They don't shame pregnant women or send them to cruel homes for unmarried mothers anymore. We're more civilised now.'

'Think so?' asked Gertie. Her expression became serious. 'Then why don't we go and find out?'

They went together to the centre of Pendurran village, although Gertie insisted on driving, claimed that Maddie still looked a bit on the peaky side.

The first place they tried was about to close for the day. It was a quiet time of year and the Old Forge was more of a teashop than a restaurant, locking its doors before the sun went down, leaving evening meals to the village pub. It was an arrangement that suited both places. The Boar's Head didn't sell toasted teacakes and the Forge didn't sell beer. That way everybody got along.

The bell tinkled as Maddie pushed open the door. Rachel, the young waitress, moved swiftly from behind the counter, ready to head off any late customer at the pass.

'Oh, it's you, Miss Madeline. We're not serving...'

'That's fine, Rachel. We've not come for food. That young man who was in here this morning...?'

'The one what tried to help when you got poorly?'

'Did he?' asked Maddie.

'Did he what, miss?'

'*Help.*' Maddie tried to be patient with the waitress but Rachel's head was more often stuffed full of useless facts about celebrities and film stars than it was with weightier subjects like world hunger or how the universe worked.

'He left, Miss Madeline. Right after you came round a bit.'

'Any idea where he went?' asked Gertie, sharply. She didn't have Maddie's patience, figured life was too short to waste any of it.

'Maybe he went to your place. I gave him your address. Hope I did right, miss.' Rachel bit her lip.

'It's okay, Rachel. Don't worry, we'll find him,' Maddie said. 'You just lock up and go home.'

The girl looked relieved, and Maddie headed for the front door, her friend in her wake.

'Not the Brain of Britain, is she?'

'Head in the clouds,' said Maddie, 'but she's a good kid.'

'Wouldn't have lasted five minutes in the regiment,' said Gertie. 'She'd have been on jankers most of the time. They're building kids real soft these days.'

'Jankers, is it?' laughed Maddie. 'And wasn't it you scrubbing barrack room floors when we first met? If anybody knows about jankers, Private Gertrude Adams, it's you!'

. . .

They found him in the farmhouse yard, throwing sticks for Wilma. *How happy he looked*, thought Maddie. *How young*.

'Maybe it's time we had a talk,' she told him. Not unkindly. She couldn't imagine anyone wanting to be unkind to this lad. It would be like hurting a puppy. His face had an earnest, innocent look. It spoke of a lack of guile, a naivety. But the eyes gave lie to that. They were deep-set, probing eyes, which didn't belong on his face. Experienced eyes that had seen too much. Been hurt often. And their colour?

Dear God, they were the coolest blue.

They were Rudi's eyes.

'We can speak, then?' he asked her. 'I'd like that very much,' he continued, eagerly. 'We've so much to talk about. I've waited years to hear your voice.'

'Yes,' Maddie nodded. 'We *must* speak, you and me. We need to sort this out. Clear up the confusion.'

51

1 OCTOBER 1957

CORNWALL

Maddie drove the car in silence. She didn't feel like speaking about any of it, about either the meeting with the young man who called himself her son, or the way her friend Gertie had forced her into this trip to St Agnes. To the house that held such potent memories for her.

She found his extraordinary story far-fetched, hard to believe. Travelling to Germany from Cornwall and him only fourteen years old? Searching for Rudi in Bavaria? *Fiction*, she thought. A vivid imagination at work. Yet there were parts of his story that seemed credible, like the fact he had been given away by his mother at birth and had lived much of his young life under the brutal regime of a heartless orphanage.

His claim that he had finally traced his birth back to Rosemundy House might of course be true. Lots of babies had been born there. Maddie had seen many of them. And his date of birth! If it was true, it was the very same day her baby had been stillborn. But then several mothers had given birth that day. She'd heard their screams as she lay next door in the lying-in room, tears for her lost baby choking her, her body shaking with the shock of it.

But one part of this young man's story was so obviously *untrue* that it convinced Maddie the whole thing was simply a fantastic tale he'd pulled from his imagination. A fantasy he'd wanted to believe. Why had he done that? A sad young man living in an orphanage looking for someone to love him... you could understand, perhaps, that he needed a family to replace the one that had rejected him.

The weak link was so glaring, in fact, that she hadn't even wanted to go to Rosemundy to find out, but Gertie had pushed her into it. For the young man had spoken in such glowing terms about the matron that it was obvious to Maddie he had never set foot in the place – 'A wonderful, sensitive and caring woman,' he'd said. They'd spoken for a long time, he claimed. He made the dreadful woman sound like a saint.

That was when Maddie had told him to leave her house.

Gertie produced a loud, theatrical sigh. 'Nearly there, are we?'

Maddie didn't answer. She had a mind to turn back and forget the whole stupid business. The last place she wanted to visit was a home for unmarried mothers in St Agnes. That's if it even still existed.

'What you make of it?' Gertie tried another tack. 'The lad. What he's calling himself, I mean.'

'Anybody can call themselves what they like. That doesn't mean anything.'

'Yeah, but Charlie Brady?'

'He picked my name out of a hat, Gert. Who knows what his game is?'

'I know, but... well, he seemed such a nice young man. Not like a fraud.'

'You'll see. Once you meet Miss Robertson, you'll understand,' said Maddie.

'Who?'

'This saintly woman he claims he met in St Agnes. She

doesn't exist. Only in his head. The matron,' she added bitterly, when Gertie looked confused. 'The place was grim. And it was her fault. She was the one in charge. Miss Robertson believed in punishment, not kindness. A religious zealot, the Old Testament kind. But she was the devil, not a saint.' The hate exploded from Maddie's lips and surprised her. Her face reddened with embarrassment and shame. *How could the woman still make her this angry after all these years?* Maddie was upset, mostly with herself, that such an ancient hurt still had the power to wound her.

'Blimey!' said Gertie. 'She sure did a job on you, Madds.'

'Sorry. No point going off like that.' Maddie shrugged her shoulders. 'But it's hard to forget. Even harder to forgive.' Maybe she never would.

'So, they were all witches, like her?'

'No, not all. Some of the girls were nice, others were real bitches. But looking back, I guess they had their reasons. Many of them were just scared at being pregnant and lonely. Away from home for the first time. Some had parents who threw them out, disowned them.'

'And the staff?'

'Sister Bennett! She was the midwife, not a friendly woman.' Maddie gave an ironic shrug.

'No?'

'*Vindictive. Sadistic.* Pick one,' said Maddie. 'I guess she was even worse than Matron, because she made it her business to make you suffer. Especially when you were in labour. "*Pain is cleansing.*" That was one of hers. She thought we all deserved the pain. We were sinners, had brought it on ourselves by being so wicked.'

'God Almighty! *They* were the wicked ones.'

'Not all of them. There was one angel.'

'There was?'

'Sure. One special angel. A nurse. A young girl, around

eighteen. She was better than the whole lot put together. A really sweet girl. Ethel, her name was.' Maddie screwed her face up, tried to remember the girl's last name. 'Nurse Ethel Ryder, that was her,' she said in triumph. 'She never judged you like the others. And she was kind – sometimes she got in trouble for it, but it didn't stop her. We talked for a long time, the two of us. About our lives, our families. People we loved. And she used to sneak food into me when I'd been confined to my room as punishment. Sister Bennett believed in punishment; did I tell you that?'

A plump tear suddenly made its way down Maddie's face, stung her cheek. *Stupid, silly woman.* She hadn't meant to cry.

'Blimey,' said Gertie with passion. 'I'm sorry, Madds.'

'What for? You didn't do anything.'

'For pushing you to come here. If I'd known how grim it was, well – I'd never...'

'No apology needed. We're mates. You did it for the best. And, who knows, maybe it'll work out fine and I can lay this bloody ghost forever.'

'We're here?' asked Gertie. 'Pretty place. I've never been to St Agnes before.'

'Nearly there,' said Maddie.

She turned the car into Rosemundy Hill, past the cottages and granite homes that looked the same as she'd last seen them. And a weird feeling worked its way through her. A powerful sort of déjà vu. But not a good remembering: it took her to an upsetting and eerie place in her head that had nothing to do with logic or reasoning.

And there it was at the bottom of the hill. She didn't know what she'd been expecting. That a bomb had fallen on it? That the place had been demolished?

Maddie drove the car in through the entrance and stared up at the building in front of her in disbelief.

Gertie let out the breath she'd been holding onto. 'This it? This the place?'

Maddie could hardly speak. The trauma of being there again, and the surprise at the change in it. She grabbed her friend's hand as they headed to the huge front door. Her own hand was trembling.

'Yes, this is it. But it's not the same,' she said.

'Things change, I guess,' said Gertie. 'The war and everything.'

'It's beautiful. *Majestic*,' said Maddie. She breathed in the cool air, the scent of pine trees.

The old house was no longer a crumbling wreck, and the grey stone that had been so depressing had transformed into a sparkling white. Tubs of winter flowers splashed their colour against the gleaming white walls, vivid yellow pansies vied for attention with the red and purple of cyclamens. The change was breath-taking.

'There aren't any prams on the lawn. They used to always put the babies out in the air every day after their feeds. Spring, summer, autumn, even winter. Didn't matter, long as it wasn't raining. Matron reckoned it was good for them. Hardened them up.'

'What, like putting your seedlings outdoors to harden off, you mean?' Gertie laughed.

'The laundry,' said Maddie, and she tugged at Gertie's sleeve. 'I worked in there.' She pointed at a spot on the far lawn where the lean-to for the laundry had been. 'It's gone,' she said in amazement.

'But this is definitely the place?' asked Gertie.

'Rosemundy House,' she said, reading the brass plate on the front door. 'That's new, but this is the place, all right.'

'Right then,' said Gertie, and she pushed the front doorbell.

Then it was too late. There was no turning back, even if Maddie had wanted to.

52

'Are you expected?' asked the girl who answered the door. She looked very young, as if she'd just become a teenager, but then all young people looked like that to Maddie now, a symptom of getting older maybe.

'I shouldn't think so,' answered Maddie.

'We'd like to speak to someone in charge,' said Gertie. Her voice held the familiar note of authority that it sometimes did when she wanted to cut to the heart of things.

Maddie was glad of it. Glad her friend had taken the reins and seemed to be in charge. She was still finding it hard to control the tremble in her hands and had balled them into tight fists.

'Matron, you mean. I'm not sure if she's in her office or on rounds. I haven't seen her this morning.' The girl finally smiled. 'But if you'd like me to look...'

'Maybe we could come in,' said Maddie, her tone polite.

The girl had been standing in the entrance, holding onto the door, barring the way like a sentry on guard. Like another sentry Maddie remembered from long ago, less friendly than this one.

'Oh, yes. Sorry.' She opened the door wider and directed them to the upholstered chairs in the reception hall, then scuttled away to find the woman in charge.

Matron. She was the last person on earth that Maddie wanted to see or speak to; she was having a struggle to stop her breakfast forcing its way up her throat. She fought hard to control the dark feeling of impending doom that being in this place re-ignited in her.

And it was foolish, for this woman could no longer hurt her, had no power over her now. So why should she allow herself to be terrorised by it all? Being back there, she supposed. But it was different now, and she was no longer alone, having to face the anger of this matron or the hurtful barbs and jibes of Sister Bennett, the midwife. Now she had Gertie. A friend tried and tested and true. An ally ready to do battle.

Maddie's eyes went to the floor beneath her. She'd been on her hands and knees scrubbing those stone flags until her hands had lost all feeling, her back ached and her knees were rubbed raw.

She got up from the seat and began to pace.

The young woman returned and looked at them both in turn, unsure who she should address.

'Yes?' said Maddie.

'Matron would like to know the nature of your visit.' She looked again from one to the other. 'And who may I tell her is calling?'

'You may tell her that Madeline Brady would like to see her.'

'*And* Gertrude Adams,' added Gertie, haughtily.

'Regarding what?' the girl asked.

'Just tell her one of her old girls has come back for a visit,' said Maddie. 'Always good to chew over old times, don't you think?' Maddie winked. She didn't usually resort to sarcasm.

Maybe I should, she thought. Because, suddenly, she felt a whole lot better. A whole lot chirpier.

'Oh, I see. Well, they sometimes do that.'

'They do?' asked Maddie, shocked.

'Some of them are quite nostalgic,' said the girl. 'They bring their children back to visit.' She smiled and bustled off again to the matron's office.

Maddie gave up her pacing and slumped back down into the seat. Chirpiness could only get you so far.

'I'm coming in with you, Madds.'

'You don't have to. I've come this far, I might as well face the old witch in her den.'

'Yeah, but you ain't doing it alone. I'm the one dragged you here. And after what you told me about the old bat, I want to match her eyeball-to-eyeball.'

'Don't worry, Gert. She can't intimidate me anymore.'

'I'm pleased to hear it,' said a voice from behind them. 'Now, if you ladies would like to follow me, I think this is a conversation best carried out in my office.'

They stood up to follow the woman, and Gertie threw a questioning look in Maddie's direction, mouthed the words, 'Who is she?'

Maddie just shrugged, as she had no idea who it was.

They followed her into an office marked *Private*. Maddie and Gertie each took a seat on one side of a large paper-strewn desk, and the young woman settled herself behind it, picked up a telephone. 'Tea, ladies?' she asked, her voice friendly.

The enquiry threw Maddie, for she'd been readying herself for full battle mode. But she nodded and the woman spoke into the phone.

'Ah, Cook, tea for three in my office? And if you could run to a few biscuits as well, that would be lovely. Really? You're a gem. I'm sure these ladies would be delighted to sample your saffron buns.' She looked directly at Maddie. 'Lilly makes the best Cornish saffron buns you'll ever taste,' she said, and returned the phone to its cradle. 'Now, would you like to talk before we have our tea, or wait until our mouths are stuffed full of saffron buns?' she laughed.

'I don't know quite where to begin,' said Maddie. 'It's confusing. I was expecting to talk to the matron, and it's a bit of a delicate matter.'

'No doubt it is, Maddie,' the woman said.

'*Maddie*? You know me?'

'How could I ever forget you, Maddie Brady? And I *am* the matron.'

'But I don't understand. The matron, she was old and crusty and...' And then it came to her. How stupid she'd been to worry about seeing Matron again. Even *then* the woman had been ancient, of course she wouldn't be there after all these years. But the trauma and the memory of this place had been preserved in Maddie's mind, trapped in amber, as if nothing had changed.

'Matron was harsh, that's true. She was a bitter old woman, Miss Robertson. And she often took out her own frustrations on the girls. At times, this wasn't a happy place. And I've made it my job to change all that, Maddie.'

'You knew her? Did you work here, then?'

'You've forgotten me. Or maybe you don't recognise me. Sixteen years can change a person a lot. I was young. I'm older and maybe a little wiser too. Enough to know that a place like this can be run properly and thrive on love rather than fear.'

'But how—?'

'We talked such a lot, you and me. I was a young nurse then, but I've never forgotten how you fought to keep your baby when Matron tried so hard to persuade you to give it up. That's why I couldn't understand what happened.'

'You're *Ethel*? Nurse Ethel Ryder?' asked Maddie. 'What – and now you're the matron, is that what you're saying?'

'Hold on,' interrupted Gertie. '*You're* Maddie's angel?'

'Maddie's what?' asked Ethel.

'Madds told me everybody here was a witch, apart from one real angel called Nurse Ethel. And is that you?' Gertie asked. 'I'm confused.'

'Looks like you're not the only one,' said Maddie. 'I can't believe this. Maybe what the lad said was true. He said he met with the matron, a wonderful, caring woman. And I didn't believe him. Because Miss Robertson was never a caring woman.'

'No, I don't suppose many would describe her that way,' said Ethel, and she sighed. 'But we've all got our reasons for being how we are. And that's why I didn't judge her. Or *you*, Maddie, when you did what you did. Although, I must admit that it surprised me. Especially knowing how much you'd looked forward to having your baby. I just couldn't believe you would give him away like that. But, like I said, no judgement. Who are we to judge each other?'

'What! You think I gave my baby away?' said Maddie, angrily. 'No!' she screamed. 'That's a lie! And you weren't even here. You were off looking after your mother when I went into labour. I prayed you would come, but you didn't, and that awful, sadistic midwife just laughed every time I had a contraction. You think I'd go through all that and then give my baby away?'

There was a knock on the door and the tea arrived, carried in by the young girl who had opened the front door to them. She carefully set down the buns on separate plates as if she were a waitress in a teashop and then left quietly. Maybe she was glad to leave. Had felt the tense atmosphere in the room. Maddie wished she could have left too.

'Look,' said Ethel Ryder, 'you must calm yourself down. I

didn't mean to upset you, but it seems that some wires have been crossed here. Some simple miscommunication has taken place.'

'You bet it has,' said Maddie. 'I went through a long and painful labour only to have a stillborn baby. And that witch of a midwife told me that my dead baby was God's retribution for sinners.'

'Wait. Sister Bennett told you your baby had *died?*'

'It *had* died,' said Maddie. 'She smacked its bottom and it didn't cry and she gave me something to make my milk dry up. Then they packed me off to Redruth hospital.'

'I see,' said the matron, thoughtfully. 'And did she ask you to sign anything, before you went to Redruth?'

'Yes,' said Maddie. 'Some sort of discharge thing. Sister Bennett said it meant I could leave here. She said it was a release that I needed to sign.'

'And you didn't read it?' asked Ethel.

'No, I didn't read it. I was upset. I'd just lost my baby and I wanted to leave.'

'So, Matron – what did Maddie *really* sign?' asked Gertie.

'Papers releasing her from any more connection with her baby. Adoption papers. You gave your baby up, Maddie. Although they never managed to find anyone to adopt him, and he ended up in an orphanage.'

'You mean that heartless midwife tricked me – and my baby was alive? And the poor little mite thought I gave it away?' Maddie sat in silence, stunned by the monumental news.

'The cruel cow,' said Gertie. 'Why would she do that?'

Maddie forced herself to remember. Her voice came out in a flat, emotionless monotone and as she stared hard into Ethel Ryder's calm face, her own face felt frozen: 'God's retribution for sinners, the woman told me. And she was so superior, standing there in judgement.' Maddie's voice faltered now. 'I smacked her across her smug, self-righteous face.'

'Good for you,' said Gertie. 'She deserved it.'

'Yes? But maybe if I hadn't done that, she'd have given me my baby. Instead, she told me I'd be sorry. I didn't know what she meant.' Maddie clasped her hands tightly in her lap. 'That's when she gave me the papers to sign.'

Ethel Ryder cleared her throat discreetly. It was either that or give way to the tears that threatened to overwhelm her. She'd taught herself to be strong, for her job there was often a challenge that brought sadness in its wake.

'I'm so sorry, Maddie,' said Ethel. 'But it makes sense to me now. It didn't before and that's what I told Charlie Brady when he came to see me. I couldn't understand why you put the lad up for adoption when you wanted your baby so much, had fought desperately for him. I told him that! But I don't know if he believed me. Because he said he was going to look for his father, instead of his mother. For how could a mother give her son away? That's what he asked me, Maddie. And I didn't know what to tell him. Many women here have been broken-hearted, have had to give up their babies, not because they wanted to, but because they had no choice. But you – you were so adamant that you would not give up your child! And I couldn't understand what changed your mind. *But I do now*. And I'm so very sorry.'

'So, you're telling me that this young boy really is my son? Is that what you're saying, Ethel? Absolutely no doubts?'

'No doubt about it,' said the matron.

'Dear God!'

'Hey, Maddie, you're not gonna faint again, are you?' said Gertie.

She didn't. She felt bitterness and anger towards the midwife who had cheated her of years with her child. And guilt as well. For Charlie Brady had been cheated too, of people who would love him. But anger was such a negative emotion and exhausting to keep up, so she exchanged it for happiness. Found a smile.

She had a *baby*. A rather tall baby, one with a voice that had already broken and spots on his face. But the best bit was that he had Rudi Fischer's eyes. She and Rudi had a baby. How could she possibly top that?

53

They all drank their tea and ate their saffron buns. Maddie didn't even taste hers – she was in a dreamlike state.

'So many questions,' she said. 'I've got so many that need to be answered. Confusing things that I can't get straight in my head.'

'I imagine so,' said the matron. 'And I'll try my best to answer them, but some things I can only guess at. You'll have to fill in the blanks yourself.'

'And this witch of a midwife – she needs to come in here right now and face the music,' said Gertie, angrily. Her face was getting redder and the large port wine stain on her neck had deepened in colour and intensity: it was her battle face.

Maddie was proud to have her as a friend. *A loyal companion who would walk through fire and flood for you.*

'I understand your passion, Gertrude,' said Ethel Ryder, 'but unfortunately there's no way we can speak to Sister Bennett. Her methods weren't the kind I encourage, and our philosophies varied greatly.'

'You're saying you gave her the push?' asked Gertie.

'She was unkind; it wasn't the sort of treatment I could

tolerate. Our girls are already frightened enough about giving birth without an intolerant midwife making it worse. So, yes, I asked her to leave.'

'Maybe you're happy to leave it there, Matron,' said Gertie. 'But we ain't. She needs to answer for what she did. Face to face. And I got some questions for her, even if Maddie don't.'

'Then I'm afraid you'll need to shout,' said Ethel. 'For Sister Bennett has left us for the hereafter. I went to her funeral last year. Not many did.'

'Well, I hope the man upstairs forgives her,' said Gertie, raising her eyes to the ceiling, to some invisible kingdom. "Cause I for one *never* will. Not for what she put my friend through. The pain and the anguish of losing a child, and all the time that poor little kid was out there thinking his mother hated him.'

'It's okay, Gert.' Maddie smiled wanly at her friend. 'But I want to forget her now. I need to think about this lad. My son. *Our* son,' she said in wonder. 'He knows who his father is. How does he know that? And how did he get Rudi's photograph?'

'Charlie found his birth certificate in the orphanage files; he told them he was going to leave, and it looks like they didn't care whether he stayed or left. He said he never fitted in, and when he saw that he was born here, he came looking for the place and to find out about his father. The certificate registered the father as *unknown*.'

'So, he asked you about his father?' said Maddie.

'You'd told me his name, remember?' said Ethel Ryder. 'Rudi Fischer from the beautiful Alpine village of Ramsau.'

'You remembered!' said Maddie.

'Of course I did. You were in love with the man. It didn't matter that he was a German, or a prisoner of war. So, if it didn't matter to you, why should anyone else sit in judgement?'

'And the photograph?'

'When I came back and you were gone, I took it from Matron's office. Kept it safe.'

'Even though you thought I was a bad mother?'

'I didn't understand what made you change your mind, Maddie, and give him up for adoption. Still, something told me there must be a good reason for it. But you know what they were like, Matron and Sister Bennett, they didn't encourage questions. I was young then, maybe not as courageous as I should have been. I regret that, but I've tried to make up for it.'

'You were always kind,' said Maddie. 'It must have been difficult. You sometimes got in trouble for helping us, so you can't blame yourself.'

Ethel Ryder simply shrugged. 'The past is the past. It's gone. All that matters now is how we deal with the present and make things better for the future and the next generation. What will you do about your son?'

'Well, if he still wants to see me, I'll try to build some bridges. Ask him to forgive me. I sent him away. Told him I didn't believe him. Going to Falmouth, working his passage on a ship to Hamburg? At just fourteen years old? It sounded like a fiction, a lie. And how did he make it to Bavaria to find Rudi? Fantasy, that's what I told him. Pure fantasy.'

'Then ask him to explain,' said Ethel. 'And do what other families do. Just love him, and support him.'

Maddie nodded, but she had no idea what other families did. Her own family was hardly an outstanding example of love or support. Would they take an illegitimate child to their bosom? A young man whose father had been a captured German prisoner of war? She could think of no circumstance where her mother would welcome such a grandson. Phyllis Brady would consider it a disgrace, an embarrassment, and her bosom would be the same icy place it had always been. There would be no warmth or protection that being part of a family implied. But the loss would be her mother's.

And as for Maddie, she would try and make up for the past. For the hurt she'd caused this young man, Charlie Brady. If he still wanted her, that was. If she could find him. She'd told him to leave her house.

'Thank you for your kindness, Ethel. And for stealing Rudi's picture back. And being my angel when I needed one. The world still needs angels,' said Maddie. She went over and hugged the matron.

'That's a lot to live up to,' said Ethel Ryder. 'But I'll do my best.'

They had had another cup of tea and talked of other things, all three women doing their best to find a calm after these revelations.

'Right, we're going home,' Maddie said to Gertie. 'I need to go and find my son. See if he still wants me.'

'Would you like to look around, meet some of girls before you leave? You could visit the nursery. You'll find it a whole lot sunnier than it was before. We painted it yellow. And we've just had two beautiful new arrivals. Twins,' said Ethel, proudly. 'A boy and a girl. Sweet as buttons. They've been holding each other's hands through their cots.'

Maddie thought about the friend beside her. It was many years since Gert had lost her baby, but it wasn't something you could easily forget. Looking at someone else's children in a nursery – it was a pain she couldn't inflict on her dearest, most treasured friend. Maddie had discovered her son, but Gertie would never see her daughter, Alice. Would never hold her in her arms.

'A nice thought,' said Maddie. 'Maybe another time.' But it was a lie. The kind of white lie you told when the truth might hurt.

'You're welcome anytime, both of you,' said Ethel, kindly. 'Don't forget us. The home can always use good friends.'

As she headed to the car, Maddie looked back over her shoulder. One final look at Rosemundy House. The matron's words still echoed in her head: *Don't forget us*. And while it was true that Maddie would never forget the place, she knew that she would never go back there again.

54

Maddie didn't argue with Gertie about who should drive them home to Pendurran. Instead, she settled back into the passenger seat and allowed everything she'd just learned to filter through to her senses. All these new and novel thoughts needed to marinate in the soup of her brain.

It wasn't easy to put emotions aside. To be logical and rational. But she would need to, because getting angry with the midwife who had tricked her would be useless. The woman was dead.

When they got home to the farmhouse, everything seemed fine. No fire engulfing the place. No flood. No escaping hens, or goats pulling washing from the line. All things she'd conjured up in her head when she thought about leaving the others in charge. Instead, there was an air of tranquillity over the house and a note pinned to the door: ODD JOB MAN ROUND THE BACK FIXING WINDOWS, it said.

She headed for the back of the farmhouse and the odd job man who had arrived out of nowhere. She hadn't booked a handyman. She couldn't afford to pay one. Most of the stuff that went wrong at the centre was either given a bodged fix by

Maddie herself, or some kind, willing person from the village would barter their services in exchange for eggs.

Gertie, panting, as if this next breath might be her last, finally caught up. 'Nobody here, Madds.'

'No, but look at the window frame. That's a new piece of wood in there, and look at that.' Maddie touched the putty around the glass. 'It's still wet.'

'Yeah, but how...?'

'The disappearing handyman,' said Maddie. 'I don't know who's paying him. But it's not me.'

'Well then,' said Gertie, 'we need to find him. Maybe he's checking the place out, ready to come back and turn it over.'

Maddie laughed. 'You see anything here worth stealing?'

'I don't know. One man's meat and all that. Maybe he's interested in the chickens.'

'A chicken rustler? You think he's a chicken rustler?'

'Or the pigs,' added Gertie, darkly.

'A pig rustler, now?' Maddie laughed again.

She found him in the barn. He'd lifted the lid off a metal dustbin, was peering inside. He turned when he heard her come in, a guilty look on his face, but she watched it turn into a smile. Saw him drop his head, unsure of where to go from there.

'Sorry,' he said. 'I was curious.'

'Food for the livestock,' said Maddie. 'The metal keeps the mice and rats out.'

'I see,' he said.

She thought of this strange, mundane conversation and what she really wanted to say. Important things. Like asking forgiveness for when she'd sent him away. Saying sorry for the years she'd missed of his life, years when he'd been alone. And for not believing him.

'You fixed the window,' she said. 'Thank you.'

'I came to see you. And when I saw the window...'

'You fixed it,' she said. 'It was kind of you.'

'So, you don't mind? It's okay?' he asked.

Maddie smiled. 'It is *very* okay, Charlie. And maybe you'd like to stay to dinner? We could talk.'

'I should like that very much,' he said.

'Yes,' said Maddie. 'I would too. I'd like you to come and eat with us, like a family.'

'You would?' He looked pleased; except he clasped his hands tightly together in front of him. A nervous habit, Maddie was to discover. Something he did when he was unsure. 'But one thing...'

'Yes?'

'Can I ask you to use my name? I told you Charlie, before...'

'I don't understand,' said Maddie. 'Your name's not Charlie?'

'That's the name on my certificate,' he said.

'Birth certificate?'

'Yes. I thought maybe *you* named me this when you made the register so I tried not to upset you, told you I'm Charlie. You understand?'

'Not really,' said Maddie. 'There's not too much of this I understand. Why don't you tell me?'

'Charlie is the name written down, but *now* I call myself by the name my father told me he wanted for his son,' he explained.

Maddie's breath caught in her throat. 'Your name... your name is Gunter?'

'Yes.' He smiled. Seemed happy that she understood. '*Mein name ist* Gunter Fischer-Brady.'

'Gunter Fischer-Brady,' repeated Maddie. 'Well, Gunter Fischer-Brady, I am truly *very* happy to meet you.' She offered her hand and the young man shook it rigidly. And then he did something quite extraordinary, but so wonderful that it felt to Maddie as if the universe had tilted slightly on its axis.

Self-consciously, Gunter Brady hugged his mother. It was something he had hoped to be able to do one day, since he realised he had been abandoned. During all his years in the orphanage in Bristol, it was a moment he had secretly imagined.

Although they had told him he was an orphan, Gunter had never truly believed it. He desperately longed for parents. And in his heart, he knew that somewhere out there was a mother and a father, and at the age of only fourteen he had set out to find them.

55

NOVEMBER 1957

PENDURRAN, CORNWALL

'I don't know if I can do it, Gert.'

'What?'

'Gunter thinks I should write to his father. But I don't know if I can.'

'If that ain't the daftest thing I ever heard you say...'

'That's not fair.'

'What happened to the feisty woman who stole a staff car so I could have a twenty-first birthday to remember?'

'*Borrowed*,' said Maddie. 'Only borrowed.' But she smiled all the same.

'See?' said Gertie. 'I knew she was still in there. And that woman would never let fear get in her way.'

Gertie went home. At heart, she was a big-city girl – 'I can still be a friend from London,' she said. Maddie felt lost, but of course she couldn't keep her friend there forever. Gertie didn't live there anymore, and it had been selfish to keep her away from Arthur, the lovesick baker, for so long. Besides, Christmas wasn't far away – Gertie always came at Christmas, it was a tradition, and she stayed over for New Year.

Maddie wrote the letter to Rudi. Maybe the most important

letter of her life. Said she would love to meet him again, that he'd never left her head, *or her heart*. Told him that she'd finally met Gunter, the son they shared. And she was happy to go to Bavaria if he would like her to. It seemed surprising that Rudi was still single after all these years but there was no wife – and no one else in his life. Gunter had told her so.

She posted the letter and waited for him to reply.

And while she waited, she spent time with her son. They gradually grew closer, more used to each other's ways. They worked together during the day: he fed the animals and put a new roof on the chicken coop. And at night, they talked. He told her about the orphanage, how he'd felt different from the other boys, out of place, didn't feel like an orphan. That's why he'd searched their files, found his birth certificate and left for Rosemundy, clutching the one document that was proof of his being.

'And no one tried to stop you,' she asked. 'Even though you were only fourteen?'

'No one cared. They were happy for me to leave, I think. When I ran away, no one came after me.'

'So, you made your way to Rosemundy House, and Ethel Ryder gave you the photograph.'

'I'm sorry I believed what they told me there,' said Gunter. 'That you gave me away. It made me sad. But to find out who *mein Vater* was. To have his face in a photograph – that made me happy.'

'They tricked me, Gunter,' she said, 'told me you were dead. But it was *my* fault. I should have read the paper that I signed.'

'No, you were brave. To have a baby alone like that? There's no fault.'

He told her about his journey to Germany. She'd called his trip a fantasy, something his adolescent mind had conjured up, for how could he, so young, travel across a foreign land when speaking no German? But it was no delusion, it was real.

Maddie was amazed at her son's enterprise. His strength of mind and resilience. His courage.

'In Falmouth, I found a ship to Hamburg. I worked at everything they told me. All the *bad* jobs,' he said and laughed, remembering.

'It sounds awful,' Maddie said.

'It wasn't so bad,' said Gunter. 'I found a friend. Someone who took pity on me. A German sailor, from the engine room. An old man. He taught me a little German and lots of things about the ship. Where all the different pipes in the engine room went. One night we traced them all.'

'A friend?'

'He'd been a sailor in the *Kriegsmarine*, the German Navy, and was a captured prisoner of war. His wife was killed in Dresden, so the sea was his life. All he had. He knew I wanted to go to Ramsau, so he travelled with me to Berchtesgaden, said he wanted to see Hitler's home, the Berghof in the Obersalzberg.'

'And did you go there?' asked Maddie.

'There was nothing left but crumbling walls. He was disappointed. Then he put me on a bus from Berchtesgaden to Ramsau – it wasn't far.'

'And you found your father?'

'He was easy to find. Ramsau's a very small place. And everybody knew Herr Fischer.'

'Your father.'

'No, my grandfather, Gunter,' he said, with pride. 'The house was his.'

'Your grandfather...' said Maddie.

'He *died*. In a camp,' he told her, and allowed her to take his hand. To console him for the loss of his family: his grandfather, his uncle Werner.

'And Rudi?' she asked him. 'He lives there? In this house?'

'With my grandmother. Now the miracle of finding *you*,' said Gunter, 'that was my grandmother.'

'Your grandmother? But how...?'

'She wanted me to find you. She told me a son should know his mother, and a mother should know her son.'

'That's what you told me when we first met,' said Maddie. 'I remember.'

'Yes. And my grandmother got a friend to look for you. At least, the daughter of her friend. Magda, a girl from München. She works in a newspaper there. She wrote letters. Searched records in Cornwall,' said Gunter.

'But Cornwall? Why? That was a leap in the dark. I could have been anywhere,' she said.

'*Vater* – he said you liked it there. And Magda, she thought it would be a place to begin.'

'Magda, she sounds clever,' said Maddie.

'She is,' he said, emphatically.

'So, you lived with your father and grandmother. No one else?'

'Just the three of us,' he said.

And had Rudi talked much about her? she'd asked. And yes, it seems that Rudi Fischer had told their son about her, but Gunter's eyes had been unable to meet hers when he spoke of it.

And that's when she knew: the boy was hiding something from her. Maybe trying to shield her from pain.

Now Maddie waited for a letter, not with the excitement that she'd known, but with dread. Felt the chill of fear swamp her optimism. Tried to ignore the curious premonition that sadness, not celebration waited for her.

———

The letter, when it came, was full of grief and blame. She'd betrayed him, it claimed. Her hands shook as she read about the suffering he'd gone through in the camp. And she was to blame, for she'd given him up, the letter accused. An intelligence officer said that a lady soldier, a private in the ATS, had been responsible for his capture.

She had read about the camp at Cultybraggan. It sounded grim. There had been a prison riot and he'd been forced to take part.

And that was where he'd been hurt. Ribs broken, kidney ruptured, injuries that healed eventually, but the knife wound on his face had taken longer to mend. It had become infected, the swelling making him look like a monster. Some of the other prisoners had called him Quasimodo, like the hideous hunchback, repulsive and ugly.

Maddie tried to imagine him as ugly. And the dark moods that he spoke of. How he'd become a bitter man, his only consolation hate. Hate for his captors. For the German SS thugs, and for Hitler. He had tried to hate her as well, it seemed. But he couldn't do it. Still, he swore he could never love her again. Never wanted to see her. So, no! She could not come to Ramsau, to his home. She would not be welcome there.

The vicious letter made her cry.

When her son found her, he stayed beside her, helped her settle down.

'*Betrayal*, Gunter,' she said. 'That's what he accused me of. I would never have betrayed him! I loved him.'

'So why is *Vater* so sure?' he said.

'What?'

'Why does Father believe you gave him up?'

'An intelligence officer told him,' she said.

'A British officer?'

'I assume so.' Maddie shrugged. 'He was interrogated when they recaptured him.'

'So, this officer – he knew your name?' asked Gunter.

Her brow furrowed into deep lines as she thought about it. 'I'm not sure. Your father didn't say so, only that they'd been given information by a *lady soldier* – a private in the ATS. And

I was a private in the ATS, Gunter. And I'd just spent two days with your father. The dots connect, except—'

'—Except you didn't do it. You've told me you didn't, and I believe you.'

'Thank you,' she whispered. She had been beginning to doubt her own mind.

'So, we must find out,' said Gunter. 'I'll go.'

'Go where?' asked Maddie.

'I'll go to *mein Vater*. We must know what happened after you left him in Cornwall. Somewhere between then and the British taking him up again, there must be an answer.'

'Yes, but what?' said Maddie. She shook her head in despair.

'You were one woman soldier during this war, one private in this...'

'ATS,' she told him. 'The Auxiliary Territorial Service,' she added, proudly. 'The women's branch of the army.'

'And were there many women in it?' he asked.

'Oh, yes. Over 250,000 of us.' It was still incredible to think of it. All those women, all doing their bit to help towards the final victory.

'That's a lot. You must be proud.'

'I am,' she said.

'And many *privates*, you think? Were there many of those?'

'Many thousands, I should think. Though I can't be sure of the exact number.'

'So, if it wasn't *you* – you think maybe he could have met one of these thousands?' Gunter asked, a smile rolling across his face. 'It's not impossible.'

'No, not impossible,' she said, slowly. The thought had never crossed her mind. But just how plausible was it? True, the ATS had a lot of women just like her, scattered all over the country. But the idea seemed a little far-fetched. Like clutching onto a very thin straw and hoping it would hold you up.

'So – I shall go.' He stood up.

'You will?'

'Of course. We're family, yes?' Her son reached for her hand and held it.

'Yes,' she said. 'We are family, Gunter. Thank you,' she whispered.

She took him to the station. It was a sad goodbye, and she would miss him. Miss their conversations and his company. But Gunter said it was something he must do. His father needed to hear the truth: that his mother was innocent. Face to face, it was the only way to make sure. To convince him.

Maddie struggled with the jumbled, conflicted mess of emotions that the letter brought out in her. *Anger* that Rudi could think her capable of betrayal. *Sadness* that he seemed a bitter man. It made her heartsick that she'd been rejected, but she would accept it with dignity. For pride was Maddie's most powerful emotion. Pride and self-esteem. She had her pride, she would not beg for love.

56

DECEMBER 1957

PENDURRAN, CORNWALL

Gunter had been gone for a month when his letter came. He'd wanted to spend Christmas in Pendurran, he said, and he missed her. But his grandmother was ill. So, he would stay in Bavaria for the holidays and come home in the New Year.

Home, he'd called it, and the thought made her glad.

But no mention of Rudi's name, nor how things had gone. Except to say she might expect an extra Christmas gift from a German that she knew. But she wanted no gift from him. Only an apology, for treating her like a leper. And some thanks, for refusing to give him up all those years ago. She was a patriot who loved her country, but if loving Rudi had made her a traitor, then it was a price she'd been prepared to pay. A secret she'd been happy to keep. Still, life wasn't always fair.

Christmas was a quiet time. Somehow her heart wasn't in it. Still, she'd put up some lights and dug out the Christmas tree, but then Gertie had phoned. She couldn't make it, was feeling ill. But she and Arthur would be down for New Year's Eve as usual.

New Year's Eve was always a special celebration at Pendurran Farm. The villagers came, and there'd be pasties and cider and a barn dance. It was Maddie's way of paying back the kindness that she'd found in those around her: neighbours in Pendurran who had helped her find a new life and those who had scratched their heads when she explained what a 'retreat' was, but had still given her advice about the pigs and bought milk from her goats. Even when they could have bought milk cheaper from the shop.

————

He was waiting at the kitchen door. A shock she hadn't prepared for.

He looked different. Maddie tried not to stare, but her eyes fixed on his face. Although the penetrating blue of his eyes hadn't changed, it was a face that had been transformed. A scar ran down the side of it, from his left eye across the cheekbone to the bottom of his chin.

She allowed him into the kitchen. Watched as he filled the kettle for tea. Waited for him to speak. He tried to hold her hand, but she pulled away, and he nodded, seemed to understand. That it wouldn't be that easy.

'I've asked myself if I'd be brave enough,' said Rudi.

'Oh? To do what?'

'To ask for your forgiveness,' he said.

'I see,' said Maddie. 'And what did you decide?'

'That it was something I must do, something I owed you. An apology for being a proud and bitter man.'

'And judgemental,' she added.

'Yes,' he agreed. 'And I was wrong and misguided. A foolish man.'

'Betrayal, you said!'

'Yes, it was cruel. And unkind,' said Rudi.

'And untrue,' said Maddie.

'I blamed you for my capture,' he said. 'Now I'm ashamed.'

Maddie listened to the story of the young ATS private who had served him in the cookhouse at Predannack. How she had fussed over him, given him extra-large helpings. She had flaunted her charms in front of him. It was obvious to Maddie what the woman had wanted in return. But her sexual overtures had been wasted on Rudi, and he claimed her anger had been a puzzle. Until now.

'So, what changed?' she asked.

'Gunter was the key. He prompted me to remember, to see things a different way.'

She called him stupid and naive, and he agreed, took it on the chin. But she forgave him all the same, and her scorn had been short-lived. Not that it was easy. For either of them. Rudi had been bitter about those hard years behind the wire. He was reluctant at first to talk about his recapture, or where he had gone when Maddie left that morning in February 1941. She could see how hard it was for him to relive the trauma. But, slowly, the story emerged: his time at the airfield at Predannack, how he'd been beaten up in Helston and taken prisoner again. And the harsh camp at Cultybraggan.

She invited him to stay. But not in her bed. Didn't know if she could love him like before, for dark moods haunted him, and he seemed a different person to the one she'd first met in Church Cove: the man prepared to risk his life to rescue a young boy from the minefield.

Now, Rudi Fischer was a man who needed to be healed.

They spent the days together working on the farm. Decorating the barn with Christmas lights. Getting ready for New Year's Eve.

Her eyes moved to the man beside her. She recalled the Rudi from long ago. A fine man with strong values and principles. But he was only a man, not the *superman* she had built up in her mind. A man with feet of clay, unlike the one she had placed up there on a pedestal. But a good man all the same. A man who had lost his way. Now he was starting to find it again. His humanity, his humour, slowly coming back.

He seemed happier now. He still had dark moods and Maddie sensed she must be patient with him. But she thought it could be worth it. That she could learn to love him again.

And he too – she could see it in his eyes, that his love had come out of hibernation. Was slowly waking up, and with nurturing, it could be strong. Maybe even strong enough to build a future on.

She watched his eyes study her. Let him hold her hand. She told him about being pregnant, how she'd worried at first, and then the joy when she realised that a part of Rudi would always be with her. About carrying their baby through all the trying times in the mother and baby home. How his photograph kept her company, helped her stay strong.

'I should have been there,' Rudi said, sadly.

'You were,' said Maddie. 'You *always* were.'

'Have I told you what a magnificent woman you are? Bold and fearless,' he said. 'That's what I thought when you stood up to me that day on the cliffs. And beautiful, of course. I meant to tell you that, but I don't think I ever did.'

'And you—'

'—A man with false pride. A stupid man.'

'No,' she said.

Rudi looked at her, shook his head. 'Did Gunter never tell you how I treated him when he first sought me out?'

'No, he didn't say.'

'I don't suppose he would. He's a special young man, he wouldn't say bad things about me to you.'

'So...?'

'I feel ashamed. But I rejected him, refused to believe he was my son – *our* son.'

'But he had your photograph,' she said. 'And my name on his birth certificate.'

'I know. And in my heart, I knew it must be true: we are so much alike.'

'Two peas. One pod,' she said. 'So – you made it up to him?'

'I tried. Taught him how to rebuild an engine. How to chop wood.'

'He's an exceptional young man,' said Maddie.

'Yes, and none of our doing,' he said. 'We should have been there for him.'

'Nobody's fault,' she said. 'It was the war. We did what we could. And now we can make up for it. There's still time.'

'Sure, *time*. We've still got time,' said Rudi. 'Let's make the most of it.' He squeezed her hand.

And the kiss that followed was gentle at first. Maybe even a little tentative. It reminded her of that first kiss, back in the barn in Gunwalloe. And as their lips joined together, his passion grew, along with Maddie's.

When she looked into his eyes, she could see they were no longer grave, but smiling.

The man she had loved was back.

57

NEW YEAR'S EVE 1957

PENDURRAN, CORNWALL

They all sat around the farmhouse table having lunch. And it reminded Maddie of another New Year's Eve, many years ago now, back at the billet in Sunnyfield.

They'd laughed and sung and danced the conga and got in trouble over the blackout. And the miracle of the steak and kidney pie. And Betty's fabulous pickled onions. Who could ever forget that? Such small things had made them excited – and grateful.

'Dig in,' said Maddie. 'It's a help-yourself sort of lunch.'

The atmosphere was cheerful and convivial, friends breaking bread together, sharing jokes, happy to be alive. Rudi was the most relaxed she had seen him: the dark moods seemed to have fallen away. Now, apart from the scar on his face, he looked like the man she remembered from all those years ago in Gunwalloe. He smiled just as easily. And when Maddie told the others about his unsuccessful attempts to catch a fish for them in Church Cove all those years ago, Rudi laughed along with everyone else.

'My fishing skills are much improved,' he said.

'We would have starved,' said Maddie. 'If it hadn't been for some meat-paste sandwiches.'

'And those wonderful pasties. You still have those here?'

'They, like your fishing, are much improved – they've got meat in them now. We're having pasties at the party tonight,' she said.

'I look forward to eating one,' said Rudi. 'And that wonderful beer. You have that too?'

'Spingo,' explained Maddie to the rest of the table. 'No, I'm afraid we don't have any. Lots of cider, but no beer. I could always pop over to Helston and get some.'

'Really? That would be wonderful,' said Rudi. 'We could go together, maybe. It would be strange to see the place again. But if it's okay, I should like that.'

'Why not? Give me an hour and we'll go.'

'I go to the barn then,' said Rudi. 'Make the decorations for tonight.'

'Bales,' said Maddie.

'Bales?' he asked.

'Most of them go to the far end for the bandstand. And a few around the floor for folk to sit on.'

'The bandstand?' he said, confused.

'Alf Bingham – he plays his accordion, and Ted Trevelyan calls the dances. It's a barn dance.'

Later, Gertie helped clear the plates away.

'Need to talk to you, Madds. How would you like to be a bridesmaid at last? Although there ain't more than one, so I guess that makes you a maid of honour. And me a poor miserable cow with only one friend!' Gertie laughed.

'He's asked you to marry him? The romantic baker? But that's great.'

'Maybe it'll be catching,' said Gertie, and smiled.

. . .

Maddie drove Rudi to Helston. And they walked arm in arm through Coinagehall Street. *Like an old married couple.* The thought was a happy one. She could easily be content with this man beside her. They understood each other, had things in common. And they both had flaws. No one was perfect. She remembered someone telling her that years ago, but she couldn't remember who. And if people could recognise each other's imperfections, could make allowances, and live with them, give each other equal respect... *Well, it might make a partnership work.*

That kind of tolerance might even allow countries to get along better. Cut down on idiotic wars.

'I can hear your brain knocking,' said Rudi.

'Is it that loud?'

'Not so much. But there's a quirky little thing that you do with your eyes when you're concentrating. It's kind of sweet.'

'*Sweet!*'

'You don't want to be sweet?' asked Rudi.

'Sounds sappy,' said Maddie. 'And sickly,' she added.

'Okay,' he said. 'So, no sappiness allowed. How about attractive? Can I say that – that you look attractive? And intelligent – *obviously*. When you're thinking.'

'That'll do. Intelligent is always good.'

Rudi blew out some air. Slowed down their pace a little. 'Helston seems to be made of hills.'

'What? You don't have hills in Bavaria?'

'Proper ones,' he said. 'And we call them mountains.'

'Show off! Right, shall we get this beer, then? The Blue Anchor's right over there.'

'Why don't I buy it, and meet you at the hotel you told me about? We could have some tea,' said Rudi.

'Fine,' she said. 'You'll need to go out back to the pub yard – that's where they brew the Spingo.'

———

It took Rudi a while to find the kind of shop he wanted and the piece that was perfect for her. But when he'd found it, he knew: it had Maddie Brady's name written all over it. He hoped she would understand and that this wonderful woman would be pleased.

Buying the beer was easier. Four crates. He hoped he hadn't overdone it.

The Angel Hotel was easy to spot. He'd been outside it once before. It was the place the two policemen had jumped him years before, and beaten him up. The moment he'd lost his freedom. He hadn't been certain how he would feel, seeing it again. But he needed to do this – ghosts from the past couldn't be allowed to haunt the future.

'Don't let the past ruin the future.' That's what Maddie had told him. And she was right. 'You have to face up to your fears, spit in their eye,' she'd said.

And that's exactly what *she* had done. Refusing to give him up to the police or the camp guards. Putting her job and her freedom on the line for him. Choosing him over her country. Now he truly understood that sacrifice, knew how much she loved her country. And the courage it had taken to have their baby. All alone, facing the stigma of being unmarried, refusing to have the child adopted. She was single-minded. A brave and feisty woman. It was part of who she was, why he loved her.

———

Maddie was waiting at a table in the restaurant. When she saw him coming, she ordered tea for them both and a toasted teacake.

'Just the one teacake?' asked their waitress.

'Just the one,' said Maddie, then looked at Rudi as he sat down. 'Ghosts all gone?' she asked him. She'd guessed going there might have stirred up memories for him.

'Vanquished,' said Rudi.

'Conquered?'

'Beaten off with a stick.'

'Good,' she said. 'And the beer?'

'A very pleasant Cornishman promises to deliver it.'

The tea arrived and Maddie poured. Tea in delicate bone china cups. Bluebells decorating them and splashes of gold on the handles. So very different from the tin mugs of her ATS kit, but the tea had always tasted like heaven back then. Even though the taste had been watered down, tea leaves used over and over again.

She watched him struggle to get his large fingers through the tiny handle, saw him shrug and wrap both hands around the cup.

'Made for delicate Victorian ladies,' said Maddie, looking at her own cup. 'I prefer mugs.'

'Me, too,' said Rudi.

The waitress came back with the teacake. Put it in front of Maddie and gave them both a fancy pastry fork, along with a lace serviette.

And so they sat drinking tea and sharing a huge, toasted teacake the size of a dinner plate. It felt intimate, both eating from the same plate. An unspoken declaration of love. *And trust*, thought Maddie. Trust was the most important thing to share with the man you loved.

'Home?' she asked, when they'd finished.

'Home,' Rudi agreed.

They held hands all the way back to the car. And when she started it, and released the sticky clutch, he laughed.

'I might be able to fix that for you,' he said. 'Dodgy clutches, dodgy boot latches. My speciality.' He tried not to smile. 'I could be a useful chap to have around.'

'Never doubted it,' said Maddie. And she *did* smile.

Driving back to Pendurran, it was hard for Maddie to keep her eyes on the road. To stop herself looking at him, checking he was still there. That this miracle was real.

When they returned to the farmhouse, Rudi uncorked a bottle of wine for them. They walked together up the stairs, two minds sharing one thought.

'Your room or mine?' asked Rudi.

'It makes no difference,' she said. 'I've waited a long time for this.'

'I hope you won't be disappointed,' he said.

She wasn't.

EPILOGUE

'Never seen Arthur like it before,' chuckled Gertie. 'Normally, he ain't much of a singer. And wild horses couldn't have dragged him up on a stage.'

'Powerful stuff is Spingo,' said Maddie. 'Put all but the strongest man on his back.' She remembered Lizzie Retallack's words, an echo down the years.

'Well, that's where the silly sod is now,' said Gertie. 'Flat on 'is back. And when he does drag hisself out of that pit, he'll have one hell of a headache. Mind, he weren't the only one knocking back the ale last night. That young Rachel from the Forge – she reminded me of Sissy when she'd had a few. And the way she was coming out of that dress...'

'And falling into old Alf Bingham like that,' said Maddie. 'Made his night, I reckon.'

'Though can't have done his accordion any good,' laughed Gertie.

'Anybody listening would think we'd had an orgy in there, instead of a plain old barn dance,' said Maddie. 'But a brilliant night. One of the best.' They'd all sung 'Auld Lang Syne'. Some more tunefully than others, Maddie had to admit, and then

Gertie had led a bizarre and slightly wobbly conga line around the barn and out into the yard. 'And Rudi enjoyed himself,' she said. 'But then everybody was so welcoming. Don't think he expected that.'

'Why ever not?' asked Gertie. 'He's a smashing bloke.'

'Him being German... he was worried – some people have long memories, won't let the war go.'

'Like who?' said Gertie.

'Rose Trevelyan for a start. She doesn't like Germans and she's not that keen on the Japanese either. A hangover from the war. Her brother was killed on D-Day.'

'Well, she's a bigot and an idiot then.'

'But she shook Rudi's hand,' said Maddie, in amazement. 'Maybe there's hope for us all.'

The kitchen door opened, and Rudi Fischer appeared. 'Good morning, lovely ladies,' he said. 'Can I interest anyone in a walk? The first day of a brand-new year. And the sun is shining. A small miracle. Does that happen often here?'

'Miracles?' said Maddie. 'Every day in Pendurran is a miracle.' She laughed. 'You must stay and find out.'

Gertie coughed discreetly. 'You pair go for a walk. I'd best check on my Arthur.'

'He has a fine voice,' said Rudi, generously. 'I much enjoyed his song about the elf.'

'Sure.' Gertie smiled. 'Arthur has hidden depths. Go on, you pair. Clear off!' She shooed them away.

'You know where I should especially like to walk?' said Rudi, as they walked across the yard. 'The cove with the small church and our barn in it.'

'Really? That's where you want to go? It wouldn't make you feel sad?'

'Sad? No. I should feel very, *very* happy to visit there.'

. . .

It wasn't far, and didn't take as long as that first time Maddie had driven from the POW camp at White Cross. She'd been there many times now, but that day felt different. Throughout the short journey, she was in an odd surreal bubble, as if she'd entered a time machine and wound the clock back to 17 February 1941.

A lot had happened to her since, but even so, the sights and sounds and smells of the ocean below them and the rugged landscape with its jagged granite cliffs felt the same, unchanged by the hand of man.

All except the dunes in the distance: they were different.

She saw Rudi glance towards them. 'It's gone,' he said, surprised.

'It has,' she said, knowing instinctively where his mind was. They seemed to do that quite naturally, as if the pair of them could jump into each other's thoughts. 'They took the barbed wire down years ago, after the army bomb disposal chaps had cleared the minefield.'

'Poor little lad, I never forget his face,' said Rudi.

'*Harry*. He was a proper character. I sometimes wonder what happened to him,' said Maddie.

'Lucky lad,' said Rudi. 'Unlike the unfortunate rabbit.'

'No, we shouldn't forget the rabbit,' she said. 'It's what brought us together.'

'You think so?' He pulled her towards him and held her tightly. 'I thought that was my natural charm.'

'You trying to steal my staff car, you mean! Poor old Harriet, you broke her boot.'

'What? I fixed her boot, if you recall.'

'I recall every bit of it,' said Maddie, her voice husky, her eyes moist.

'Happy?' asked Rudi.

'Very,' she said.

He walked her over to the barn. *Their* barn. 'Can't believe it hasn't fallen down yet.'

'New people in the farm now,' said Maddie. 'I think they must be fixing the old place up. Going to rebuild the barn, turn it into a place for holidaymakers, I hear.'

'No! They can't do that,' said Rudi. 'That's our special place.'

'Well, then,' she said, a challenge in her voice, 'let's go in there one last time.'

'What – break in?'

'Sure, what can they do to us?' said Maddie. 'It's only a rickety old barn. And it's not like we're stealing anything.'

The bench had collapsed and the hole in the roof had got bigger, but the walls were still there, thumbing their nose at the passage of time.

'I'm glad we've come back,' said Rudi. 'This is the place where I first knew I loved you. That I could not possibly in my lifetime love anyone else in the same way. So, I wanted to ask you something important. I have no wish to shame you, but...' He stumbled over his words, searching for the perfect ones that would reflect the seriousness of the moment. Of the intensity of his feelings.

'What, Rudi, what?'

'My face,' he said, and touched the scar with his fingers. 'It does not upset you? You are not ashamed of it?'

'Your face,' said Maddie, 'is that so important to you? It's what's underneath that counts. But it just so happens that I love your face – your eyes, your nose, your lips, your cheeks, but especially your beautiful eyes.' She caressed his face as she took inventory of each separate piece of it.

'You do?' he asked, surprised. 'And is this a face you could look on every day?'

'*Every* day,' she said, emphatically.

'So, this Madeline Brady, a woman of fine beauty and

extreme intelligence, would she be happy to take this' – he fumbled in his pocket and brought out the ring he had purchased in Helston – 'and marry a man with such a face? A man who would love her above all else – above himself.'

It was all that she'd hoped for. Everything she wanted. But still, it took her by surprise. And she paused, allowed the silence to settle before she replied.

She wanted to scream at the top of her voice, shout *yes* a hundred times, but she only said it once and in a quiet voice.

Still, it was enough, for Rudi smiled, seemed happy and relieved. He put the ring on her finger. 'I'll look after you,' he said. His voice was earnest, his expression solemn, as if this was a promise he'd thought seriously about. Needed her to know that.

'*We'll look after each other*,' said Maddie. 'And where shall we live?' she asked.

'Anywhere you are will be my home,' said Rudi.

'Pendurran? Could you live at the farm?'

'I like the farm and the countryside and the ocean. I will miss my mountains and my Alpine lakes, but maybe we could go there sometimes.'

'*Heimat*,' she said. 'Homeland.'

'You remembered.'

'I remember everything you told me. And of course, we'll go there,' said Maddie. 'We *must*. We'll see your mother and our son and walk around the lake. We can work it out,' she said. 'And now, do you mind if we go down to the ocean?'

They walked hand in hand along the path Maddie had trodden so many times before. Back to where their lives together had begun. To the beach at Church Cove. And every so often, small ripples of pleasure and excitement made their way through her, as she thought about the ring on her finger, felt its presence, told herself that it was real and not some romantic fiction she had conjured up.

'The ring,' said Maddie. 'It's beautiful. And the dolphins...'

'Not too sweet, too *sappy*?' he asked.

'Just right. And the band, I don't think I've seen anything like it before,' said Maddie.

'Just in Cornwall, that's what the jeweller told me. And I know how much you love this land. They mix tin and gold together to make a special ring. I hoped you would understand,' he said. 'The two different metals. Like us.'

'So, which one are you?' she asked.

'Tin – *obviously*.'

'Really?'

'Tin is good,' he said. 'Tin protects lots of other metals. It's important.'

'So, that makes me gold.'

'And *very* precious.'

'Well, I don't know if I can live up to that,' said Maddie. 'But I'll try.'

She studied his face as he gathered small pebbles from the beach, skimmed them along the wave tops. Watched his look of concentration turn to joy at the achievement. Maddie smiled. Such simple things: they were always the stuff of life, of happiness, the things you remembered. The longer she lived, the stronger that belief became.

'Did you see?' he asked her. 'That was a triple,' he said. 'Definitely a triple.'

'Two bounces,' she teased him. 'I only saw two bounces. You'll need to practise. But then we'll have time.'

'Yes,' Rudi agreed. 'We will.'

She wound her arm around his waist. 'Can I ask you something, a very special favour?'

Rudi pulled her closer. 'A favour for a favour,' he said, and kissed her firmly on the mouth, his tongue probing, sending small frissons of excitement through her.

Maddie shuddered. His lips were moist in the cold air, and

an invitation. Reluctantly, she pulled away, for she wanted to hold nothing back from him. Wanted them to be honest with each other from the start, an equal partnership.

'You can say no,' said Maddie. 'And maybe you'll think it's a strange thing to ask so I'll understand if you don't feel comfortable with it.'

'Now I'm intrigued,' said Rudi, 'and a little nervous.'

Maddie stroked his face gently. 'Nothing serious, I promise. And you might think it's frivolous, but you know that Gertie is my best friend? I love her. Not the way I love you, of course. It's a different kind of love.'

'I know,' said Rudi. 'And I understand. A comradeship. Hans and I had much the same. You've been through a lot together. Friends like that are special. And I would never come between the two of you. So...?'

'Would you think it really silly if I wanted to have a double wedding?' She put her fingers to his lips to stop his sudden reply. 'At heart, you see, I'm a romantic. A sucker for a happy ending. And in my head, I saw my wedding like the end of *Pride and Prejudice* when Jane gets to marry Mr Bingley and Elizabeth finally gets her Darcy. You, my love, are my wonderful Mr Darcy, only better than him. Much better. Braver, more handsome, the love of my life.' She took her hand away from his lips. Her breath was coming in short bursts now, and Maddie couldn't believe she'd told him all that. How ridiculous would he think her now?

'You believe in happy endings. I remember that. It's part of who you are. And why would I want to change one tiny part of you, Maddie Brady? Apart from that name, of course. Will you be happy as Maddie Fischer, do you think?'

'Very, *very* happy. I'd be proud to have your name. You've brought nothing but honour to it. And the wedding...?'

'Let's see what we can do. Maybe the vicar would give us all a discount,' he said.

A joke. She smiled, relieved. Gertie had joked about it too.

Maddie released a contented sigh and looked out once more at the ocean. Today was one of those tranquil days in the cove, the rhythm of the waves soothing as they glided peacefully to shore, leaving behind tiny traces of pure white foam. She had always thought of the ocean as timeless. And neutral. It held no grudges, knew nothing of man's idiocy or his wars. Every day it was there without fail, sweeping everything clean. Asking nothing in return, except respect for its power. And its beauty.

She glanced at the man beside her, the man who would be part of her life. He picked up another smooth, round pebble, weighed it in his hand. 'This is what triples are made of,' he said, smiling. 'You just watch.'

The stone skimmed the water and Rudi Fischer jumped up and down on the sand, his face crinkled in delight. He might have been eight years old instead of thirty years older. 'See,' he said, 'your man has skills! That bounced three times.'

Maddie smiled right along with him. 'A four,' she said. 'Easily a four.'

She pondered once more on the joys, the frustrations and the sadness that life sometimes threw at you. And she knew that she was right. Simple things held the greatest joy. They were the vital DNA of life, the most important stuff that built memories.

One thing she was certain of: she and Rudi Fischer would build lots of memories.

They joined hands and turned their backs on the beach, walking slowly up the hill to the car. Back to Pendurran and the start of a new life.

A LETTER FROM ELAINE

Dear reader,

I'm thrilled that you chose to read my book *Be Brave for Me* and I want to say a huge thank you. I hope you enjoyed joining Maddie in her world and if you did and would like to keep up to date with all my latest releases, just sign up at the following link. Your email address will never be shared and you can unsubscribe at any time:

www.bookouture.com/elaine-johns

I hope you loved *Be Brave for Me* and if you did, I would be very grateful if you could write a review. I'd love to hear what you think, and it makes such a difference helping new readers to discover one of my books for the first time.

I love hearing from my readers because it's YOU, the reader, who truly brings a book to life by investing your time and enthusiasm in it. Until you pick it up and get involved with the characters and their lives, the book is only words on a page. So, I'm very grateful to you and if you would like to get in touch, I would be delighted to hear from you via my website, or FB page.

In writing about Maddie and Rudi, I wanted to highlight some of the positive things that might come out of war. War is a brutal, terrible thing, but as well as showing the dreadful acts that we humans are capable of, I also wanted to think about the kindness and humanity that people show to each other. How they help each other through the trauma. Often, good things come out of bad. And there are many examples from both the First and Second World Wars when folk pulled together and carried on with life courageously and often with humour.

Many relationships were built, and couples found each other; found love. I wanted to think about how two people like Maddie and Rudi, supposed enemies, could be thrust into each other's orbit, and find love instead of the hate that they were expected to feel. I hope you were rooting for the pair of them and felt their joy and their despair the way I did when I was writing about them. Love conquers all – that's what I hoped. And I believe it did.

I initially had the idea of turning enemies into friends and then lovers when I remembered that strange occurrence from WWI when at Christmas in 1914, British and German soldiers sang carols together and then came out of their trenches to play a game of football. It was something that for me underlined the idiocy of war, but also shone a light on the humanity of the soldiers. All of them, wherever they came from, were simply men.

Although this is essentially a positive book about love and the romance of Maddie and Rudi, I was especially interested in highlighting the important issue of women who society forced into giving up their babies when they became 'unmarried' mothers. There were many sad women whose whole lives were affected by the pain of having to give up their children. There were many mother-and-baby homes all over the UK and in Ireland and the cruelty of *some* of these places is still coming to light. Hopefully, society is a much kinder and less judgemental place now. However, I wanted to show that Maddie, although in that situation, could still be strong, resilient and above all keep her self-respect throughout her ordeal. I hope I've done that, and I hope you agree that she is a force to be reckoned with, but also someone who deserves to find love.

Thanks,

Elaine

elainejohns.com

 facebook.com/elaine.johns.79

ACKNOWLEDGEMENTS

Writing a book is never a solo endeavour. There are many people I would like to thank for their help and support in getting this book to readers. First of all, and most importantly, you – the reader – have my thanks. Until a reader opens a book and brings his or her own life experience and reading history to a work of fiction, then that book remains simply words on a page. But it finally becomes 'alive' when you, the reader, take it on. So, many thanks to you all, for taking the time and giving my book *life*.

Many people have been supportive. My thanks to my editor, Ellen Gleeson, for her tireless and enthusiastic work and all the good folks at Bookouture. Thanks also to my agent, Judith Murdoch.

Thanks also are due to Anne, a good friend and alpha reader who has patiently and honestly read and critiqued manuscripts over the years, taken me on coastal walks, and makes a fine runner bean chutney. And to Sally for her knowledge of smallholdings and feisty hens; also, Lesley and Kevin Finan and Helen Watson.

Thank you to the fine gentleman, who works at ex-POW Camp 115 in White Cross, St Columb Major, for the tour and his insights into this wartime prisoner-of-war camp near Newquay. Only the water tower remains and a couple of the original huts, and the football pitch in my book has now been taken over by static caravans as the site is currently a holiday park. Cultybraggan Camp, near Comrie in Perthshire, is one of the few remaining intact POW camps left in the United Kingdom.

Lots of folk have helped in my research and I thank them; any errors are mine.

I am grateful to the following books for research and inspiration:

REFERENCES

Sherman, M. *No Time for Tears: In the ATS* (London: George G. Harrap & Co. Ltd., 1944), p. 13.

BIBLIOGRAPHY

Benney, C. *The Secrets of Rosemundy House* (St Agnes, Cornwall: Wheal Hawke Publications, 2014).

Quinn, R. *Hitler's Last Army: German POWs in Britain* (Stroud, Gloucestershire: The History Press, 2015).

Cornish historian Clive Benney's book on Rosemundy House contains some fascinating insights into this historic St Agnes Hotel, which began life in 1780 as a private house, became a mother and baby home for unmarried mothers from 1922 until 1964 and is currently a country house hotel.

However, *my* Rosemundy House is fictional, as are ALL its characters and staff. None of the midwives were called Miss Bennett nor the matrons Miss Roberts. Speaking to several St Agnes' residents about the history of Rosemundy House, I found differing opinions about how harsh the regime was there, but these were subjective and mainly hearsay. I personally make no judgements as to the real character of the people in charge of the home and neither does Mr Benney in his fascinating and deeply researched book into the house's history. But this house for unmarried mothers seems to have been a product of its time, which was often unforgiving to pregnant women who had their babies out of wedlock. It was a time when society forced some of these sad, unfortunate mothers to give their babies up against their will. I, for one, am very glad that those times are gone and *hopefully* society is now slightly more humane and understanding.

If any readers are interested in information about the home and mothers who had their babies there, there is a link below:

www.facebook.com/RosemundyHouse

Thank you all for the time you've taken to read my book,

Elaine